Alex21
Enjoy my first
work! There are diamonds
in this rough.

INFERNAL SHADOW

LEGACY OF THE ARAHANA
BOOK 1

TAYLOR CROOK

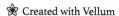

For my dad, who started me on this journey of fantasy and has supported me on this journey of writing. Through first drafts and edits, this one's for you.

B'ARAD

DORSETTI PLAINS

AQUI

GATLING

BARRISTON

THE DARK WOOD

ITHADORE

HANNC

THE SALTMARSHES

TANNERHORN

CASEA

PREC

STLE VEES

GRANISTON

MERIDIAS

ITADEL
LIGHT

THE NOMAD'S PASS

HAVEN

PROLOGUE

~

The winds howled relentlessly across the cracked and broken landscape that was once a lush and diverse world. They howled as they descended from the peaks of mountains that cracked and shuddered as earthquakes ravaged the land. They howled through the ever-churning oceans that spit and crashed against rocky beaches. They howled across vast deserts turned to sheets of glass by the cascading lightning strikes from the ever-present storm clouds above. They howled until they broke upon a sphere of perfect calm surrounding the last living being on this plane.

Within this prefect sphere sat what used to be a man, but could now only be described as man-shaped. Over ten feet tall and nearly as broad across the shoulders, Its skin was matte black and tough as boiled leather. No features could be discerned in Its face, but perhaps through some trick of the mind when looking at something that should be human, it seemed possible to see the faint traces of a brow and a nose. No eyes were visible, but those who were unfortunate enough to feel Its gaze upon them always seemed to know when they had Its attention. The sphere itself was an infinitesimal use of the being's power to keep the rain, wind and lightning at bay, something done more out of habit, from a time when It felt things. Or feared things. A time when It was a man.

The being gave a brief moment of thought to that concept. It supposed It used to be a man, but It was so much more now. It was far beyond the constructs of mortal species. The pitiful creatures that used to plague this land, the creatures on which It had fed to gain Its power, used to call It something.

Umbra Infernalis.

The thought bubbled up from the depths of Its mind almost involuntarily. A memory triggered by thoughts It had not had in some time. It remembered the name with fondness, or more accurately, remembered the man It had been, being fond of the name. After It had absorbed their first champions, one who was all brute strength and one who could hide like a shadow, Its skin had turned into the dark hide that covered It now. That's when they started to fear It.

The Infernal Shadow.

Umbra would do fine. It could feel Itself getting close. Close to leaving this plane that It had sucked dry and making its way into another. It would need something to call Itself. A name for them to fear. Their life force always tasted so much sweeter when it was tainted with fear.

Yes, Umbra would do fine.

Throughout these brief thoughts, the rest of Umbra's consciousness had been focused on needling its way through the fabric of time itself. A fabric that separated the tiers of existence. None of the beings in this plane had the ability to travel though the tiers, but fortune had been with Umbra the day a traveler passed through. The traveler had been smart and fast, however, and Umbra had only been able to absorb a tiny speck of his power before he destroyed himself, and most of his own world, in an attempt to keep Umbra here.

Fortunately, for an eternal being like Umbra, that speck of power was all that was needed. It had been at it for centuries, but Umbra could feel Itself getting close. It was almost through. Soon It would be able to exert some influence on this new world.

1

THOMARAS

❧

"One hundred, ninety-nine, ninety-eight..." Thomaras counted softly under his breath.

"A'course, my third wife was my favourite wife," the disheveled man that shared his cell continued in the clipped, mush-mouthed cadence that the poor and downtrodden always seemed to adopt.

"Mhmm, of course," Thomaras offered, only half-listening, "... ninety, eighty-nine, eighty-eight..."

"She had hair like fire and thought I was the most handsome man she'd ever met. She always said it!"

"... eighty-three, eighty-two, eighty-one..." Softly, and then louder for his companion's benefit, "Yes, she would say it."

"When do you think the bartender will be back? I could use another drink."

Thomaras rolled his eyes at the old man's drunken ramblings but left it at that; he still had seventy steps to wait.

"I once arm-wrestled a Granite Ogre and won!" The man seemed to have drifted into another story.

It was fine. Soon Thomaras wouldn't have to listen anymore. He had already risen from the crouched position he had taken up against the wall. Lithe and catlike. He gently stretched his long limbs, which were manacled and chained to the wall. His tightly corded muscles didn't noticeably bulge but were as hard as iron. A combined result of hard training and, if what his degenerate father had told him could be believed, the genetic disposition of his mother's people. All the while, he counted steps.

"... fifty... forty-nine, forty-eight..."

At this point, Thomaras was barely mouthing his count. The man was prattling on about some nonsense, but Thomaras was almost completely focused on his next moves.

The dungeon that he was locked in belonged to the city of Tannerhorn. This particular dungeon was square and patrolled by one guard, a guard that Thomaras had discovered to be wonderfully predictable. He walked at the same pace. It took him 120 steps to complete a circuit of the jail, and in the same direction every time. The room that acted as the antechamber to the dungeon, and that also held Thomaras's weapons, was forty steps in the opposite direction. That meant that Thomaras had eighty steps once he reached that room to pick the lock and find his daggers.

"... forty-three, forty-two... forty-one..."

Thomaras crossed most of the distance to his jabbering companion and stopped once he reached the maximum length that the manacles would allow. Raising his wrists to his mouth, he used his teeth to pull out the small iron needle that was embedded in the callus he had developed in the web of skin between his thumb and index finger.

"... but I say, if the moon is up at night and the sun during the day, how do we know they aren't... What's that?" the drunk asked, finally taking notice of what Thomaras was doing as he deftly picked the lock on each manacle.

"Nothing," Thomaras said. "In fact, I'm not even here. You just dreamed me."

"Dreamed you?" Any lucidity in the man's eyes had quickly faded back into a drunken haze.

Rather than answer, Thomaras put his finger to his lips in a universal gesture for keeping quiet. The man returned the gestured before falling down in gales of laughter and then promptly passing out. Thomaras shook his head but was relieved he wouldn't have to silence the man himself. Poor fool was already going to have a headache tomorrow.

Thomaras returned his attention to the guard and the crunch of leather soles on the dirt floor of the dungeon confirmed that he had just finished his circuit and was moving past the door again. As quietly as possible, lock pick in hand, Thomaras reached his long and thankfully slender arm through the bars of the door's viewing window and started to work the lock.

Click.

Thomaras opened the door about a foot and a half wide. He'd made a note on his way in that the hinges didn't begin to squeak in protest until the door was opened about a foot and three-quarters wide, so as long as it didn't get any wider there would be no need for the door to complain. Silent as fog, Thomaras moved his slim frame through the door and shut it behind him.

Moving through the hallway, Thomaras kept the count going in his head but was confident that he had more than enough time to get to the antechamber and get his daggers. His greater concern was silence, a concern addressed by years of training and a healthy dose of Arahana blood in his veins. The blood of his people seemed to account for a lot of his skills.

Well, his mother's people, Thomaras supposed.

Thomaras focused his thoughts on the task at hand as he approached the door to the antechamber. The dungeon must have been commissioned to the Engineers Guild in Granniston, the capital city of Meridias, the eastern kingdom of the continent, as most dungeons were. All the rooms and hallways were dug seamlessly into the bedrock under the city, a skill that only those engineers could accomplish. The doors were all made of iron and fitted, quite cleverly, into the rocks on hinges. Fortunately, every obstacle, no matter how strong, had a weak point to attack. In this case, it was the locking mechanism and with two hands at his disposal, this lock fell even quicker than the last.

Wasting no time, Thomaras strode into the antechamber, not worrying about any protest from the door, as this one was well maintained due to its more frequent use and thus less disposed to petty griping. Using his near perfect memory, Thomaras located the chest that contained his weapons and set to popping the lock.

Strapping the daggers across his lower back, Thomaras stuck his lock pick into the pocket of his trousers and soundlessly drew one of his daggers.

Waiting by the door of the antechamber, Thomaras listened for the clomp of the guard's boots down the hallway. As he heard him pass, Thomaras silently swung the door open and crept up behind him. Years of training made his footfalls strike the ground as soundlessly as a moth landing on a leaf. Once he had closed the distance,

Thomaras quickly placed the steel on the throat of the man in front of him.

"Shhhh," Thomaras whispered into the guard's ear as intimately as a lover. "Make a sound and you die," he continued, much less like any lover he'd had. Well, less like most of them.

The man nodded as much as the dagger at his throat would allow.

"We are going to take a little walk into the antechamber and then you're going to ask your partner on the other side of the door to open up. Got it?"

Again the man nodded and Thomaras thought, not for the first time, how much more persuasive he was when he held a person's life in his hands.

The walk to the door, or more accurately the awkward shamble, didn't take too long, and the guard seemed more eager to live through the night than to prevent whatever was happening.

"Hey Griff, open up, gotta take a leak."

Despite his position, the man managed to sound somewhat natural. Not that it really mattered; even if this Griff suspected something, he would open the door to see what was the matter and that's all Thomaras really needed.

"Danno, you have a child's bladder, you know that?" Griff chuckled good-naturedly as the various clicks and clanks indicated he was opening the heavier and more complex lock system. Given enough time, Thomaras could have picked the lock himself, but he needed both guards on this side of the door anyway.

"I swear, my wife can hold it longer than you and she... argh!" Griff cut off abruptly as Thomaras struck lightning quick with his dagger and sliced his hand.

Sensing an opportunity, Danno spun away from Thomaras and went to draw his own sword, but Thomaras was faster. He drew the second dagger from his sheath and cut a shallow gash across the man's cheek. Danno staggered back and tried to complete the draw he had started, but before he could, he was startled by his friend falling to the ground beside him.

"What's the matter Gwiff? It wath juth a scrath... Uh, why can't a talk?"

Thomaras spun his blades in his hands and tucked them into their sheaths as Danno followed Griff's lead and fell to the ground. The paralyzing agent that coated his blades would only last a few hours, but it would render the guards unconscious and make their memories of the evening fuzzy. That all suited Thomaras just fine, as he had no interest in them being able to identify which prisoner escaped their custody with another prisoner in tow.

Wasting no time, Thomaras made his way into the dungeon, calling the name of his quarry as he went.

"Ashea? Ashea?" he whispered into each cell window as he went along.

He received many responses in gruff voices telling him how they felt about his interrupting their sleep. One gentleman even had a colourful suggestion about what he might be able to do to him better than Ashea could if he could get him out of there. Thomaras ignored them and kept moving. Finally, he heard a response from a cell, quiet but full of confidence.

"I'm Ashea."

Thomaras got to work on the lock, which quickly surrendered with a satisfying pop. He swung the door open and entered the room.

"Hi," he said to the small woman manacled to the wall.

2

ASHEA

~

"Hi," the tall, slender man said, as if he were a neighbour coming over for tea.

"Hi," she replied, unsure of what else to say.

"I've been paid to get you out of here. We have to move quickly. We have two unconscious guards to undress and then we need to be out of this shitty little town before they wake up or the shift changes," her rescuer said as she stared awkwardly at him.

At first glance, the man's face seemed fairly generic. Longish dark hair framed a slender face with a close-cut dark beard, a look popular on Haven for most men. Those who were provided the opportunity to stare awkwardly at the fellow, however, would notice that his features weren't as generic as the man attempted to make them. His ears were longer and just slightly pointed under his shaggy hair and his long nose complemented his angular cheekbones that were also longer than the average person's. All this alone wouldn't have meant much to Ashea, but then she caught the light of the torch in his ice-blue eyes and just for a moment, and saw a perfect square of white framing his triangular pupils.

"Arahana." She breathed the word to herself.

"Right, first we need to get these off you," he said, closing the distance to Ashea.

"Do you have the key..." she started to ask as the manacles made an audible click and fell to the floor.

She rubbed her chaffed wrists while he tucked a slim piece of metal back into his trousers.

Before she could ask how he did that, the man was hauling her up to her feet. He was definitely stronger than he looked.

"Hey now!" she protested as he began to pull her towards the door.

"I told you we have to move quickly. We need to get those guards' clothes off and get them over our own so we can get ourselves out of here," he said, and continued to pull her out of the cell.

At this point, the slightly less musty air in the hallway was a welcome relief from the very musty air in her cell.

"Okay, but..." Ashea began to protest, but the man interrupted her.

"Shhh. We have to be quiet," he said at a normal volume. Seemingly, his own exposition was not subject to these noise constraints.

"Fine," Ashea whispered, "but that doesn't change the fact that..."

"Once we're dressed like the guards, we just walk out as if it's shift change. Then head out of town and..."

"I'm four feet tall!" Ashea exclaimed as loud as she dared while stopping dead and wrenching her arm out of his grip.

He turned to look at her and, had she not just spent the last three days in this dungeon for reasons she didn't understand, she would have laughed at the slack-jawed expression on his face.

"Um, right..." he said, eying her up and down. "The guard's clothes won't fit you."

He finally put that together, despite the stupid look on his face. "So, new plan?"

"New plan," he agreed. He recovered quickly. She'd give him that.

"You're going to stay a prisoner for a little longer." He motioned for her to follow and began walking again.

Ashea had a brief moment of panic that she'd end up back in her cell before she figured out what he was talking about and hurried after him.

She was relieved to find that she was holding it together and still using her brain.

When she stepped into the antechamber after him, she saw two guards on the floor and there was a slightly acrid smell in the air. Her rescuer was busy stripping the clothes off of the larger of the two guards and pulling them over his own. While he was doing that, she wasted no time pulling a pair of manacles off the wall and grabbing the keys from the other guard's belt. Once she had them unlocked, she grudgingly put them around her sore wrists.

Still holding it together.

"I know we don't have time for you to tell me why you're here, but can I know your name at least?"

As the man's head popped through the guard's tunic and he began to straighten the fabric over his own clothes, he spared her a quick glance.

"Davin," he said as he belted the tunic and picked up the guard's helmet.

"Probably not your real name," Ashea declared.

"Probably not," he agreed.

"Well Davin, I suppose thanks are in order," Ashea said while she watched him pull the helmet low over his face. The fit wasn't perfect, but she suspected that at this time of night, most of the guards would probably be half asleep anyway.

"You're handling this all pretty well. Are you often saved from dungeons in the night by mysterious strangers?" Davin asked, pausing for the first time the efficient pace that he'd set since he had first crept into her cell.

"Oh, all the time," Ashea replied lightly. "This is a typical Saturday night for me."

Davin merely raised an eyebrow at her sarcasm.

"Sorry, truth is I'm terrified, but I can be terrified out of that cell just as easily as in it. I may not know what you have planned for me, but I do know I wasn't ever leaving that cell. I'd rather face whatever is out there than die quietly in the dark."

She watched Davin's eyebrow lower as he considered her for a moment. "That's terrible advice. I could be taking you someplace far worse," he said with a wink.

Ashea laughed, and it seemed to relieve the pressure of emotion building in her chest. "Maybe, but if that's the case, I'll just escape from you once we get out of here."

"That's the spirit," Davin said, chuckling. "You're tougher than you look."

Ashea just smiled. She had spent her early teens with her foster mother and father deep in the salt marshes of the east. Their home was isolated so even though her mother was a medicine woman, they would rarely have clients visit, and more often travelled to them offering their services. Her parents had been her teachers and her only friends. She was sixteen when she fled her home in the marshes, and had been on the run since.

Being tough was a prerequisite for that kind of life.

"Okay, you ready?" Davin asked.

"For what?"

Instead of answering, Davin turned towards the door that exited the antechamber. "Better get in here. I think something's wrong with Danno."

After a moment, the door opened, and an annoyed-looking guard walked in. Before she could fully register what was happening, Davin spun his body and buried the back of his fist into the guard's temple with a sickening thud. Before he could collapse, Davin completed the rotation so that he was now facing the man and caught him so that he could ease his body to the floor. He then poked his head out the door to make sure that no one else was coming. Once he was sure the coast was clear, he pulled his head back in and sighed audibly before pulling the unconscious man to lie next to his other companions. Ashea marveled at how economical each movement was, how practiced.

Davin gestured towards the empty hallway, following behind her as she entered.

"Okay, almost there. Only one more door to go and we're out of here. Just walk ahead of me and look scared." Davin's instructions were a whisper across the back of her neck and she only nodded slightly, sensing that their brief reprieve was over and remembering what was at stake. Escaping a dungeon was not an offence that was generally taken lightly.

The walk from the antechamber to the dungeon's exit didn't take very long, but it was tense and grueling. With each step, her heart pounded harder in her chest and her breath got a little more ragged. There was no one in the hallway, but once they got to that door they'd have to knock on it and when they knocked on it someone would open it and they'd have to talk their way out of here and what if she said the wrong thing? Or they saw through Davin's disguise? Or they looked at his shoes? Oh no. He hadn't taken the guard's boots! She began to turn to tell him, but he gently put a hand on her shoulder.

"Easy there. I know I said act scared, but you can tone it down a little."

She could hear the gentle teasing in his voice and it calmed her, as did the confidence.

He knows what he's doing, she reminded herself. *Just let him do his thing.*

By the time they got to the door, she was feeling like she probably only looked the appropriate amount of scared rather than the dead panic she had been in moments ago.

I sure hope he's not taking me out of here just to murder me and do weird stuff to my corpse, Ashea thought. *He's actually starting to grow on me.*

Davin knocked on the door and it sounded to Ashea like the deliberate routine of someone who'd done the same thing a million times. *Did he practice knocking for this? Who was this guy?*

Ashea was startled out of her thoughts when the viewing slat slid open and a pair of eyes stared out at her.

"What?" the eyes asked as they looked back and forth from her to Davin. She felt the panic rising again.

"Taking this one out. I got orders."

His voice sounded exactly like one of the guards that she'd heard outside her doors. Griff, maybe? How did he learn to imitate him so fast?

"At this time of night?" He sounded highly skeptical. "On whose orders?"

The eyes were brimming with skepticism now too as they squinted down at her, and she felt her heart sink. He might be able to sound like Griff, but how could Davin know who gave these guys orders? She swallowed hard and tried not to wince as Davin cleared his throat.

3

THOMARAS

∽

"Captain Typhin himself," Thomaras, currently Davin and impersonating Griff, said as he gave the guard on the other side of the door a pointed look. "He wanted to ask this one some questions personally." He nodded his head towards the attractive figure beside him.

The eyes behind the slat at least had the good grace to look uncomfortable with the implications before the slat slid shut and the clicks and clacks of a complicated lock being opened commenced.

He could feel Ashea startle a little and sag in relief as he gave the correct answers to a stranger in a place that he'd never been before. In order to prevent her from speaking, he whispered quietly in her ear. "A few well-placed coins to the right people can provide a wealth of information about any organization."

He then tightened his grip on her arm slightly, hoping she understood its meaning to stay quiet. To her credit, the girl simply nodded, almost imperceptibly, in acknowledgment of the information. She also relaxed a little more. Good. She'd handled all of this well, but had started to panic a little as they approached this final hurdle.

The door completed its complicated ritual and Thomaras's eyes quickly adjusted to the change in the light as it swung open. Despite his ability to adjust to almost any change in light, instantly he squinted the way anyone else would when going from dark to light. A civic employee who spends most of his time guarding drunks and brawlers in for a night to sleep it off probably wouldn't notice something as small as that, but better safe than sorry. Thomaras was nothing if not careful.

"How's your shift been?" the guard asked.

"Fine. Ask Danno to tell you the joke I told him earlier. Made him laugh until he passed out," Thomaras suggested as he walked past the young man, keeping his head tilted down behind Ashea's opposite shoulder as if he were checking her restraints.

He might sound like Griff, but his face was still his own.

"Alright, but I doubt he'll do it any justice," the man chuckled. "Danno can't tell jokes for shit."

Thomaras simply raised a hand in the air in acknowledgment as he continued on his way. He had to walk the line between acting natural and giving the guards too many chances to see through his ruse.

From here on out, it would be simple, though. None of the guards would want to ask too many questions about their captain's interest in a female prisoner at this time of night.

Thomaras didn't want to think about it much himself.

"Griff," the guard at the door said with a nod as Thomaras walked by.

Thomaras gave him a mock salute in return that

doubled as an effort to cover his face just as he moved through the torchlight.

And with that, they were free. He tightened his grip once again on Ashea in anticipation of her giving herself away while they were still in view, but he was again impressed to note that she didn't need the reminder and maintained the body language of one person at the mercy of another.

Thomaras continued for about five minutes towards the guard captain's home until they reached the bridge that spanned the river that ran through town.

"As soon as we cross the bridge, we are going to make a hard left and jump down to the river bed. Don't move your hands yet." He unlocked her manacles as he said this last part, but held them against her hands as if he were still guiding her.

She kept her hands behind her back but couldn't resist flexing her fingers at her new-found freedom. That was okay. Thomaras had moved closer to her in anticipation of exactly that. It was doubtful anyone would see them this time of night, but again, Thomaras was always careful.

Case in point, he had chosen this spot to break from his stated trajectory because the torches in the middle of the bridge hadn't been properly maintained and were currently out, putting darkness at his back. Anyone watching him go across the bridge would simply see him disappear into the dark and assume he reappeared on the other side.

"Now," he whispered as he let her go and jumped down the slight incline, landing silently and shifting his feet quickly so as not to disturb any rocks or topsoil and send them tumbling into the water.

Ashea landed slightly less silently, but due to her small size, she was still quiet enough that the sound of the river would obscure any noise. She did not, however, move her feet fast enough and ended up sliding more than running down the bank. Fortunately, Thomaras had been here the last few nights, silently scraping away any loose topsoil and scree on the bank to avoid this very issue. Like her landing, the scrape of her boots down the bank was easily covered by the river's churning waters, and no rocks splashed in.

Thomaras noticed Ashea sway a little on her feet as she stood beside him and motioned for her to sit. She slumped down on a rock without protest and rested her head on her knees. Sleep didn't come easily in a dungeon cell and all the fear and adrenalin from the break-out had likely sapped her body's remaining energy. Without a word, Thomaras turned and unfastened a leather sack that he had hidden under the bridge. He pulled out two dark cloaks and tossed one on top of Ashea's dozing form. She startled a little, but didn't bother moving. He dropped the other to the ground and quickly stripped off the guard's clothes and stuffed them into the sack, which he promptly threw into the river. It bobbed in his view twice before the current took it out of sight. In one fluid motion, he picked up and donned his cloak, then walked over to Ashea.

"I know you're tired, but we have a bit of a walk ahead of us yet."

As he spoke, she pulled the cloak off of her head and looked at him through bleary eyes.

"Here, drink this." He produced a small vial out of one of the many pockets sewn into his cloak and handed it to her. Her nose wrinkled as she took off the stopper and smelled it.

"What is it?" she asked with a wary expression.

"A tincture made of herbs and oils. A friend of mine is an herbalist and keeps me stocked up. It'll give you some energy."

She sniffed the vial again before taking it in one shot. "Ugh, that's bad. My mom used to make something similar, though. Ginseng root for sure, maybe some mushrooms in there," she said as she licked her lips a little to, who knew why, get more of the flavour.

"If you knew all that, why did you even ask me?"

"Just wanted to make sure you knew the source. And more importantly, didn't make it yourself," she said, winking at him.

Looked like she was feeling better already.

"Okay, then, how far is this walk?" she asked, hopping up and donning her cloak.

"About ten miles north. A small mining village called Hannover. There's an inn there where the man who paid me to get you out is meeting us. We'll take the river until it doglegs to the east and then continue the rest of the way through the scrublands," Thomaras explained, noting that she appeared to be committing everything to memory.

"Alright, then," she stated simply, and turned to begin walking.

"No no," Thomaras said, gently grabbing her arm to stop her, "in the water." He stepped ankle-deep into the river. The tug of the current wasn't too bad this close to the bank, but it was still uncomfortable.

Ashea sighed audibly and then stepped into the water behind him. "Hounds?" she asked in a resigned tone.

"Hounds," he agreed.

Thomaras started walking, then he looked back over his shoulder and asked, "Nothing fazes you much, does it?"

"When you've had a life like mine, it just takes a lot more than for most. You see..."

"That's okay," Thomaras interrupted before she could

continue, "we'll only be travelling together a while longer now. The less I know, the better."

"Fair enough," she responded, unsurprisingly unbothered by the comment. "Answer me one question, though. You didn't take Griff's boots. Weren't you worried they would notice?"

The question amused Thomaras slightly. "Nope."

"Why not?" Ashea pressed.

"First of all, they wouldn't fit. Secondly, no one is going to notice something like that. Seriously, how often do you really look at a man's shoes?"

4

THOMARAS

~

They heard the city bells ringing about two hours after they started their soggy trek through the river. Much like the threat they represented, the bells were distant and faint, the sound barely reaching their ears. Ashea heard them slightly after Thomaras and gripped his arm in panic. He smiled and explained that they were already too far for it to matter. The guards had no idea which way they had gone, only that they said they were going to Captain Typhin's and never arrived. The river would cover their tracks and scent from any kind of hunting party and they had left the river about an hour ago, so even if they tried following the river on a hunch, they would have no idea where they were heading now. On top of that, neither Thomaras nor Ashea could be described as high-profile criminals. Thomaras had been booked for allowing himself to be caught stealing tomatoes from a vegetable farmer's market stall and was reasonably certain that Ashea's incarceration was the result of some palms being greased to hold her in a cell and forget about her. Any search party would be a token effort lasting an hour at best.

They had been silent since then. The tincture that Thomaras gave Ashea had probably worn off half an hour ago and although she hadn't complained, she likely didn't have energy for much more than putting one foot in front of the other. No matter, they could rest soon. The scrublands that they travelled were fairly flat, but the tall, weed-like grass made for great cover when travelling. The camp that Thomaras had made before heading into the city was nearby.

Dawn was just breaking on the horizon when Thomaras led them into a small copse of trees that had managed to eke out an existence in a small valley between two hills. Thomaras gestured to a log in front of the small fire pit he'd made and Ashea sat down with a satisfied, if exhausted, sigh.

He strode over to a dead tree that he had hollowed out and removed a leather backpack and a large, oiled animal hide. He placed the animal hide roll behind the log and then sat down beside Ashea, rummaging through the pack as he did so, and handed her a waterskin and some dried boar meat. She drank greedily from the skin before sinking her teeth into the meat with equal vigour. Thomaras chuckled and set to work on his own jerky with slightly less enthusiasm. He tapped Ashea's arm when he wanted the waterskin so as not to break the silence that had settled comfortably between them.

When he was done with his meagre dinner, he passed Ashea a second strip of the dried boar and then reached behind him to grab the animal hide. Ashea ate as she watched him unroll the hide, revealing a soft quiver filled with arrows and an unstrung bow about six feet tall.

Thomaras heard the chewing beside him stop and when he glanced over, he saw that Ashea was staring at the bow. He could understand why. The bow was a thing of beauty. He had crafted it when he was a young man from a very rare Osage Orange tree that grew near his village and, as far as Thomaras could tell, nowhere else. The wood was strong but supple, which allowed Thomaras to create a bow that was much more powerful than it looked. His range with the weapon was limited only by his far-above-average eyesight and, as for power, he had once punched a hole through solid iron plate mail from about three feet away. Not a maneuver he was keen to try again, but it was good to know he could.

"You should get some sleep," Thomaras said, voice straining as he bent the bow down to finish stringing it. "I should be able to bring down a rabbit in time for us to eat before we have to head to Hannover. Your saviour is meeting us at the inn at nightfall." He stood up and slung the quiver on his back so that the arrows popped up over his right shoulder.

"Okay, but I have to pee first," Ashea said, then stood up and started walking out of the trees for some privacy.

Thomaras tested the tension on his bow while he waited. A man his size shouldn't have even come close to drawing a bow this large, but as with many of the things that made Thomaras unique, thanks to his mother's bloodline, he was stronger than he had any right to be.

His thoughts wandered to his mother, or more accurately, what he had heard about her. His father claimed that she was a full-blooded Arahana, but considering they had been wiped out centuries ago, that seemed unlikely. Jacob was, of course, a liar and that was one of his better traits, but Thomaras couldn't deny that he was different. His mother must have had a healthy dose of Arahana in her, but Thomaras suspected that her being full-blooded was just a drunken boast from a drunken fool. Still, he had searched for answers about the mysterious woman his father had bedded and always come up empty. There was certainly something special about her...

Thomaras was startled out of his reverie as Ashea burst through the trees. He cursed himself for not paying more attention. He had heard her coming for thirty seconds, but had been too lost in his thoughts to notice.

"I think there's a wild boar hunting me," Ashea gasped as she tried to catch her breath.

"Um, sorry?" was all Thomaras could manage as he tried to process the absurd words he was hearing.

"I know, I know. It sounds crazy, but I was peeing and I heard something snuffling around in the distance. When I finished, I got up and looked through the trees and there was this boar sniffing around." The look on her face suggested there was something more, but she didn't want to say it.

"And? Sure, boars can be aggressive, but the most they'll do is run you off. They don't hunt you and it doesn't even sound like this one saw you." Thomaras made sure his tone encouraged her to let out whatever she was holding in.

"No, it didn't. I mean, I think it didn't, but..."

Ashea trailed off, but Thomaras just waited in silence. Sometimes it was better to let people get to where they needed to get by themselves. Ashea collected herself for another moment. "It was saying my name," she finally blurted out, looking as if she knew exactly how crazy she sounded.

Thomaras started to formulate a protest, but made a conscious effort to tamp down his incredulity. So far, this woman had kept a level head through circumstances that would have thrown most people for a loop. Why would she suddenly start to panic now? Besides, worst-case scenario, they go out there and find a perfectly normal boar and have meat for their next meal. Thomaras would even have time to butcher the whole thing before they left. The last time he was here, all he'd had time to do was carve and salt some of the meat for the jerky he just finished. He hated wasting that much of an animal.

"Okay, lead the way," he said as he slung his bow over his shoulder.

Without hesitation, Ashea turned back the way she came and led Thomaras out of the trees and up the small hill opposite the way they had come in. As she reached the crest, she crouched beneath the tall grass and pulled it back so they could look down the other side.

Below them, sniffing through the grass, was indeed a wild boar. Its hide looked matted and covered with dirt and the way it was jerking around while it walked seemed... wrong. Like it was being controlled by a puppet master that didn't quite understand the way this particular marionette was supposed to move. The wind turned in their direction and the unpleasant smell of old mothballs wafted into his nose. The whole situation was a little strange, but Thomaras thought that it could very well just be an old animal that had lost most of its motor function. He turned to Ashea to tell her as much when the boar, which had been mostly looking towards them head on, turned to its left and began its awkward shuffle in that direction.

Thomaras's heart dropped into his stomach.

"Right, you should head back to the camp. I'll deal with this," he said to Ashea, pulling her back from the crest of the hill.

"But you haven't even heard it yet. It said my name a couple of times, I swear!" Ashea's voice was pitched low, but the panic that he didn't believe her was evident in her tone.

"Honestly, that's the least of my concerns." Thomaras quietly pulled an arrow out of the soft quiver over his shoulder.

"The least of your concerns? How could that possibly be the least of your concerns?" Ashea asked.

"Because I killed that boar two days ago. Those strips of dried meat in your belly? You can see on its flank where I cut them off before I buried it." Thomaras never took his eyes off of the boar while he spoke. "So, if it's okay with you, I'm not going to wait around to see if this thing can do any other tricks. I'm just going to put it the fuck down." His last statement was greeted by a silence that Thomaras took for tacit agreement.

Focused solely on his quarry now, Thomaras began to move slowly away from their vantage point on the hill, keeping pace with the... thing below him. After about a dozen paces, Thomaras raised himself up on one knee and nocked his arrow. He took a deep breath, lined up his shot, and pulled his great bow back as far as it could go. At this range, he probably didn't need this much force, but he'd never had to kill an animal twice before, so he figured he'd be as certain as possible.

As he had a million times before he released his breath and let the arrow fly. His shot was true, and the arrow struck the boar right through the ribcage, piercing its heart with such a forceful impact that it knocked the large animal over, breaking the arrow as it rolled along the ground and then lay still.

Thomaras sighed and lowered his bow. When the boar staggered to its feet again, Thomaras wasn't surprised. Even a shot to vital organs took a little time to bleed an animal to death.

Good shot, Thomaras thought.

When the boar turned and looked in the direction from which the arrow had come, he was a little more surprised.

Probably just a coincidence.

When the animal clearly saw him, squealed in rage, and then charged at him, Thomaras was very surprised.

Oh fuck!

After that, he didn't have much time to think at all. The boar moved impossibly fast, particularly for an animal that should be bleeding to death. Its stride was still awkward and wrong, but that didn't seem to hamper its unnatural speed. Thomaras was fast but there was no time to pull another arrow, aim and have any hope of drawing and shooting something coming at him at that pace. Instead, he dropped his bow and drew his daggers. He wouldn't be able to get completely out of the way in time, but when this thing hit him, he was going to finish the job he started.

So long as he avoided those tusks.

Too late, he realized just how bad his plan was.

5

___

ASHEA

~

Ashea watched in horror as the boar charged at Davin. She couldn't understand what she was seeing, but she knew if she didn't do something, Davin would be gored.

She raised her hand and visualized a cube of pure fire. She imagined it forming at her fingertips.

There was only a flicker at first, as the same doubt she always felt flooded her mind and she felt her will bump up against the same invisible wall it always did.

Then she saw the boar was almost upon Davin.

Conviction flooded her mind instead, drowning the doubt and suffusing her outstretched hand with enough will to crash through the block.

The cube formed.

She willed it forward into the boar as fast as he could imagine. It smashed into the nightmare creature and knocked it backwards. It thrashed for a moment while the fire consumed it and then lay still.

Davin looked back at her in disbelief before moving to

check on the burning boar. Over the crackle of the flames Ashea could hear the thing saying her name, over and over, in a voice like stone scraping across stone.

Davin brought his foot down swiftly on the boar's head, silencing it.

They stared at each other in silence for a moment while a sickening combination of charred pork and mothballs assaulted her nose.

"You can use magic?" Davin finally asked.

"A little," Ashea said, too shaken to explain any further.

"A little? That looked like more than just a little magic to me."

"I've... I've never done anything like that before. The most fire I've ever conjured was barely enough to light a candle." Even as she explained herself a familiar, ghostly memory of using magic played across her mind. One she could never be sure was a dream or reality.

Davin looked at her for a moment and she could almost hear the calculations going on within his head before he came to a conclusion. "Lucky me, I guess. Those tusks would have done a number on me."

Ashea gave a mental sigh of relief. She wouldn't have been surprised if he opted to leave her right then and there. It wasn't that magic was completely unheard of within Haven. In fact, most people had seen it in some form or other. It just usually only came from the council of mages. Anyone using magic who wasn't already part of the council would likely draw their attention and Ashea had learned enough about Davin to know that was the last thing he'd want.

"My pleasure, and the least I could do, considering," Ashea said. "My father used to hunt, and I watched him shoot his fair share of game. I've never seen an animal get up from a clean shot through the heart like that. Not for more than a few steps, anyway. How did that thing charge you?"

As she asked the question, a slight chill settled between her shoulders and she could see in Davin's face that he was feeling something similar.

This place suddenly felt very exposed.

"I don't know, but I've also never seen something I've killed, butchered and buried resurrect itself and call for someone by name. Let's assume it wasn't playing by the same rules that we are and get out of here."

"Davin, that's your best idea yet," she said, falling into step beside him.

"Thomaras," he said without looking at her, and she got the sense that she was being let in on something that not many people knew.

"Thomaras," she repeated, hoping some gratitude came through in her voice, but not wanting to push the moment too far.

As he gathered his things from the camp, Ashea could see that Da— Thomaras had switched back into professional mode. Just like in the dungeon, his movements were precise and efficient and in a matter of minutes he was leading them back out of the copse of trees and into the scrublands. Ashea was tired. She'd only had time to pee, and even that got interrupted, but her desire to put space between them and that thing overrode her exhaustion. For the first time in her life, she was anxious to get to a place that had more people in it. Strength in numbers was an age-old adage for a reason, she supposed. As they left the little camp behind, the wind blew across her shoulders and the smell of mothballs made her nose wrinkle in distaste.

It was close to midday when Ashea finally saw some

structures on the horizon. As they drew closer, she could make out a small town at the foot of a mountain which, she assumed, housed the mine. Shops and inns dominated the village. She couldn't see any residences anywhere.

"Where are all the houses?" Ashea asked, breaking the silence for the first time since Thomaras had shared his name.

"Aren't any. The proprietors live in their inns or shops and the rest of the miners come up here to work for a spell before they move on or head home. It's a village of transients, a perfect place for a couple of faces to get lost in a crowd," Thomaras said.

Ashea wasn't terribly familiar with this area of Haven. After fleeing Meridias as a child, she'd spent most of her time in the western kingdom of Ithadore with her first true family in the salt marshes. Hannover, though close to the border with Ithadore, was still the first city in the northern kingdom of Aquilo she'd visited.

"Isn't Aquilo more tightly policed than any other kingdom?" Ashea asked.

"Oh yes. I avoid working jobs in the north altogether, but Hannover barely counts as the north. The granite that they mine out of that mountain is mostly shipped up to the Granite Ogres on the plains and they pay mostly in game meat and skins. Since Aquilo is essentially the bread basket of Haven, most of the cities have their own local sources for food and skins. I would guess that more than half of the work and trade done in Hannover is done by citizens of the salt marshes. Leaves a lot of room for guys like me to operate."

It appeared as though he had operated here a few times before, as he was very familiar with the geography of the town. Even though he seemed slightly more relaxed now that they had reached the village, he was still glancing over his shoulder and, on a number of occasions before reaching their destination, had stopped their journey to circle around and make sure they weren't being followed. When he did, he was like a ghost, disappearing into the tall grass silently and reappearing the same way a few minutes later. Ashea hadn't had the courage to ask if he was looking for guards from Tannerhorn or something... else.

When they got to the edge of town, Thomaras put his hood up and motioned for her to do the same. For such a small town, there were people everywhere and the clatter and din were a harsh contrast from the miles of silent fields they had just travelled. Smoke rose from cook fires along the street, but the blackest column rose, along with the clang of metal on metal, from the blacksmith's shop. The smells of food, sweat and dirt assaulted her nose and, to her disgust, made her stomach rumble.

This many people made her nervous. This many dirty, hard-looking men in mining gear made her cling close to Thomaras. Just when she thought that she had reached her limit, Thomaras turned down a side street and angled towards a tavern and inn on the other side of the road, picking his way deftly through the crowd. A large woodcut sign on the front with a cross-looking, well-endowed woman on it read "The Jilted Maiden Inn." There was something in the expression on her face that seemed to imply she might not be a maiden after all.

"Almost there," Thomaras said as he gripped her wrist and weaved them through the last of the crowd.

Being pulled by her wrist was not normally something Ashea stood for, but under the circumstances she was grateful for the guidance. How did people stand being so close to so many other people?

A short distance away from the inn, Thomaras stopped abruptly as a fight broke out. Actually, "fight" might be a generous term for it. Three men, seemingly drunk, took exception with the doorman and decided to try to push their way in. Ashea gaped as the doorman, who must have stood an impossible eight feet tall, grabbed the first two men by their faces and, one in each giant hand, picked them up fully off of the ground and tossed them back into the street almost disdainfully. The third man, having seen this, thought better of the head-on approach and instead swung his pickaxe at the unarmed doorman. Though only slightly off balance from throwing the first two assailants, the giant was still too close to properly get out of the way of the swing and had to settle for throwing his forearm up to block the blow. Ashea cringed and waited to see blood explode from the hole in the man's arm, but instead she shielded her eyes as sparks flew and with a loud crack the pickaxe's iron spike snapped off, bounced back the way it came, and embedded itself in the attacker's forehead. Ashea saw the blood she had expected earlier as the man stiffened and fell backwards.

"Ha, bad luck there. That's some kind of armoured bracer he's got on, though. Wonder if it's enchanted or..." Thomaras abruptly cut off his thought and quickly let go of her arm for a second before putting his hand back on her wrist.

While he spoke, Ashea's heart leaped as a fourth unseen man had raised his pickaxe above his head, ready to smash it into the back of the large doorman. Before he could finish the motion, he stiffened and dropped the pickaxe, falling to the ground as he clutched at a dagger in his throat. The doorman turned, faster than someone that big should be able to move, saw the man fall and then looked at Thomaras and nodded. It took her another full second to realize that Thomaras had thrown the dagger. She probably wouldn't have realized at all had he not been holding onto her arm.

"Not over yet," Thomaras said as he let go of her arm again.

The first two men had gotten back up, dusted themselves off, and were now picking up their own pickaxes and sizing up their foe.

"Torin, you want your hammer?" a voice from inside the inn called out casually.

"No. No need," the doorman, Torin, responded. He nonchalantly cracked his massive knuckles, a sound that echoed down the now almost silent alleyway, and turned towards the remaining drunks. His voice was deep and clear, but the words were spoken with a heavy accent. The common tongue was not his first language. Ashea felt herself getting more and more curious about this boulder of a man and tried to make out his face, most of which was hidden under a wide-brimmed hat and a bandana that covered his mouth.

Were his eyes red?

The men screamed as they charged, bold with ale, swinging their axes clumsily. It was over almost before it started. Torin parried the swings with his bracers, the cloth from his loose-fitting shirt shredding as the metal sparked against his armour, then simply grabbed the two men once they were off balance and clunked their heads together. The men went slack as Torin let them fall to the ground.

By the time city guard came down the alley, the spectators were breaking up and dispersing. Torin saw them coming, waved casually, and walked back towards his post by the door. As he walked past the body that Thomaras had felled, he bent down and picked it up, carrying it over to the other dead man and placing it down beside him. It was almost too quick to see, but as he stood up, Torin pulled Thomaras's dagger out of the man's throat and slid it into his pocket.

"Did he..." Ashea began, but Thomaras interrupted her.

"He did. I've seen him working before, but never in action. Quick hands for a big guy. Let's go. Don't need to be seen by the guards."

Thomaras was already walking across the street, so Ashea followed. When they got to the entrance, Torin put one giant hand on Thomaras's chest.

"You're Erica's friend. No trouble. Yes?"

That deep bass voice seemed to rumble in Ashea's chest, not altogether unpleasantly.

"No trouble," Thomaras replied with a wink and continued on after Torin removed his hand.

Ashea followed and intended to smile at the giant as she walked in, but he was already turning to speak to the guards that approached.

"I thought he saw that you helped him. Why would he think you'd cause trouble?" Ashea asked.

"He doesn't, just needed an excuse to get close enough to give me my knife back," Thomaras responded, patting the cleverly hidden bracer of knives that was strapped to his chest.

Quick hands indeed.

Thomaras strode up to the innkeeper and slapped some coins across the bar. "One room, two beds if you have it, and dinner and drink brought up in an hour." Thomaras's tone was all business. Not rude, but certainly not inviting any chitchat.

The innkeeper took a quick glance at the coins before palming them and smiling back at Thomaras. "Of course, master Darrius. I'll have the boy bring you up right away. Young Ben!" the innkeeper bellowed.

It didn't take long for Young Ben to come running, a gawky, awkward youth who would probably never be considered handsome, but whose eyes flashed with bright intelligence.

"Right this way." His voice was quiet but confident, and Ashea got the sense that he wouldn't be stuck in this town too long.

"Thank you," Thomaras replied and then followed him up the stairs. "Have you worked here long, Young Ben?"

"Just Ben is fine. Only a few weeks at the Maiden, but I've been helping out at the inns in Hannover for a couple of years now," the boy replied without looking back.

"Ben, then. So you would probably recognize someone that doesn't fit in with the usual crowd around here?"

"I would." The boy still didn't turn, but there was interest in his voice.

"Well, I'm waiting for someone like that. Older man with dark hair, a moustache and bushy eyebrows. He'll be dressed fancier than most. As soon as he arrives, can I count on you to come and knock on our door?"

As Thomaras finished the question, they arrived at their room and Ben unlocked the door, opened it and handed Thomaras the key. "I can try, sir, but we do get mighty busy here at night." The look on Ben's face suggested he was open to negotiation.

Thomaras smiled and pulled a small coin purse from one of his many pockets. He reached out to put it in the boy's hands, but as Ben reached for it, he pulled it back. "In addition to that man, you'll come let me know about anything else you see that's out of the ordinary?" Thomaras raised an eyebrow.

"Indeed, sir, upon reflection, we don't tend to get *that* busy at night." The boy winked, and Ashea saw that intelligence flash behind his eyes again.

"Good lad," Thomaras said and clapped him on the shoulder before heading into the room.

The room was small but neat, with two beds on either wall and a window looking out to the rear of the inn. Ashea walked to the window and was surprised to see a stable in the back.

Thomaras noticed her looking and walked over. "Any time I'm here, I get this room. The inn-keep, Earnest, knows me well and makes sure I get it. I like to be able to see who is coming and going."

As Thomaras kicked off his soft leather shoes and reclined on the bed, Ashea had to suppress a chuckle at his long legs as they fell off the end of it.

"Sounds like he's a good friend," Ashea said, watching Young Ben run to the stables on some errand or other.

Thomaras snorted a laugh. "The only thing he's friendly with is my coin. He knows I pay double for everything, including his discretion. You must be tired. Get some rest — dinner won't be up for awhile yet." Thomaras's eyes closed.

Almost as if his words were an invocation, Ashea's body seemed to remember how tired it was and she grunted her agreement as she closed the drapes, kicked off her own shoes, and crawled into the small bed. She started to ask Thomaras if one of them should stay up and keep watch, but she was already drifting away, and the last thing she remembered was mumbling unintelligibly about half-eaten boars before she fell asleep.

6

THOMARAS

~

Thomaras opened his eyes again after a few hours, feeling fully rested. He didn't need much sleep; about two hours every couple of days was generally enough, and it didn't need to be consecutive. Another attribute of his Arahana blood. Although he earned his living taking less than savoury jobs from high-paying people, usually whose faces he never saw, Thomaras's spare time was spent trying to track down any information he could on the Arahana.

Little was known about the Arahana. They were once the dominant race on Haven and even the least magically inclined Arahana could do things with magic that most of the current mages could only dream of. The mage of elements probably wielded more elemental power than the average Arahana, but the average Arahana could also wield any other branch of magic. Something no current mage could do.

It was assumed that there was some overlap with the Arahana and the humans that currently occupied Haven, but it must have been at an extremely early stage of development since there were no written records of any interaction, just some crude artifacts and paintings. It seemed as though the Arahana used the early tribes as a labour force. Slaves might be a strong word, but they certainly weren't equals.

Over the years, historians had put some of the puzzle tougher. It seemed the magic found in the bloodlines of humans today was a result of crossbreeding between the two species. These were working theories. There wasn't much to go on as most of the history of the Arahana was wiped out after the Cataclysm, along with the Arahana themselves. The consensus was that the humans that currently populated Haven were those that returned after heading east into the wastelands before the Cataclysm. The only reason anyone could come up with that people would willingly head into that mess was that they were forced to go. Likely by the Arahana, who fraternized with humans and created half-breeds. It was assumed that the Arahana wanted to keep their bloodlines pure and sent any bastard children away with their families. Thomaras found it funny that even beings as advanced as the Arahana wanted to fuck the help.

After Haven recovered from the Cataclysm, the nomadic peoples of the wastelands, and the generations of banished Arahana bastards who interbred with them, returned to fill the void in Haven left by the Arahana. Those people who returned to Haven all agreed that they felt the pull of the infinity prism, drawing them back to what they felt was their true homeland. While most couldn't explain exactly what that pull was, there emerged a select few who could interpret signs that gave them clarity. Some from dreams, others through nature itself, and some even told of messages coming to them through the weather or their campfires at night. Whatever the medium, all the messages added to the same story of the infinity prism, drawing them home.

The infinity prism was almost an entity itself, maybe not conscious in the way that people were but aware of its own existence and ever-fixated on maintaining balance. Within the infinity prism was the tiled plane: an infinite line of realities separated by the fabric of time itself. Balance within these planes kept the worlds from crashing in on each other.

The one constant that all of those who were sensitive enough to see the messages agreed upon was a large spider-like creature who acted as an agent of the prism and who would be their protector should they return to Haven. Not all the Nomads returned; likely those with less or no Arahana blood and who didn't feel the pull remained, seeing in those returning only the same made-up gods that people outside of their desert followed blindly.

Now, diluted Arahana blood was part of the peoples of Haven, and mages were, according to their own historians, the result of those seers returning to the place where their magic could grow into its full potential. Most of this speculation was pieced together from Arahanan ruins or tribal human cave paintings that historians have found over the years and referenced with the earliest history of the recolonization of Haven. It made sense, as timelines jibed with oral histories of the Nomads that remained out east when their "softer" brethren traded in a life on horseback for agriculture and cities.

What didn't make sense was Thomaras.

As far as he could tell, he was half Arahana. His eyes, his build and all the strange attributes that he benefited from spoke to his blood being fully mixed. Not diluted over generations of breeding. Which should be impossible. The Cataclysm happened thousands of years ago and, although the Arahana were long-lived, all historians agreed it was a lifespan of centuries, not millennia.

So Thomaras tracked down even the most dubious leads, relics, ruins or people that had anything to do with the Arahana.

A knock at the door startled him out of his thoughts. Thomaras sat up and stretched a little before walking to the door.

"Yes?" he said quietly so as not to disturb Ashea's sleep.

"Master Darrius, a gentleman just sat down in the common room. Dressed in finery and doing a poor job of trying to look less nervous than he is. Thought you'd want to know." After delivering the message, Ben's footsteps faded down the hallway.

Earnest must have told Ben his name, which was exactly why Thomaras always used a fake. Earnest was a good man, but your average person couldn't always be counted on to keep the 'utmost' in the level of discretion that Thomaras paid for.

Thomaras pulled on his cloak and checked that he had the room key before stepping out the door, locking it behind him. He moved down the hallway and into the common room. There was still light outside, but the sconces were being lit in anticipation of the coming dusk. Thomaras's stomach rumbled as the smell of dinner, likely a stew and hearty at that, hit his nose. Earnest saw him come down the stairs but paid him no mind; a better example of the discretion that Thomaras relied on him for.

Thomaras spotted the man he was looking for right away. He'd only met — was it Joseph? — once, but he would have recognized him as being out of place even if he'd never seen him before. His clothes were bright red crushed velvet with gold and brass buttons and trimmings. His riding cloak was dark black, to hide the dirt, and lined with fur. Fashion over function this time of year. He was doing a passable job of looking more haughty and judgmental than nervous, but Ben was right; you could still see it on him. As he saw Thomaras walking over, he moved to stand up, but Thomaras motioned that he stay seated.

"She's upstairs sleeping. It was an exhausting journey. After dinner, I'll bring her out to the stables and you can be on your way."

"Excellent. I would rather leave now, however. Can you bring her out immediately?" The man's nerves were clearly frayed.

Perhaps his journey here hadn't been so great either.

"You're better to leave after dark. That way, you'll miss the masses heading out after their shifts. A mark like you in this town could be too tempting, even with your guards." Thomaras was about to stand up but Joseph gestured with his hands that he stay. He then looked around conspiratorially and leaned in close to Thomaras.

What an amateur.

"About that. The guards I hired to bring me here refused to take me back. We ran into some... trouble, and the superstitious fools think the whole errand is cursed. Would you be willing to act as an escort for me? I've already convinced the brute at the door to come along, but I could use someone that I know I can rely on." Joseph looked around again and blew out his moustache as he leaned back in his chair.

He really was shaken.

"Guard duty isn't really my thing," Thomaras said curtly.

The truth was that he was getting too close to this job.

He had told Ashea his real name, ostensibly to make her feel more comfortable, but the truth was he was starting to like her.

That was far too close to the job.

"Sorry, this will be where we part ways. Good hire, though," Thomaras said, nodding his head towards the door. "He's more than just size. He can handle himself."

Joseph nodded, resigned, as Thomaras turned around. Whether he was just too defeated to persist or he could read the determination in Thomaras, he didn't press the issue.

Thomaras headed back up the stairs, the din of the common room receding away to nothing as he reached his room, unlocked the door and entered. For a moment, he stood there and looked at Ashea.

She was pretty, but not his type. No, it wasn't that kind of attraction that was causing Thomaras such trouble with this one. He'd never had family or friends; this type of business required solitude to be successful and his father had been human garbage. Perhaps what he was feeling for her was more along the lines of friendship? Kinship? Thomaras shook his head. Weakness was a more accurate description.

He crossed the room and began to gather his things. He opened his pack and began to put the throwing knives that he'd left behind into the various hiding places on his person.

Thomaras felt a little better knowing that the giant doorman would be going with Joseph and Ashea. He made a mental note to have a word with Torin before they left. As a professional courtesy. Joseph appeared to be attracting some kind of trouble and that boar was still an unsettling weight on Thomaras's mind.

For a second time that night, Thomaras's thoughts were

interrupted by the door and, more pleasantly, the smell of dinner.

"I have your meals here, Master Darrius." Earnest's voice came from the other side of the door, along with the sound of a tray being placed on the floor and footsteps receding down the hallway.

Thomaras opened the door eagerly and bent down to pick up the tray. Two bowls of stew, two mugs of ale, and some crusty bread sat before him. Not a feast fit for a king, but a damn sight better than the devil boar jerky that he had earlier.

When he placed the tray on the small table between the beds, the scent of food seemed to pull Ashea out of her slumber. "Smells good," she said, sitting up before her eyes had even fully opened.

Thomaras handed her a bowl, took the other for himself and for a moment they sat in companionable silence while they ate.

"The gentleman who hired me to get you out is here to collect you," Thomaras said without looking up from his food.

"Oh, okay. Does that mean this is where we part ways?" Ashea's tone betrayed the expression of hope on her face that Thomaras was studiously trying to avoid.

Hope that he would disagree with her statement.

Misplaced hope.

"It does. Good news, though. He hired Torin to escort you to wherever you are going. I have no doubt he'll keep you safe," Thomaras said around a mouthful of bread. He kept eating to give the impression of professional detachment. Not something he normally needed to fake.

"Oh yes, that's good. He looks very... capable."

Something in her tone gave Thomaras the impression

that capable wasn't the word she was thinking of, but he resisted the urge to look up at her or push the issue.

Detachment.

"Right, so when you're all done, you can get a couple more hours of sleep and then meet me in the common room. I'll introduce you to Joseph and you can be on your way," Thomaras said, standing up before she could answer and walking to the door.

"Sounds good. Thanks, Davin," he heard from behind him and, as his hand rested on the door handle, he couldn't help but smile.

Utmost discretion, and he didn't even have to pay her.

"It's Darrius here," he said and turned to give her a wink. "Davin will work anywhere in the southeast, though, if you ever need to hire me." *Maybe not detachment, but at the very least, I managed to keep it professional.*

Ashea only smiled and went back to her meal. Her eyes still looked tired, and he imagined a few more hours of sleep would do her some good. Thomaras closed the door behind him and headed down to the common room.

Erica's shift should be starting any time now, and he was eager to see her again.

7

THOMARAS

~

E rica's deep breaths told Thomaras that she'd fallen asleep, her naked body curled pleasantly against his in the small bed in his rented room. He'd been friends with Erica for a long time. They would always chat when he passed through Hannover, and it was always the highlight of his stay. About a year ago, she had suggested they spend some time together after her shift. It came as no surprise to Thomaras, who had noticed a connection early on.

The surprise was that he kept coming back to her.

Ashea had come down to the common room shortly after Erica's shift had finished, and the three of them sat and talked for a while. Thomaras was pleased to see the two women getting along so well. Perhaps in another life, the two of them could have been friends. When Thomaras and Erica retired to his room, Ashea had been sitting with Joseph as they waited for Torin's shift to finish.

He wondered if he'd ever see her again. Not that it mattered. The job was done. He'd been paid and found some fun for the evening on top of it. Torin had said he'd be done "soon" when Joseph last pressed him, so Thomaras assumed they'd probably left by now.

A scream of terror made Thomaras bolt upright in bed, causing Erica to be unceremoniously dumped to the floor.

"Um, what was that?" she asked, more concerned about the scream than her fall.

"Nothing good," Thomaras said as he rushed, naked, to the window. "I would get dressed if I were you." Not something Thomaras normally said to a beautiful woman in his bedroom, but extreme circumstances made for strange times.

Fumbling for his trousers, Thomaras peered into the darkness. Horses were whinnying in fear and running from the open doors of the stables. In the light of the torches, Thomaras could just make out the scene below him. Joseph, the author of the scream, was being dragged into the stables by the stuff of nightmares. Dark, hairy and with too many legs, Thomaras thought they looked like insects of some kind, but they were each the size of a small wolf. On the right side of the stable, Torin had pinned Ashea behind him and was swinging a torch like a tiny club in his massive hands, fending off four more of the creatures. He connected with one of them, sending it spinning backwards, and as it landed, it raised its forelegs in challenge.

Spiders.

Thomaras's pants fell to the floor, forgotten. Giant spiders? Thomaras's thoughts briefly went back to the not-dead, dead boar thing that they had fought, but these looked different. They were moving how you would expect spiders to move. Were those spiders eighty pounds and organized against you? What was happening today?

There was no time to answer that question even if he

could because at that moment Thomaras's keen eyes picked up three more spiders on the roof of the stables. Suddenly, Torin and Ashea looked very much like a couple of flies that had wandered into an ambush.

"Give me my bow!" Thomaras yelled, hand extended out behind him, not daring to take his eyes off the spiders on the roof.

"Why? What's out there?" Erica asked.

"I would say the less you know, the better at this point," Thomaras responded, as the bow slid into his grasp. He quickly passed it into his other hand and reached out again for the quiver. "Let's just say..." he began as he grasped at the air. "So, I'm going to need those arrows, too."

Thomaras did his best keep his voice measured, as shouting would only scare her more. He heard her whisper the word "shit" under her breath as she crossed the room again, but he barely noticed. The first of the spiders had gracefully slid over the edge of the roof and had begun descending towards its victims on a gossamer strand that Thomaras could just barely make out in the light of the torches.

As the quiver hit his hand, Thomaras smashed the glass out of the window, hoping his intended targets would be too distracted to notice the sound. Torin now had one spider by the top of the head and was doing his best to keep its five-inch fangs from finding flesh. The other hand was still swinging the torch in a large arc, keeping the other spiders at bay. Ashea was gamely throwing rocks at spiders and although more often than not her aim was true, the projectiles barely seemed to register.

Thomaras drew his bow and fired at the first spider. At this range, Thomaras didn't need a full draw, so by the time the first arrow smashed through the creepy monster's thorax and pinned it to the wall, Thomaras had already drawn and loosed two more arrows. The next arrow hit the spider on the left, who had not yet started its descent, and sent it flying into the gloom. The last arrow missed its mark when the now-descending spider, with shocking speed, dropped itself from its webbing and began to fall to the ground. It wasn't quite fast enough, though, and Thomaras's arrow took off the back leg that had guided its descent, sending it pinwheeling to the ground and tumbling into the bushes that lined the stable.

Without thinking, Thomaras leapt out of the window, bare-ass naked, and braced himself for impact. While hanging in midair, Thomaras briefly thought about how strange it was that he was, quite literally, jumping into the fray to help what amounted to two complete strangers.

Then he was hitting the ground and rolling and he didn't have any more time to think about how many of his own rules of survival he was breaking.

When the two spiders, one dead and one maimed, hit the ground beside them, Torin and Ashea looked up to see Thomaras rolling to his feet with his bow at full draw in his hands. Torin simply nodded, red eyes giving nothing away behind his bandanna as he held an eighty-pound spider by the head with his arm fully extended. The man was strong.

Thomaras let his arrow fly, and it hit the spider that Torin was holding with such force that it broke apart, leaving Torin holding the head in his hand, which he promptly smashed, fangs first, into the head of the spider closest to him. It too collapsed to the ground, twitching.

The remaining spiders turned their nightmare faces towards Thomaras and backed towards the open stable doors, stomping a complex dance as they did. Torin grabbed Ashea, and they both ran towards Thomaras.

"No pants," Torin said simply, and Thomaras got the sense from his tone that he was acknowledging the bravery involved leaping into battle naked. Thomaras could really only acknowledge the stupidity at this point, since the only thing that he could think of that was worse than fighting giant spiders was doing so completely naked.

"Yes, well, I do some of my best work without pants on," Thomaras quipped grimly and Ashea snorted a laugh that was so genuine that Thomaras couldn't help but chuckle himself.

"Trouble," Torin rumbled, pointing towards the stable doors.

Emerging from the gloom were four more spiders. Presumably, the little dance was some kind of communication to call their brethren. Thomaras didn't want to think of what had befallen Joseph after he'd been dragged inside.

"Shoot them, please," Ashea said, any mirth in her voice gone and replaced by fear.

Thomaras thought that was a grand idea and loosed the arrow he had nocked. He began to draw another, even as the first impaled one of the spiders.

"Shit," he hissed under his breath as he tossed the splintered arrow to the ground. It must have broken during his heroic leap. "Got any weapons on you, big man?"

"Hammer," Torin said and pointed again towards the stable.

"Not a great spot for it. Maybe I can draw them away so you can get in there and grab it?" Thomaras asked.

"There might be more inside," Torin responded.

"Any thoughts, Ashea?" Thomaras spared a glance at Ashea, but she didn't respond. Sweat was starting to bead on her forehead.

Finally she said, "Torin, get ready to catch," and her eyes snapped open.

"Catch wha—" Thomaras began but stopped when he saw the largest maul that he'd ever laid eyes on come flying, seemingly of its own volition, out of the stables. The spider directly in its path ducked out of the way just in time as the hammer flew right into Torin's outstretched hand.

"Thanks," he said, apparently nonplussed at his massive weapon jumping into his hand.

Torin tossed the torch to Thomaras and with a practiced gesture, spun the hammer quickly in one hand, spinning it on its axis in his hand rather than spinning it around in a circle, and looked the weapon over.

The thing was about six feet long. Its iron handle was wrapped in worn leather and it looked as though it was one solid piece. Thomaras couldn't see any joints where the handle met the head. The head of the hammer itself was intimidating to the point of being terrifying. It was shaped like a wolf's head, and the two wicked-looking spikes on the back had been wrought to look like fur bristling on the hackles of a wolf's neck, while the business end of the hammer was shaped like the wolf's open mouth, complete with teeth etched into each side of the hammer's face.

Thomaras let out a low whistle. He'd seen mauls like that wielded by knights before, but even the largest men he'd seen had needed two hands to swing the ponderous weapons. All power and no speed. But in Torin's hands, it moved more like a stave. As he walked towards the spiders, he tossed it from hand to hand, waiting for the right moment.

"Forgot about that magic of yours. How'd you do that?" Thomaras asked, glancing down at the exhausted girl crouched down beside him.

"Air," she panted. "Just made it thick enough to scoop it up."

"But you could barely light a candle before?" Thomaras asked.

"Are you complaining? I don't understand it any more than you. All I know is using this much magic is exhausting."

Thomaras got the sense that something about using magic was bothering her more than she wanted to admit but didn't press the issue. "Seems like you're always tired," Thomaras said nonchalantly. "You should consider getting yourself into better shape."

"Shut up."

Torin closed the distance on the spiders and the carnage began. The first spider that leapt at him was smashed to the ground in a blur of iron that was a two-handed overhead swing. As a second spider looked to take advantage of Torin being bent over his victim, Torin simply flicked the hammer out one-handed to the side and got it with the top of the hammer's head, sending the creature flying. One of the spiders had moved around behind him, looking to flank, but Torin's practiced eye caught the movement and he spun around backward, looping the hammer low and catching the spider with the spiked butt end of his weapon. The speed with which the giant man moved was uncanny.

"How did he even see that one?" Ashea asked, now able to stand beside him.

"When you're that big, people try to gang up on you, attack you from behind. Torin must be used to it by now. I wouldn't guess he's lost many fights," Thomaras explained.

"Makes sense," Ashea responded, and then added, "Cold out here?"

"Hey," Thomaras said, sparing her a glance, "my eyes are up here."

The last three spiders had skittered away from the death-dealing mountain in front of them to try to regroup, but Torin didn't give them the chance. Rushing forward, he threw the hammer with one hand at an unsuspecting spider. It flew end over end until it squished the monster into the ground with a thud. Not breaking stride, Torin grabbed the closest spider to him with both hands, raised it over his head and smashed it to the ground. It stopped moving immediately.

The last spider was on Torin as soon as he straightened up, but he was ready and managed to catch the spider's deadly fangs on those impressive bracers of his. The fangs stuck into them and Torin lifted the spider up one-handed, ready to smash it on the ground. Unfortunately for Torin, the spider's abdomen was right at face level and before Torin could bring it down for a final blow, it began to spin its web around him. The silken strands looped around the back of his head, trapping his outstretched arm against his face. As strong as he was, Torin couldn't get any leverage to rip his arm free, and his whole head soon disappeared underneath a mound of webbing.

"Son of a bitch!" Thomaras exclaimed and began to run towards his suffocating companion.

He closed the distance quickly and raised the torch, ready to club the foul beast off of Torin. Before he could bring his arm down, he felt an impact in his chest and went flying. Lightning-quick, the spider had kicked him. Thomaras tried to get back up, but the wind had been knocked out of him and just getting his breath back seemed impossible, let alone getting to his feet.

The air above him seemed to sizzle as a cube of fire flew

by and hit the spider, engulfing it in flame and sending it into the side of the stables where it stopped moving. Calming himself mentally, Thomaras began to catch his breath to the point that he could get himself up and over to Torin.

The big man was on his knees, pulling uselessly at the webs that coated his head. Concerned about his ability to breathe underneath all that web, Thomaras pulled one of his ruined arrows out of his quiver and grabbed Torin by the shoulder.

"Stay still!" he screamed, hoping Torin heard him.

Torin immediately went still and Thomaras began to saw away at the webs at the back of his head. Slowly the strands gave way until Thomaras had created enough space to get both of his hands inside the webbing and heave. It didn't come away all at once, but when he heard Torin start gasping, he knew he'd done enough to break the seal.

"Pull your arm free!" Thomaras yelled again and stepped back as Torin ripped his arm away from his face, pulling most of the webbing away.

As he did so, the balaclava and hat that he always wore ripped away and fell to the ground. Thomaras bent down, picked up the wrap, and then froze when he looked at Torin's uncovered face for the first time.

Torin's eyes were red and deep-set into a broad face. A bald head gave way into what looked like bushy sideburns but were actually thick fur that ran down the side of his face from ears to jawline but stopped where his cheeks began. His nose was broader than most, but was proportionate to the rest of his face. Seeing Thomaras look upon him for the first time, Torin smiled shyly, exposing what looked like small tusks that curved slightly out of his mouth.

"That's why you're so big. You're part Granite Ogre, aren't you?" Thomaras asked.

"Half," Torin responded.

"Mom or Dad?" Thomaras asked without thinking. Frankly, he was baffled by the logistics of it either way.

"Dad." Torin didn't seem embarrassed by the discovery, despite having hid his face.

"Your mom must have been some lady. I didn't think a human could survive conception with a Granite Ogre, let alone birthing one," Thomaras blurted out as he handed Torin back his balaclava.

"She didn't," he said.

"Oh, I... sorry." Thomaras mentally cursed his lack of filter, but Torin waved the comment away.

"Leave her alone!" Erica's scream saved Thomaras from further awkwardness, but any relief was quickly dashed when he turned to see what was happening.

Erica was leaning out of the now opened window of his room, half naked, and pelting the seven-legged spider that Thomaras had winged with an arrow earlier with Thomaras's belongings. The scene was so ridiculous that it took him a moment to notice that the spider was attempting to drag Ashea's unconscious body away.

Almost in unison, Torin and Thomaras charged at the spider. Upon seeing them, it looked quickly from Ashea to them and back to Ashea again, a behaviour so human that Thomaras made a note to laugh about it later, before turning abdomen and fleeing.

"Is she okay?" Erica asked when they got to the body. "I think it bit her."

"No shirt," Torin said, his tone slightly different from when he had commented on Thomaras's lack of clothing, but no less appreciative.

"Eyes down, big man," Thomaras said as knelt beside Ashea.

Her breathing was shallow but steady and she had gone extremely pale. There was a nasty-looking bite on the back of her leg.

"We might have a problem here."

Thomaras was familiar with poisons of all sorts, but his strength was more in administering them than removing them.

"Venomous?" Torin asked.

"Looks like it. We need to get her to a healer quickly," Thomaras said in a rush.

"I know someone. Pants," Torin said, pointing at a pile of Thomaras's clothes that had been tossed from the window.

"Yes, pants," Thomaras deadpanned.

8

THOMARAS

~

Thomaras dressed hastily while Torin gently picked Ashea up in his arms. The tiny woman looked almost like a doll clutched against the half Granite Ogre's giant chest. Erica had disappeared from the window and Thomaras cursed himself for not telling her to stay put. They could very well still be in danger and he didn't need her death weighing on his mind.

Motioning for Torin to follow, Thomaras quietly moved into the gloom of the stables, daggers drawn, eyes quickly adjusting to the darkness as he scanned for more of the spiders hiding within. He jumped slightly when movement caught his eye, but relaxed when he realized it was Joseph raising one bloody hand to him.

"Darrius... thank the prism. Is the girl okay?" Joseph's voice was weak and full of pain. Thomaras was frankly a little surprised at his concern over Ashea.

"One of those things bit her. She's alive, but

unconscious. Are *you* okay?" Thomaras knew the answer to the question even as he asked it.

Bending down beside the man, he could see that the spider's large fangs had literally ripped his guts out. Thomaras had once watched a butcher remove the intestines from a pig and a cold, detached portion of his brain was surprised at how similar they were to the human intestines before him.

"No, I don't think I am, but that doesn't matter. You have to get her to my employer. He can help her." Joseph's voice was still reed thin and weak, but his grip on Thomaras's arm was strong with desperation.

"I don't even know who employed you, Joseph. Torin knows someone. He's going to bring her to them." Thomaras gently pried Joseph's hand off of his wrist and the man clutched his hand instead, pulling Thomaras down to his face.

"NO! She must make it to him. Bring her to the mage of reflections. Our world depends on her making it to him. He can help her." Thomaras turned his face away from the dying man's breath, the fetid smell of blood, bile and death heavy on each word he spoke. "Bring her... bring her to him..." Joseph's grip on his hand slackened and his head rolled to the side, his final strength spent.

Thomaras rocked back on his heels. *The mage of reflections? The leader of the council of mages. The man that stood between Haven and disasters that only he can foresee. What does he want with Ashea?* Thomaras suddenly felt that all of this was far, far above his pay grade. Maintaining anonymity and delivering a human package to the most powerful man on the entire continent didn't exactly go hand in hand.

"Darrius?" Torin's voice was a low rumble that shook him out of his reverie.

"Right, well, it's up to you where you want to take her. The mage of reflections resides in the capital to the north, but it seems like her condition is time-sensitive. How close is your person?"

"Closer, west of here," Torin said. His words seemed to be laced with accusations of being abandoned.

Of abandoning Ashea.

"Seems like that's the move, then. I'm sure Joseph wouldn't mind you borrowing his cart."

"You aren't going with them?" a voice from behind him said, making him cringe. These words weren't just laced with accusations, they were *dripping* with them. "How could you do that? They're going to need your help. You can't just abandon them!" Erica's voice was firm and cutting without being shrill. All those drips of accusations had finally coalesced into the real thing and Thomaras didn't like it.

"Why not?" Thomaras turned to face Erica. "I was hired to do a job. I did it. I don't see anyone here offering me more money for another job, do you? Even if they were, this is way over my head. I survive by keeping a low profile. This situation has the profile the size of... of him!" Thomaras gestured angrily towards Torin, punctuating his final words.

"You're so full of shit." The volume may have dropped out of Erica's tone, but the quiet only served to accentuate the anger that remained. "I watched you jump out of a window, ass naked, to fight giant spiders in order to save these two. Now you're saying you won't help save Ashea's life because it might draw *attention*? That ship may have already sailed, dumb-dumb!" Her voice did rise a little at the end and she made her own punctuating gesture towards the group of tavern patrons that were milling about, gasping in horror at the dead spiders strewn about the stable yard.

"All the more reason for me to cut and run now."

Erica laughed at him. "You aren't just going to leave these two to fend for themselves."

"You can't just berate me to get me to do what you want," Thomaras retorted.

"It's not what I want, silly, it's what you want. You just aren't willing to admit it."

"What I want to do is take the money I collected for this job and move on." *Wasn't it?*

"I know you've got this image you want to maintain, but you can drop it. You're among friends."

"I don't have friends!"

"What about me?"

"I told you when we first got together, it wasn't serious. That I go where I need to go and can't be tied down."

"And I believed you. Until you made excuses to come back again and again," Erica said with a warm smile.

"There's always work..."

"There's always work in Hannover," Erica cut him off with his own words. "You always say that and I never call you out on it, but at some point I'd have to be an idiot to think you weren't coming around for me."

Thomaras did his best laugh derisively. "For all you know, I have girls like you in every town."

"Do you?"

He didn't.

"That's not important. What does any of this have to do with these two?" Thomaras knew his anger was undercutting his greater point about not caring, but couldn't help it.

"My point is maybe you aren't as big an asshole as you

like to pretend," Erica said, holding up a hand to forestall his protest, "and maybe the reason you've never cared about people before is because they were never the right people."

"I don't even know them," Thomaras asserted.

"No, you don't. But isn't one of your great skills reading people? I know it's one of mine and these are good people. Good people that could use your help."

Erica had walked across the stable while they argued, and now she was standing close to him and looking up into his eyes. He looked at her upturned face and tried as hard as he could to believe she was wrong. That she was seeing something in him that wasn't there.

"I can hire you," Torin rumbled in the silence, "if that helps."

"Fine, I'll go. But it's only because of the coin," Thomaras lied.

"Of course it is, baby," Erica purred.

"Fuck," Thomaras said, and as he leaned in to kiss her, she intercepted him with a thumb and forefinger on either side of his chin, each gripping one side of his cheek so his lips were stuck puckered out like a fish.

"Good boy," she said with a wink, and kissed his nose.

Thomaras couldn't help but smile as she walked away. What fun was a woman who couldn't put you in your place from time to time?

"Well, looks like everyone has their stuff. Let's say we get out of here before another one of my nightmares comes true and tries to kill us," Thomaras said while picking up his pack and checking his bow. He removed the broken arrows from his quiver and tossed them aside, replacing them with fresh arrows from his travel pack.

Torin nodded and gently went about settling Ashea in the back of the cart. That done, he picked up their packs and laid them beside her. Erica simply patted Torin on the arm and they shared a smile. Thomaras could see it was the easy smile of two people who had been acquaintances so long that their bond was maybe even stronger than friendship. They may not have ever spent time together outside of The Jilted Maiden, but had shared so many experiences in that building that they had become something akin to family. Their silent farewell completed, she walked towards Thomaras and before he could say anything else kissed him hard on the lips, one hand cupping the side of his face, and all thoughts went out of his head.

"You take care of them, okay?" Her tone was earnest and her expression matched it.

"I mean, the guy is eight feet tall and about a million pounds — pretty sure he'll be taking care of me."

"I know. I just wanted to make you feel all tough and manly before you left. You want my real advice? Hide behind Torin," Erica said and slapped his butt.

Thomaras laughed and looked back at Torin, who had finished hitching up the horses and was giving him, or more accurately Erica's advice, a thumbs-up. "Just remember who got their face all webbed up there, big man."

Torin simply waved the comment away with another smile.

"Looks like the town guards are here. They're asking around the crowd, but I'll go give them the hysterical lady routine and make sure they're distracted. There's a road that leads into an alley behind the Maiden. Take it until you hit the main street and you can get out of town from there. Not sure if the guards would slow you up, but best not to risk it, right? Good luck, you guys!" And with that, Erica ran, wailing, into the stable yard, turning every head.

Thomaras hopped up onto the cart and started to drive

them out into the yard. Torin walked beside them and Thomaras didn't need to ask to know that he wouldn't be riding on the cart with him. He was just too big.

"You going to be able to keep up with us?"

"Horses have to keep up with me," Torin said.

Thomaras wasn't sure if Torin had a great sense of humour or a lot of trouble with the common tongue, but he was beginning to suspect the former.

Erica was as good as her word and was holding both of the guardsmen by their arms and dragging them to the front where she "was just *certain* one of those awful, awful things had gone." He led the coach the other way and into the alley, taking a final look back at Erica's retreating form.

At the only person he'd ever loved.

He thought he'd better tell her that next time he saw her.

Weaver (Interlude)

She was unnerved. That in itself was... unnerving. She was many, many things. She was ancient; she was wise; she was powerful; she was immortal. Or close to it. She was never unnerved.

It was unpleasant.

The humans, whether they believed she existed or not, called her the Orb Weaver. She supposed it was as good a name as any. Her true name was far too long and complex for the humans to comprehend. It was a name filled with power, a name older than she was, a name passed down for generations.

The name Orb Weaver was fairly clever, she had to admit, if inaccurate from an entomological perspective. She was not truly a spider, though she did look like one. However, the orb weaver spider was not the genus that her predecessors had based their form on. Her shiny black carapace, large at the abdomen and tapering down dramatically in the thorax and head, surrounded by long, delicate legs, was far more reminiscent of a black widow spider. She did not, however, have the trademark red hourglass marking on her. Such warnings seemed a trifle unnecessary when you were the size of a large cart, your legs ended in razor-sharp claws and your face was adorned with three-foot mandibles that curved like scimitars and could cut twice as easily.

No, what was clever about the name was how she read the reflections of the future that bounced off the walls of the infinity prism and returned to be seen by those attuned to it. Much like a spider, she did spin silk from her spinnerets, but the main purpose of hers was to read the reflections of future events from the infinity prism and, when things went according to plan, weave them into the form she wanted. Some clever human must have heard the name orb weaver somewhere and attributed it to her. Now when they referenced the guiding force of the infinity prism, they would often reference her as well. Unfortunately, things were not going to plan, and she wasn't weaving much out of this reflection at all.

The reflections were not an exact science. Much like light bouncing off of a real prism, these reflections of possible future returned refracted and distorted. It was up to beings like her to sort out their true meaning.

She sighed heavily, an action that caused her entire body to expand and contract, and tried to calm herself down. Her connection to her brood was telepathic and instantaneous, and the last thing she had seen through the eyes of her final offspring was that smallish ogre and the half-breed who had just killed the rest of her brood charging in to finish the job. She chose a tactical retreat rather than sacrifice her remaining spider in what would have been a foolish attempt to fight them off. Creating more would take time and energy she did not have. This way at least she could keep an eye on the girl and these two... developments.

The word tasted ashy in her mind, like it shouldn't be there. In her world, there weren't "developments." She weaved the webs and read the reflections and acted accordingly to keep her interests satisfied. Everything else had been correct. The girl was where she was supposed to be. That foolish mage — the prism reader, he called himself — had sent his men exactly where she had expected and she had influenced events so that when he got to that little mining town he would be without his guards. Everything, as usual, had gone according to plan.

Then these two... developments showed up. They were supposed to simply be the last of the guards employed by the prism reader. Every reflection of the future she had woven had said they would fall to her brood like any other.

They had not.

Calming herself with another sigh, she instructed the final spider to continue to follow them. The girl would need attention soon. The ogre said he knew someone to heal her and the Orb Weaver was fairly certain she knew who that was. She turned to her webs and started looking over what had been woven. A massive tapestry of silken strands filled the large underground chamber that was her weaving grotto. Hundreds of feet of web filled the room. Patterns and designs that would look nonsensical to any but her filled every inch of the walls. Most of the tapestry was dedicated to an over-arching reflection, the equivalent of a rainbow whose beams had been spilt thousands of ways, that sprung from the Cataclysm which had cleared out the original occupants of Haven and stretched all the way to the present. This was the reflection that the prism wanted disseminated among the people of Haven and acted as a warning against another cataclysm. It was the reflection that created the original pull that drew the magic-sensitive descendants of the Arahana back to Haven and was the reflection that had become as close to a religion as the people of Haven came to following. There were no shrines, though a few statues had been made in her likeness, and no clergy to speak of, but all the people here felt the pull from time to time and understood that the infinity prism often had plans for them. For decades, the Orb Weaver had flexed her influence to prevent various paths of the reflection that led to another disaster. Of late, most of what the reflection warned against was an entity of enormous power.

One that she had yet to be shown.

She reviewed the silken strands quickly, moving with a beautiful, fluid grace. Once the information from a reflection had occurred and could no longer be re-woven, the webbing would disintegrate and fall away. When new paths of the reflection occurred, she would feel it and weave the will of the reflection on her walls. Once there, it was hers to manipulate to a point. Subtle shifts were best, she had found. A light touch. It was best if no one suspected she was there. Though, as was evidenced by her dispatching her brood, sometimes a more direct approach was necessary. That *child* who called himself a prism reader was also able to read reflections; how, she did not know. She doubted he pulled silk out of his butt and threw it on a wall, but even *his* powers were unable to detect her meddling. She had to admit, grudgingly, that the mage had been doing an exceptional job of leading his people in the right direction. Of late, she had very little work to do. That all changed when the girl showed up...

Finally, she found the place where the reflection picked up again. Her mandibles twitched with relief and she rubbed her front legs together in satisfaction. They were going to see the Druid. Aside from her, only he and maybe one other would be able to heal the venom. She certainly wasn't planning on visiting these would-be heroes, so best to let the Druid handle the healing. She was almost certain the Druid wouldn't kill for her. He had drawn that line in the past, but he would heal the girl and detain them for a while. Once they left him, however, she could arrange for a nasty surprise.

More than a little relieved that things were back to normal, the Orb Weaver began plucking and mending strands to arrange for some trouble to befall her prey. As she was working away, a feeling of dread suddenly filled the pit of her stomach. She ignored it while she made the last arrangements on her silken tapestry and then suddenly she was falling. Her legs, normally able to cling to the webs without thought, let go. The strands she was weaving were almost at the top of the grotto, and while a hundred-foot drop wouldn't kill her, neither would it be pleasant.

Fortunately, some ancient ingrained instinct that had bled over from her arachnid form had set a guide strand of webbing and she found herself suddenly swinging like a pendulum rather than falling like a stone. Though this was not the primary use of her webbing, it was a skill with which she was just as adept and her legs gracefully gripped the guide strand as she let more out and lowered herself to the ground.

What had caused her to slip and why?

Before she could complete the thought, nausea gripped her so deeply that she almost blacked out. It felt like something was trying to burst through her abdomen.

Something dark and evil.

In desperation, she began spinning out webbing. It came out normally at first, and then the white silken strands started to get darker and darker until they were such a black obsidian that it seemed to swallow the light from the torches completely. Frantically she kept spinning, wanting nothing more than this evil out of her body. Finally, the web abruptly returned to a silken white, and she stopped spinning. She simply stared at the black mass before her. Maybe fifteen feet long, she dared not put it on the wall. Surely something like that had no place within the tapestry of the world. Not wanting to look at it anymore, she gathered up the silk and stuffed it into an old chest that she sometimes used to hold items for her human agents. When the lid closed, she was so relieved that she slumped down, one leg lying across the chest.

She sat this way for some time, recovering from both the nausea and the altogether different, sick feeling she had from seeing that stuff come out of her. Once she had recovered, she realized that she could feel something... wrong through the box. She laid another leg on the box and the feeling intensified. No, that wasn't right.

It clarified.

Suddenly, all of that nausea she had felt when the mass was inside her was in a form that she could parse. She was right not to put it on the wall. This was no reflection to be read — it was a warning for her. The connection that she had to the prism, the one that knew her name and passed knowledge to it, was warning her. Something was amiss.

She continued to feel the evil from the mass, to sift its intentions... yes, it was starting to form a little more clearly. It was still just a feeling, but there was something... it felt like... like someone was knocking on the wall? Knocking on the wall of this plane of existence? That made no sense. She felt it some more... No, not knocking. Digging?

Her stomach dropped.

Someone... no. Something.

Something was trying to get in.

9

TORIN

≈

Torin walked easily beside the cart as it bumped and jostled down the dirt road out of Hannover, his long legs matching the pace of the draft horses without a problem. His size, strength and stamina all came from his Granite Ogre father. Full-blooded Granite Ogres were much larger than him, standing twelve feet tall to his eight and weighing almost twice as much. They were also far more ponderous, however, an advantage that Torin had over his full-blooded brethren. His human side made him smaller, but quicker and more coordinated as well. Torin wasn't sure if this had more to do with being half human or growing up as the smallest, and most different, member of his society. Any contest of strength, the primary type of a physical contest that Granite Ogres participated in, he would lose. So, early on, Torin learned to be quicker and better than his opponents.

His life amongst his father's people hadn't been any more difficult than most. As a child, he was picked on for being different, but that happened anywhere. In his mind, it strengthened him and taught him how to survive on his own. Once he became an adult, however, he was largely accepted for what he was; a small ogre who worked hard and had a quick wit. The ogres weren't the brutes that many assumed they were, based on their appearance and ferocious strength. They loved to wrestle and compete, but who didn't like to test their strength in physical competition? They were fierce warriors when the time called for battle, but the humans were the ones that had forced the aggression between the two races.

Torin shook himself out of his reverie. That was a painful history to dwell on, and if he was going to continue living among these people — his people, he had to remind himself — then it was best not to think of the atrocities of the past. Instead, he glanced over at his new companion. Darrius? He thought that's what Earnest had called him. Definitely a lone wolf, but he'd twice now helped Torin when the odds were against him. Honourable... or at least honourable in his own way, and fairly funny as well. Probably not as funny as Torin, but, in Torin's own estimation, that was a high mark to hit.

Feeling Torin's gaze upon him, Darrius turned to look his way. Sitting upon the cart, he was eye to eye with Torin for the first time. "Whatcha thinking about, big man?" Darrius asked in his rapid common tongue.

Torin had no trouble understanding the common tongue, but speaking it was a little more difficult. Not that he didn't know all the words. Languages came easily to him, but words in Common were difficult to form around his tusks. He had to speak slowly and even then some words would come out slurred or mushed. For this reason, Torin tended to use as few words as possible.

"Big. Not a man," Torin replied, giving Darrius a pointed look.

Another specialty of Torin's, as the balaclava he used to hide his tusks forced him to use his eyes to express most of his non-verbal intentions. He certainly wasn't ashamed of what he was or how he looked. Many female ogres had thought his tusks were quite handsome, and he agreed, but he didn't like to scare people, and his size, combined with the tusks, tended to do just that.

"Well, technically you're half, and that half is a better man than most I've known." Darrius looked uncomfortable saying these kind words to Torin.

"You *are* handsome, but I am not interested." Torin couldn't help but twist the dagger a little at his discomfort. To his very pleasant surprise, Darrius smiled at the joke.

"You're breaking my heart, Torin. Have you any idea how hard it is to find someone taller than me? Just once, I'd like to be the little spoon." Darrius finished the last words with a wink, and Torin boomed out a laugh that echoed into the night.

"You're pretty funny, Darrius. Not as funny as me, but funny," Torin said after he'd finished his laugh.

"Thomaras, actually. Seems like we're in this together for at least a little while, so you might as well know my real name." Thomaras looked uncomfortable again at this revelation, though this time it seemed more like the discomfort of a carpenter who had used a specific tool for so long that using a new one was throwing him out of his rhythm.

"Thomaras." The name was a little harder to say than Darrius, but if he took his time, he could say it clearly. "It suits you. You are pretty tall... for a human."

It was true. Thomaras stood a head taller than most men

around him at any given time, though he was still much shorter than Torin. He also blended into the crowd remarkably well for someone who should stick out like a sore thumb, or like a half Granite Ogre, in a common room. Earlier that day when he had thrown the dagger from the crowd it had taken Torin's keen and practiced eye longer than normal to find him and see where it had come from, and even then he had a sneaking suspicion that had Thomaras wanted to remain a face in the crowd he could have.

"Yes, well... my mother was a tall woman, I'm told," Thomaras said.

Torin couldn't quite put his finger on it, but he thought there was something in that statement. If it was a lie, it was a very practiced one. Maybe there was more to that story than he was letting on? In any case, his tone certainly suggested that the matter was closed and Torin didn't want to push his new companion too hard too soon. He agreed with Erica that they would need his help and he still wasn't sure how committed Thomaras was to sticking around. Not to mention he liked the confident man and could maybe even consider him a friend one day. It had been a long time since Torin had someone he could call a friend. Not since he'd been back on the plains with his father's people. He did have some companions at The Jilted Maiden that he was fond of. Erica, who Thomaras had become close with, and Rolph, who was the doorman that worked whenever Torin didn't, were both work friends, but this seemed different.

"So, where are we headed and who is this giant-nightmare-spider venom expert we're going to see?" Thomaras asked smoothly, changing the subject before it could even become a subject.

"Druid. Good healer. Head west of Tannerhorn. Into the

Darkwoods." Torin explained the directions and Thomaras nodded, clearly familiar with the area.

The Darkwoods, although they sounded sinister, were so named for the remarkable colours that the trees took on. Ranging from light, normal-looking wood all the way to the darkest wood stain imaginable, the trees there grew naturally in different colours and were one of the few natural resources found in Ithadore. Many craftsmen traveled great distances to harvest wood for projects for which they could charge huge sums of money.

This was not to say there weren't dangers in the woods. They were vast and deep and many predators roamed there, but the same could be said for any good-sized forest. There were legends of the forest defending itself against those who took too much at one time, but no one knew if they were true or simply a tale made up to protect the natural splendour and incredible resource that was the Darkwoods.

"So if this Druid lives out in the woods, is he still a part of the council?" Thomaras asked.

"Not sure. I know he doesn't like big indoor places," Torin answered. He didn't know the Druid that well, but he had mentioned on many occasions that while he supported and understood the need for a council, that traveling to the capital every moon cycle and sitting in the opulent meeting hall made him feel ill. He was far more comfortable out in nature, a sentiment that Torin could get behind.

"Makes sense, I suppose. Compared to all of this, the council chamber of Castle Vees probably seems a little less grand," Thomaras said, indicating the clear, pre-dawn sky still dotted with shining lights and wide-open country that spread before them. "I've always felt more comfortable on the road, though a city is a useful spot to find some companionship," Thomaras finished with a grin.

"Like Erica?" Torin asked.

"Like Erica... or any other woman one can find in such establishments. No need to limit oneself." The second part came out in a rush, as if the speed of his mouth could physically move his thoughts away from Erica herself.

Torin smiled and said nothing. He had known Erica a long time and never once seen her join a patron in their room, though not from a lack of offers. A few who offered a little too persistently had gotten some one-on-one time with Torin instead. They rarely offered again. Torin sensed something between the two humans, but kept his mouth shut. His mind wandered to Ashea and how it had felt to hold her tiny but womanly frame.

The rest of the trip continued in the companionable silence of two people who had spent years together as opposed to hours. Torin noticed this strange comfort but said nothing. It was obvious that Thomaras had as well, and there was no point in drawing attention to it. Torin was a man of few words anyway.

The sun was just beginning its journey over the horizon behind them when the forest came into view, vast and dark. The trees looked like an army arranged in haphazard battle formations. As they approached, the rising sun cast strange shadows from the trees and even Torin's keen eyes played tricks, for it looked as though shadowy figures were detaching themselves from the edge of the forest and lumbering awkwardly towards them.

Too awkwardly, actually.

Torin turned to ask Thomaras what he saw and his mouth went dry at the sight of the lithe man beside him.

Thomaras's face had drained of all colour and a single bead of sweat dripped from his hairline down toward his temple. He made no move to wipe it. He made no move at all, sitting stock-still in his seat and staring at the shadows Torin had seen.

Not bothering to ask what was wrong, Torin unlimbered his hammer from its place strapped across his back. The familiar weight of it in his hands eased the growing dread that had been creeping in his stomach, but did not remove it entirely.

Torin's movement beside him seemed to shake Thomaras out of his shocked state and he immediately pulled up on the reins to stop the horses and readied his own weapon. The giant bow looked as comfortable in Thomaras's hands as Torin's hammer felt in his own and the dread receded a little more.

"You know what these are?" Torin asked in a quiet rumble.

"No earthly idea, but I've seen something like them before and am very disappointed to find out it wasn't just a bad dream."

Thomaras seemed no less scared but had put on a professional visage that satisfied Torin.

Looking back towards the woods, Torin could see more clearly that the shapes approaching were animals. Or the bodies of animals? Deer, moose, bears and wolves — there were about eight of them in all. They shambled awkwardly, and as they came closer, he could see that some of them were missing limbs or had gaping holes in their flesh or broken bones protruding through their mottled fur.

The group of animals was about thirty feet from the edge of the forest and maybe fifty feet away from them. They were all sniffing around awkwardly, and Torin could hear them all making a similar sound.

"They saying something?" Torin asked and was

immediately answered by the *twang* of Thomaras's bow string.

He turned in the direction of the creatures just in time to see the closest wolf's head explode in gore as Thomaras's arrow struck home.

"You don't want to know," Thomaras answered without looking his way.

He was already lining up another shot as the things looked around to identify their attackers. The moose went down next, an arrow through the eye dropping it with an audible thump, and Torin allowed himself some relief. He wasn't particularly looking forward to testing his hammer against an angry moose-thing. His relief was short-lived, however, as the keen-eyed deer noticed them and, seemingly as one, all the remaining animals started to run towards them in a herky-jerky gait that, despite its awkwardness, was very fast. Torin's flesh crawled as he watched.

Three wolves, two deer and the bear bringing up the rear. Torin started to walk towards them deliberately.

"Torin, make sure to smash their heads!" he heard Thomaras call.

"How else?" Torin answered as he held the hammer up and spun it in his hand without looking back. He thought he heard Thomaras bark a grim laugh.

He kept his pace even, resisting the urge to charge into battle. He wanted Thomaras to thin the herd a little before he got there.

Twang.

The lead wolf suddenly appeared to trip and fall, rolling over and over until it finally stopped, an arrow protruding from its head.

Twang.

The deer right behind it fell out of the air mid-bound, its head a mangled mess. At this range, Thomaras's arrows were more like ballista missiles.

Twang.

The second deer was almost upon Torin when the arrow took it in the chest, knocking it backwards onto its side. As amazing a shot as he was, this close and moving as fast as they were, Thomaras had to eschew head shots for the more reliable centre mass target. Up close, Torin could see that the creatures were not only mottled and dirty, but their fur and flesh had taken on a matte black quality that seemed to swallow the light. Remembering Thomaras's instructions, Torin casually stomped the skull of the deer with his giant foot. The sickening, squelching crunch turned Torin's stomach, but he pushed on. This close to the animals, there was a prominent smell of mothballs that caused Torin to wrinkle his nose in displeasure.

The remaining wolf, hobbled by a badly broken back leg, was upon him first. It may not truly be a wolf now, but some remaining instinct caused it to circle low behind Torin, trying to hamstring the large prey and bring it down.

Unfortunately for it, Torin had never been prey in his life.

Swinging his hammer underhanded, he felt a satisfying *thunk* as the flat of the hammer connected under the chin of the beast, its head exploding as the momentum carried it flying into the bear, which stood up and swatted it away, staggering slightly at the impact.

Lots of pieces of skull and fur but no blood, Torin had time to think grimly before he turned towards the bear-thing.

The bear was big. As it drew itself onto its hind legs, it came as close as any opponent in recent memory to being eye to eye with Torin. It gave up less than six inches. It opened its mouth but instead of a roar, a single word came out in a voice that seemed strained and gravelly, like it struggled with the sound it was making.

"Ashea."

Torin was so shocked that he didn't immediately react when the bear charged, and by the time he came to his senses the beast was so close he was forced to drop his hammer and catch a massive foreleg in each hand as the bear reared up and tried to maul him. As he fell backwards, it was all he could do to keep the massive clawed paws away from his face, his arms fully outstretched and straining to keep a mouth full of razor-sharp teeth off of his neck.

This close, the smell of mothballs was almost choking Torin, but he didn't dare stop his steady breathing. If he held his breath, even for a moment, he might never get it back.

He heard Thomaras's bow firing repeatedly, but the bear didn't seem to register the arrows and the tangle of their bodies was probably making a headshot almost impossible. Torin thought back to his days wrestling the bigger ogres back home. The weight of the bear was massive, but if he could get some leverage...

Twisting his own hips, Torin managed to get a knee up into the bear's. This move caused the bear's mouth to get unpleasantly close to his face, but only briefly. Twisting his whole body into his knee, he was able to flip the bear's hips as he rolled and as the bear's hips went, so did the rest of its body. Now straddling the massive animal, Torin could bring his full strength to bear. Still gripping both forearms, Torin bent them until they snapped. The bear made no indication that it had felt anything at all, but its paws now hung, limp and useless, from its arms. With two of its weapons neutralized, Torin's arms were now free. The bear had been trying to wriggle free and buck him off, but all of Torin's considerable weight was sitting on its hips and he could control any of its movements from there.

Not wanting to feel those teeth, Torin simply jammed his forearm into the beast's mouth. The enchanted granite that infused his arms and gave his people their name easily snapped the teeth of the beast he sat astride. The animal continued to attempt it bite his arm, seemingly unaware that it had literally lost its bite. As strong as he was, Torin couldn't smash this thing's skull with one bare hand, but he didn't want to let the beast up. Who knew what else these things could do?

Thomaras appeared in front of him and his conundrum was abruptly solved as Thomaras plunged his dagger, two handed, into the beast's head. The bear went still and Torin slumped in relief. He noticed for the first time that the bear's eyes were completely missing. Empty sockets stared back at him. *How could it have seen us?*

"No time to relax, big man." Thomaras's words interrupted his thoughts, and he looked up to see him pointing towards the forest.

They were only about thirty feet away now, and he could just make out more shambling forms emerging from the woods. The space between them and the woods was also littered with the bodies of these creatures, arrows jutting out from their heads. Torin noticed Thomaras's empty quiver and realized that he hadn't been trying to shoot the bear earlier. He had been holding back another wave.

"Fuck," Torin said.

10

THOMARAS

~

Thomaras didn't wait to see if Torin was getting up before retreating back toward the cart and Ashea. He hadn't liked leaving her alone, but he hadn't wanted to leave Torin to fend for himself against that thing either.

He reached the cart with Torin on his heels and they both turned to face the creatures who, at this point, were mustering their forces at the tree-line. He barely had time to register the absurdity of what he was thinking. Aside from the wolves scattered amongst the group, none of these animals would know how to work together amongst themselves, let alone in mixed company. What was going on here?

"Working together?" Torin's question rumbled out beside him as if echoing Thomaras's own incredulity.

"I guess?" he replied.

Thomaras was eying the woods warily. He counted about fifteen of these things, all told. Without any arrows left, he didn't like their odds.

"Run?" Torin asked.

"I doubt it. Those things move unnaturally fast and those draft horses aren't built for speed. You smash, I slice?" Thomaras asked as he dropped his bow and took out his daggers. Even as he suggested it, he didn't like the plan. Torin smiled.

Fortunately for both of them, the plan didn't need to be tested. Both men started as the sound of creaks and groans filled the air. It was similar to the sounds occasionally heard in the woods: the pop or crack of tree branches swaying or shedding snow in the winter. A single note breaking out amongst the soft sounds of the forest like a musician rising above the sounds of a crowded common room.

Except this was an entire symphony.

Though they made no sounds, the creatures were clearly in disarray. In unison, the trees nearest these nightmares seemed to spring to life. Some of the lower branches swung around and wrapped the animals up, holding tight against their squirming. Some that were farther away grew at incredible speeds and impaled the creatures, sometimes two or three in a row, before curling up on themselves and holding them. Some just swung down and clubbed the largest animals repeatedly until they stopped moving.

Thomaras and Torin watched in stunned silence as the forest, as if it were an avatar for nature itself, came to life in response to the abominations that were desecrating its hallowed grounds.

As abruptly as it started, it ended.

Those animals that hadn't had their heads destroyed thrashed futilely against the almost eternal strength of the trees that held them. The threat was ended, and it seemed to Thomaras that they had the forest itself to thank.

"Maybe those legends about the forest protecting itself

were true?" Thomaras offered up, more to break the silent tension than for any other reason.

"Nope," Torin responded anyway, and pointed towards the woods.

Two figures emerged, and at this distance all Thomaras could make out was that they were both men, one light-skinned, one a darker bronze, speaking solemnly as they emerged from the woods.

"Is that the Druid we're here to see?" Thomaras asked.

The lighter-skinned man certainly looked the part. He was wearing brown leather trousers and a leather jerkin with a dark green cloak falling over his shoulders. It was hard to tell at this distance, but it looked like the cloak was clasped around his neck with vines — not dead and crafted into a clasp, but alive and clinging to each other to hold his cloak on. In one hand was a large, intricately designed staff that also looked more like it had grown into its shape rather than been hewn. It looked like a collection of roots had woven themselves together in a tight braid to form the body of the staff, and then opened up and wrapped themselves around the largest, most roughly cut emerald Thomaras had ever seen.

"Looks like a Druid. Not the Druid I know," Torin responded.

At this point, the men had ceased their discussion. The presumed Druid's companion had unsheathed a wicked-looking curved sword and began systematically removing the heads from the creatures that were still moving.

"That one is dangerous too," Torin observed in a detached, professional tone.

Thomaras tended to agree. The man had jet-black hair matching an equally dark and neatly trimmed beard that framed a handsome face. His clothes were also simple and earth-toned, but the trousers and jerkin were covered by what looked like boiled leather. Judging from the armour and the way he handled that curved sword, its twin rested in its sheath at his hip, Thomaras guessed he was one of the desert people, the Nomads. Strange to see one in Haven. As their name suggested, the nomadic desert folk generally kept to themselves, but were more than willing to help travelers from Haven navigate their harsh homeland for the right price. They were celebrated swordsmen, training from a young age. Perhaps the Druid had managed to hire one as a guard.

"Well, let's go see if this Druid can help out Ashea. Sound good?"

Torin nodded and slid the hammer back into its holster on his back.

By the time they had gotten the cart moving again and closed the distance to the woods, all the abominations were still and the two men were standing side by side, waiting for them. Thomaras, not wanting to appear aggressive, pulled up the reins about ten feet from the men and gave a friendly wave. "Well met, strangers; I assume we have you to thank for the... floral assistance," Thomaras said in his most charming voice.

The Druid remained still but his companion immediately drew the second curved sword and crouched, very slightly, into what looked to be a very practiced stance.

Okay, perhaps it wasn't his *most* charming voice.

The Druid gave an exasperated sigh. "I've had a rather foul day, gentlemen. It started when I spilled my tea all over the kitchen table, which, I will admit, probably had nothing to do with you two, and has now progressed to me having to expend a terrible amount of energy to kill what appear to be animals that had already died within my forest, with my forest, which, I will add, is my least favourite way to use my forest and, based on the two of you showing up when you did, most likely *does* have something to do with you. All of this before I'd even had a chance to eat the breakfast that was going to go onto the kitchen table that I spilled my tea all over, which, once again, I realize has nothing to do with you but it really bothered me and definitely did not put me into a great frame of mind to deal with everything else that this day has thrown at me." Thomaras and Torin could only stare at the diatribe the Druid directed towards them. "Now would be a good time for an explanation or an apology. Maybe both," the Druid finished, much more succinctly.

"Sorry about the tea," Torin rumbled, eliciting a raised eyebrow from the Druid and a far more appraising stare from his companion.

"Yes, and more importantly, if we brought any trouble upon you," Thomaras added diplomatically. "I fear that we may indeed have been the intended target of these creatures. We did not know, however, that we were being targeted."

There was a brief moment of silence as the four men assessed each other. Then the Druid sighed and placed a familiar hand on his companion's shoulder.

"It's okay, my heart. I do not think they come seeking trouble." Both men relaxed, and both swords were sheathed, though the staff remained in the Druid's hand. "Please excuse our rudeness; as I've said, it's been a difficult day."

"Spilled tea." Torin commiserated.

"Yes... well, among other things, but yes, damn it!" The Druid thumped his staff on the ground as he said this and then seemed to collect himself. "My name is Felix, and this is my husband, Az'an. We are the stewards of the

Darkwoods." Felix slipped his hand into his husband's, seemingly without thought.

"I'm a steward by marriage. It's his forest," Az'an added with a familiar smile that seemed to indicate that this was a shared, and very commonly used, joke between them.

Thomaras was surprised that instead of his customary cynicism towards such displays of affection, he was smiling at the simple comfort these two found in each other's presence.

"Okay, great," Thomaras said, his odd feelings making him awkward. "I am Davin and this is Torin. We have a friend who has a very serious spider bite. We were hoping you could help?" Thomaras gestured towards Ashea in the back of the cart.

"Spider bite? Most herbalists can take care of something as simple as that; you needn't have come all the way out to see me." Felix was already moving towards Ashea as he said this. "But you did, so I suppose I should take a look. Where is the bite... good Gaia!" Felix recoiled so far he would have fallen off the cart had Torin not caught him with a steadying hand on his back. Felix barely seemed to notice.

"The wound on her leg is enormous. How big was the spider that did this?" Felix looked back and forth from Torin to Thomaras as he asked.

"Big," Torin responded.

"About the size of a small wolf. There was a pack of them," Thomaras filled in.

"A pack? Spiders don't hunt in packs," Felix said as he pulled a handful of long blades of grass from a pouch and started to lay them across the wound. The emerald on his staff began to glow with a green light that the blades of grass matched. As they glowed, they fastened themselves over the wound like a bandage.

"They don't typically come in plus sizes, either. Can you help her?" Thomaras tried to keep his voice calm. Felix was coming into this whole thing cold, but he was worried about Ashea and it was giving his comments an edge.

"Fair point. This will stop the venom from spreading further and bring down some of the swelling, but to clear the rest of the venom, we'll need to bring her to my home. May we ride with you on the cart?" Felix asked.

"Sure, but I don't see how this thing is going to fit into the woods. They're far too dense," Thomaras responded.

"You let me handle that; just drive," Felix said as he reached a hand down to help his husband onto the cart.

Thomaras clicked his mouth to get the horses going and Torin fell into stride beside them.

As the cart approached the woods, Felix raised his staff slightly, and it gave off the emerald glow once more. Just as the tips of the horses' noses were about to hit the trees, they began to peel backwards, creating a path wide enough for the cart and Torin to pass comfortably.

"You can make them move like that?" Thomaras was stunned to see the trees appear to shuffle backwards, their roots never leaving the ground, and then shift back into place with what Thomaras could only describe as what a sigh would sound like coming from a tree.

"More like I'm asking them nicely. Trees are very stubborn. You need to be careful about how you make requests of them," Felix responded with a smile.

They continued on in silence, the trees creating a path that Thomaras had no choice but to follow, so there was no need for directions from Felix. After about twenty minutes, they came into a small clearing, just big enough for the cart to sit in without any movement from the forest, at the base of the largest tree Thomaras had ever seen.

The trunk itself was at least a hundred feet around and when Thomaras looked up, he could see where the branches jutted out from the massive trunk, but they were each so thick themselves that he couldn't see where the topmost leaves joined the rest of the canopy. He saw something descending from the top.

"Is that..." Thomaras began but trailed off.

"Our lift up, yes," Felix answered.

Thomaras could now see that a platform was being lowered by thick green vines, uncoiling themselves slowly from the top of the tree.

"Torin, would you be a dear and gather up your friend?" Felix asked. "I think we'll leave the horses down here. Our home is above. Not sure how you are with heights, Davin, but there is no need to worry; I assure you it's quite sturdy," Felix added as he patted the tree.

Thomaras simply nodded. Heights didn't bother him, but he wasn't sure how far he trusted these vines. Once the platform reached the ground, he waited until Felix and Az'an had stepped on it before he followed. The four vines to came together in a coil before separating and attaching themselves to four posts on each corner of the platform. Once they were all aboard, the vines gently began to retract and the platform rose smoothly, spinning slightly as the vines folded back up in such a manner that no tangles occurred.

Their ascent did not afford much of a view — there was a clearing, yes, but the dense forest all around blocked any vista their height would have provided, and Felix and Az'an's "house" was within the canopy.

The home itself was incredible. The phrase 'tree fort' sprung to Thomaras's mind, but he immediately dismissed it as almost disrespectful when describing the structure before him. The already wide tree widened just before the branches of the canopy spread out into the sky. The home was hollowed out from the inside of the tree. The platform came to rest at the front door, which was inset from a porch that encircled the entire tree. Various windows, again cut directly from the tree, indicated different rooms and that it was a two-story dwelling. A warm glow came from the home and cut through the shadows created by the forest canopy.

"This tree didn't mind you carving a house out of it?" Thomaras asked Felix.

"Ha! Oh, it wouldn't have agreed to that, I assure you. No, I simply directed the tree to grow in a specific way for us. No sharp edges required." Felix almost managed to hide the smugness in his tone. Almost.

Thomaras whistled through his teeth and heard a slow grunt of appreciation from Torin.

"My predecessor had cultivated this tree for this very purpose when he was a much younger man, a shame that he never got to see his dream fully realized, but I have a hunch that he never truly expected to. He was a great man, and I assume one of you knew him? Not many people know of my healing abilities. They travel to the mage of light for that." Felix's questioning expression bounced from Thomaras to Torin.

"I knew him. Many years ago. Was your age," Torin replied.

"Ah, then you *are* part Granite Ogre? It's hard to tell with your face covered, but given your size and that you are much older than you look, a Granite Ogre heritage stands to reason." Felix seemed satisfied with his deduction. "Perhaps when this is done, you can share some stories about him? Cornelius was always tight-lipped about his younger days," Felix added hopefully.

Torin simply nodded. "Didn't know him well."

"I hate to break up the trip down memory lane, but should we get started on healing our friend?" Thomaras cut in.

"Not to worry, the grass is doing its job, so she is stable, but your point is well taken; no use dallying. Az'an, show Torin to the guest room. I'll gather my things. Davin, you may make yourself comfortable in the sitting room." Felix then turned on his heel and entered the house, Az'an and Torin close behind him.

Thomaras noticed that the grass that Felix had laid on Ashea's wound, once green, was now brown and dead in the middle and that the edges were almost completely black.

Thomaras, last to enter, was shocked at how beautiful the interior was. They entered into a small foyer that had hooks, grown directly out of the tree for cloaks, and shelves grown into the wall to hold one's shoes. The foyer opened up into what appeared to be the sitting room. All the furniture was grown out of the tree itself, and there was even a fire pit and chimney in the corner. Thomaras imagined they had to be extremely careful with that, but part of him also sensed that there would be some kind of magical fireproofing available to someone who could grow a house out of a tree. The rugs and throws on the couches and floor all appeared to be made from woven leaves, still supple but multicoloured as if they had been harvested at the peak of autumn, just as they had changed colour but before they dried up. It smelled of spices, apples and the crisp, clean air of a fall day. Thomaras couldn't imagine a more comfortable place to live.

Unsure how he could help Ashea, Thomaras settled down into one of the wooden chairs and was pleasantly startled to find it had a spongy quality to it, as if it had been grown out of moss and made to look like wood. Despite the comfort, he found himself fidgeting and glancing into the hallway that the group had disappeared into. Finally, he stood up. Surely he could do something to help? Just as he was about to make his way down the hall, Torin emerged, followed by Az'an, who had a pipe in his hand.

"Rest, friend. Felix has it under control," Az'an said as he cupped the pipe with his hand and lit a match, puffing as he applied it to the bowl. "You'll only get in the way." The pleasant smell of tobacco filled the air as he exhaled smoke around his words.

"I suppose you're right," Thomaras conceded and flopped back into his seat. He noticed Torin stretched out on a couch that almost fit his prone form.

"Good lad. Now, why don't you tell me your real name before I decide that you and I have a problem?" Az'an's tone never changed as he sat down and he still smiled placidly, but Thomaras felt a familiar flare of energy within him when he realized that the smile never touched his eyes. "You're a good liar, that's for sure. Just not quite good enough," Az'an added.

Thomaras's vision swam as more of that pleasant-smelling tobacco smoke filled his lungs. Too late he noticed that Torin wasn't just stretched out, he was unconscious.

Something... in... the smoke...

His thoughts were coming slowly now, like they were wading through molasses.

"Now then, why don't you tell me about yourself?" Az'an, still smiling placidly, leaned forward, elbows resting on his knees, and exhaled into Thomaras's face. He felt himself drifting. Not into sleep, but into compliance.

And then he started talking.

11

ASHEA

~

Ashea strode through the corridors of the foster home. She was eight. The nobles she stayed with were kind enough in their own way, but they mostly left her to her own devices. She was a symbol for them. An embodiment of their kindness and generosity that they could dress up and show off around town, so that everyone knew what good people they were. Ashea didn't hold it against them — she was used to being used. Most people who adopted children had their own reasons for doing so, and rarely did those reasons benefit the child. These nobles would enjoy her for a while and then, when she became inconvenient, they would toss her back. For now, she was eating fine foods and wearing fine clothes, so she might as well enjoy it.

Scratchscratchscratchscratch.

There was that sound again, coming from up ahead this time. She'd been hearing it for a while now. Ashea continued to walk forward until the sound got louder and put her head on the wall where she thought it was coming from, ear pressed against the hard wood like she was trying to hear the ocean in a shell.

Nothing.

Strange, she was sure it was coming from there. She turned left down the hallway towards her room, only her room wasn't there. The doorway stood where it should, but instead of looking and seeing her bed and dresser, there was nothing. Inky blackness filled the doorway, so complete that she could almost *feel* the darkness.

Scratchscratchscratchscratch.

She could hear it clearly now, coming from the other side of the darkness. No need to press her ear up against it. In fact, her whole body recoiled at the very thought and she felt a cold sweat break out all over her all at once. Why was she trying to find that sound? That sound was wrong... it was off... it was...

"Easy now, easy." A kind, lilting voice seemed to come from above her and all around her at the same time. She started to relax and an emerald glow filled her vision until it was all she could see.

Felix was beginning to worry. Even with a bite as large as the one that Ashea had, his magic should have extracted the venom with no problem. It *was* extracting the venom, but there was something else. Something trying to... break through? Into the woman? That didn't make any sense.

"Easy now, easy," Felix said as Ashea began to sweat and thrash.

He gently removed the long strands of grass that he had fed into the wound and through her body. Channeling his will into the grass, he caused it to absorb the venom while at the same time using it as a catalyst to suffuse her body with the glowing warmth of his magic. The stone resting in the staff glowed brightly even though the staff itself leaned against the wall. As the last of the grass came out of the wound, it went from black to brown to green. Good, the last of the venom was out.

Why, then, was she still stuck in this fever dream?

He sensed it again then, something trying to break through. But from where? And how? The Orb Weaver had let him know she was coming. Let him know that she was sick with the venom of her brood so that he could be prepared and save her life. Felix didn't tend to ask questions of her, but this whole situation smacked of a plan that had spun out of her control and he had never once known that to happen to her.

He felt Ashea start to slip again and did his best to calm her mind. His power was still within her, replacing the venom in her veins. He began to sweat with effort as he attempted to calm her down and wrench her away from whatever it was that was pulling at her consciousness. That's when he heard it.

Scratchscratchscratchscratch.

What was that sound? How was it in her head...

The cool, clean water of the lake felt wonderful against her skin. The summer was hot, and the water washed away what felt like layers upon layers of sweat and grime from her person. She was thirteen years old. She had managed to run away from her foster family three days ago and hadn't slept much. Her foster father, mean when he was sober and even meaner when he was drunk, had finally gone too far.

She was tipped off when he was kind and gentle with her after their evening meal. Telling her what a good job she did scrubbing the dishes and touching her hair affectionately. He was never kind, and he never touched her unless it was to smack her. Her foster mother, a weak and scared woman, wouldn't look at Ashea and made some excuse about going to visit a friend down the road. It was in that moment that Ashea decided she would leave.

She was always locked in her room. There was no window and no other way out, but she knew tonight he would be coming to visit her. A child's intuition, perhaps, born from years of bouncing from family to family. After he put her to bed and she heard the lock click into place, she went to her dresser and pulled out a rock, about the size of an apple, that she had snuck into her room one day. At the time, she didn't know what made her do it, but in truth, she had always thought she might need it.

One day.

Lying in bed, curled up in the fetal position, she clutched the rock in her hand and waited.

She didn't wait long.

She heard the door open and listened to his heavy, irregular breathing. He was a large man, broad-shouldered and strong from a life of labour, but his belly protruded out past his belt line from a life of drinking and eating. For a moment she hoped he would leave, just turn around and lock the door, but he didn't. He closed it behind him instead.

She heard his heavy footsteps, felt his weight on the bed and smelled the booze on his breath. As soon as she felt him looming over her, she pivoted her body and meant to swing the rock against his head. Unfortunately, his weight on the scratchy blanket caused her arm to tangle, costing her the element of surprise and her only advantage.

He caught her arm easily and squeezed until the rock dropped from her numb wrist. She heard it fall to the floor with a thud. In her mind's eye, she was oddly aware of where the rock landed. In her desperation, she almost felt like she cupped it with the very air in the room.

"You little bitch," her father slurred, his face pressed against hers. A day's worth of stubble scratched her cheek. "You dare try to hurt me? After all I do for you? After all the love I show you." The reek of booze hit her full in the face.

Some part of her mind snapped then. She didn't know exactly what he was going to do, but she knew it was wrong. She knew that it had something to do with the cries of pain that she heard from her foster parents' bedroom at night. Her mind recoiled at the idea so viscerally that she imagined the air thickening around the rock, picking it up and slamming it as hard as she could against his skull.

Thunk!

She could almost hear the sound of it against his head. Almost feel the blood splatter onto her face.

It wasn't until he slumped off of the bed and fell to the floor, until she saw the rock, covered in something dark that she couldn't quite make out in the low light, that she realized she had in fact moved the rock.

Impossible.

But she didn't waste time figuring it out. She could see his chest, still rising and falling with erratic, shallow breaths. She grabbed the small bag she had packed and ran for the door. She had slept in her clothes so as not to waste any time. The door only locked from the outside and she pulled it home with such enthusiasm that she practically ripped it off its hinges.

Standing in the kitchen was her foster mom.

They looked at each other for a moment and then she

looked past Ashea and towards the bedroom. The haunted, broken look in her eyes seemed to disappear and was replaced with a deadly hardness.

"Run along now," was all she said, walking to the kitchen and picking up the long knife she used to cut vegetables.

Ashea didn't wait to see what happened next. She ran through the front door and into the night.

She bobbed in the cool water until something shook her out of her memories.

Scratchscratchscratchscratch.

Was the sound coming from under the water? How strange.

Ashea took in a deep breath and dove. The lake wasn't very deep, and the water was crystal clear.

Scratchscratchscratchscratch.

She had meant to go under, take a look around and come up for air, but suddenly realized she could hold her breath for a very long time. Maybe forever! Excited by this newfound ability, she swam deeper and deeper, right to the floor of the lake.

Scratchscratchscratchscratch.

What could be making that noise? It was so clear, like someone scratching lightly at a door. Like they were trying to dig through the door and had all the time in the world to do so.

Scratchscratchscratchscratch.

She was at the bottom of the lake now; her lungs didn't ache at all! It seemed the sound was coming from the mud that coated the lake floor. She was about to press her ear to the ground, to try to hear better, when she saw that it wasn't mud on the floor of the lake. It was too black, too thick. It seemed to swallow the light.

Scratchscratchscratchscratch.

All at once, she wondered why she would have wanted to know what that sound was. It wasn't a good sound; it wasn't even a right sound. In a panic, she realized that she couldn't hold her breath forever. What made her think she could? She very much wanted to be out of this lake.

Lungs burning, she began to swim to the surface. She dared not push off on the floor of the lake because she knew, in the same way she knew what her foster father was about that night, that if she touched that blackness she wouldn't be able to escape.

So she flailed her arms and pulled herself upward. Her lungs were burning. She was moving so slow! Finally she got to the surface, stuck her neck out as far as she could so that her face would break the water and pull in a delicious breath of air!

She broke the surface.

She still couldn't breathe. She was above the water and she couldn't breathe. She kept pushing her face forward, trying to take in air, but she couldn't. Irrationally, she thought if she went under and came up again, maybe it would work. She put her head in the water and saw that the inky blackness was reaching up to her. Long, black tendrils that would pull her down forever.

She broke the surface.

She still couldn't breathe.

"To the side! Turn your head to the side."

An urgent voice was calling to her, but she couldn't see where it came from.

"Turn your head!" it screamed again, but this time it seemed like each word was accompanied by a pulse of emerald light. That light seemed so good, so natural. Somehow it smelled of a fresh field of flowers in the spring. She turned her head.

Ashea gasped as air filled her lungs! She had done it! She broke the surface! Immediately, her head swam with disorientation.

She was dry.

She was lying on her stomach.

She was in a soft, warm bed that smelled of autumn leaves.

"Easy now, you're safe. And breathing."

It was the kind, lilting voice from her memories. No, from her dreams. The dreams were fading already but the feeling of reliving forgotten memories still lingered. As if someone had been trying to look through her eyes in order to sift through her memories.

Ashea looked around and realized what happened. In her dream, she'd been swimming upwards to get out of the water. She had been close to waking, so her body had pushed upwards as if it were swimming. This had caused her face to be pushed into the pillow. She'd been suffocating herself.

"Th-thank you."

Her throat was dry and her voice cracked, as if she had slept for a long time. She did not feel rested, though.

"Of course, my dear. You had a rather nasty spider bite, but you're okay now." He patted her arm gently.

She jumped, but not at his touch. The spiders! They were huge! She had cast her magic to help Torin and Thomaras and that's when she had felt her thigh turn to pure fire. She twisted herself around, kicked the covers off, and looked at her leg. All she saw was a bandage that was made out of... grass? Strange, but now that she was aware of it, the grass felt cool and tingly on her leg, as if it were healing it. Then her head started to swim, and she lay back heavily.

"It's okay, I took care of the venom and your leg should heal just fine. What you need is some sleep. I can't imagine the dreams from the fever were all that pleasant. I assure you any sleep you have now will be unhindered by such things," the man said.

He was slender and handsome. Longish auburn hair framed a face that was clean-shaven save for a neatly pointed goatee that covered his chin. His eyes were the greenest she had ever seen, dark green like a forest, and his pupils were golden and glowed slightly.

"Thank you again. They were awful. There was this terrible scratching, like someone was trying to get into... into... well into me." Ashea's eyes were already closing, and she was drifting to sleep, so she didn't see the man's face turn a ghostly pale.

"Yes, well, no need to worry about that now. Just rest." But his tone did sound worried.

Had she been less exhausted, she would have opened her eyes and asked why he was worried, but the bed was so soft and so warm. As she drifted off to sleep, she heard him talking to someone as he left the room.

"Az'an, how are... Az'an! What did I tell you about using that smoke on our guests?!"

She heard the words as she drifted off, but they meant nothing to her.

12

THOMARAS

~

H is vision swam, and his head was foggy, but Thomaras did his best to hold on to his thoughts. He knew he was being drugged by something that made him want to speak. Overwhelmingly, he wanted to answer the questions that Az'an was asking him. He also knew that there was nothing he could do to stop himself from talking, so he did the only thing he could think of. Instead of answering the questions, he talked about Erica.

On and on he went, describing everything he could think of. How she looked, how she smelled, how she made him feel, how he hoped he made her feel. If he was in his right mind, he would have been terribly embarrassed, but in his drug-addled state, all he knew was that the more he talked about her, the less he gave up about himself.

"Az'an, how are... Az'an! What did I tell you about using that smoke on our guests!" Felix's voice startled Thomaras a little more out of the fog and his mind sharpened enough that he snapped his mouth shut mid-sentence.

"I haven't been able to get anything out of him. I've never seen someone able to resist darkroot like this." Az'an turned to Felix and looked a little chagrined at his lack of response. "Well, he's clearly lying about his identity, so I..." Az'an began, but was cut off by a withering look from Felix.

"A man like this has many reasons to keep his identity secret. You could have let me talk to him before you did something rash like this. How will they trust us now?" Felix's voice was calm, but it was clear the point he was making was something they'd discussed before. "I've helped their friend. She's stable now; perhaps that will be enough to calm any tensions that may have been caused," Felix finished.

Az'an looked contrite, but before he could open his mouth, he and Felix were swept off the floor in an explosion of movement. Torin, moving at his shocking pace, had jumped off the couch and picked up both men by the throat. He pinned them against the wall. Az'an was kicking futilely at Torin's stomach, but if he felt anything, Torin's stony expression didn't show it.

Torin had knocked the pipe out of Az'an's hand and the last of the smoke cleared out of Thomaras's brain. Shaking his head, he stood up and put a hand on Torin's shoulder.

"At a guess, I would say our friend here misjudged just how much of whatever drug he gave you it would take to put you out, am I right?" Thomaras asked, his tone friendly on the surface but all steel beneath.

"Badly," Torin replied. Neither his expression nor the grip on the two men wavered.

"Just wanted to wait and make sure that Ashea was okay before you voiced your displeasure with our treatment?" Thomaras continued as he walked over to Felix and fixed him with a hard stare. Felix's eyes were calm, as if he were happy to let them get all this out of their system.

"Yup," Torin agreed.

"Well, let's just remove their toys and then maybe we can sit down and have a more civil chat," Thomaras said.

He pulled the swords from Az'an's belt, noting the excellent balance on both weapons as he did so, and put them in the corner where Felix had leaned his staff. That done, he nodded at Torin, who dropped both men simultaneously, allowing them to fall unceremoniously to the floor gasping for breath.

"Understand that the only reason I didn't suggest he kill you both is that you helped our friend. That being said, if you give me any reason to change my mind, I won't hesitate to do so." Thomaras left the steel in his voice but didn't feel as much anger as he could have.

It seemed as though Az'an was trying to protect their home and Thomaras *had* shown up as the target of some weird animal abominations.

"I understand your feelings and appreciate your forgiving nature. Sometimes Az'an is a little overzealous in his role as my protector. Love will do that to a man," Felix said. "Your friend needs rest. Please, remain with us for the day and night at least before you decide what you'd like to do."

Az'an remained quiet. Not a sullen silence certainly, but that of a man who recognized he'd made a misstep.

"Not sure we want to stay in a place where we've already been secretly drugged," Thomaras said.

Torin grunted his agreement.

"I understand that, but please, you have my word that we mean you no harm. I get the sense that your journey is important for reasons larger than our own here in these woods. We won't keep you from it, but your friend needs rest," Felix said.

Thomaras got the sense that Felix reiterated the last part not as a tactic, but as a reminder for them as to what was really important here. A caregiver putting his patient first.

"What kind of assurances do I have for our safety?" At this point, Thomaras was just covering his bases. The reality was that Ashea did need to rest, and so did they. Even he could only go so far on so little sleep.

"This is no threat, simply the truth: I am a Druid and you are a guest inside my home. A home designed by me in the heart of the forest I protect. Do you think I need that staff to channel my power here? Of all places? My husband was wrong to do what he did, though his heart was in the right place, and for that reason, I allowed your large friend to accost us. Please know that it only happened because it was allowed. This entire tree is a weapon for me; contingencies are in place. If I had wanted to stop you instead of talking to you, I could have. Is this enough for you to know that I am your ally and not your enemy?" Felix continued to gaze placidly at both men.

Thomaras understood the nature of having the advantage. Here, he did not. He glanced at Torin, who nodded.

"Well, gentlemen," Thomaras said, picking up Az'an's weapons, "I think we understand each other." He tossed the swords to their owner, who deftly caught them both and sheathed them.

"I believe you have some stories to tell me about my late mentor," Felix said as he walked over to Torin and laid a hand on his forearm, gesturing for him to sit. Torin did so.

"No hard feelings, lad. I may have overstepped," Az'an said as he extended his hand towards Thomaras.

Thomaras looked at him for a moment, eyes hard, arm

at his side. The moment dragged on and just as Az'an was about to drop his hand, Thomaras grabbed it.

"I get it. You saw me as a threat. Don't worry, he's not my type." Thomaras winked.

Az'an surprised everyone with a bellowing guffaw, not an unpleasant sound at all. "Oh, I know. Seems like this Erica person is the only one on your mind," he said through laughter.

"She's nothing special. I simply needed something to talk about, so I didn't tell you anything important. That's all. Tell them, Torin," Thomaras spluttered.

"No," Torin responded without hesitation and this time both Felix and Az'an burst out laughing, followed shortly by Thomaras.

"Torin, hold that story. Let me get us some food. I think it's time we all ate." Felix was already walking into the kitchen.

Thomaras sat down and actually relaxed a little. He was a pretty good judge of people, and these two did seem to be true to their word. Any lingering doubt was erased by the smell of venison roasting over the spit on the fireplace. Thomaras's stomach growled.

After they ate, the rest of the day was surprisingly pleasant. Torin told one brief story about Cornelius — Thomaras couldn't imagine Torin being anything but brief when speaking — and then Felix regaled them with several more.

Az'an, presumably having heard all the stories before, abruptly stood up and laid a hand on his husband's shoulder. "Alright dear, I'm going to go hunting. We are nearing the last of our venison." Felix patted his hand and nodded, then continued on with his story.

"Why don't I join you?" Thomaras surprised himself by asking.

Normally he wouldn't seek the company of another, but he was starting to feel a little cramped. Az'an nodded, and the two men walked to the door.

"I'm afraid the best I can do is spot for you. I exhausted my arrows during the fight with those things and didn't have time to check for any I could salvage," Thomaras said, slinging his bow across his shoulders anyway. He felt better with it nearby.

"Please, help yourself to some of mine. Felix is rather adept at making arrow shafts, as you can imagine, so all I need to do is fletch them and add the arrow heads. I have a deal with a blacksmith in Hannover and he keeps me well stocked." Az'an gestured to a closet near the door.

Inside were a few travel cloaks for colder weather and a chest on the floor. Thomaras opened it up and found hundreds of arrows, all very well made.

"Wow, someone's been busy," Thomaras exclaimed, helping himself.

"Yes, well, being the steward of the Darkwoods allows for more free time than my husband is willing to admit," Az'an said wryly, and Thomaras found himself starting to like the man, drugging aside.

In his line of work, if you couldn't forgive someone a little drugging, you'd end up with no friends at all.

Once again, Thomaras found himself surprised at a pleasant afternoon. The men spent most of the time in silence. It was the only way to spend time on a hunt if you want to actually kill anything, but just being out in the woods, in his element, was relaxing. Thomaras was impressed at how quiet Az'an was. Not as silent as

Thomaras — he'd yet to meet anyone who was — but still very good. If Az'an was silent as a breeze, Thomaras was a dead-still night. They easily bagged a deer, Thomaras giving Az'an the shot, and then headed back to the house.

Az'an and Thomaras butchered the deer, dividing the meat between what needed to be used fresh and what could be salted and dried. Then Az'an stretched out the skin so that it could be turned into leather or used for the hide. This, along with some of the fresh cuts, was the deal Az'an had struck with the blacksmith. He'd head into town the next day for the exchange.

"I'm going to ask around as well, see if anyone else has seen these strange beasts or if we're the only lucky ones," Az'an said as they headed back up the lift. Thomaras snorted out a laugh but said nothing else.

By the time they were in and washed up, Felix and Torin had dinner on the table. It smelled delicious and the four men ate, chatting a little. As they cleared the last of the dishes, Ashea emerged from the bedroom, fully dressed but still looking a little weak.

"You should still be in bed, child! If you're hungry, we can bring you a plate there," Felix protested. He swept across the room to aid her, but stopped when she held up her hands and recoiled shakily. Torin and Thomaras shot to their feet reflexively, but Az'an remained seated.

"NO!... No, thank you. We have to go. Thank you for everything you've done, all your hospitality, but we need to go. I've had some more dreams." Ashea said the last part in a rush, as if she didn't want to admit it out loud, as if saying it out loud would mean she couldn't let them fade away into whatever recesses of your mind that nightmares go to.

"What were they about?" Thomaras asked as he walked

towards her, offering his hand. He was strangely relieved when she took it and leaned her tiny weight onto him.

"It's hard to say, but something is coming. Coming for all of us. And I think it's trying to get here... through me."

13

ASHEA

Ashea stood, leaning slightly on Thomaras and taking comfort in his presence. The details of her dreams were already fading, but the information she had gleaned from them was still very much in her mind. They were different from the feverish nightmares she had suffered while she fought off the spider venom. In those dreams, something had made her relive horrible childhood memories in order to weaken her mind, to allow it in. These dreams were calming — there was still someone there, but he wasn't trying to force anything onto her. He was there to help.

"We should be going," Ashea said again.

"You really should be resting, Ashea, but if you wish to go, of course you may do so," Felix said. He had sat back down, perhaps noticing her reaction to seeing him, and seemed to truly only be concerned with her wellbeing.

Ashea looked from Felix to Az'an and back to Felix. Any comfort she had found in the kind, handsome face of the slight Druid was gone. His visage was merely an attractive mask hiding the enemy within.

"Thank you, for your concern," Ashea marveled at how steady she was able to keep her voice, "but I'll be fine. Thomaras, Torin? Shall we?" Steady as it was, Ashea knew her voice was too casual, straining to remain normal, but she just needed out.

"Okay, we're off, then. Thank you for your help, gentlemen. Felix, do you need to accompany us or can you create a path through the trees from here?" Thomaras asked as he led Ashea to the door. Torin was collecting what few items they had brought up.

Felix took an extra moment before answering, looking from his three guests and back to his husband. "No, no need for me to come along. I would be happy to escort you if you'd like, but I can move the trees from here. Would you like to be returned to where you entered?"

His tone remained pleasant and calm. He appeared to be thrown off by her behaviour more than anything.

"That works, thank you. No need for you to come along; we've already imposed enough."

Thomaras also seemed calm and pleasant, but he too seemed to be reacting to her energy. She was incredibly grateful that his reaction was to do exactly as she wished and get them out of there.

They gathered their things and headed out the door. Az'an wrapped some fresh-looking cuts of meat in burlap and handed them to Thomaras, who shook his hand and thanked him. Ashea's head swam when she stepped out the door and saw the huge drop in front of her. She clutched Torin's arm, and he patted her hand gently. His strength was reassuring, and she relaxed enough to step onto the platform that would take them down.

To her dismay, Felix insisted on taking the ride with them and he chatted with Thomaras companionably about his hunting and the impression he had made on Az'an. When they reached the ground, the party bid an awkward farewell and, in spite of her fears, Ashea genuinely thanked Felix for his help. He had saved her, after all. Even if it was to serve someone else's purposes. She was even more surprised when he swept her up in a gentle hug. His skinny arms wrapped around her so quickly she didn't even have time to tense up and in that moment, where her fear was forgotten, she actually found the embrace quite pleasant.

"May I say one thing before you go?" Felix asked as the embrace ended.

Ashea, not trusting her voice, nodded.

"Whatever he told you in your dreams, just know that he will do whatever it takes to achieve what he believes is right."

"Are you saying I shouldn't trust him? Because the other interested party is the one that sent giant spiders after me," Ashea snapped, anger helping her find her voice.

"I will be the first to admit that the Orb Weaver's tactics are not always pleasant either..."

"So you do work for her," Ashea interrupted. "He said you were her agent."

"I am no one's agent. My loyalty is to my husband, these woods and the natural world. I will, from time to time, aid her in her plans if I deem her requests appropriate. Healing you, for example. I used to work for Dafoe and his expectations for obedience were much higher."

"So you're telling me to go to her instead?" Ashea asked.

"I am telling you to weigh your options. You need help with your blossoming powers at the very least, but where you find that help is up to you."

"I'll keep that in mind," Ashea said, her earlier conviction fading.

"You could stay here. Within these woods, I can guarantee your safety." His was voice was low, meant only for her, and his calm tones mixed with the fresh, earthy smell of his robes made her consider for a moment what she had seen in her dreams.

Then a snippet of her dreams returned to her. *He has the power to calm and confuse your mind. Resist! He works for the enemy.* The echo of her dreams in her mind immediately put her guard back up, and all she could manage was a weak smile.

Thomaras and Ashea hopped up onto the cart, presumably taken from Hannover after she fell unconscious, and Torin walked beside them as they began to drive through a trail that appeared as the trees themselves moved out of the way. Ashea shuddered at the power that the Druid wielded and hoped that the messenger in her dreams was correct about him being unwilling to tip his hand just yet. She looked back and saw the platform ascending, the Druid standing with a small smile on his face. He almost looked sad.

"Okay, Ashea, what do you know? I'm all for beating a retreat if that's what you want, but we are very much still in his house. If he means us harm, what's stopping him?" Thomaras asked, not unkindly.

"He's working for someone else, someone that wanted us there but who, more importantly, wants us alive. He won't risk keeping us here if it means a fight," Ashea said with a certainty that came right out of her dreams.

"Drugs," Torin said and Ashea looked to Thomaras for clarification.

"True," he answered Torin first and then continued to

her. "Az'an tried to drug us after Felix took you into the other room to heal you. Tried to put the big man to sleep and fog my head, said it was to get answers from me, but Torin woke up and my head cleared. We had Az'an at our mercy and Felix came out of your room to calm things down. They claimed it was some kind of misunderstanding, Az'an being overly protective, but it could be as you say. The need to avoid conflict so that we remain unharmed."

Thomaras didn't sound entirely convinced, and Ashea recalled the familiar way that he had taken Az'an's arm when he had said farewell. She prickled slightly. "You don't believe me? What, you became friends with them after they drugged you? Think for a second! He's got magic! He uses it to calm you down and fog your mind. Thomaras, you're the most suspicious person I know and you just turned around and forgave them after all of that?" Her tone was sharper than she'd intended and she felt a little bad.

"Suspicious, yes, but I'm also a good judge of people. I've been doing dangerous work for a long time and wouldn't have survived this long if I wasn't." Thomaras's tone was also sharp, and a little defensive.

Torin grunted quietly and gave Thomaras a look.

"That being said, I do my best to avoid magic and don't have much experience with it, so you could be right. The important thing is that we're on our way out of here, right?" He looked at her and she saw an olive branch in his expression. One that seemed to say, no apologies needed, let's just move on.

"I suppose you're right, so long as we do get out of here. Kind of creepy that he can do that with the trees." Ashea shivered a little as she looked around.

"On the way in I was impressed, but now that you've called his character into question... yeah, it is a little creepy,"

Thomaras said, glancing around little nervously. "Maybe we keep the conversation to a minimum until we're clear of the forest? Should only be a few more miles from what I recall."

Ashea nodded and glanced at Torin, who didn't need any encouragement to stay quiet and was currently scanning the woods.

Thomaras's instincts proved correct, and they reached the edge of the forest in short order. As they broke the tree line, a raven burst from the trees, cawed, circled once as if in farewell, and headed back into the woods.

"Let's head back towards the main road and then we can chat," Thomaras said.

Before she could answer, Ashea's mouth went dry. Strewn across the field in front of them were the bodies of animals that looked just like the boar that had come after them.

"Oh, right. While you were asleep, we had some company. Felix and Az'an actually helped us fight them off. Not sure what we would have done had they not come along," Thomaras said a little sheepishly.

"Made us trust them," Torin said, and Thomaras nodded at the point.

Ashea wasn't sure if he believed it or not, but could tell he was considering it. "Well, I can't speak to their motivation, but it does line up with the dreams. He said that the being that wants to take me would use means that we can't even imagine to catch me." Ashea forced her voice to remain steady as she spoke, but the more she remembered the dreams, the more she remembered how terrified they made her.

"Who told you that? You keep talking about these dreams like someone was in your head communicating with you," Thomaras asked as calmly as possible, but she could see the impatience bubbling under the surface.

"Dafoe," Ashea spat the word out, as if saying it quickly would lessen the effect it had on Thomaras.

"Dafoe? More commonly known as the prism reader? The leader of the mages council and the most influential person in Haven? That's who's talking to you in your dreams?" Thomaras's calm tone made her more nervous than any yelling would have.

"Uh... yep," Ashea said sheepishly, looking at Torin. The amusement she saw dancing in his eyes made her feel better.

"Which, I suppose, means we need to head north to Vees for an audience with his mageliness?" he asked again, tone equally calm.

"Not a word but... yep," Ashea said, and again the tension in her chest receded as Torin had to fake a cough to suppress his laughter.

"Yep. That seems about right," Thomaras sighed and shook his head.

Torin was laughing out loud now and Thomaras shot him a withering glare that only made him laugh louder.

Ashea's relief was palpable. She wasn't sure why a man like Thomaras was willing to stick with them through all of this, but she was happy that he was.

Perhaps he, too, was happy to be in the company of friends.

"They're out of the forest now, heading back to the main road," Felix said and turned towards Az'an, though he couldn't see his husband yet. His eyes were still seeing what the raven saw.

"Babe, you know it freaks me out when you do that," Az'an said.

"Does it? I'm not sure you've mentioned that before," Felix said, amused.

He had. Every time. That's what made it so amusing, after all. Felix understood. When he used his far sight technique, his irises and pupils disappeared completely and his eye sockets became dull, milky pools. He'd seen his mentor do it; it was definitely freaky.

"Do you think it was the prism reader that was visiting the girl's dreams?" Az'an asked, all business this time.

"I do."

"And you think it's okay to let her go to him?"

"I think she should be free to choose."

"And the Orb Weaver?"

Felix sighed. "I don't like her methods either."

"What about her cause?"

"It's the one thing she shares with Dafoe; the defence of Haven and the infinity prism within which it resides. Unfortunately, the two of them refuse to see that."

"What did she request of you when she told you about the Asheal?" Az'an asked, and Felix knew where he was going.

"To heal her, make sure she lived."

"And the other two?"

"She didn't mention them."

"You see why I drugged them now? She leaves you in the dark. For all we know, they were sent to kill us and she wouldn't bother to warn you."

"I know you don't trust her, Az'an, but I do. Sometimes

that has to be enough. Now come, I have a feeling that they may need our help. I'd rather stay close."

"Okay, fine. We'll head through Hannover, since I need to bring the venison to Walter, the blacksmith. What about the scratching?" Even Az'an's usually implacable tone showed some nervousness as he broached the subject.

"I... don't know. I would rather speak to her about that in person... or never think of it again," Felix said, only half-kidding about the last part.

Whatever that scratching was, it wasn't the Orb Weaver, nor was it Dafoe. If pressed, he would have said it was from somewhere outside their plane of existence. Fortunately, he wasn't pressed. He thought if he had to say that out loud, he might go quite mad.

14

THOMARAS

～

Thomaras cursed himself mentally for even taking this job. When Joseph had approached him, he had made it seem like a simple snatch and grab, something he'd done a million times. As soon as he'd mentioned a human being was what he was snatching, he should have known better than to get involved. The money was good, though. The bulge in his coin purse was proof of that. But was it worth it? Magic, after all, was unpredictable and more powerful than he liked to think about. No, he made up his mind. The money was decidedly not worth it.

Good people that could use your help.

Erica's words echoed in his mind.

He hated when she was right.

"Did you make your bow?" Torin rumbled the question.

"I did. Cut it from a tree near the village I grew up in. Haven't found it's like anywhere else in Haven," Thomaras replied.

"Orange Osage. They are rare but can be found in the Dorsetti Plains. Ogres use them for bows too."

"Huh, I didn't know. Most people that see me use it ask if it's enchanted, like your bracers, but they've just never seen a properly made bow before."

Thomaras was confused when Torin started laughing and raised an eyebrow at him questioningly.

"No bracers," Torin said, holding up his arms so that his loose tunic sleeves fell down to his elbows.

"So, how did you block those pickaxes back in Hannover?" Thomaras asked.

"An enchanted material that starts out as granite, but once the shamans are done with, it is similar to iron, only far stronger. It's where they get their name. Granite Ogres." Ashea's voice startled them both, and she smiled at them, though she still had her eyes closed and continued to lean against Thomaras's shoulder. "I thought you were some worldly traveler, Thomaras? What did you think they were using all that granite that comes out of Hannover for? I put that together right away," Ashea said mockingly.

"I just assumed they used it for tools and weapons. I'm still confused, though. What does the granite have to do with you blocking metal with your bare arms?"

"Maybe you should field this one, Torin. I only know what little my mother told me about your people," Ashea suggested.

"Around the time that we grow into adulthood, Granite Ogres learn the ability to hibernate. We can do so for up to a year but rarely have need to sleep so long. Mostly the ogres hibernate for a few months during the lightning storms that drive all living things on the Dorsetti Plains into hiding."

"Wait, a couple of months? The village I grew up in

bordered the plains and we could see the edge of the storms, but they only lasted a few days," Thomaras said.

"The storms begin in the south, but they move north and east and rage there for a few months. The storms are constantly moving. It's the only thing that stops the cascade of lightning from turning all the plains into charred desolation. Every year, the ogre tribes gather in our mountain fortress, B'aradure, and wait out the storms. By hibernating, the adults allow more food for the younger ogres, which means less stockpiling each year. A feat that is not easy for a people who primarily hunt their meat and gather berries and vegetables where they can."

"Okay, so you hibernate. What does that have to do with magic rocks?"

Thomaras felt Ashea sit up, presumably to get a better look at Torin as he chuckled at Thomaras's question.

"Once we reach our adult size, any ogre who wants to be a warrior will have the granite infused into their bodies by the shamans. This happens during the annual sheltering and is done while the ogres hibernate. It's safer, less painful, and allows for easier recovery."

"So, you're telling me that you have magic rocks in your arms that can stop a pickaxe? What, being twice as big and four times as strong as everyone south of the plains wasn't enough for you? Sounds nasty though, good thing you were asleep for it," Thomaras said with a laugh of his own.

Torin smiled slightly, but it didn't reach his eyes the way it normally did when he found something funny. Thomaras got the sense that he had said something wrong, but he didn't know how to fix it. Thankfully, Ashea did.

"Whatever it is, you can tell us if you want to. If not, you don't have to."

Her words were simple, honest, and full of love. Torin

still didn't smile, but after concentrating briefly, a resolved look crossed his face.

"I think I have to start at the beginning," Torin said and then launched into an uncharacteristically long story...

Torin's birth was the first of the many curse-filled blessings that would come to define his life. After his mother was raped by a Granite Ogre, Torin's mere conception was a miracle in itself. Through years of brutal raids, no human woman had ever conceived a child from an ogre. Most didn't even survive. Torin's mother Talia, however, was an exceptional woman.

Standing well over six feet tall with broad shoulders, even at a young age, she was larger and stronger than most men in her village. She didn't fit in with the women and was teased mercilessly. Seeking acceptance, she found kindness from the local blacksmith who taught her his craft. Eventually, Talia earned the respect for the village when she took over from him.

Talia's village was on the border of the great Dorsetti Plains. Decades had passed since the last raid by the Granite Ogres and most of the ogres wanted to move on from the wars and raids that made up the more recent centuries of Haven's bloody history. There were small groups, however, that still felt that humans needed to be punished for the crimes of overzealous settlers who had once sought to take the plains from the ogres.

Dagros, Torin's father, was one such ogre and led the raiding party that attacked Talia's village. The battle was short as the ogres easily overpowered the peaceful villagers, who mostly relied on patrols from Vees, Aquilo's capital city, to settle matters of violence. Very few of the villagers even fought back, but of those who did, Talia was the most ferocious. She even managed to kill one of the ogres with her great mallet and would kill another with a hidden dagger before she was restrained. Dagros was so impressed with her bravery that he granted her two rewards. First, he allowed her, and the wizened blacksmith she was protecting, to live. Second, she would have the honour of bedding him.

He took her in front of his raiders in the middle of the small village Talia called home. Talia fought just as ferociously against Dagros as she did defending her village, but he was large even for a Granite Ogre and the scratches and bruises she left on him only seemed to encourage him.

Satisfied with the violence they had wrought, Dagros led his ogres out of village and rode home — the miracle fetus's conception completely unknown to him.

Nine months later, Talia's life was finally claimed by Dagros and his raid as the giant half-breed child destroyed the body that bore him. Unsure how to care for such a child but unwilling to let him die, the villagers dispatched their swiftest riders to find some of the nomadic ogres before it was too late. Fortunately, it was nearing the season of storms, so the ogres were heading towards their annual mountain fortress and were not hard to find.

The riders approached the first group of ogres they came across and explained the situation. The ogres, ever the survivors, immediately rushed to care for one of their own and thanked the riders for bringing him to them and not killing him outright as an abomination. The ogres soon found a new mother among the other groups travelling and the baby was cared for as a newborn should be.

The years were not especially kind to Torin. Though the ogres would not let one of their own die, that didn't mean that his half-human heritage was completely overlooked. Children teased, adults pitied and bullies bullied. Add to that the fact that Torin was often passed from tribe to tribe among his father's people and he was ever the outcast.

As was often the case, this harsh childhood shaped Torin into a stronger person than most and, in truth, Torin always considered his poor treatment an advantage in what was a harsh world. He was isolated, and in that isolation learned that silence and thought, ever the traits of his ogre heritage, could be powerful tools. Tools he used so much that even amongst his stoic brethren, he gained a reputation for being as still as the rocks from which they took their name.

The bullies were always bigger, always stronger, and always had the advantage of numbers over him. So, he worked twice as hard to hone his skills in fighting, both hand to hand and with the massive quarter staff that he favoured as a weapon and would eventually inform his skills with his massive hammer. Never having the advantage of size taught him he had to be faster and better than his assailant. Never having the advantage of strength meant he had to learn to use their strength, and his own wits, against them. Never having the advantage of numbers meant he had to learn how to persevere and put down his attackers with so much brutality that they never wanted to attack him again.

By the time he began to feel the pull of adulthood, he had earned the respect of his people. Despite an absentee father, Torin became more competent than most young ogres. Instead of one figure to teach him about fighting and tactics, about living off the land and about the most important of all ogre traits — survival — Torin had many teachers. He learned wherever he could and from whomever he could. Torin never felt he lacked for guidance or learning.

No, what he lacked was a sense of belonging.

It wasn't hard to figure out who Torin's father was; Dagros was a notorious criminal among his people and his raiders were the last of their kind. The tribe that raised Torin was honest with him about what happened to his mother and how he was conceived, and that was enough for Torin. He never felt the need to seek out his father and assumed that Dagros felt the same about him. Many tribes had sought to find Dagros and put an end to his violent ways, but his group was elusive when tracked and deadly when found. They didn't even show up at B'aradure to wait out the storms and most ogres assumed that they headed south, into human territory, to wait out the violent months of weather.

After years of pretending that being disconnected from his father didn't matter, Torin finally accepted that what it had created was a disconnect from the ogres. They had never felt like his people, and more and more Torin felt the urge to go in search of those who did.

There was one more rite of passage, one more gift bestowed upon his people, that he hoped could connect him to the Granite Ogres. Once he stopped growing, Torin travelled to B'aradure and informed the shamans he was ready to accept the granite. They led him into the traditional chambers, carved into the very walls of B'aradure, and gave him instructions on how to slip into hibernation.

"Don't worry if you can't enter hibernation on your own the first time. For many ogres it can take two or three years before they are able to do so without aid from a shaman. Most first-timers require the aid of a shaman." Shar'duk's calm and comforting tone matched the wrinkly smiling face gazing down at Torin and he immediately relaxed. He began to combine the breathing exercises that all ogres learned at an early age with the instructions he had gotten from the shamans.

Torin relaxed some more, and he waited to slip into a deep slumber.

And waited.

And continued to wait.

"Don't worry, Torin, just let me help you." Shar'duk's voice was accompanied by a large callused hand on his forehead. "Just keep breathing and I'll guide you into the hibernation."

Torin lay still for what felt like an eternity and on multiple occasions felt the pull into a deeper slumber than he'd ever thought possible, but as much as he tried to let his mind run free to that place, it stubbornly refused. Finally, he felt the hand leave his forehead.

"I'm sorry Torin, I don't think you can hibernate."

Shar'duk exchanged a sad look with his assistant before meeting Torin's gaze once more.

"We can only assume it has to do with your human blood. I'm sorry, Torin, we couldn't have known."

"What does this mean? Can you give me something to sleep through the granite infusion?" Torin asked, confused.

"It's not something that you can sleep through. Only the deep slumber of hibernation can keep you unconscious through the trauma that infusing your body with the granite requires," Bar'nuk, the apprentice, explained gently.

Torin, for the first time in his life, raged against the unfairness of it all. He screamed and bloodied his fists against the cave walls. He bellowed in wordless anguish, in a rush of emotion and insecurity that he had long suppressed in his attempt to believe he wasn't *that* different. His size didn't matter *that* much. That he could, through study, through will, through patience, become just like the other ogres.

But he couldn't.

He couldn't do the one thing that defined his people. His rage was so fierce that the shamans could barely calm him down, and when they did, his knuckles were pulped and bloody.

Breathing heavily, Torin finally calmed down enough to speak.

"Do it anyway."

If he wasn't truly a Granite Ogre, then he would prove he was stronger.

The two shamans looked at each other, and Bar'nuk started to speak hesitantly. "Torin... you wouldn't, I mean, the chances of survival..."

The wizened Shar'duk cut his apprentice off. "Prepare the stone, Bar'nuk." He spoke softly, but the words jerked Torin's head up like he'd been slapped.

Hope lit up in his eyes.

"As you say," Bar'nuk said simply and left to prepare the stones.

"You aren't going to try to stop me?" Torin asked.

Laughing gently, Shar'duk shook his head and looked down at the kneeling miracle before him. "When has anything been able to stop you, Torin? You never should have been able to be conceived. You never should have been able to grow in a human's belly. You never should have survived the birth and you never should have survived the day-and-a-half ride it took to get you to a mother's milk. And all that when you were just a baby. So tell me, Torin? Now that you are all grown, how would you suggest an old man like me stop you?"

Once again, tears filled Torin's eyes as he looked up at the old shaman, but this time they were gentle tears, tears of relief and gratitude. They didn't speak again. The respect and acceptance of this powerful ogre calmed Torin enough that he was content to wait for what was to come.

In the end, even Torin's indomitable will could only stretch the limits of his flesh so far. Using the mysterious tools of their trade, the shamans cut and shaped the enchanted rock to fit from the back of his hands to where his forearm met his elbow. They chose this area because it would serve as the best defence and was some of the least traumatic areas of the body to work on. Even so, once the skin had been flayed, the rock embedded, and the wounds treated and bound with poultices, Torin was barely hanging on. The shamans wanted to end there, but Torin insisted they infuse his abdomen. Partly a request out of pride and partly as added protection for the vital organs there.

The shamans worked carefully. This was a difficult and sensitive area and without the recovery of hibernation, their margin for error was slim. Torin mercifully passed out after the first few cuts and when he woke, he was in a bed, arms and stomach on fire, but with a sense of great peace in his chest.

"What will you do now?" Shar'duk asked, startling Torin out of his reverie.

"What do you mean?" Torin asked, though he knew exactly what the old shaman meant, just not how he had guessed.

"Come, Torin, we both know you aren't staying here. You may have proven that your ogre blood, diluted as it may be, is as strong as anyone's, but you also proved that there is an entire side of your heritage that you don't know. So, what will you do now?" There was no smugness in his voice.

Smugness wasn't really a shaman trait, Torin supposed. He just sat there looking at Torin calmly.

"I'm going to head south, to learn about the humans. Maybe I'll find more of a home there than I have here."

"Very wise, Torin, very wise. Rest, recover. I will see to it that you have all the provisions you need. I know little of the human kingdoms. The only guidance I can offer is to head southwest. There is a village that was briefly your home but that you never knew. A blacksmith there understands our granite to a certain extent." As he said this Shar'duk produced a medium-sized leather sack. He put it on the table with a thud. "These are some of the stones that we imbued with our magic, but that we couldn't get into your body. The blacksmith knows how to shape it the same way he shapes other metals. Just tell him I've prepared it for his use. You may choose to create what you will with it, though admittedly there is not much." Shar'duk pushed the sack towards Torin as he finished.

"Thank you, my friend. You've done so much for me," Torin said.

Shar'duk merely smiled that knowing smile and patted his shoulder. "I'm sure you'll find what you're looking for."

Torin paused briefly and looked at his companions watching him silently.

"And then I came south. I found the village Shar'duk sent me to, Hastings, and spoke with the blacksmith there. Turns out he was my mother's apprentice and the nephew of the blacksmith that taught her. He was the one who filled me in on the details of the attack and my father. Then he made me this." Torin hefted the giant maul in one hand.

"So wait, that thing is as strong as your arms?" Thomaras asked.

"Not quite. There wasn't much granite, so he ended up blending it with iron to make a mixture of the two metals. Stronger than iron but weaker than true unchanged granite. Does the job, though," Torin finished with a grin.

"That it does. Well, if I wasn't going to do so before, I'll certainly remember to stand behind you whenever we run into trouble."

Torin smiled sheepishly, almost as if he was aware of just how many words he put together in a row. "Getting sleepy," was all he said.

"Yes, I suppose you haven't had much rest the last few days," Thomaras said.

He hadn't either, but he had a suspicion that he needed less than even the sturdy Granite Ogre. They'd left Felix's house as the sun was setting and had probably been on the road for two hours now. Something at the top of a ridge on the south side of the road caught his eye.

"Let's pull off into that copse of trees up ahead and I'll take the first watch," Thomaras said and touched Ashea's shoulder gently to get her to stop staring at Torin in wonder. "Here, take the reins."

Thomaras didn't wait for her response. Instead he hopped off the cart and started walking beside it. Some rest would do them all good.

15

RYGAR

~

"What did I tell you?" Talon said and slapped Rygar hard on the back. "A wagon with one guard. Ripe for the picking. My gut never steers me wrong." Talon slithered back down the crest of the hill from where they were watching the road, not taking any chances despite the cover of darkness.

Rygar sighed. He couldn't argue with Talon's gut — it had been right on many occasions — but that didn't make him want to put a knife in it any less. He'd been second in command of these men for years and had aspirations of taking the lead himself. He had been about to do so, in fact, and then Talon and his damn gut showed up. Rygar had put in his time. The men trusted and feared him in equal measure, and he'd talked to enough of them to know that he would have had their support once he took care of Mandar, their old leader.

Then, about six months ago, Talon ruined it all. He joined up like any other man, put in some time, but then he started getting these gut feelings: where easy marks could be found, where buried treasure might be unearthed, and started to gain the ear of Mandar. By this time, all the men were suitably impressed with Talon, who wasted no time in killing Mandar and securing command. Who could argue? He'd led their merry little band of thieves to riches they couldn't have previously imagined. No, Rygar couldn't argue with Talon's gut, but he sure fucking hated it.

"Let the men know the plan," Talon ordered as Rygar finished his own shimmy down the hill. Talon was strapping on his great sword and putting on his ridiculous horned helmet. Best to look intimidating, Talon always said.

Rygar shook his head and turned to the men. "Alright, boys, spread out in a semicircle on either side of the road. They're going to make for the small copse of trees on the other side, so we'll stop 'em before that. You all just make sure you stay low and quiet in the tall grass and the dark will take care of the rest. There's two of them and seven of us, so I don't expect a fight, even if one is a biggin'." Rygar efficiently doled out the orders.

The men nodded and went about their business. Thieves and brigands they may be, but they knew their craft. Rygar had made sure of that. Even when Mandar was in charge, it had been Rygar, trained himself first as a hunter and then a soldier, who'd turned their crew from the usual rabble that made up bandit groups into a successful unit. Maybe not as successful as Talon and his damn gut, but still successful. Their crew had grown under Rygar as well. The seven that were here were his best, an elite raiding party. The rest of the men, twenty in all, remained in their camp a day's ride north of Hannover. Rygar allowed himself another small fantasy of stabbing his dagger into that gut and then moved to join Talon.

It wasn't that Talon was an especially bad leader. Gut feelings aside. He knew the game: how and when to discipline and when to let the animals be animals. It was just that he swooped in and took over all of Rygar's hard work. Then he acted like he didn't even know that the seeds of a coup had been sown for him. Then, to add insult to injury, he allowed Rygar to stay on as second in command. Like Talon somehow had the right to *allow* Rygar anything.

"The men should be in position. Shall we go introduce ourselves?" Talon asked with a wolfish grin and, Rygar had to admit, at least a little, that the horned helm and the pommel of that great sword sticking up over his shoulder cut an imposing figure.

"Aye, let's go."

Rygar kept his voice curt and professional, as always.

Talon clapped him hard on the back, as always.

Holding his torch out in front of him, Rygar led the way onto the road and waved for the cart to stop. They'd stopped them after they'd started to angle towards the trees on the road's north side. Perfect. They'd put three of their men on one side and the other two would come from the south side and close the circle on these poor bastards.

"HOLD! HOLD, GOOD SIRS!" Talon bellowed as the cart approached. "Tis late to be on the road. Perhaps you'd like to join our fire for some food?" Talon's voice was perfectly pleasant and Rygar had to admit, even just a little, that maybe he was good at this part, too.

"No thanks," a deep voice rumbled from the direction of the cart, appearing to come from the larger man riding on the passenger side.

"Well now, I'm afraid that I have to insist." Talon put some menace in his voice now and Rygar loosened the one-handed mace that was sitting on his hip.

"Still no," the voice rumbled again, seemingly unfazed by Talon's voice at all. At his point, both he and Talon drew their weapons.

"Well then, you shou—" Talon's voice caught in his throat and both men took an involuntary step back as what appeared to be the silhouette of a tree with a head on it detached itself from the cart. It took them a moment, but both Talon and Rygar realized simultaneously that the large man wasn't sitting on top of the cart. He was *standing* beside it. They glanced at each other quickly, and their resolve stiffened.

"You should know that we have numbers on our side! My men are lying in wait for you right now. Crossbows trained on you both!" Talon's voice was back to its menacing timbre.

"You sure?" The large — no, huge — man rumbled again.

"Ha! Come on out, men," Talon ordered.

Rygar began to feel better when he saw Corys and Chris step out of the grass, crossbows trained on the large man. He glanced to the other side of the cart, expecting the remaining men to step out, weapons drawn. When they didn't, his heart sank a little.

"OY! Come on out!" Rygar barked, thinking maybe they'd missed the order.

Nothing.

His heart sank a little more. He glanced at Talon and leaned in so that their prey wouldn't hear him whisper.

"Maybe they..." He stopped mid-sentence as William, at least he thought it looked like William, tough to say in the dark, staggered into the road clutching at his throat as his blood flowed down the front of his boiled leather like a waterfall.

"Guuuuuurg," William reported to his commanders before falling forward onto his face.

After a moment, his training kicked in and Rygar took a step towards the cart, weapon ready, but before he could take another he heard the telltale sound of arrows flying through the air and watched as Corys and Chris went flying back into the tall grass almost in the same instant. He barely had time to register that, however, as a third arrow hit the ground right in front of him. He took a step back, heeding the obvious warning.

"I thought you said there were only two of them! Now there are three more archers in the woods? What good are our scouts?" Talon roared.

Not much now, Rygar thought as he spared a quick glance towards the grass into which his scouts' corpses had just disappeared, but he kept the thought to himself.

"Don't be too hard on them. They were only off by one." A voice came from the darkness beside the road and both Talon and Rygar unconsciously leaned forward to peer into the gloom.

"Over here, gentlemen," came that same calm voice, but this time it was in the middle of the road. How could he have moved that quickly? That quietly? They looked to see a tall, lean man with a shaggy beard emerge from the shadows, pointing a gigantic longbow at them.

"Now, it would appear that we have taken the advantage here, wouldn't you agree? That question is rhetorical. That means you don't have to answer, by the way. Don't fret, though. I'll let you know when you need to answer. It was a pretty good plan. Might have worked too if your men weren't so noisy. Found them in the grass pretty quick with all their mouth-breathing. Oh, and you might want to tell your scouts to cover up their metal buckles, too. Moonlight flashes off them and it's like a torch in the night for eyes like mine. I saw them before they saw us, I'd reckon," the lean man espoused.

"Listen, you—" Talon started but was cut off by an arrow that landed between his legs.

"Tut-tut-tut, I haven't asked you to speak yet," the man continued in his insufferably calm voice, but the flames of Rygar's anger were tamped down when he noticed that he already had another arrow at full draw. Rygar had barely looked away. Instinctively, he dropped his mace on the ground and raised his hands in front of him slightly.

"Now there's a reasonable chap. How about you, horns, care to drop your sword too?"

Talon glanced from the man to Rygar and sneered. "You'll have to take it from my corpse!" he screamed, but before he could take his first step, the air went out of his lungs and he dropped to his knees, clutching his stomach.

"You... bastard," he managed as he realized that it was Rygar's dagger that had plunged mortally into his gut.

His precious gut.

"You did this. Your gut brought us here to die! We shouldn't have been hunting this close to the Five Points Road, but you insisted. Now they're all dead and I mean to survive." Rygar hissed the last words through gritted teeth and slit the throat of the man he'd hated since the day they met.

He savoured the moment only briefly before tossing aside the dagger and raising his hands again.

"Right, well, seems like you two had some issues of your own. Hope you can still answer my questions," the man with the bow said, his draw unwavering despite the strength it must have taken to hold it.

"Ay, I'll answer your questions. Never cared for him

much. Took too many risks and took part in a little too much of the celebrating, if you take my meaning." Rygar kept his voice steady and amicable.

"Not sure that I do," the man responded coldly.

"The women, I mean. I never took part myself. I'm a man, not a dog, you know? The dogs, they need feeding from time to time, so I'd abide it, but never took part myself." Rygar hoped his honesty about his honourable nature would be enough to save his skin.

"Hmmm. So you'd abide it but never took part yourself?" the man asked.

"That's right, I find it distasteful," Rygar replied.

"I bet the women found it distasteful as well. Wouldn't you agree, Torin?" the man asked his companion.

Rygar had almost forgotten about the huge form beside the cart. He stepped forward now and though his face was covered, he thought he could make out red eyes under his wide-brimmed hat.

"Very distasteful," Torin rumbled again, his eyes never leaving Rygar.

"Well, yes, but some evils are necessary so that men can function. It's a law of nature!" Rygar felt this conversation was getting away from him and he started to panic.

"Oh, don't worry, we understand you completely. Right, Torin? In fact, why don't you bring our new friend over to the cart? Now that we've seen what kind of man he is, I think we don't need this anymore."

Relief swelled in Rygar as saw the man lower his longbow.

As Torin walked towards him, arm extended, he moved to meet him halfway and shake his hand. But instead of grasping his hand, the giant grasped his entire head, lifting him right up off the ground.

"Hey! What! What are you doing!" Rygar spluttered.

"Right, I figured an arrow through the chest is too quick for scum like you, and Torin's been looking for a workout lately, haven't you?" The man's tone was light, but his eyes were hard as flint.

"Hardly a workout," Torin said.

"Now, maybe you still get out of this. Maybe. If you're honest with us right now. Can you do that?"

"Yes!" Rygar bellowed, legs kicking in the air like he was some toddler instead of a full- grown man.

"Perfect. Did someone send you after us?" he asked.

"No! No, I swear. Talon, he gets these gut feelings. He knows when there are easy marks around. Like something is guiding him." Rygar tried to pour all the sincerity he could into his answer.

"Didn't work out so well this time, did it? Too bad you killed him. Maybe he could have supported your story." His interrogator looked thoughtful for a moment. "What do you think, Ashea? Your dream messenger say anything about our enemies using bandit guts?" he asked, looking back at a small young woman that Rygar noticed for the first time.

"Not specifically, but he said she could influence people without them knowing it. I'd wager these gut feelings could mean he was a tool of that kind of influence."

Rygar didn't understand half of what the girl was saying, but it seemed to support what he was saying and he began to hope a little.

"Hmmm, okay. Alright, good sir, say you'd been successful here. What would have been the play? Kill the two of us and keep the girl for sport?" The man's mocking tone made Rygar a little uneasy, and he briefly considered lying, but the big hand on his head seemed to sense it and started applying pressure slowly, like his head was a melon in a vice-grip.

"Aghhhh, okay! Okay! Yeah, that's the play. Keep the girl around for a while!" Rygar let his breath out in a rush when the pressure stopped, but his relief was short-lived as he looked into the eyes of the man holding him. They seemed to indicate that what he had felt was just the tip of the iceberg when it came to the force he could generate.

"Makes sense. When those spiders came, they didn't seem worried about us, just wanted to get you out of there, Ashea. I'd wager a few more would have shown up to grab you once these fools had you," said the thin man. He spoke to his two companions as if he'd forgotten Rygar was there. He couldn't decide if that was good or bad. The spiders sounded familiar. Hadn't Corys reported being followed by some giant spider thing?

"Um... sir? If I may?" Rygar asked with as much dignity as he could, given his current state.

"You may call me Thomaras. Go ahead."

Ah! A name. He might get out of this yet. "One of our scouts reported us being followed by what looked like a giant spider. Said he didn't get a good look but that he noticed it only had seven legs. Looked like one had been hacked off or some such. We all thought he was going crazy, but maybe not?" Rygar delivered the information as if he were a friend of theirs and not being suspended by the head.

"Waiting till we're out of the way," Torin said, looking between Thomaras and Ashea. "All done?" he asked, gesturing with Rygar as if he were some tool they were going to toss.

"I'd say. Thanks for the information. Now Torin is going to squeeze your head until it pops." The absolute lack of emotion in Thomaras's voice threw Rygar into a panic.

"Wait, wait! You can't!" His eyes glanced around desperately and landed on the girl. "Please, talk some sense into them. You don't want to see me killed!" he wailed.

"What do you think, Ashea?" Thomaras asked.

"You said that you never raped anyone?" she asked him.

"No! Never!" Rygar answered for this life.

"But you watched, didn't you? Watched your men brutalize those women? Don't lie to me." The young face grew hard as she asked the questions, like a mask from her past had descended upon her beautiful features.

"I mean... I... well, yes. I suppose. I am a man, after all!" Rygar somehow knew lying wouldn't help him.

"And then you would go to your tent and pleasure yourself. Right? Too shy to do it in front of your men, so you hid behind some kind of righteousness. Right?" The mask had settled so firmly over her face that even her companions looked a little nervous.

"I, please, I never hurt anyone myself! I swear." He knew his lack of admission was admission enough. How had she known?

"But you watched. Seems like I owe it to all those women to watch as well. Go ahead Torin." Her eyes never wavered from his.

"Wait..." He started to protest, but then the pain came. He started to scream. He beat and clawed at the iron talons that seemed to have engulfed his head. Slowly, he felt his skull begin to crack, his scalp spilt, and a wet flap of skin slapped down across his forehead. Blood was running into his eyes. He screamed until his voice was hoarse. His vision went from white to red to black nothingness as the pressure in his skull popped his eyes out of his head. Then there was only pain.

Then there was nothing.

16

THOMARAS

~

"Well, that was gross," Thomaras said as the lifeless bandit corpse fell to the ground.

Torin nodded his head in agreement and wiped the blood and brains off of his hand on the dead man's tunic. He looked to Thomaras expectantly.

"I think we need to get off the road. I know we're all tired, but we need to push through to Hannover. I would guess that the remaining members of this bandit group won't take too kindly to what we've done here. It's only a few more hours." Thomaras didn't wait for an answer before hopping back up on the cart.

He led them away from the corpses and drove them down the road for a while in silence. Ashea was quietly staring into the night.

"You okay?" Thomaras asked.

"I'm fine. Just thinking."

"I know it's hard to see people die like that but it was us or them," Thomaras began, but Ashea cut him off.

"Oh, I know. My life has not been so easy as to shield me from men like those. As far as I'm concerned, you and Torin made the world a better place today. Still, watching the world get made a better place can be tough."

Thomaras just nodded. Ashea understood what happened here and nothing more he said would change how she felt about it.

"Let's hurry," Thomaras said.

"Erica's in Hannover," Torin rumbled.

"She is. It'll be nice to see her," Thomaras responded nonchalantly. No need to keep playing into Torin's teasing.

The ogre and Ashea shared a grin anyway.

"The bigger question remains what we do after we get to Hannover?" Thomaras said, directing the question to Ashea.

"Continue on to Vees and Dafoe. Don't we?" Ashea's answer became a question.

"I know you dreamed about him or whatever, but I think we need to consider if that's the best idea. Felix seemed to think the prism reader's intentions weren't necessarily altruistic."

"You heard that?" Ashea asked.

"I've got good ears. Stop avoiding the question. What do you think we should do?"

"Well, I'm not super eager to meet up with the person that sent giant spiders to collect me, if that's what you're suggesting," Ashea snapped.

"Well, I'm not eager to introduce myself to the de facto leader of all of Haven. I like to operate beneath the notice of the powers that be," Thomaras snapped right back.

"We don't know enough." Torin's calm tone made Thomaras realize how heated he and Ashea were getting.

"What do you mean?" Ashea asked, her tone now matching Torin's calm.

"The Orb Weaver poisoned you and sent the bandits. Dafoe had you locked up—"

"No, he didn't. I was locked up in Tannerhorn," Ashea interrupted.

"For what?" Thomaras asked.

"The guard said they don't take kindly to drifters..." Ashea stopped as realization struck her.

"I'd wager he had a general description of you and there were orders sent down to lock up anyone matching it."

"Until he could have me collected," Ashea finished the thought.

"So, both of our options stink. What do you propose, Torin?" Thomaras asked.

"Research. Find out about the Orb Weaver and Dafoe. Make the choice after."

"Counterpoint: we don't go visit any mages or eternal beings and instead get ourselves lost somewhere. The salt marshes are a big place," Thomaras suggested.

"No."

Ashea said the word so quietly that Thomaras and Torin looked at her.

"Whatever his intentions, Dafoe wasn't lying about the fact that something is coming for me. Something dark and powerful. Whatever it is, I need someone's help."

Torin grunted.

"Okay, someone *else's* help," Ashea said, and managed a chuckle.

"Felix seemed to know a lot about the Orb Weaver," Thomaras suggested.

"True, but he also works for her. At least sometimes. I'd rather find the information through a neutral party. At least a party that doesn't know about me," Ashea said firmly.

Thomaras was once again impressed with Ashea's

composure. This job was becoming less like babysitting all the time.

"The mage of light isn't far from Hannover. She's long been separated from the council and is almost as well known as a scholar as she is a healer," Thomaras suggested.

"Okay, maybe we can get some answers from her about Dafoe as well?" Ashea asked.

"Two birds with one stone. I like it," Thomaras said with a grin.

Ashea smiled back and the familiar contentment that accompanied the formation of a plan settled over Thomaras. He looked at Torin, who nodded his agreement before returning to his constant scan of the road ahead. The clouds above covered the stars and moon and the dark was pervasive. Nevertheless, Torin remained vigilant and Thomaras had to assume Torin's eyesight in the dark was nearly as good as his own.

Thomaras felt Ashea's head flop onto his shoulder and shortly after heard the even breathing that accompanied sleep. Whatever rest she had gotten with Felix wasn't enough and Thomaras was content to let her sleep the rest of the way to Hannover.

By the time they parked the cart within the stables of The Jilted Maiden, most of the guests had left. Thomaras flipped a coin to Ben and asked him to run ahead and arrange quarters for the three of them.

"Three rooms, sir?" the young man asked.

"Two is fine, Torin and Ashea can share."

Ben nodded and walked off briskly.

"I have a room in town," Torin said.

"I'm sure she'd feel safer if you were close," Thomaras said.

Torin nodded and kept his face impassive.

Torin carried Ashea in his arms as they entered the Maiden. Ben returned to lead them to their quarters, but Thomaras remained in the common room as Torin and Ashea went upstairs. He found an empty table and sat down gratefully.

"I didn't expect to see you again so soon," Erica said and sat down across from him.

"Well, I missed you."

"So you ran into trouble?"

"Big trouble."

"How long are you hiding out?"

"Not long. We need to head to the Citadel of Light tomorrow."

Erica rose slightly out of her chair. "Is Ashea getting worse?"

"No, no, she's fine," Thomaras said and raised a hand to motion Erica to sit back down. "We just need to get a little information."

"On what?"

Thomaras smiled. One of his favourite things about Erica was that he could bounce plans and ideas off her without ever worrying about her discretion. Not only that, but she often had information or just a fresh point of view that helped him.

"Oh, we just have to decide which omnipotent being to bring Ashea to. We're worried that if we choose wrong, it might cost her life."

"So no big deal, really?" Erica asked.

"Nope. I know the mage of light is a scholar, so we figure we can ask her about the Orb Weaver," Thomaras said.

"The Orb Weaver? So there really is an omnipotent being that wants Ashea?"

"Yup. Since she's a mage, we thought she could tell us a little about Dafoe as well."

"Of course, the other interested party is the prism reader himself. Well, I wouldn't ask the mage of light about him."

"Why not?"

"I'm assuming you want a neutral opinion? When she left the council of mages, it was ugly. Like when Hedgrid's wife found out that Hedgrid's 'apprentice' wasn't just working the forge. Remember that?"

Thomaras snorted a laugh. "I do. Okay, so biased opinion. I guess we'll have to figure out another way to find out what Dafoe's all about."

"Hmm, if only you had a well-traveled friend that used to live in Aquilo and whose parents were still up north..."

"Sounds pretty good. She'd need to be beautiful too, though..." Thomaras said with a shrug.

Erica threw her hands up dramatically. "Well, aren't you in luck! I'm the total package."

Thomaras chuckled. "It could be dangerous and we don't have a lot of time."

"Perfect, we can leave tomorrow. Torin and Ashea can go to the citadel and we'll head up to Barriston. They're about the same distance away from Hannover."

"Maybe I should go alone. Perhaps I can find out more through my normal methods than from your parents," Thomaras began.

"I get that working alone is your natural state, but we'll get information faster together. Outside of coming to Hannover, you avoid the northern kingdom like the plague, but it's my home. My parents will be able to tell us something about Dafoe. Their farm is large and profitable and as such they are often involved in the politics of the kingdom. My father has even had occasion to meet with Dafoe."

"Okay, fine. I'll let them know tomorrow."

"Good, I was getting bored with all this talking, anyway. Give me twenty minutes to get closed up down here and I'll meet you in your room," Erica said before leaving across the table and kissing him deeply.

"Sounds good," he said once he'd recovered, but she was already walking away.

Realization struck Thomaras. "Wait, am I meeting your parents?" he called after her.

Erica just smiled over her shoulder.

∿

Umbra (Interlude)

Wind and lightning buffeted the sphere of energy surrounding Umbra. It sat placidly, unaware or unbothered by the ferocity of the storm that whipped up around It this day. It was at Its work and such minor distractions were below Its notice.

Umbra's influence had grown as It continued to try to work Its way into the next plane. A very small, almost forgotten part of Its mind, the part that still maintained a little of Umbra's previous human nature, cursed the Arahana who had gotten away before It could drain more of his powers. Had Umbra been a little quicker, a little less sure of Itself, It would have the ability to travel through the planes already.

This small part of Umbra's mind was forgotten as quickly as the idea that had flared into Its consciousness.

The Arahana that had travelled the planes was centuries ago and Umbra was patient. Patient in a way that only those who were eternal could be. What small portion of the Arahana's power It absorbed was enough. A tiny needle, yes, but one that Umbra could use to dig through.

Already Its influence was growing. It had been able to reach through the tiny hole It had created between the planes and use Its powers to raise the dead. The animals that It controlled were clumsy but did Its bidding as quickly as Its thoughts could come. It had almost succeeded, too. The girl would have been his had that foolish magic user not stepped in.

Mage.

The word echoed in Umbra's mind, springing from that place that used to be human. Yes, the mages, ever a problem but ever the source of Its power. Once Umbra had the girl, It would have no need of any mage again. It would snuff them out wherever It found them. She was the answer.

No matter, Its influence in that plane was small, but It had flexed that influence to do many things.

Contingencies.

The boy who thought he could read the reflections, thought he could control the future, was indeed only reading what Umbra wanted him to read. This mage of reflections, this prism reader, as he called himself, thought he was working to protect his realm from a great evil.

In truth, he was inviting It in.

Then there was the eternal, the spider. She was more of a problem, but that only meant she would require a lighter touch. Umbra had dealt with her kind before and proven the fallacy of their name. Eternal was a moniker fit only for Umbra. With any luck, even the small influence that Umbra had should prove enough to have the two of them deal with each other in the end. If not, once It had the girl there would be nothing stopping Umbra from snuffing out the pitiful eternal Itself.

Suddenly the massive, matte-black shoulders of the eternal being hitched up in pleasure as It took a deep breath, the first It had taken in centuries. It savoured the pleasure, something It hadn't thought of or felt in so long, of the moment. That tiny hole had broken through just a little more. Its influence just got a little stronger.

If it were possible for a grin to spread across that featureless face, the visage would have been so terrible as to drive any human looking upon it insane. Nonetheless, It felt the pleasure of the moment, springing forth from that long, deep-buried human part of Its brain, as It began to cast out Its influence in a new and different way. Not so direct as controlling dumb animals. More subtle, more guileful, It sought out a human mind that it could nudge in the right direction.

Ah, there.

Contingencies.

17

STOBACK

⁓

S toback sat in the shade of one of the leafy palms that lined what was generously called the main street of the tiny island town. Acta, was it? Rocksburg, maybe? He wasn't sure. He was fairly drunk when he'd taken the escort contract and was still fairly drunk now.

The climate this far south was tropical, and even in the shade, Stoback was sweating into the filthy leather jerkin under his rusted chain mail. The sweat didn't concern him. He rarely washed his clothing, or himself, for that matter. In point of fact, aside from pissing, shitting, or fucking, he rarely removed much of his armour at all. A dunk in the river every month was more than enough cleaning for Stoback, maybe two months if it rained. Looking out over the ocean, though, Stoback considered making an exception. He'd never been in the ocean, never been this far south in Haven.

The southern islands of Haven made up an archipelago, but only the four largest islands had cities on them.

Preolia is both the name of the island and the city. The thought surfaced through the drunken haze of Stoback's mind. *Now, what am I doing here?*

This wasn't an overly concerning thought for Stoback. He often blacked out and ended up in places with little memory of how he got there. He was usually able to piece together what happened after a while, sometimes on his own and sometimes with the help of the local authorities who would come to try to arrest him for whatever trouble he'd caused.

Merchant. More of his fuzzy thoughts were starting to coalesce into memories.

He remembered taking the escort contract, a caravan from Meridias down to the island, Preolia, which was the capital of the southern kingdom of Casea. Wares mostly, some struggling merchant who was moving his operation down south, a handful of guards that Stoback would command, and the merchant's wife and her handmaidens. The merchant himself was riding down a day later after he'd settled his affairs in the east. He had taken the job for little coin, as he often did, for the promise of a chance to do some killing. Traveling across that much of Haven, even on the Five Points Road, ran the risk of bandit raiding parties or even some aggressive wildlife. The merchant had hired him, as they often did, because he was cheap and his reputation as a swordsman was known across Haven.

There was no action, though... His mind was feeling decidedly less fuzzy. Once he figured out exactly what happened, he'd seek to remedy that situation.

Stoback had been disappointed when they were a day out from the southern shore of Haven, where they would meet the ferry that would take them to the island, and it was looking like there would be no action at all. He started to get bored.

Oh, right. His head seemed to clear completely as the rest of the memories came rushing back at once and the familiar trickle of excitement began to fill his body.

This was going to be one of the times that involved the authorities.

Stoback attempted to get back up but was foiled when all the blood in his body seemed to rush to his head and he plopped back down on his arse. Giving his head a moment to clear, he used the point of his unsheathed great sword to prop himself to one knee before making the rest of the journey to his feet.

Looking around, he guessed that it was nearly midday. The sun was hot and all the productive citizens of Preolia were giving him a wide berth as he stood at the edge of the main drag. As his own unwashed scent wafted around him, he supposed he couldn't blame them.

The smell was only part of it, however. Though not a particularly large man, he was well muscled if not terribly broad across the shoulders, and stood a little below the average height of men in Haven. He was intimidating in the way that those who appear unbalanced are to the general public. His rusted chain mail was partially covered by a threadbare brown cloak that had never been washed in its existence. The great sword that he carried had no sheath and while the rust on the blade spoke of its age, the dented and chipped edge of the sword showed just how little care had ever been given to it. The lank, filthy brown hair hung to his shoulders, almost always concealing an equally filthy and pockmarked face. His facial hair grew in patches and never seemed to get much longer than a five o'clock shadow. His brown eyes were so dark they almost appeared like black pools in his pasty white face. A bulbous nose that was red from years of drink was matched in size only by his ears, which poked out of the hair that fell in disarray around them. Thin lips curled up at the edges in a constant parody of a smile that only served to make him look more insane.

Time to go. Head north and west. Some of the drink must have been coming back again because that thought hadn't sounded entirely like his own.

Setting out down the road, Stoback decided that this particular trip had ended with enough action and he'd best start heading back north. His leather boots, or what was left of them — both big toes stuck through holes — made little noise on the wooden planks that made up the road, but the tip of his sword dragging along behind made a constant scrape that people around him couldn't help but glance at before quickly averting their eyes. Stoback much preferred the sound of the steel on cobblestone that made up most of the roads in Haven, but they had to use wood over the sandy ground that made up most of the island.

After about five minutes of walking, he had reached the edge of town and turned towards the place where he dimly recalled being dropped off by the ferry.

"Stop!" a voice behind him bellowed, and that trickle of excitement turned into a surge.

Spinning around, sword still limply at his side, Stoback saw the merchant who had given him the contract and six armed men in uniform, likely the city guard. Had the merchant been a day behind him as he was planning, he would have come across the scene of Stoback's carnage. Not seeing Stoback's body among the corpses, it was a logical leap for the merchant that his hired sword of questionable repute was responsible. His excitement started to rise some more.

Now why did I think I'd had enough action? Stoback thought as the familiar howl that came to his ears at the promise of violence set in and his manic grin grew from a slight curl of the lips to a wide gash across his face.

"That's him. That's the man I hired to guard my caravan. Stoback."

The merchant practically spit the word and his hand was in a white-knuckled grip around the ornate handle of a sword that he'd likely never used in a fight.

"Stoback, you are under arrest by order of the captain of the guards of Preolia. You stand accused of murdering all members of the caravan you were paid to escort. Have you anything to say in your defence?" One of the guards bellowed out his lines from memory in a bored monotone. He probably thought that six against one were good odds and whatever happened here, his job would be done shortly.

Stoback grinned. He would disabuse him of that notion.

"I'll take your silence as an admission of guilt and that sword you're holding as resisting arrest," the largest of the guards said, drawing his own sword.

He clearly wasn't the commanding officer, but the tone had shifted in the face of Stoback's insolence and the guards silently agreed with their righteous companion by drawing their own swords and advancing.

Perfect, Stoback thought as the men drew a circle around him.

Make it quick! You have places to be. The maniacal smile faltered briefly as another thought that wasn't his own floated into his head.

The smile reappeared quickly as the largest man, the one that had first drawn his sword, closed the gap. He was handsome, square-jawed with light green eyes that seemed to sparkle in contrast to the dark brown skin that the locals of the islands all had. He made a quick cut towards Stoback, not recklessly, but with skill and training behind it. He knew what he was doing. He was maybe even good.

But Stoback was the best.

Faster than any man should be able to move a great sword, particularly with one hand, he parried the blow. Though surprised at the speed, the guard's form was solid and he was able to bring his sword around for a second cut when it appeared that the weight of Stoback's sword had caused him to overbalance. The second cut was perfectly aimed at the back of Stoback's neck, and the youth seemed to smile a little as he prepared for the killing impact to reverberate through his arm.

His blade tasted only air.

Stoback used his momentum to roll to the ground, ducking under the killing blow and bringing him to his feet, with his sword extended in front of him, face to face with the commanding officer. The whites of his eyes were wide around dark brown irises as he stared down into Stoback's almost black eyes. He coughed once. Blood spilled into Stoback's face, coating his filthy teeth and turning his rictus grin a blood red. Disdainfully, Stoback shoved the man off of his rusted, chipped sword and he slumped to the ground, dead.

Stoback started laughing.

It was a low giggle at first and it seemed to shake the rest of the guards out of their shock. As one, they closed in on him, but with lightning speed he parried their blows, stumbling and rolling through them as if he were still drunk. Each time he cut one of his attackers, his laugh grew in pitch and volume.

He parried a blow, seeming to trip backwards as he did

so, only to spring up off of one hand, spin in the air, and slice the man flanking him almost in two.

His laughter grew.

Thinking his blade would be stuck with the force of the blow, two of the men attempted to run him through the back simultaneously. Stoback's blade, however, slid out of the dead man like butter, and he spun quickly, blocking both blades with such force that both of the men were knocked to their right. Rather than stop his momentum to prepare another attack, Stoback simply continued to spin until, on his second rotation, he brought his sword from the left side of the stumbling men. Their momentum to their right and Stoback's spinning blow from his left caused the sword to slice through both men, cutting their bodies cleanly in half.

He was cackling now, high-pitched and without a trace of sanity.

"Your sword is enchanted," the large guard who'd initiated the attack said with derision. "What skill does it take to wield a magic blade?" He spat on the ground.

Stoback ignored the comment and continued his laughter, advancing towards the guard and his remaining companion. Behind them, the merchant was clutching his sword. He'd managed to draw the weapon, but that only confirmed for Stoback that he had no idea what to do with it.

The large guard cursed as his last remaining ally looked between Stoback and his dead friends, sheathed his sword, and ran. To the big youth's credit, there was no hesitation as he advanced on Stoback, this time in a more conservative stance.

Whatever skill the young guardsman had meant nothing. One-on-one, Stoback cut him down in three quick, successive attacks. One to put him on the defence, one to put him off balance and the last to cleanly remove his head from his body, the handsome face contorted in a rictus of surprise and pain.

He stood over his fallen victim, his laughter slowly getting under control, the howling in his ears slowly abating.

"Hyugh!"

The telltale hallow thud of his enchanted armour rang in the air as the impact in his back knocked the wind out of Stoback and he whirled around, instinctively backhanding the merchant who had crept up behind him.

The merchant crumpled in a heap on the ground, his gaudy sword broken in half. He looked up at Stoback with pain and confusion in his eyes.

"Sneaky one, aren't you?" Stoback half-wheezed and half-giggled as he tried to get his breath back.

The merchant only stared at him in shock. His jaw was likely broken, and he didn't look like the type who was used to physical altercations.

"Bastar—" the merchant began, but Stoback ran him through the chest, causing him to sputter out blood in lieu of his intended insult.

Stoback's giggle rose in pitch before he could get it under control again. He looked around at the dead bodies of the guards and then simply turned and continued walking out of town and towards the ferry, his sword dragging behind him, leaving a trail of blood that slowly dried up until it was gone. No one from Preolia followed him.

Good, he thought, *I have places to be.* This time, the thought seemed almost like it was his own.

18

ASHEA

~

Ashea woke in a cozy bed to the sounds of light rain outside her window. The smattering of drops against the window made her doubly happy that Thomaras suggested they push through the night to get to Hannover. The last thing she remembered was passing out on his bony shoulder, and she wondered how she'd made it here.

Torin's dozing form in a chair beside her answered her question.

A warm feeling spread through her chest and into her face at the thought of the stoic ogre spending the night in a chair that was far too small for him. He was probably just making sure she was safe, but it was nice to imagine he did it to be close to her. Even if it wasn't true.

"Torin," she said softly.

The ogre's eyes opened immediately, and he smiled broadly, revealing the handsome tusks on either side of his mouth. The warm feeling seemed to invade her face once more, and she stretched to cover it up.

"Where are we?" Ashea asked once she was done stretching.

"Jilted Maiden."

"I thought so. Thomaras was probably eager to see Erica again. Want to go get some food?"

Torin nodded and stood up, treating himself to a stretch as well. Ashea helped herself to an eyeful of his giant form before getting out of bed. She wasn't fully recovered from the spider bite, but she felt like she was close.

When they entered the now familiar common room of the Maiden, Erica and Thomaras were already eating at a table. They motioned for Torin and Ashea to join them.

"About time you woke," Thomaras teased. "Sun's been up for hours and some of us like to be productive."

Before Ashea could respond, Erica cut in. "Don't listen to him. I dragged his ass out of bed five minutes ago. He would have slept past noon if I let him."

Thomaras smiled, shrugged at her and then took a bite of bread slathered in honey butter. "I do my best work at night. What can I say?"

"You must be starving," Erica said to Ashea after she rolled her eyes at Thomaras. "Dig in!"

The pair had clearly ordered for all four of them. Eggs, bacon, sausage, potatoes, and bread were crammed onto the table. Ashea's stomach rumbled in response before she could even sit down. "I am, thank you."

For a while, the four of them ate in silence. The innkeeper that Ashea had met the first night she was here came by with coffee, and she gratefully accepted. For a few magical moments, she forgot all about what had brought the four of them together and just enjoyed the togetherness.

Thomaras seemed to sense her contentment and gave her an apologetic look before interrupting it. "Are you rested enough to leave today? We can stay another night if you want, but I think we should get moving. At some point, either Dafoe or the Orb Weaver are going to make a decision for you, and I don't think we want that."

"I'm fine. I wouldn't mind a bath before we go," Ashea said.

"That's fine. We can leave around noon," Thomaras responded. "But there's been a change in plans. You and Torin will be heading to see the mage of light. Erica and I will be heading into Aquilo to do a little research of our own on Dafoe."

Ashea's heart sank as the familiar feeling of being abandoned weighed it down. Torin, somehow, seemed to sense her concern and rested a hand on her shoulder.

"Why can't we stay together?" Ashea asked, feeling a little juvenile as she did so.

"With the mage of light so close, many people around Hannover have seen her for various reasons," Erica answered. "Because of that, I've heard a lot of stories. Her fallout with the mage's council was messy. You can still ask her about the prism reader, but I think her opinion will be unfavourable, to say the least."

"So you two want to get some less-biased information?" Ashea asked.

"At the very least, biased in the opposite direction. The citizens of Aquilo all seem to revere Dafoe as a leader. Maybe we can find some truth in the middle?" Erica said with a chuckle.

"What do you think of him?" Torin asked Erica.

"I was fairly young when I left home, a teenager really, so it's hard to say. I grew up knowing that Dafoe was a force for good and balance in the world. That he stood for the protection of the infinity prism and all who dwelled within it. When I moved to Hannover, I started to realize that he was as much a man and a politician as he was a magical protector. I believe his intentions are to protect the realm, but he's only human."

Ashea smiled at the worldly opinions held by Erica. "In the salt marshes, we didn't worry about the mages as much as we did getting sleeping sickness from the mosquitos."

Erica laughed and laid her hand on top of Ashea's. "Trust me, that's probably better than dealing with the politics of Haven."

"So, you two will be okay traveling alone?" Thomaras asked.

Ashea did her best to hide the colour in her cheeks. "I think we'll be okay."

Torin nodded and Thomaras returned it, accepting the matter as closed, but Erica caught Ashea's eye and gave her a knowing smile.

"The rooms at the citadel can be expensive. You two had better plan to share one," Erica said.

"Probably safer that way too," Thomaras added, though Ashea got the sense he was oblivious to what Erica was suggesting.

"We'll be fine," Torin rumbled and continued eating.

Was that a hint of a smile she saw?

"Torin!" a voice bellowed, causing the few patrons to jump in surprise.

"Rolph!" Torin bellowed back with unexpected enthusiasm.

Torin, it seemed, had returned to Hannover to find an old friend. Ashea watched as Rolph approached. Instead of towering over them like Torin, Rolph was probably a head shorter than the average man, but twice as wide. His shoulders were almost comically broad and the thick muscles of his forearms looked like cords of wood. The bright red beard he wore was braided and went down to his belt and swung back and forth every time he looked one way or the other. When he saw Torin, his eyes lit up.

"You left so quickly I had to hear about it from Ben! Are you back now?"

"Not back, leaving soon," Torin rumbled after embracing his shorter friend.

"Bah! Well, that's fine. I could use the extra coin, anyway. Hi Erica," Rolph said with a smile.

"Hi Rolph, join us for breakfast. We have plenty."

"Don't mind if I do!" Rolph said, and dug into the food with enthusiasm.

After introductions were made, Rolph shared stories with the table about Torin that made Ashea blush even though she was no maiden. She couldn't stop thinking about how nice it was to learn more about her large, silent and, she was finding herself thinking more and more, handsome friend.

For another few hours, Ashea was able to enjoy the togetherness.

19

THOMARAS

~

After breakfast, it didn't take long for Erica to get her hands on a couple of horses for their trip. They belonged to one of her regular customers who asked only that they returned the animals in one piece. Thomaras was impressed with how well connected Erica was.

"I'm not connected. I'm just kind to people. You'd be surprised how willing people are to help you out when you're willing to help them," Erica explained.

"I'll take your word for it," Thomaras said, smiling. "I'll stick with getting coin into the right hands."

"Sounds expensive. My smile is free," Erica said, demonstrating.

"Not in my experience," Thomaras quipped back and dodged away from a retaliatory punch.

"What are you implying?" Erica demanded with mock indignation.

"Meals, jewelry, that trip we took down Preolia..."

Thomaras punctuated each item by extending a finger from his hand.

"Based on what I've heard of my smile, it sounds like you're getting a deal."

Thomaras sighed heavily. "You're probably right."

Erica laughed and looped her arm through his. They walked to the edge of town where their horses were waiting, and they found Torin and Ashea preparing to leave. Torin saw them and gave a wave.

"Don't you two look happy," Ashea said with a wink at Thomaras.

"Why wouldn't I be?" Thomaras replied. "I'm going to meet a woman's parents. I'm only living a reoccurring nightmare of mine."

"Don't be nervous. They're almost certainly going to hate you, so what do you have to lose?" Ashea said reassuringly.

"Torin, want to trade? I'd rather deal with a mage than this," Thomaras asked hopefully.

"Already met them, they love me," Torin responded.

Thomaras just shook his head. "Listen, you two be careful. Stick to the Five Points Road and if you see any of those animal things, run. Or the spiders. Or a Druid. Just be careful..." Thomaras trailed off.

"Very articulate warning. We'll be fine. You two take care of yourselves as well," Ashea said.

Torin nodded and Thomaras surprised himself by embracing the Granite Ogre. It was like hugging on an outcropping of rock. He gave Ashea a quick, awkward hug as well and bade them farewell. Once they were up on their horses and heading down the road, Erica reached out and touched his thigh lightly.

"They'll be fine. Torin can take care of himself and, even if something else is after her, both the Orb Weaver and

Dafoe have a vested interest in Ashea. I doubt they'll let anything happen to her."

Thomaras readied a sarcastic comment but found he didn't have the taste for it. He was genuinely worried about his friends, and Erica's words made him feel better. He just smiled at her and nodded instead.

Barriston wasn't far from Hannover as the crow flies but if they took the Five Points Road it would add at least a day to their travel. Fortunately, Aquilo's reputation for order and safety, even on backcountry roads, proved to be true, and they reached their destination unmolested.

"See, you were nervous for nothing," Erica chided, as they connected with a more populated road that lead into Barriston.

"I wasn't nervous, I was just paying attention. I still am."

"I guess I've never seen you in work mode. It's kind of intense."

Thomaras felt a momentary flutter of panic at revealing this aspect his life to Erica. It wasn't for everyone. "Sorry."

"No, don't apologize," Erica said before leaning into him from her horse. "It's also kind of hot."

The panic receded and Thomaras felt the way he always seemed to around Erica.

At peace.

The peace didn't last too long.

"Hold, travelers," a voice full of authority boomed from behind them.

Thomaras and Erica pulled up on their reins and turned on their horses. Three soldiers in golden armour were arrayed on the road before them. The leader stood slightly ahead with his men flanking him.

"What can we do for you?" Erica asked before Thomaras could say anything.

"Two daggers and a longbow," the leader said. "That's a lot of weapons for one man. What's your business in Barriston?"

Thomaras mentally cursed himself for insisting on bringing all his weapons, but he knew that the risk of cutting through the backcountry was too high to go unarmed. He'd have to deal with the consequences of that caution. By the prism he hated Aquilo.

Erica's warm laugh filled the air. "See honey, I told you they looked real! You even fooled these trained soldiers. Sir, please accept my apologies. These are prop weapons. My boyfriend here is an entertainer."

Somehow, Thomaras managed to keep the surprise of his face. Instead, he broke into a grin and stood up in his stirrups. He threw his hands in the air and bowed. "Well met, gentlemen, well met. I am Fabulous Flournoy."

"An entertainer? You don't look much like an entertainer. What kind of act do you perform?" one of the soldiers asked.

"Why, feats of skill. Behold!" Thomaras drew his daggers with a flourish. He spun them in a complicated routine that would serve no purpose in real combat before making them disappear into his robes so quickly they appeared to simply vanish.

"And the bow?" the leader asked.

"Trick shots, of course. Erica, toss an apple into the air."

Erica obliged and Thomaras drew his bow and nocked an arrow. Then, on impulse, flipped himself around so he was dangling on the opposite side of the horse. His height allowed him to stretch between the horse's back and front legs before letting his arrow fly and piercing the apple. He then pulled himself back up to his saddle and bowed to the men.

The soldiers flanking their leader were smiling, and one was about to clap before he remembered himself. The leader looked impressed but kept any other emotion off of his face. "Impressive. Just keep those daggers wherever you hid them, okay?"

"Very good, sir," Thomaras responded.

"Where will you be performing tonight?" he asked.

"Oh, unfortunately, we're not here for business. My boyfriend here is meeting my parents," Erica responded without missing a beat.

"I see. Well, best of luck," the leader said. Thomaras could have sworn he sounded disappointed there wouldn't be a show.

The soldiers moved past them and Thomaras and Erica continued at a slower pace until they were out of view.

"You're lucky I can improvise," Thomaras said.

"I was worried you were going to say you were a hunter. I needed to do something."

"I probably would have. Usually a good excuse for a bow," Thomaras conceded.

"Hunters in Aquilo need to have a license. Dafoe doesn't like people walking around with too many weapons. I should have remembered, but it wasn't a law before I left. Mom mentioned it to me in some letter she wrote. I honestly haven't thought of it again until now." Erica was clearly frustrated with herself.

"Hey, you did great. Would have been messy if I had to kill them."

"Thanks. We're almost at my parents' house. We can find out what other laws have been put into place," Erica said with a smile.

Barriston was a clean little village bustling with activity. The market was in the centre of town and the sounds of hawkers mixed with the smells of various foods gave it the feel of a much larger city. As they rode through, a few people greeted Erica and one even invited her out to the local tavern to meet up with some old friends. Thomaras smiled as he saw Erica's past come to life in front of him. A past filled with friends and family.

"You okay?" Erica asked.

"Yes. It's just a very different welcome than I would receive if I ever went back to my home village," Thomaras said.

"How come?"

"I'll tell you about it another time," Thomaras said and was surprised to find he meant it.

Sharing his past was not something he normally did.

Erica's parents lived just outside the village on a rather large farm. Their home was expansive and beautiful.

"I see your parents do well for themselves," Thomaras said.

"Yes, it's the largest farm in the area, and my father knows how to use it. He not only supplies most of the food for the surrounding cities, but provides jobs as well. They want me to take over the business someday."

"But you'd rather serve tables in a tavern?" Thomaras asked.

"I'd rather make my own way. At least for now."

Thomaras's heart swelled for her once more.

"Alright Thomaras Qu'aran. Are you ready to meet my parents?" Erica asked as they reached the front door.

Thomaras was happy to find that he was.

20

ASHEA

~

Ashea allowed herself to get lost in the small pleasures of her journey. The sun was shining and warm on her face, though she could see an angry storm brewing above the Dorsetti Plains. The Five Points Road was busy enough that she could get lost in the crowd without a press of humanity invading her space.

And the company.

Well, the company might have been the best she'd ever enjoyed.

Torin strode along beside her. Solid and quiet. His was a presence that seemed to absorb stress and danger and radiate pure calm. She knew the only reason the walk was so pleasant was because he was there. She was still being pursued by forces she knew almost nothing about, but she felt like with Torin by her side, she could handle whatever came.

"Have you ever been to the citadel?" Ashea asked. She

had figured out pretty quickly that any conversation she wanted to have would need to be initiated on her end.

"No. It's hard for me to get hurt," Torin replied.

Ashea laughed. "Yes, I suppose even in your line of work, you dispense the beatings more than you absorb them."

Torin smiled and Ashea could just make out his tusks pressing against the fabric of his balaclava. Not for the first time, she felt a flutter in her chest. "Do you really need to hide your face like that? Depriving the world of your smile seems a shame."

Because he spoke so little, it was hard to tell when Torin was at a loss for words, but based on the colour creeping across his face, Ashea was fairly confident her words were having their intended effect.

Then he pulled his balaclava down and flashed her a smile that made her miss a step. She could tell by the warmth in her cheeks that her colour was matching his.

And that flutter in her chest had descended decidedly lower.

"It's easier to travel with my face hidden. I'll make an exception for you," Torin rumbled gently.

Ashea just smiled back at him and let the silence fall between them. Silence thick with anticipation and a physical need that she hadn't felt for a long time. And never so poignantly.

She was pleased to see that her take-charge approach to flirting was appreciated by Torin. She'd learned that most men were intimidated when she was forward with her intentions. She'd also learned that those men weren't worth her time.

She was happy that Torin would be.

"You and Rolph seem close," Ashea offered, and was rewarded with another of Torin's rare smiles.

"Very. He's like family."

"Do you ever miss being around your people?" Ashea asked.

Torin was silent for a long time and she began to worry that she'd pushed him a bit too far. After a moment, though, he looked down at her and shook his head.

"Not really. I never really fit in with them anyway. There, I was a burden. Smaller and weaker in their eyes, no matter how hard I worked to fit in. Here I may be different, but there are a few who see me for who I am. Rolph. Erica. Hopefully others," Torin said with just the whisper of a question in his tone.

"Thomaras? Yes, I think he likes you just fine."

Torin rumbled a deep laugh that made Ashea's heart skip a beat. She could get used to a sound like that.

"Good. I was worried my feelings would go unrequited."

Now it was Ashea's turn to laugh and as she did, she grabbed his arm around the elbow and leaned her head into his bicep like it was the most natural thing in the world.

"I see you, Torin. Don't worry about that."

The rest of their trip was as pleasant a time as Ashea could remember since fleeing the salt marshes and the only real family she'd known. She felt safe with Torin in a way that she couldn't quite define. As if his mere presence was enough to ward off anything that came her way. In terms of physical threats that might have even been true.

Unfortunately, the real threat stalked her dreams.

By the time they saw the citadel creeping up over the horizon, the sun was well on its way to setting. The impending dusk only served to show the sconces that decorated the citadel and the walls that circled it. They cast light against the encroaching darkness through the night. When Torin and Ashea walked through the gates and into the courtyard, the moon was on the rise. A tall man with a shaved head and wearing tan robes greeted them with a ledger in hand.

"Greetings travelers. Solaire has retired for the night. Are your wounds life-threatening?"

"No," Ashea responded, unsure if she should try to explain that she just needed to talk to the mage.

"Very well. Do you require a remedy for any pain or to help you sleep?"

Ashea got the sense that he was reciting a standard list. "No."

"Very well. I will put you on the list for tomorrow. Name?"

"Ashea."

"Excellent. And do you require one room or two?"

"One," Torin said.

Surprised by his quick response, Ashea glanced up at the ogre, who smiled at her slyly.

Ashea felt that flutter again.

"Perfect. Take this, it will let you into your rooms," the man said, handing her a perfectly round stone hanging on a leather thong. "Just follow the path. Have a pleasant evening."

Ashea looked around for a path, and then the stone in her hand began to glow light blue. In front of her, a blue path mirrored the glow, and Ashea could see that it stretched through the courtyard and into the citadel.

Torin and Ashea shared a look and began following the path. The courtyard was beautiful and peaceful. Here and there, she saw people sitting and waiting to be seen. Some had obvious injuries, while others looked ill or feverish. Their path took them around a tree and Ashea took a startled step back when she saw a huge black bear lying beneath its branches. The bear just looked at her and laid its head back down beside a mangled-looking front paw.

"She heals animals?" Ashea asked Torin.

"I guess. All I know is that there is no violence permitted on this land. It seems the edict extends to the animals as well," Torin said, pointing at a buck with a clearly broken leg.

"But how do they know the rules?" Ashea asked in wonder.

Torin shrugged. "Same way they know they can come here to be healed. She's the mage of light. It seems her light extends to all beings."

Ashea smiled at the notion and wondered if the mage's light could banish the shadow that stalked her dreams.

She doubted it.

The interior of the citadel was plainly appointed with the odd flower or plant. The rooms were just as neutral, but Ashea was pleased to see that the bed looked large enough for Torin. She was even more pleased to see a tub of steaming hot water in an adjoining chamber.

"That bath looks perfect right now," Ashea said.

"You can go first."

Ashea flashed him a smile and walked into the room, leaving the door slightly ajar.

She slipped off her traveling clothes and stepped into the hot water. The feeling on her skin elicited a sigh, and she dunked her head beneath the surface. Then, she stepped out of the tub and arranged her long hair so it fell down her back.

She stepped into the doorway. Her ample breasts were glistening with a wetness she knew was already reflected between her legs. She turned slightly at the hips so that all of her curves were on display. "Torin, I could use some help in here."

Torin turned from his pack and Ashea was rewarded by his jaw momentarily dropping open as he took her in from head to toe.

Then he crossed the room, removing clothing as he did. A laugh bubbled up from inside her and she retreated back to the tub of water coyly.

Torin would definitely be worth her time.

21

THOMARAS

~

L ying in Erica's bed with his legs dangling off the end,
Thomaras gave silent thanks for his ability to operate
on little sleep. They had arrived the night before as Erica's
parents were eating dinner. Introductions had been a little
awkward at first, but once they had gotten over the surprise
of their only daughter bringing home a strange man
unannounced, hospitality had kicked in.

Thomaras had eaten his fill of one of the finest meals
he'd ever tasted and the four of them had laughed and joked
long into the night. Mostly because Erica had left him no
choice, Thomaras had given his real name but had told Erik
and Syl that he was a courier. It was one of his most used
fake professions.

Now, with the sun just barely creeping over the horizon,
Thomaras could hear Syl and Erica in the kitchen cooking
and Erik out in the fields giving instructions to his
labourers. Certain no more sleep would come, Thomaras

heaved himself out of the bed and dressed quickly before heading down the hall and into the kitchen.

The smell of frying bacon hit his nose, and his stomach started rumbling. "Syl, that smells divine. Is it possible that you've outdone last night's dinner?"

"Ah, handsome and a sweet talker. I see why you like him, dear. Have a seat, Thomaras. How'd you sleep?" Erica looked so much like her mother that Thomaras would have sworn the two were sisters when they'd first met. A life of hard work had cut lines into her face, but she wore them well and, like her daughter, had a smile that could guide ships to dock on a dark night.

"Just fine, thanks. I guess I should have expected a house full of early risers on a farm. Erica usually sleeps as late as me."

"She knows the rules. We let guests sleep late, but if you're going to make a habit of coming around, you'll have to get used to getting up for the chores," Syl said, and placed a plate of food down with a smile.

Unsure how to react to the assumption that he would be returning, and the fact that he enjoyed it, Thomaras instead shoveled food into his mouth and moaned at how delicious it was.

"Leave him alone, Mother. You'll scare him off," Erica said and leaned in to kiss Thomaras's cheek.

"Fine, fine. Teasing aside, Thomaras, you're welcome back anytime, but Pa will be in for breakfast shortly and I suggest you drop that courier horse dung you were feeding us last night. We can look the other way if a guest wants to lie to us, but if you're sharing our daughter's bed, you'd best shoot straight," Syl said, pointing a spatula at him.

Thomaras was so surprised he had to remind himself to

keep chewing. With an effort, he swallowed his bite so he could give the response Syl seemed to expect. "Yes ma'am."

Syl just nodded and went back to cooking. Thomaras shot Erica a look, but she just gave him a shrug.

Right on cue, Erik burst through the door, gave his daughter a kiss on the cheek, swept his wife up in a big hug, and then sat down to eat.

"Finally awake there, old bean?" Erik asked Thomaras.

"Uh…" Thomaras started.

"I'm kidding! Relax, though I'm sure my lovely wife explained the rules?"

Thomaras couldn't help but smile. "Yes sir. Next time, I'll be up to help you in the fields."

"Bah. Doesn't look like you'd be much help out there. I'll take Erica and you can help Syl with the cooking." Erik's smile danced brightly in his eyes. Much like his wife, the proof of hard work decorated his face, but the intelligence there was unmistakable. It was no surprise his business was so successful.

"I fry a mean egg," Thomaras deadpanned, eliciting a laugh from everyone in the kitchen.

He'd have to remember to tell Ashea just how much Erica's parents liked him.

"Now, out with it, man. You two came here to ask us about something and knowing my daughter, it wasn't for my permission to marry. What's on your mind?"

Thomaras smiled at the direct tack Erik was taking. He may be an affable farmer, but he was also a shrewd businessman. Someone you underestimated at your peril.

"Dafoe. Is he the benevolent ruler he claims to be?"

Thomaras could be direct as well.

Erik laughed. "I didn't figure you for a courier. In the decade that Dafoe has ruled Aquilo, the infrastructure has improved, the economy has doubled and I haven't seen a bandit since there was still colour in my beard."

"But?"

"No buts that I can see. The man appears to be as advertised."

"Which means you don't trust him," Thomaras inferred.

"In ten years, he's accomplished more than any prism reader before him. Rather than have a proxy rule his kingdom while he manages the affairs of the mages council he's taken on both roles and excelled. If his farm bordered my own, I'd be sure to keep an on eye on him."

"An ambitious man is rarely satisfied," Thomaras said with a nod.

Erik smiled. "I can see why Erica likes you."

"Everyone keeps saying that like it's a surprise. So, you don't trust him?"

Erik was silent for a while. "I don't know. He's never publicly claimed nor denied a desire for more power, so technically he's not lied about anything. His only claim is that he works for the betterment of the world. I've never seen evidence to the contrary. Am I concerned that his ambition might lead him to make a move for more power? Maybe. But the bigger question is this: would that really be so bad?"

"Civil war has always been avoided in Haven at all costs. There are theories that it caused the Cataclysm," Thomaras suggested.

"True. But what if there was no conflict? Would anyone object if Dafoe extended his rule west and made the salt marshes into something more than a den for bandits and thieves?"

Thomaras could think of a number of people, actually,

but he had to admit that popular opinion would likely be of a mind with Erik.

"Thank you. You've given me a lot to consider."

"You're welcome. I don't know what you're up to, and I don't want to know, but can I ask you to consider something?"

Thomaras nodded.

"Don't answer now, but whatever you decide, if you have to stand against Dafoe, will it be for the right reasons?"

Thomaras nodded again. It was a good question and one that he had maybe never considered in his life. Was it good for him? Could he get away with it? How much would he earn? Those were all questions he'd asked.

Was it for the right reasons?

That was a new one.

22

ASHEA

~

Torin and Ashea sat in the courtyard of the citadel sipping on tea and eating fresh egg sandwiches provided by one of the tan-robed attendants that bustled around the area. The sun was still low in the sky and although the telltale smell of rain was on the air; the day promised to be a pleasant one.

"How's your breakfast?" Ashea asked Torin.

The giant smiled at her and held up the sandwich, which appeared tiny in his giant hand. "Might need seconds."

Ashea laughed and reached out to touch Torin's arm. He took her hand and squeezed it gently. She had been impressed at how gentle Torin could be for one so strong.

She'd been even more impressed when he wasn't so gentle.

Before she could suggest they head back to their chambers, the small stone that acted as their room key pulsed twice and a line of matching light flickered to life, leading them into the citadel.

"Guess she's ready to see us," Torin said. The disappointment in his voice suggested his thoughts were matching her own.

"Looks like," Ashea sighed.

A woman in a tan robe appeared beside them. "Solaire will see you now."

"Thank you," Ashea said, but the woman was already off on her next task.

They followed the path of light through the citadel and into a small receiving room on the main floor. The room was the least appointed of any she'd seen yet, containing only a modest desk with two chairs on the side closest to the door.

On the other side sat a woman that could only be described as statuesque.

Even seated, it was clear that she would have towered over Ashea. Though not as tall as Torin, she would likely have been fairly close to looking Thomaras in the eye. Her dark skin indicated she was from Preolia, a fact confirmed by the loose-fitting single-piece garb that was worn there. Her hair hung down past the middle of her back and, at first glance, appeared tangled and matted. Upon closer inspection, the effect was intentional, the strands woven together and quite beautiful. She smiled and a fierce, if weary, intelligence shone through.

"Hello, Ashea, Torin, my name is Solaire, as I'm sure you know. I'm sorry I couldn't see you sooner, but it's been a busy few nights. A madman is hacking and slashing his way up the Five Points Road. I understand you aren't here for healing?"

Ashea felt a pang of guilt. The mage must be on call at all times. "Yes, I'm sorry. We just had a few questions."

"Don't be sorry. A moment's rest from my usual work is a welcome reprieve. Ask away."

"We came to ask about the Orb Weaver. We heard that you are well schooled on the subject."

"The Orb Weaver? I don't think I know more than most. Legends speak of her as an eternal being that acts as the protector of the infinity prism inside which our world resides. Is there something specific you'd like to know?"

Ashea felt her cheeks colour as the mage of light stared at her expectantly. Was she supposed to just ask this woman if she thought a legend was real? Besides, the Orb Weaver wasn't what she was really interested in.

"What do you think of the prism reader?" she blurted.

Solaire raised an eyebrow. "If you came here to gossip, I'm not sure I can help you. As tempting as that might be."

Ashea shook her head. "No, that's not what I mean..."

Solaire continued to stare at her as she struggled. She'd been certain of her purpose when she'd come here, but now she would have to give up her secret. To a mage of all people.

Torin placed a hand on her arm and smiled.

"I can use magic. I've never told anyone, but now it appears the prism reader knows and has taken an interest in me," Ashea finally said.

"Ah, well, I see why you were hesitant to tell me. No need to worry that I'll turn you in, though. I haven't been a part of the council in years. I'm not sure I can help you, however, unless your skill is in healing?" Solaire asked, and her tone almost sounded hopeful.

"No," Ashea answered and decided if she was going to trust this woman then it had to be with the whole truth. "I can control the elements."

Solaire laughed. "Just like my sister. No wonder Dafoe is

so interested in you. Another woman wielding the elements for his cause would suit him just fine."

"Your... sister?"

"I'm sorry, child. I'm letting personal feelings interfere with your questions. The mage of elements, Luness, is my sister. She is the prism reader's most trusted general. Given how I feel about the man, it can be a sore subject for me. I'm guessing you want to know if you should go to Dafoe?"

"Yes."

"I don't see that you have much choice. Unfortunately for most mages, membership in the council is hardly optional. You can choose how much you want to participate, but if you can wield magic, then it is best for Haven if the council can keep tabs on you at the very least. I'm surprised you're so hesitant. Dafoe has worked hard to cultivate an image that draws magic users to him like bees to honey."

"I was warned against it," Ashea admitted.

Solaire raised an eyebrow. "I see. By whom?"

"The Druid."

"Felix? I would ask how you met, but my guess is that the spider he works for is involved."

"You know Felix works for the Orb Weaver?" Ashea asked.

"Yes. After my split from the council, she approached me to serve her as Felix does. I refused."

"You refused a god?"

"Hardly a god, my dear. Immortality should never be confused with omnipotence. I believe her work is important, though. Just as Dafoe's is. My services, however, must be available to everyone. The healing I can offer must be a universal right, otherwise my gift is squandered. Serving either one of them was too high a risk for compromising that neutrality. So then, you're asking who I think you should go to?"

"I might not have been so direct about it," Ashea said with a smile.

"My falling-out with Dafoe wasn't pretty. I was trying to maintain an objective position, and he thought I was turning my back on the council. Despite the fact that our last words were contentious, he allowed me to do as I wished because, I believe, he knows my abilities are too important to risk losing. Not just for him, but for everyone. I may not agree with his methods, but I do believe that he has the greater good of Haven in mind."

"And the Orb Weaver?"

"I believe her goals to be the same, but she sees mortals as tools she can bend to her will. I'm certain that despite his service to her, Felix has done much to challenge that belief, but at the end of the day she is always going to know, in her heart, that she is something more than any of us."

"But you refused to work for either of them and they both just let you go. What's the difference?"

"When I said no to the Orb Weaver, I ceased to exist in her mind. I was a game piece that was removed from the board. Inconsequential. Dafoe ensures that I am supplied both by the mages council and the kingdom of Aquilo itself so that this place can continue to serve its purpose. He doesn't benefit from what I do, but knows this world does, so he makes sure I am able to function. I can't tell you what choice you should make, but I speak only the truth."

Ashea looked at the tall, earnest woman and decided to trust her with one more thing. "I have dreams where something is chasing me. Dafoe says he can fix that. Do you think he can?"

Solaire considered her for a while before speaking

again. "Dreams are largely the realm of the prism reader. If anyone can help, it's him."

"Thank you. I appreciate all of your help," Ashea said.

"You're welcome, child. Just be careful in your travels. Your companion appears more than capable, but there is someone very dangerous out there right now. I've seen too much of his handy work not to take him seriously."

"I won't let anything happen to her," Torin said.

"I believe that, but you alone may not be enough. Ashea, how much of your magic can you control?"

"It comes and goes. I don't know why. Sometimes it seems like in times of great need I can use it, but I was recently locked up and try as I might, I couldn't blast my way out. Right after that, a boar was charging someone, and I was able to call a fireball to kill it," Ashea said.

"Have you used it since then?" Solaire asked.

"Just once. I used air to bring Torin his hammer."

"From where?"

"It was inside a stable filled with giant spiders. He was going to charge in and get it."

"Well, my sister knows more about the elements, of course, but magic itself comes from our will. We have a latent talent, but it's our ability to bend that to our will that makes our magic potent. It seems as though something might be standing in the way of that will. At least some of the time."

"How do I fix that?"

"That, unfortunately, I do not know. Issues like this creep up in novice mages, but can usually be addressed by another mage proficient in the same type of magic. I am certain my sister could help you. In the meantime, just give it some thought. It seems to me that any time you've used your magic, it was to protect someone else. Now, I must attend to my other appointments. You are welcome to stay as long as you wish."

"No, thank you. We have friends we need to meet."

"Very well. Travel carefully out there. Good luck."

With that, Solaire stood and left them alone in her office. Ashea shared a look with Torin, who smiled in return.

"Going to see Dafoe, then?"

Ashea sighed. "I think so."

"Thomaras is going to hate this," Torin said.

Ashea laughed. "Yes, at least there's a bright side to all this."

23

TORIN

~

The storm that had been gathering for days to the north finally broke as Ashea and Torin strode into Hannover. The sunset against the angry storm clouds descending upon them had an ominous beauty that made Torin appreciate the roof and walls that would be surrounding his slumber tonight. Ashea slipped her hand into his and leaned against him.

Well, whatever slumber he managed to get.

Torin thought back on the previous day's journey and all that had happened at the Citadel of Light with wonder. Ashea wasn't the first woman that he'd slept with. He'd been with a few ogres before he'd headed south and there was no shortage of human women in Haven that found his size and strength appealing. No, what made Ashea so different was how much he had enjoyed all the mundane things they'd done before and since they'd shared a bed. Even just walking from Hannover to the citadel and back with her was more fun than he'd had with even the most adventurous of his previous partners.

"Let's run!" Ashea laughed as the rain started to fall in earnest.

Torin smiled and allowed her to drag him by the hand through the muddy streets of Hannover. He tried to keep some perspective on Ashea. He'd only known her a few weeks and for all he knew, she was only interested in sex. Which would be just fine with him, but it was better not to get too wrapped up in feelings that were probably just excitement over someone new and attractive.

So, so attractive.

When they burst through the doors if The Jilted Maiden, the sconces were low and the common room was all but deserted. Torin and Ashea did their best to get the rainwater out of their hair.

"You made it!" Erica's voice rang out from a table in the corner of the room.

"Earnest!" Rolph's voice boomed out drunkenly. "Bring towels! And ale!"

"No more ale!" Thomaras chimed in. "It's time for whisky! None of that local shit, either. Bring us The Bard's Tears!"

Earnest emerged from the back with towels slung over his shoulder. The man looked exhausted and ready for sleep but if Torin knew anything about him, it was that the prospect of even a little more coin would keep him here all night.

"Here are your damn towels," Earnest said and threw them at Torin and Ashea. "And I'll bring the whisky when you show me your coin! This stuff isn't going on your tab, Rolph."

Earnest's demands were met with roars of laughter from

the two men and as Ashea and Torin made their way to the table, Thomaras tossed a coin purse on the table with a heavy thunk.

"How'd it go?" Thomaras asked. His speech was surprisingly slurred.

"Good," Torin said with a smile.

"She gave us a lot to think about," Ashea elaborated. "It seems as though she doesn't really trust either the Orb Weaver or Dafoe, but..."

Thomaras cut her off with a wave of his hands. "That's too much information for how drunk we are. Just tell me where we're going next."

Ashea laughed and shook her head. "To see Dafoe."

"Well, fuck. I guess a mage is better than a giant spider anyway," Thomaras said.

"It's okay, you don't have to come," Ashea said. Torin looked at her in surprise, but she shook her head. "No, it's okay. I've already asked so much of you and honestly, I can't afford to pay you anyway."

"I want to come," Thomaras said quietly.

"What was that?" Torin asked.

Erica laid one hand on top of Thomaras's and nodded encouragingly. "I want to help. I've lived by a set of rules for a long time and they've kept me alive, sure, but they've also kept me at arm's length from anyone else. I think maybe it's time for that to change."

Thomaras looked around quickly and then back down at his hand, covered by Erica's.

"I think I'll help Earnest with that whisky," Rolph said tactfully and got up.

"What changed?" Torin asked, sensing that Thomaras had more to say.

He was silent for a moment before looking at Erica

again. "Her. You two. The knowledge that something is happening out there centered around the two most powerful beings on Haven and I can do something about it. I don't know, I just... I think I'm done being angry."

"At who?" Ashea asked.

Thomaras looked up and smiled. "My father, Jacob, was an asshole. There really isn't any other way to put it. He was a small-time fence that lived on the border of Ithadore and the Granite Ogre lands in a village called Gatling. He wasn't terribly well-liked, but he did have a way with ladies, and was generous with his coin at the local tavern when he had it. According to him, my mother was as close to full-blooded Arahana as he'd ever seen. She was passing through the town on her way back into the Granite Ogre lands when he seduced her. Now, the main thing I know about Jacob is that he was a liar and his opinion of himself was far greater than it had any right to be. Naturally, these things went hand in hand. Once I was old enough to start thinking for myself, I always just assumed my mother was a tall woman that he'd convinced himself was an Arahana. She likely had a little of the blood in her, but so do many in Haven. One thing I could never understand, however, was why he agreed to raise me after she returned to him with a two-year-old boy. Whenever I pressed him on the matter, he would look a little spooked and tell me not to worry about it."

"Wait, your father openly admitted to being forced to raise you? He told you he didn't want you?" Ashea asked, incredulous.

"When I was too young to be of any use to him, my father would leave me at the local brothel and the women there would take turns caring for me. They tried to shield me from the terrible things that some of the patrons would do to them, but they couldn't hide everything from me. I think they were worried that if I was exposed to degenerates at a young age, I would learn to be a degenerate. What I actually learned was the strength that a woman can find inside herself in order to put food on the table for her loved ones. My father and I came to an understanding when I was about eight years old that I was a burden on him, and if I didn't make myself useful he had no problem taking me into one of the other kingdoms and leaving me to the system. Fortunately for me, I had some natural talents that made me very useful. As I said, my father was a fence, but he would also engage in some other criminal activities from time to time if the money was right. He taught me how to pick locks and pockets, how to move about quietly and sneak into places I wasn't supposed to be. Whether it was the Arahana blood he claimed came from my mother or just natural talent, I quickly surpassed him in most of these pursuits and together we began to make him a lot of money. Jacob's real talent wasn't in any of the actual criminal skills he taught me, but in knowing how to keep a low profile. Knowing the right jobs to take and which ones to turn down, no matter what the pay might be." Thomaras paused, taking a long sip from his glass.

"Sounds like someone I know," Torin said good-naturedly.

Thomaras laughed and pointed at the big man in agreement.

"Indeed, he was an asshole, but he certainly taught me how to survive and how to best use my skills. Unfortunately, the asshole part was getting worse and worse as I got older, and by the time I was sixteen, it was unbearable. The camel's back finally broke after a particularly heavy night of drinking. He returned home with a woman who, when she saw me sharing the one-room cabin we lived in, decided she would rather sleep elsewhere. He tore into me, telling me I had ruined his life and that he would have been happier if I'd never been born. I certainly wasn't pleased with the arrangement either, and let him know it. We eventually came to blows, and while he was a tough and crafty old man, he was still an old man and no match for me. I don't regret the beating. He deserved it and would have survived the night if I'd stuck around. But I left; I needed a drink to calm myself down. I returned to the cabin an hour later to find my father with a knife in his belly. Some enemy he'd made had decided to come by that night to settle a score. No matter how careful you are, ours is a risky business. Maybe if he hadn't just taken a severe beating from his son, he would have been able to fight them off. Maybe if I'd been there, I could have helped. I don't know, but I do know that in the state that I'd put him, he had no chance."

"Still not your fault. You didn't put the knife in his belly," Torin said.

"No, I didn't. And I don't know if I would prefer him alive today or not. I left Gatling that night. Gathered my things and the little money Jacob's drinking allowed us to save and set out to make my own way," Thomaras said.

"Wait, you said there was a knife in his belly. Was he dead when you got there?" Ashea asked.

Thomaras looked at Ashea for a moment and then down at his glass for a longer one. He sighed deeply, as if coming to a decision.

"He was alive. Barely. He took my hand and apologized for being a shit father. I told him to go fuck himself and he laughed. Then he got very quiet and looked me dead in the eyes. After a moment he said, 'Thomaras, I know you don't believe me about your mother and that's by design. I tried to make it sound like drunken boasting, but I have to tell you the truth, for your sake. Believe me or not, it's up to you, but I have to tell you. Your mother wasn't partially blooded, she was a full-blooded Arahana. She and the few that remain hidden in Haven are the last of their kind. She made a mistake, slumming it with me, and by some miracle, if you want to call it that, she got pregnant. Not supposed to happen very often between our kind and theirs but it did. I, of course, had no idea. She was simply gone the next day, and I was left with the memories of sleeping with a god. Two years later, she comes back and tells me I have to raise you. That her people will kill you if they find you. She'd been hiding from her own people, claiming to be on some mission or other, until you were old enough that I could handle you. I told her no, I wasn't going to let her ruin my life. Well, she threatened to do some terrible things to me if she ever found out I gave you up. Then she demonstrated, with her magic, how she might do those things and I decided I'd best listen.' And he did. His last words were a tacit admission that he didn't want me," Thomaras said, slamming his glass onto the table.

"But did you believe him?" Ashea asked.

Thomaras sighed again and finished his drink in one swallow.

"Absolutely. Just another reason I try to keep a low profile."

"I don't know. I think you've got every right to be angry with him," Ashea said.

"Oh, I'm not angry at him. I don't care about him, never have. I'm angry with myself. I let him turn me into someone that couldn't be close to anyone else. Someone that couldn't trust. I'm done with all of that."

With that he got up, kissed Erica on the forehead and walked towards the stairs.

"I'm sure you're both aware of this, but you are now as close to a family as he's ever had," Erica said.

"We know," Ashea said, and Torin nodded along.

"Good. Now, I'm going to go make sure he doesn't murder anyone."

Torin looked at Ashea as Erica walked away.

"That was intense," Ashea said.

"Yep."

"Is Thomaras our friend now?"

"Yep."

"Huh. Feels like that's going to be a lot of work."

Torin laughed out loud and then leaned in and gave Ashea a big kiss. "Come on. There's something in my room I need to show you."

The smile Ashea gave him made him forget about everything else in the world.

24

ASHEA

~

Ashea nuzzled further into Torin and groaned dramatically. "Do we have to get up?"

"Only if you want to start the journey," Torin replied.

"What I want to do is stay in bed with you for a week."

"That's fine, but we may get interrupted by a mage. Or an eternal spider. Or both."

Ashea sighed. "I know, I know. I need to choose before they choose for me. I get it. Maybe one more day?"

Torin looked at her seriously. "You were having a nightmare last night."

"Oh, yes, that happens sometimes."

"I couldn't wake you up, so I just held you."

Ashea's heart melted at the simple statement of kindness, and she kissed him. "It's okay, I'm fine."

"But Dafoe might help make them go away, right?"

"You're right. But he might also tell me what's causing them. What's hunting me, and I don't know if I can handle that," Ashea blurted out.

"We can," Torin said calmly.

And just like that, Ashea realized why she'd been so hesitant. Why she'd jumped at the chance to take another day to decide her course of action. Where she went today would signify the first steps taken in the direction of the problems she'd run from her whole life. She didn't know if she could handle what she saw when she finally faced them.

But with Torin by her side, at least she wouldn't be alone.

"Okay. But first we need to tell Thomaras about us."

"He can't guess?" Torin asked.

"You know him. He's a loner. He might be able to read a mark like a book, but interpersonal dynamics are going to fly over his head. I think he thinks of me like a kid sister or something and he seems to have some brothers-in-arms connection with you. It might feel like a betrayal if he knew... whatever we are. Especially after he opened up to us like he did."

"Okay. I'll tell him."

Despite how well she'd gotten to know Torin over the past few weeks together, she was still sometimes taken aback by his unerring calm.

"Good. I was going to make you do it anyway. Hungry?"

Torin grinned and nodded. The two of them gathered their few belongings and then headed down the stairs. The smells of breakfast filled their noses and for a little while Ashea's concern about Thomaras's reaction fell away.

Now, sitting in the common room, plates empty before them, Ashea's heartbeat jumped a little as she saw Thomaras come down from his room. She was nervous, even if it was Torin doing the hard part. Erica had been up and about, serving them their meal, long before Thomaras had come down, but the colour in her cheeks and the spring in her step told Ashea that they too had likely made the most of their last morning together. When Erica saw Thomaras come down, she first smiled at him and then gave Ashea an encouraging wink before making herself scarce.

Looking their way, Thomaras started to head over, but hesitated as Torin reached over and squeezed Ashea's hand before kissing her lightly on the cheek and standing up. Thomaras's face was priceless and would have normally been cause for a stinging comment from Ashea, but she was too nervous to do anything but stare back, dumbly she assumed, at him.

Torin walked over slowly and put a giant hand on Thomaras's shoulder. She couldn't hear what he was saying, but from time to time Thomaras would peek his head around Torin's mass and give her a strange look. Slowly, after a few nods and awkward laughs, Thomaras clapped the giant on the shoulder and smiled broadly at the Granite Ogre. Torin was smiling himself.

"All good," Torin rumbled as he came over and picked up their belongings.

"Thank you," she said quietly and smiled.

Torin headed out the door into the light rain to load up their trusty cart. As he passed by, Thomaras clapped him on the shoulder again before heading over to Ashea.

"So... you two are... Torin just said that... uh..." Thomaras stuttered uncharacteristically.

"We're fucking?" Ashea said, finding comfort in his sheepishness and being unable to help herself from making it worse for him.

"Oh god, can you not? He said that you two were in a relationship. He, at least, has some class." Thomaras's exaggerated grimace only seemed about twenty percent real. Falling into their old patterns put him at ease.

"Oh, he's definitely the classy one in the relationship. At least in public," Ashea responded with a wink and was rewarded with another pained look from Thomaras.

"Goodness, woman, I don't want to think about it. The sheer mechanics are baffling," Thomaras said with a laugh.

"Oh, I don't mind the challenge. It's rather like climbing a tree... one that gives you an orgasm when you get to the top," Ashea said as she patted his arm and walked past him. Thomaras's audible sigh was reward enough as Ashea headed towards the door with a laugh.

"Ashea, hold on," she heard Erica call out as she was about to step outside, "I have something for you."

Turning at the door, she saw Erica approach with a leather cloak lined with what looked like wool.

"I brought this travelling cloak back from home. It was mine when I was a younger girl and I thought it might fit your spritely form," Erica said with a laugh, handing the beautiful cloak to Ashea.

Ashea was at a loss for words. She and Erica had gotten close over the sporadic time they'd spent together, but she hadn't expected this kindness. She wasn't accustomed to gifts.

"Erica... I... I don't know what to say. Thank you." Her bumbling reply seemed inadequate to the gesture, but when Erica swept her up in a warm embrace, she simply hugged her back.

When the two women separated, there were tears in both of their eyes and they shared an embarrassed laugh before Erica whirled around and headed back to the kitchen. The morning rush was starting, and she had tables to attend.

Ashea watched her go for a moment before slipping on

the cloak, which fit her better than any piece of clothing she had ever worn, and headed into the drizzle.

"Nice cloak," Torin said with a smile. "Beautiful."

"Me or the cloak?" she asked with a coy smile.

"You," was his reply.

Her heart warmed at the four simple words he spoke.

"Must be nice not to have to wear children's clothes for once," Thomaras said as he walked past her.

She readied a biting retort to his interrupting a beautiful moment but saw the tears starting in the corners of his eyes and realized that this goodbye with Erica was likely harder than anything he'd experienced. She couldn't imagine having to leave Torin. She settled for a disgruntled sniff. Let him think he won the exchange.

"Let's go," Torin said, giving Ashea a knowing smile; he had seen the tears as well.

"Yes, please, let's. On to the capital and his mageliness..."

"Not a word," Ashea interjected, and Torin pointed at her in agreement.

"... the prism reader!" Thomaras continued theatrically. "I can't wait to make myself known to the most powerful man in Haven. What *are* we waiting for?"

"Is the whole trip going to be like this?" Ashea asked as she climbed up beside Thomaras.

"Oh no, don't worry. I intend to complain about the rain about half the time as well," Thomaras replied, smiling.

Ashea laughed, Torin smiled and their little family headed out of town towards the person who could give her some answers.

25

TORIN

~

Torin strode along beside the cart, his hand resting on its railing so that Ashea's could rest on his own, and could just make out a hazy yellow blob in the overcast skies ahead of them as they headed northeast. Their journey was shaping up to be a long and soggy one. Feeling the warmth of Ashea's hand on his and listening to the rain patter off of the wide brim of his hat, Torin didn't even mind that much.

"Who's this idiot?" Thomaras said with a scoff.

The comment pulled Torin's eyes away from Ashea and onto the road ahead of them. Walking towards them in the dead centre of the cobblestone was what appeared to be a drunk, or maybe a deserter of some kind. His chain was rusty and dented, his toes poked through the ends of his chewed-up leather boots and limp, tangled hair fell in front of his face as he leaned forward, dragging a pathetic-looking great-sword behind him.

"Hmmm," Torin rumbled as he considered the figure ahead of them.

"I wonder if he washed out of a city guard or one of the kingdoms' armies?" Thomaras asked, mirth clear in his voice.

As the two parties closed the distance on each other, a low grating noise could be heard and every now and then sparks would fly from the tip of the sword as it dragged across the stones. This close, Torin could make out the man's dark eyes peering through the soaking tangle of hair in his face.

"You're going to ruin your weapon if you keep dragging it like that," Thomaras called out when the figure was closer. "What's left of it, anyway," Thomaras finished under his breath once he saw the state of the chipped and dented blade.

"Trust me, it works just fine," the man said.

Torin was immediately on edge. He didn't like the disconnected tone that the man was using. He seemed... off.

"Well then, hopefully, we'll have no cause to see it in action. My name is Davin and these are my travelling companions. Who do I have the pleasure of addressing?" Thomaras asked, adding a jovial flourish to his words.

Torin sensed that Thomaras didn't like the look of the man, but he wasn't sure that he was taking the threat as seriously as he should. Torin had spent years as a doorman and had dealt with all kinds of threats. Drunk and boastful was always his preference, as they tended to be more bark than bite. The silent ones with a hard look in their eyes were worse. They were usually experienced in the trouble they were doling out and inevitably had the skills to survive the trouble they caused. The worst was crazy. You never knew what to expect from crazy, and not knowing what was coming was more dangerous than anything else.

This guy reeked of crazy.

A gust of rainy wind blew into their faces and Torin wrinkled his nose as he realized that the man also reeked. Stale, unwashed clothing mixed with what might have been weeks of body odour and dirt mingled with another familiar smell that he couldn't quite place.

"I'm Stoback. I'm here for the girl. Please, please make me kill you to get to her." Stoback said the words so calmly that it took everyone a beat to take in what he was requesting.

A beat and half later, Thomaras was letting an arrow fly. Torin was once again impressed with the man's speed with his bow. Torin himself had just gotten his hammer into his hands and the arrow was already on its way. Torin began to sigh in relief as he awaited the inevitable spatter of blood that would mark the strange man's end.

Thunk.

The strangely hollow sound that the arrow made as it struck its target was accompanied by an odd shimmer in the air around Stoback, and the arrow fell to the ground, broken, as if Thomaras had shot it into a stone wall.

Without stopping to consider what happened, Thomaras loosed two more arrows at the man in rapid succession.

Thunk.

Thunk.

The arrows fell to the ground the same as the first, and Torin shared a brief look with Thomaras before he lowered his bow.

"I always thought the bow was a coward's weapon — it takes all the fun out of the killing," Stoback said in a low giggle and began to walk forward.

"Well, big man, looks like you're up. I'll jump in if things get out of hand," Thomaras said as he dropped his bow and pulled one of his daggers.

Torin only grunted and spared a quick look at Ashea.

"Careful," she said and smiled.

Torin smiled back grimly and nodded. He spun his hammer in his hand and then tossed it back and forth a few times.

Stoback just kept walking towards him, sword dragging behind, while he giggled softly.

Torin really hated fighting crazy.

Once they closed the distance on each other, Torin didn't wait. He threw a two-handed horizontal swing at his enemy, appearing to put all his strength into it and leaning forward a little to make it look like he had overextended.

Stoback bit and ducked under the arc of his hammer in order to spring forward into what should have been Torin's exposed and overbalanced torso. Instead, Torin was able to stop the momentum of his swing, sidestep, pivot the head of the hammer skyward and bring the butt of the handle down on the back of the rushing Stoback's neck.

Except he wasn't there.

Stoback had thrown himself into a roll at the last moment, coming up behind Torin, and now he *was* overextended. He felt the sharp sting of the rusted blade on his side, where his love handles would be if he had any, and then felt the blade kick off of the enchanted granite that protected the length of his spine.

Not wasting any time, Torin rolled forward himself and then popped up, pivoting to face his attacker, hammer up in a defensive position.

Or at least it was.

Torin's arms reverberated as Stoback's battered-looking

great-sword came down with stunning force and knocked the weapon from his hands.

How had he closed the distance so fast?

Faster than should have been possible, the filthy man brought the sword over his head for a second blow and Torin only had time to throw his granite infused forearms up to block it.

It never came. Instead, the wind and rain started to spin around Stoback, stopping him with his sword up over his head as he struggled to bring it down on his intended target. The wind picked up and he gritted his teeth, trying to hold his ground. Torin turned and looked at Ashea, standing on the cart with her hands above her head and her eyes closed.

Torin reached his own arm into the wind. It buffeted him back, as if he was reaching in slow motion. Finally, slowly, he grasped Stoback's still-extended arm in a vice-like grip. Stoback's gaze whipped back to him and Torin smiled as his other hand grabbed the man's opposite arm.

"Got you," Torin said.

He began to squeeze the man's arms. He could feel them, bony and skinny, under the chain. He waited for the inevitable snap, but it didn't come.

"You're strong, ogre, but my armour is stronger," Stoback said, and that familiar smell washed over Torin again, carried on the man's breath.

Then he placed it.

Mothballs.

Pain exploded in his testicles, and any other thought was wiped from his mind. Stoback kicked him, full force, a second time, and Torin, with his remaining strength, pivoted and threw him as far as he could. Which, it turned out, was fairly far. The man was of average build, and Torin wasn't. Torin dropped to his knees. He still couldn't understand how Stoback was wielding that great-sword, especially one-handed.

Stoback flew through the air and landed at the edge of the cobblestone road before rolling into the muck beside it. That same shimmer and hollow thud accompanied his landing.

Stoback sprang up immediately and, after slipping slightly in the mud, regained his feet and started to sprint towards Torin. Torin began to struggle to his feet. The ache in his groin was incredible, but he forced himself up and began to look for his hammer.

Torin knew Stoback would be closing soon, but he forced himself to continue to look for his weapon. If he couldn't find it now, he would have no time to look once he was engaged again. With relief he saw it about two steps off the road, lying in the muddy grass. He could hear Stoback's boots slapping on the cobblestone. His giggles had turned into full-blown laughter and the terrible sound was getting closer.

Torin dove towards the hammer. He had expected to feel the cut of that rusty blade on his legs. The man was faster than he had any right to be, but instead he heard a loud bang and saw a flash of light in his peripheral vision. He scooped up his hammer and turned to see Stoback covering his eyes and crying out in frustration. Thomaras stood with a bag in his hand and winked at Torin. He motioned for him to cover his eyes, and just as Stoback seemed to collect himself, he threw the bag. Torin did as he was told and heard the sound again, which caused Stoback to cry out.

"Stop that! Goddamn it. You fight like pussies!" Stoback raged.

Torin took his opportunity and swung his hammer with all his strength at Stoback.

Stoback's instincts were incredible, matched only by his speed. The man, still blinded by Thomaras's strange bags, managed to sidestep the blow and bring his sword down with a horrific *clang* on the haft of the hammer. It was made of solid iron but snapped in half like a twig under Stoback's sword, causing Torin's hands to go completely numb.

Stoback was laughing again and Torin realized too late what he had been sprinting for earlier. He wasn't trying to close the distance with Torin; he'd been moving towards a large rock, which he now held in his hand. Before Thomaras could throw anything else his way, he hurled the rock with deadly accuracy and caught Ashea, whose arms were raised as she tried to call another spell, right on the forehead.

She fell with a sickening thud.

Thomaras immediately leapt into the fray. Though he wasn't as adept in hand-to-hand combat as he was with his bow, he was still fast and skilled and his daggers were a blur as he advanced on Stoback. The man gave ground, laughing all the time, and parrying each and every cut Thomaras made. The moment Thomaras let up his attack, Stoback was on him. Swinging and cutting in random patterns that Thomaras was barely avoiding. Parrying the giant sword with his daggers was out of the question, so all Thomaras could do was dodge the cuts. Unfortunately, the random, drunken movements made that almost impossible and Thomaras was already sporting gashes from near-misses with killing blows.

Finally Stoback backed Thomaras up against the cart. With nowhere to go, Thomaras whipped a kick out, catching Stoback in the chest and causing another hollow thud to ring out from his armour. It didn't move him back much, but slowed his swing enough that Thomaras could duck and roll out of the way.

Once again, though, Stoback had laid a trap. He pivoted mid-swing and brought his sword down towards Thomaras's exposed back with its full force.

Fortunately, Torin was a quick study. He positioned himself perfectly and as soon as Stoback pivoted his swing, he slid in on his knees and blocked the blade with both forearms raised over his head.

There was another crack in the air and this time Stoback was sent flying backwards. He landed a few paces back with his blade still in his hand.

Torin screamed in agony.

It should have been impossible, but the blade had shattered the granite that infused his forearms. No weapon should have been able to do that.

"WOOOOHOOO! That was something, big boy!" Stoback whooped, still lying flat on his back with only his head lifted up, looking at Torin and laughing.

Torin couldn't speak. The agony in his arms was more than he'd ever felt. More than when the granite had been infused into his body. He was on his knees, eyes locked on Stoback, but his vision was narrowing to a smaller and smaller point.

"Oh no, you going to sleep, big boy?" Stoback cooed.

Stoback was on his feet now and still talking as Torin's world descended into blackness.

26

ASHEA

~

Ashea was in a haze, her mind not quite unconscious but still swimming somewhere below waking. All she knew was she had to keep her grasp on the spell she was trying to will into existence. As always with her magic, the spell she had in mind came to her through sheer instinct. There was rain and wind, so she tried to harness it. It had worked and held that crazy man long enough for Torin to get a hold of him, but something went wrong and Torin had to throw him. After that, she had started to work on another spell.

Torin's scream of pain instantly wrenched her out of her daze and she sat up quickly. Immediately she lay back down as her vision swam and unconsciousness once again threatened her rattled brain. Once again, she held a mental death grip on the spell she was willing and sat up, this time more slowly. When her vision cleared, she watched as the stranger planted a fist into Thomaras's face after sidestepping an errant swipe with a dagger. Thomaras crumpled to the ground, and Stoback turned back to Torin's unconscious form.

"Let's see how much more of that granite we can smash, big boy!" Stoback crowed between bouts of maniacal laughter.

Ashea was stunned to see Torin laid out like this. He was always so strong, so reliable. It was like watching a mountain get knocked over by a gust of wind. A crazy, stinking, filthy gust of wind.

As the anger ignited in her, she realized that, in her attempt to hold on to the second spell she'd been weaving, she had never let go of the first. She directed all of her fury into the cyclone of wind and rain that she had created, now floating above the battle, and focused it into Stoback.

The cyclone snaked around parallel with the ground, and hit Stoback full in the chest. Arms outstretched above his head, sword in hand in what would have likely been a killing blow, the man was completely exposed and went flying back in the direction from which he had come. The force of the wind sent him three times as far as Torin tossed him, but she had a strange feeling that he should have been thrown farther. That her magic was somehow slipping off the man. He landed with that damn hollow thud that let Ashea know that she had done nothing but buy them time.

Knowing she had to move fast, Ashea leapt from the cart and focused her will on the ground where Stoback had landed, causing it to erupt underneath him and bury him in dirt and broken cobblestones. Ashea could still hear his muffled laughter through the temporary tomb she had created. Kneeling at Torin's side, she thought about what the mage of light had asked her. If her powers manifested in any healing magic. She'd never tried, but she laid a hand on

Torin's chest anyway. She pictured a warm, healing light radiating through him.

It worked.

When it got to his shattered forearms, it seemed to stop, blocked by some other magical force she couldn't see. She could only sense it as a roadblock to her own magic. Puzzled, she sent the healing aura around the skin on the outside, imagining it taking the pain away from him. As she did so, her own forearms exploded in agony and she cried out, falling back from Torin.

Once the pain subsided in her arms, she noticed Torin stirring slightly. As his breathing slowed, he settled into a restful sleep. Having never healed anyone before, she hoped that she had at least made him more comfortable.

"Think you can help me get him in the cart? Judging from that laughter, we don't have long to try to get out of here," Thomaras said, startling her.

"I don't think we can outrun him in this cart, but I'm working on something special. Let's at least get a little way down the road," Ashea responded.

Just as she had once done with his hammer, Ashea pictured the air thickening around Torin and then suffused the idea with her will, making it come alive. Slowly Torin began to rise up, and she gently laid him on the cart. Ashea winced as he came down with a thud. Her strength was starting to wane.

"Maybe be a bit gentle with the unconscious giant, okay? I'm not sure how you guys do it in the bedroom, but I think this situation calls for a lighter touch," Thomaras said with a wink.

His familiar teasing made her feel a bit better. These were desperate times, and she was doing what she could. "You try turning the air into a shovel while at the same time creating a pocket of freezing air above your head," Ashea quipped back.

"Freezing..." Thomaras started to ask and then looked up.

Ashea watched his eyes widen as he saw that the rain above their head was again swirling in a circle, but this time had started to turn into a wet snow.

"How are you..." Thomaras started again before shaking his head.

"I'm simply willing the warmth out of the air above me and pushing it away," she said. Ashea didn't know how else to explain it. Hell, she barely understood what she was doing.

"Sounds great, can we get moving?" Thomaras was already on the cart.

Ashea smiled and pulled herself up and then started falling backwards as a wave of dizziness washed over her. Thomaras's hand shot out and caught her, pulling her to safety.

"You okay? You're looking a little pale there," Thomaras asked, concern etched across his battered face.

"Yes, fine. Just a little tired," Ashea lied.

She was exhausted. It was all she could do to hold on to the spell above her. Fortunately, Thomaras didn't press the issue. He got the horses moving and then made a wide bend around the area where Ashea had buried Stoback. They could still hear his laughter, and the loose dirt covering him, quickly turning to mud in the rain, was moving visibly. They got another ten feet down the road before they heard him finally free himself completely.

"Nice trick!" Stoback bellowed after them. "But you're not going to be able to stop me." He started sprinting.

"That plan of yours ready?" Thomaras asked, not looking away from the horses as he drove them forward.

"Yes, but I need you to slow down or I won't be able to concentrate," Ashea responded.

The jostling of the cart and her own exhaustion was making it impossible for her to move the pocket of freezing air she had created.

"If you say so," Thomaras complied in a tone that suggested he thought it was actually a very bad idea.

As they slowed, Ashea was able to marshal her thoughts, and her will, and she began sending the vortex of cold air at the pursuing madman.

At first it didn't look like anything was happening and Stoback continued to gain on them, but slowly the effects of the spell became clear. Stoback's breath started to puff out as the temperature dropped. Then his soaking hair started to ice over. He stopped running altogether, as it became impossible for him to draw breath without burning his lungs. He tried to backtrack, but dropped to his knees as he shivered convulsively. His lips started to turn blue and ice was forming in a thin layer on his skin.

Ashea tried to concentrate on the spell, will the air to get colder and colder, but she was so tired. She could feel her magic start to slip off of Stoback once again. Stoback's shivering slowed and then ceased altogether. They could no longer see his breath. Ashea slumped down, exhausted.

"I'm... sorry. I can't hold on anymore," she croaked out.

"That's okay. I think there's some help coming," Thomaras said.

Ashea looked over her shoulder. Ahead of them in the road stood a tall, statuesque woman. Her hands were both raised in the air and one held a what looked to be three metal spheres, perfectly round, held together with a chain.

Ashea jumped as a huge crack broke the sky and a lightning bolt struck Stoback square in the chest. The air shimmered and Ashea could just make out a hollow thud, but the force of the bolt sent Stoback flying once again. This time, he was not so quick to recover.

"Solaire?" Ashea said to herself, confused.

Though remarkably similar in appearance, as they got closer, Ashea noticed some marked differences from the mage of light. The woman's head was shaved down to her ebony scalp, and she was dressed in simple, well-tailored leather armour. The face was identical, though. Her prominent cheekbones sat below very familiar bright green eyes, which stood out against her dark skin and made her both incredibly beautiful and incredibly intimidating.

Standing beside her, dressed in similar leathers, was a young man of about twenty. His head was also shaved, and he sported about a day's worth of stubble. Ashea was under the impression that it was a look he cultivated and not a result of laziness. His white skin and light blue eyes made him appear to be a pale shadow of the woman beside him. He was almost the same height but cut a much less imposing figure. He had a confident smile and Ashea could see a similar artifact held in his hands.

"Ashea, I presume? I am the mage of elements, Luness. My sister told me you were heading our way," the mage said in a calm tone, as if she hadn't just fried a madman with a bolt of lightning.

"You have to stop him first! He's not dead. His armour protects him somehow," Ashea blurted out.

"Have no fear. My apprentice will handle him. We are well aware of what his armour can do. Robert, go," the mage commanded, not taking her eyes off of Ashea.

"He may need help I..." Ashea began, but Luness cut her off.

"I know my business child, and Robert his. Now you, driver, let's get moving. Your friend in the back there is likely a bit the worse for wear," she snapped.

"Driver?" Thomaras asked under his breath but got the horses moving.

Ashea watched Robert as he strode past her and gave her a wink. He opened the hand with the three metal balls in it and they started to float above his palm. The chains connecting the spheres were taut and the whole thing had a faint red glow to it. In his other hand, a small sphere of fire was beginning to grow.

As the cart passed, the mage pulled herself up into the back with Torin.

"It may take a while but Robert will rejoin us when the problem is dealt with. Hurry along now, I've no desire to be in this rain any longer than I have to," Luness said.

Her words seemed strangely hollow and faint.

"You'd best lie down, girl. You've drawn too much power for one so unseasoned."

Ashea was about to say that she was fine when suddenly she was pitching forwards into the tall woman's embrace.

Maybe lying down for a minute would be okay.

27

THOMARAS

～

Thomaras almost let go of the reins to try to grab Ashea as she fell forward, but the mage was there so he resisted the urge. He wasn't too keen on slowing down, with that maniac still behind them. Luness laid Ashea down gently next to Torin and the peaceful expression on both of their faces as they slept in the back of the cart belied the violence that had put them there.

"Can't you move this thing any faster? We have to get to Vees," the fierce woman beside him said.

"Not sure if you noticed, but my friend in the back there is rather large. These horses aren't used to that kind of load. They're struggling just to keep moving, let alone to put any kind of speed into it," Thomaras replied.

The truth was that he was shaken. He may not have known Torin very long, but he would have been willing to wager that there weren't many in Haven that could best him in combat. Granted, this Stoback fellow seemed to have some magical gear. Thomaras wasn't sure anyone his size could lift a sword one-handed, let alone jump around with it like he did, but even without the enchantments, the man's prowess with the blade was obvious. Torin was having trouble even hitting him and Thomaras was never comfortable with someone he couldn't shoot dead from a safe distance.

"Well, he should recover shortly; the girl appears to have taken the edge off his injuries," the mage said.

Thomaras recognized the curiosity in Luness's voice and prepared himself for the inevitable follow-up.

"Any idea how she did that?"

"Did what?" Thomaras fell back on old habits of giving as little information as possible to authority figures.

"Healed your friend. My understanding was that she has a talent for the elements."

"Uh, I'll be honest; I don't know much when it comes to magic," Thomaras said.

"Yes, that's obvious, but you've known her for a while, yes? Have you ever seen her do any other healing?" she probed again.

Thomaras wasn't sure exactly what Luness was looking for but figured that maintaining an air of bumbling ignorance was probably his best bet.

"Listen, your... uh... mageliness, I—"

"That's not a word," the woman cut him off curtly.

"We told him that already," Ashea said in a groggy voice.

They turned to look at her in unison and saw her sitting up, one hand rubbing her face as if she'd woken from an afternoon nap.

"Good, you're awake, child. I..." Luness began.

"Ashea. You may call me Ashea," she said, politely but without deference.

The tall mage appraised Ashea for a moment before a smile crept across her face.

"Forgive me, you are not my apprentice and should not be treated as such. I have to admit, I am at a loss as to what you are, Ashea. Please, both of you, there's no need for honorifics. Just call me Luness."

"Well, this is usually the part where I give a fake name, but something tells me that wouldn't matter all that much to you folks. I'm Thomaras," he introduced himself reluctantly.

Luness nodded and turned back to Ashea.

"Your friend, to his credit, I suppose, has been reluctant to give me much information about your powers. How long have you been able to use multiple types of magic?"

Ashea looked to Thomaras and back to Luness but said nothing.

"You have nothing to fear from me, Ashea. My curiosity is just that. I've never met one who could control multiple forms of magic. Like the Arahana of old. You made the choice to accept Dafoe's invitation. Do you trust him?"

"Dafoe has spoken to me in my dreams. He is very concerned about the being that is tracking me, but he hasn't mentioned much about my abilities. I've heard that bad things happen to rogue mages..." Ashea trailed off.

"And would you consider yourself a rogue? The truth is that magic only manifests itself in a very few people at a time. We try to find those people immediately and guard *them* from threats. Only those who misuse their gifts are hunted down by the council."

Thomaras gave Ashea a quick nod when she glanced his way. He was a good judge of people and Luness seemed genuine in her explanation.

The question, of course, became what exactly the council considered misuse.

"So it's okay that I used magic without the council knowing?" Ashea asked.

Luness laughed. "We aren't overbearing parents that watch over every use of magic. Our concern is those that use magic to harm others for their own benefit. From what I've seen, all you've done is save your friends' lives."

"And my dreams?"

"That is something I can't answer. I'll be happy to train you in elemental magic, but dreams and reading the reflections of the prism? That falls under Dafoe's purview. I believe he can help you, though." Luness's face broke into a warm smile.

Ashea nodded, reassured. Then, the smile was gone and the mask of professionalism fell over the woman's face once more. *A beautiful mask*, Thomaras couldn't help but think, and his eyes discreetly traced the curves of her body as it swayed back and forth with the rocking of the cart.

"You're cute but I'm out of your league, driver," Luness said to Thomaras as she glanced his way, her eyes crackling with tiny lightning bolts.

Maybe he hadn't been as discreet as he thought. "Of that, I have no doubt. My apologies," Thomaras said quickly.

"Do I have to talk to Erica?" Torin rumbled sleepily from behind them.

"Wonderful timing, as always, Torin. Can't you just stay unconscious like a normal human being?"

"Nope. Not normal. Not a human being. Stop the cart, I can walk," Torin replied.

"Are you sure? Whatever he did to you, it looked serious," Ashea asked, concerned.

"No pain, thanks to you, I think," Torin said, sitting up and flexing the fingers on both hands. His forearms were still a mess of cracked granite poking through skin, but there was no bleeding and he did seem to have a full range of motion in his hands.

"I'm sorry I couldn't repair the granite, but there was some barrier I couldn't see. It stopped my magic, but it felt like... nothing at all," Ashea said.

"Shaman magic. They can fix it. I hope," Torin replied.

He stepped out of the cart and stretched his legs. Looking like someone who'd been sitting a little too long as opposed to someone who just had their ass handed to them and ended up unconscious. Thomaras marveled again at the strength of his friend.

"Shamanic magic is invisible to us," Luness explained to Ashea. "As ours is to them. It comes from a different place, I think. I've never had much experience with it. The Granite Ogres keep to themselves mostly and are particularly secretive when it comes to their shamans."

Torin nodded his agreement but said nothing. Ashea was barely paying attention to Luness as she watched Torin begin to walk beside the cart. She looked like she was worried he'd topple over any minute. Torin looked at her and smiled reassuringly. He flexed his fingers again for her, but Thomaras could see his eyes linger on the ruined forearms.

With Torin walking alongside them once more, the horses were able to pull the cart with ease, and they started to make better time. When they approached the Five Points Crossroads, for which the road itself was named, there was a contingent of twenty armoured men on horseback waiting for them.

"Sergeant Moore, it sounds like my apprentice has things well in hand, but he is fighting a particularly dangerous enemy. Please go and make sure all is well, and provide him an escort back to Vees. He's going to be exhausted," Luness ordered.

A grizzled-looking soldier with an eye patch nodded and slapped one arm over the other in the air in front of him, making an X in salute. He then began giving orders to his men, and all but five of them headed down the road at a canter. The remaining five, who were not mounted, formed up around them and they continued towards the crossroads.

The crossroads was where roads from Ithadore, Casea, Meridias and Aquilo all met. The final road was the route to the desert path that led out of Haven. Each kingdom patrolled the section of road that passed within their borders and the crossroads itself generally had a presence from each kingdom. Only the road through Ithadore was unmanned. The lack of any real resources and the fact that the salt marshes dominated the majority of the landscape had left the kingdom without a ruler for centuries.

They made their way through the crossroads, which was really just a giant roundabout, and headed north into Aquilo.

"Never been to Vees," Thomaras sighed.

"No, I can imagine a man of your proclivities would want to avoid a place of order like that. I doubt you've been to Granniston either," Luness sniffed haughtily.

"First of all, my proclivities are good drink and beautiful women. Nothing wrong with that. It's how I make my living that keeps me out of a city where the leader can see the future. The capital of Meridias is lovely, however. Lots of ways to satisfy my proclivities there," he added with a wink.

Luness stared blankly for a moment and then scowled at him.

Thomaras momentarily regretted admitting to so much

for the sake of winning an argument, but the look on Luness's face was worth it.

"Well, you have no need to fear Aquilo today. You are my guests and I am Dafoe's general. For now, you are an ally," Luness said, resuming an air of control.

Thomaras wasn't terribly comforted.

"I may need to rest a little longer," Ashea said sleepily from the back of the cart and, by the time Thomaras turned around to look at her, she was already fast asleep.

The rest of the journey took a few hours. The roads here were patrolled regularly and Thomaras was surprised at the number of soldiers he saw. He thought about asking Luness how many soldiers Aquilo had. Each kingdom was supposed to maintain a standing army with similar numbers, but Thomaras had spent enough time in the other kingdoms to know that there were more northern soldiers by far. Unless the entire army was patrolling the Five Points, which Thomaras doubted.

Finally, sodden and cold, they reached the gatehouse leading into Vees. The walls around the capital were the tallest Thomaras had seen and were thicker than he thought possible. There was a good hundred feet between these walls and a slightly smaller set that surrounded the city itself.

The guards, recognizing Luness right away, waved them through the open gates and they continued into the city proper.

The houses in the capital were all made of stone with red clay roofs. They were neatly organized and every road that Thomaras could see was cobblestone. The sheer cost of creating a city like this was mind-boggling.

As he looked up the main road, he could see Castle Vees, which served as the mage's council meeting area, the true seat of power in Haven, on a hill above the neatly organized city. In what was another line of defence, the road up the hill was narrow and winding, the sides around it sheer and impossible to climb. An invading force would have to ascend two soldiers at a time at most.

Thomaras was about to ask Luness why Vees looked like it was designed to withstand a siege when a soldier, armour dented, weapons lost and face bloodied, galloped up from behind on a lathered horse.

"Luness! Luness!" he yelled as he dismounted. Something was in his hand.

"Sergeant Moore? What is that?" Luness said, her flat tone indicated that she may have known exactly what it was.

Hesitating slightly, Sergeant Moore reached into a bag and pulled out the head of Luness's apprentice. His handsome face was contorted in fear and pain, likely the last things he had felt before his head separated from his body.

"I'm sorry, Luness. When we got there he was holding this and waiting for us. We didn't stop to ask questions, we just attacked. He cut through us all like nothing. He didn't even drop Robert's... he just held on to it and laughed while he killed us. He left me alive to send a message. I'm sorry, there was nothing I could do," Moore explained, trying to remain composed and doing a valiant job of it.

"No, sergeant, I am sorry. I underestimated our enemy. I thought Robert was ready... no, it was my fault, not his. Please, put his head back in the bag and give it to me. I'll make sure he's laid to rest." Luness got out of the cart and walked over to the shaken man.

"I tried to get Robert's body, but he wouldn't let me; he said that wasn't the message," Moore explained.

"You did well, sergeant. There was nothing more you

could do. I'll handle it from here." Luness laid a hand on his shoulder as she took the bag from him.

"There was one more thing. He wanted me to tell — sorry, they're his words — Big Boy and Slim Jim to bring him the girl. That he'd be waiting every night on the outskirts of Hannover. Each night they don't come, he'll spend at The Jilted Maiden. He said who knows what kind of fun he can get up to there?" Moore reluctantly reported.

Thomaras went cold. His only thought was of Erica. He didn't know how Stoback had found out about her, but he was certain that mentioning The Jilted Maiden was no coincidence. He shared a look with Torin.

"How do I kill him?" he asked Luness.

Holding her apprentice's head in her hands, she looked at him slowly.

"With my help."

28

THOMARAS

~

Thomaras couldn't think straight. His blood was howling in his ears as anger pumped through his whole body. Thinking of Erica in danger made him want action, want violence. Standing here doing nothing was excruciating. "Okay, let's go, then."

"That's not going to work," Luness said. "My powers don't seem to be enough to stop Stoback. Robert may have been my apprentice, but he nearly matched me in raw power. I had instructed him in exactly how to circumvent enchanted armour like Stoback's, but he still failed. We need to know more if we're going to stop him. We'll have to speak with the council."

"You speak to them; I'm going to go kill a psychopath. Come on, Torin."

He didn't have time for a meeting. He needed to save Erica now. He started walking back towards the gates. He'd be faster without the cart anyway.

A giant hand on his shoulder stopped him.

"We need help," Torin said.

Thomaras knocked the hand off his shoulder. "Fine, go get help. I'll see you after I've murdered Stoback." Thomaras kept walking.

"You need help," Torin said, infuriatingly calm.

Thomaras whirled on the giant and pointed his finger at him.

"You might be scared of him, but I'm not going to let that slow me down. I'm not going to let any of you slow me down. I wouldn't even be here if it weren't for you. I wouldn't have run into crazy-town out there and Erica wouldn't be in any danger. So I'm going to go, on my own like I always have, and save the woman I lo— and save Erica. You do what you want." Thomaras was screaming by the end of his diatribe.

"If you die trying to save her, you won't accomplish anything," Ashea said quietly.

"I won't die!"

"Really? How are you going to kill him, then? What's your plan? Your bow didn't work, and he mopped the floor with you when you got close. What's the plan?"

Ashea's words were calm and measured, but they still slapped him in the face. Thomaras started to answer, wanted to respond with the fire he'd felt before, but Ashea's words had doused it.

"Alright, you're right, but that doesn't change the fact that time is of the essence," Thomaras said once he'd gotten himself under control.

"I believe your friend will be safe for the time being. Stoback's threat was obvious, but he wants Ashea for some reason. If you are as taciturn with most as you've led me to believe, she will be one of few bargaining chips he has to use against us," Luness said, commiseration in her tone.

Thomaras didn't like it, but logic was slowly beginning

to erode the fury that drove him. "Alright then, how quickly can we meet with this council?"

"They are waiting for us now," Luness said. "Dafoe wanted Ashea to meet the council as soon as she got here. We need only continue up to Castle Vees."

Thomaras nodded and began walking towards the castle.

"Can someone tend to the horses?" Torin asked Luness.

In response, she began directing the soldiers of Aquilo to make arrangements for the horses as well as to clear a path on the busy streets leading to the castle.

Thomaras noted that the soldiers listened to her orders as if they were from one of their own superior officers.

"They listen to you even though you are from another kingdom and have your own troops there that you command?" Thomaras asked, falling into his old habits of collecting information.

"Yes. Here I am the prism reader's second in command, as he is the ruler of Aquilo. When I am home in Meridias, I am the top general of our forces and report only to King Gran himself. It is a unique arrangement, but my position on the mage's council supersedes my responsibilities back home," Luness answered.

"Does your king ever have a problem with that?" Thomaras asked.

"There are times when I'm sure it frustrates him, but Aquilo and Meridias are such close allies that there is rarely a time when the will of one would impede the other, even incidentally," Luness said.

"Sure, but wouldn't it make sense for him to find another general? Couldn't you just fulfill the role of the court mage?"

"King Gran is a wise man. He wants the best tactical

mind in the kingdom to command his forces. There is none better than mine."

Despite her high evaluation of herself, her tone wasn't boastful. She was simply stating facts.

They made their way through the main street of the capital. Like the rest of Haven, the city was a cosmopolitan melting pot. Fair skin like Thomaras's was just as prevalent as Luness's dark complexion and everything in between. When it was resettled, Haven not only called out to those with the blood of the Arahana but was also a haven for anyone brave enough to leave the comforts of their current homes to risk something new.

Thomaras did notice, however, that one group of people he'd seen in every inch of Haven that he'd explored was absent: the poor. No beggars, no enfeebled, no down-on-their-luck or dirty people were in the crowds at all. In fact, every person was dressed impeccably and their clothes were clean.

"Where are the poor?" Thomaras whispered to Luness.

"They do not exist here. Dafoe has found ways to employ any and all, care for the sick and eliminate poverty in Vees. He's truly a great man." Her voice was not only sincere, but bordering on open adoration.

"Sounds like he nailed it," Thomaras said under his breath.

He didn't trust a city with no poor. No matter what systems a ruler put in place, there would always be those who wanted to live outside of it, even if it was to their own detriment. No wonder he'd never gotten any work up here. There were very few shadows to hide in.

As they finished their winding trip up to the castle, Thomaras marveled again at the defensive structure before him. The narrow road ended at an impressive gatehouse, its walls sitting flush with the drop on either side of the path. Castle Vees was built in such a way that its outer walls also sat flush with the cliff, giving would-be attackers no way to set up siege engines even if they managed to make it up the path. The gate itself was made of thick iron crossbars and was currently raised to allow them in. Thomaras could see that the bottom of each vertical bar ended in a point that, when lowered, slid into slots cut into the rock to lock it in. The gate also seemed to have a faint blue glow to it. Thomaras looked down from the gate and over at Ashea.

"Enchanted, I think," she murmured. "Feels familiar... an aura I recognize somehow..." she continued, almost to herself.

"It is a similar enchantment to that of Stoback's armour, but I only know that because the mage who enchanted both things explained it to me. You could really feel the similarity?" Luness asked Ashea.

"Yes. It doesn't make any sense to me, but it just *feels* the same. It's..." Ashea seemed to be searching for the right word.

"Intuitive," Luness finished for her. "It seems you truly are open to all types of magic."

The awe in her words was obvious.

Once they passed through the gatehouse, there was a beautifully landscaped courtyard leading to a door that was clearly designed to look good as opposed to keep anyone out. The seemingly unending line of fortifications leading to this point allowed for the decorative choice, Thomaras supposed. Standing in front of the doors was a stylishly dressed young man.

"Luness! I'm so glad to see you," the man exclaimed sincerely.

He closed the distance between himself and Luness in a

few graceful strides and swept her up in a brotherly hug. When he put her down, he held her shoulders and, being slightly shorter than her, looked up into her eyes.

"Word was sent about Robert. Are you okay? The boy was incredibly talented and I know you cared deeply for him." The man addressed Luness as if she were the only person there.

"Thank you for your kind words, Dafoe. I will be alright. It is the burden of the master to occasionally lose an apprentice. It was my failure; I shouldn't have sent him alone." Tears glimmered slightly in her eyes.

"Stop that," Dafoe said. "He knew the risks. He wouldn't have gone if he didn't believe he was ready as well. We both know that a master is such in training only. When it comes to operations in the field, there are no orders given. The apprentice is encouraged to speak their mind and refuse a task that they're not ready for. Robert's training was almost complete and although he was confident, he wasn't stupid or rash. He wouldn't have taken on a foe he wasn't ready for. Clearly, the information we got on Stoback's magical armour was incomplete — a topic we can discuss with Thorn at the council meeting."

He had released Luness's shoulders, but his eyes were locked on her in that same way, shutting everyone else out.

Luness nodded and smiled at him. Dafoe nodded back and then turned to the rest of the group. "Ashea, allow me to introduce myself. I, as you have no doubt surmised, am the prism reader, but please just call me Dafoe. Formal titles are such a mouthful." Dafoe extended his hand to Ashea.

"It's nice to finally meet you in person. Thank you for your warnings and for sending us help," Ashea said, clearly uncomfortable with meeting the most powerful man in Haven.

"And you must be Thomaras!" he said with a smile.

Thomaras considered the man smiling before him.

He was slightly shorter than average, which made him almost a head smaller than Thomaras, but he held himself with a confidence that made Thomaras feel as though his own height was ungainly. His robes were crimson with gold trim, but he managed to wear them in a way that made them seem stylish as opposed to ostentatious, and they were expertly tailored to show a well-muscled torso beneath. He had an unruly mop of curly blond hair that once again managed to look effortlessly casual as opposed to messy. His handsome, clean-shaven face looked to be no more than twenty. His eyes were a bright blue flecked with gold and seemed to dance with good humour.

Thomaras was put off by how much he liked him immediately and elected to keep his guard up by simply nodding.

"Ha! There's that caution that's kept you all so safe. I must say, I made a number of arrangements to get Ashea here once I discovered her abilities, but you were the one that paid off the most. And I didn't even hire you! I suppose we have Joseph to thank for that. He was a good man," Dafoe said, and appeared to be genuinely saddened at the passing of Joseph.

"Glad to know my cover used to be safe," Thomaras said, annoyed again at coming under the scrutiny of one so powerful.

"Oh, it was. I had no idea you, or your large friend here, even existed. Fear not, once all is said and done, you may go back to your accustomed obscurity with my thanks. It's the least I can do for the role you've played in bringing Ashea to me," Dafoe said, and seemed to mean it. He turned to Torin. "Torin, you appear to live up to everything that's been reported to me. I've had occasion to spend some time with the Granite Ogres and while you may not be as big as most, you're clearly a force. Thank you so much for bringing Ashea safely."

He should have looked comically small standing in front of Torin like that, but his sheer presence made it seem as though he was looking the big man in the eye. Torin simply nodded. Dafoe reached out and took one of his shattered forearms, examining it.

"Shamanic magic isn't something I know well, but if there is anything we can do, we will. Thorn, our resident enchanter, may have some thoughts on how to help. Perhaps he and Solaire could even work together. They've done so in the past, right, Luness?" Dafoe asked without taking his eyes off Torin's wounded arm.

"They have," Luness responded. "Life magic seems to blend well with enchantments, though not as seamlessly as with alchemy."

"Hmmm. Well, if there is nothing we can do here, I can always arrange for an escort so you can head back to your shamans," Dafoe said, finally looking back up at Torin.

"Thank you. Not sure they can help. It's not supposed to break," Torin said with a half-smile.

Dafoe smiled at the gallows humour and patted his arm. Thomaras would have loved to believe his friend was able to joke about the situation, but he could tell the joke was forced. He shared a look with Ashea and could tell she felt the same.

"Okay, let's not waste any more time," Dafoe said, clapping his hands. "We'll head into the meeting chambers so we can get down to business. I know that you're sodden and road-weary, but we have little time to spare. I've arranged for food and drink to be brought to the chambers, as well as some towels, but I'm afraid that is all we have time for. Luness, you may join us once you've made arrangements for Robert."

Luness looked down at the bag holding her former apprentice's head as if remembering it was there again. She sighed and, without looking at anyone, headed into the castle herself, her pace taking her ahead of Dafoe and the others.

"She'll be okay," Dafoe explained without looking back. "She's a warrior, a general. She understands losing forces in battle. An apprentice is a little harder, but she is one of the strongest people I know."

Thomaras was surprised to find that, though unsolicited, the explanation did make him feel better. He'd only known her a few hours, but in that time Luness had gained Thomaras's respect. Not only that, but with Erica in danger, he was acutely aware of the pain of losing someone you cared about.

He hadn't lost her yet. *Now pay attention*, Thomaras chided himself. He began to focus on the route that they'd taken, through a grand entrance hall with tall ceilings and all the adornments of wealth one would expect from a castle, and then into a smaller hallway to the left of the entrance. So far, the hallway was a straight shot with a few turns, but no branching paths. Thomaras was sure to make a note of the layout just in case. Trust was something that came slowly to someone like him.

Dafoe was hard not to trust, though. Thomaras could understand the adoration in Luness's voice. He almost thought he'd follow the mage into battle.

Dafoe was certainly a natural leader. Charismatic while still genuine. Sure of himself in a way that made you feel like you could relax and leave the big decisions to him. A dangerous inclination.

The hallway ended at a simple doorway with two guards standing outside. Their chain mail was impeccably clean and by Thomaras's estimation they knew how to use the broadswords at their hips. Likely elite guards, a theory supported by the crimson and gold livery that matched Dafoe's robes.

The men saluted Dafoe with the same motion they had Luness, and he returned it with a nod.

"Garrett, Damian. How are you fairing today? Everyone inside?" Dafoe asked the men.

"No complaints, sir. They're all there except for Luness and... well, you can guess who," the man that Dafoe referred to as Garrett replied with a small smile.

Dafoe sighed and shook his head. "Sounds about right. How's Sarah? Did Mary send that potion along?"

"She's right as rain now, thanks to the potion. Thank you for asking, and for making the arrangements," Garrett said.

Thomaras could see the gleam of not only respect but love in the man's eyes. He was taken aback. This was not the supreme leader of Haven that he had expected.

Dafoe simply rested a hand on the man's shoulder for a moment before turning back to the group. "Alright, Ashea, are you ready to meet your new family?" Dafoe asked.

"Family?" Ashea asked.

"Well, yes, You're finally home, my dear," Dafoe said as if it were the most obvious thing in the world.

He turned and opened the door, striding in without hesitation.

29

TORIN

~

Torin watched Ashea trailing a step behind Dafoe through the door and into the chambers beyond. He was concerned about Dafoe's intentions for her. So far, both he and Luness had shown nothing but genuine interest in her well-being, and Torin was inclined to believe the sincerity in both of them. He'd just have to watch and listen to the rest of the council and make sure nothing else was going on. Fortunately, these were skills that he excelled at.

Torin entered the chamber last, ducking under the doorframe and turning sideways slightly on his way through, and took a quick look around. It was a fair-sized chamber but utilitarian compared to the rest of the castle. The large table they were seated at was carved from a dark-coloured wood. Torin's eye wasn't nearly good enough to tell if the wood was stained or the table had been commissioned in this colour from the Darkwoods, but judging by Dafoe's opulent tastes everywhere else, he suspected the latter. Aside from the table and chair, the only other furniture in the room was a matching credenza along the wall parallel to the table. At the moment, it was covered in the food and drink that Dafoe had promised, and the man himself had made his way over there as he waited for Torin and his friends to come in.

"Please, make yourselves comfortable. Allow me to introduce you to the council and then feel free to get yourself something to eat or drink as the meeting progresses. We are fairly informal here," Dafoe said.

He then picked up a honey cake and put it on a small plate before making his way to the head of the table and sitting down.

As promised, there were towels hung on the backs of three of the chairs, and Torin was happy to wipe off what felt like a week's worth of rain and mud from his body. Torin looked around at the people in the room and was greeted by the standard looks of amazement that his size tended to garner.

The chair to the right of Dafoe's was empty; Torin assumed Luness would occupy it once she arrived. Next to that, there sat a burly older man with the shoulders of a blacksmith. The muscles under his tunic were large and well defined, and in truth, the only way you could see the man's age was in the long white hair that was pulled back in a ponytail, and matched by a short, white beard on his face. There were some lines around the blue eyes, but his face looked more seasoned than it did weathered. The scars and burn marks on the man's bulging forearms suggested that his shoulders were indeed those of a blacksmith.

Next to him was a kindly-looking older woman with short, grey hair that was tucked up in a neat bun; not a strand out of place. She wore round, gold-rimmed glassed that made her brown eyes appear larger than they should have. The lines on her face were more prevalent, but they only served to accentuate the kindly smile she was directing at Torin. Her whole countenance screamed doting grandmother, especially as she sat at the table knitting.

The seat opposite Dafoe was empty, but standing on the table in front of it was a small wooden doll. It stood maybe eight inches tall and, aside from a lack of gender, was very intricately carved. All the joints looked as though they could actually move like a human's would, and the mouth, carved into a cartoonish scowl, looked very real. Even its eyes appeared to have been painted in such a way that they glowed white.

Then the eyes swiveled to Torin, making him jump involuntarily.

"Are were going to get this thing started? I have work to get done," the little doll said, it's voice that of a middle-aged man.

"Morley, I asked you to be here in person for this. I know you don't like leaving your chambers, but for those who aren't used to dealing with your avatars, they can be... unnerving," Dafoe said gently.

"Fine, give me a moment and I'll be right along. Mary, my dear, do fix a plate for me, won't you? One of each will be fine," Morley, or the doll parroting Morley, said.

As soon as he finished speaking, the doll fell over onto its back. The once intricate details had disappeared, and all that remained were a few sticks tied together with leather twine. The head appeared to be made of folded corn husks.

"How about I give you one of each of my feet in your ass, you fat fuck," Mary said under her breath.

Torin was taken aback by the harsh words coming out of the kind woman's face. Thomaras laughed out loud.

"Now, now, Mary. You know he just likes to push your buttons," Dafoe said, standing up.

"I wouldn't let that cocksucker push my buttons for all the gold in Haven. A girl's got to have standards, you know," Mary replied, only looking up from her knitting at the end to give Thomaras a wink.

Thomaras glared impatiently and Torin began to worry that his friend would soon lose his temper.

"Since you've already met Morley Swingle, or at least one of his artifices, I may as well start the rest of the introductions," Dafoe said.

He was putting a plate of food together as he spoke. It looked to Torin like one of each item for this Morley fellow. Torin was struck again at the confidence in the man. So secure as their leader that he had no problem putting a plate of food together for one of his subordinates.

"This fine picture of a lady is Mary," Dafoe said. "She's our resident alchemist. If you've ever used a potion for any ailment, it was produced by our Mary here."

"You know as well as I that I've never acted like a lady in my fucking life. And I've told you before, I'm a witch! Your fancy words don't change what I do," Mary insisted.

Her tone suggested this was a long-suffering argument between the two of them and that it was one that they enjoyed having.

"When people hear 'witch' they conflate it with those filthy women who live in the swamps to the west," Dafoe clarified gently.

"Those are hags! A witch is nothing like that," she said to Dafoe, with some heat in her voice.

"And this is Thorn," Dafoe said, clearly changing the subject. "He's our resident enchanter and the greatest craftsman I've ever seen." He placed an extremely full plate beside the now inanimate doll at the end of the table.

"Greetings," Thorn said. "Torin, is it? Sergeant Moore sent some men back to retrieve your broken weapon once he was certain that Stoback had cleared off. Once we are through here, I believe I can repair it for you."

Torin nodded his thanks, but before he could say anything else, the door opposite the one that they came through burst open and Luness came striding through.

The statuesque woman's beautiful face was a thundercloud. Her dark purple travelling cloak flowed out behind her, revealing her perfectly cut brown leather armour underneath as she crossed the distance of the room to Thorn and slapped him in the face.

"You told us how to deal with that armour you made. You drilled it into us how to stop Stoback if he ever showed up again. You were WRONG!" Luness screamed the last word into Thorn's face.

Thorn sat there and took it. His only reaction was to hang his head slightly.

"Oh my, this looks delicious!" A voice said from the doorway, as if nothing else was going on.

Torin looked up and the fattest man he'd ever seen waddled into the room. His head was shaved bald, and his pale, pudgy face was so swollen that his eyes looked like little slits above his nose. His mouth smiled greedily, showing incredibly straight, white teeth as he looked at the plate of food. Torin recognized the voice as the one that had come from the doll.

"I know, Luness," Thorn said. "I'm sorry. I don't know what happened. I *know* Robert knew exactly what to do. It should have worked."

Luness looked for a moment like she was going to

strike him again, but then her shoulders sagged as the energy her anger had been feeding off finally depleted itself.

"I'm sorry, Thorn. I know you loved Robert, too," Luness said as she went to sit down.

"Aye, he was a good man. The only report I was able to get was that Robert was... that he died. Do you know any more of what happened?" Thorn asked.

"No. By the time Sergeant Moore and his men got there, Stoback had already killed him. I felt Robert's magic, though. He executed the spell perfectly. My first blast was enough to daze him, even through the armour's protection. All Robert had to do was detonate something powerful underneath the armour and it should have killed him. I felt the fireball he formed. We heard the explosion. Aside from that, I don't know."

Now her voice was detached and professional. She was a general being debriefed.

"I don't understand," Ashea said. "That armour seemed magic-proof. It even resisted the ice I tried to freeze him in. How was Robert supposed to stop that?"

Thorn looked up for a moment, confused, but Luness answered Ashea before he could say anything.

"His armour was enchanted to stop swords and arrows from hitting. Thus, the spell was designed to stop objects moving at a fast speed. This doubled for things like fireballs or lightning bolts, as well as softening his landing when thrown with something like wind. The plan, the technique on which we had drilled endlessly, was to form the fireball itself underneath his armour. Thus, the detonation would happen within the armour's enchanted field and instead of protecting him, it would likely do even more damage." Luness looked to Thorn for confirmation.

The grizzled old man seemed not to hear her and was instead looking intently at Ashea.

"Girl, you said that you felt the armour was resisting the ice you were trying to form around him. Are you sure about that? I don't mean to question your honesty, but I know you are untrained when it comes to magic. Are you sure?"

Torin could see Ashea bristle slightly at the being called "girl," but she seemed to understand that Thorn's question was an important one. She thought for a moment.

"Yes, I'm sure. The cyclone of ice that I created should have frozen a human solid. Even with my waning strength, the air itself had dropped below freezing and at that point, the cold was sustaining itself. I was simply directing it. When it touched him, however, it seemed to bleed my will from the air and warm it just enough."

"We didn't design that armour to resist magic. Why would we? Stoback wasn't supposed to be fighting us, he was supposed to be fighting for us," Thorn said, more to himself than anyone else.

"Wait, what?" Thomaras asked, incredulous. "Fighting for you? That psychopath used to work for you?" Thomaras was almost screaming in anger.

"Easy now," Dafoe said. "We didn't know what he was until he left us. He was Thorn's apprentice for a while until his talent in combat far exceeded his talent in enchanting. It remains a sore subject for us all."

His tone was placating. He was trying to calm Thomaras down, but it also had an edge of authority. A gentle reminder of whose house this was.

Thomaras didn't seem to care.

"So, this asshole defected, took your magic toys and has been running around murdering people for what? Decades? And now you're discovering that your magic can't even top him? I think I've heard enough," Thomaras said and turned to the door.

"Wait," Torin said and grabbed his arm.

Thomaras jerked it away. "Easy for you to say. Ashea's here. Safe. Stoback has Erica and is doing who knows what? You can wait. I'm going."

"Just wait. We'll come with you," Torin pleaded.

"Will you? Plan to come along and fuck my life up some more, do you?"

"Thomaras, that's not fair. We—" Ashea tried to interject.

"Enough!" Thomaras interrupted. "All you've done since I found you in that cell is make my life a complicated mess. Now, you might have gotten Erica killed, too. So, please, stay here with your magic friends and let me take care of this."

With that, Thomaras pushed through the door. No one else tried to stop him.

"Should we go after him?" Torin asked Ashea.

"Would you let him stop you from getting to me?"

Torin shook his head. "We can't let him go alone."

"He won't listen to reason, I'm afraid," Dafoe said. "I won't stop you if you want to follow, but I think this moment calls for patience. Something is different about Stoback, and we need to figure it out. Charging into his trap is exactly what he wants."

Ashea looked at Torin and shrugged. "I think we should hear them out."

Torin didn't like it, but he had to admit that going up against Stoback half drawn wasn't going to get them anywhere.

"Okay."

∾

30

ASHEA

~

"But you better get talking, otherwise we are going with him," Ashea said.

Thorn sighed heavily. "Yes, I suppose we owe you folks an explanation, given that he almost murdered you a few hours ago. We found Stoback when was just a boy. Back then, a group of bandits had found a way to consolidate power amongst the lawless and were raiding villages all through Aquilo. From what we can piece together, Stoback's parents were farmers living on the outskirts of one of those villages. After the bandits put down what little resistance that village had to offer, they made their way out to the farm. I don't know what horrors that young boy witnessed when they got ahold of his parents, but I reckon it wasn't pretty. For some reason, maybe out of boredom or maybe just to swell their ranks, those bandits took Stoback with them. Raised him as a sort of communal pet. He was maybe three or four when they picked him up, hard to say, and he ran with those assholes for almost a year. By the time Dafoe put a force together to track down and stop those monsters, young Stoback, and we aren't even sure that's his real name, couldn't or wouldn't speak. The soldiers weren't sure what to do, so they brought the boy here."

Dafoe picked up the thread of the story. "I immediately sent for the mage of light to help him. She was able to fix the physical effects of the mistreatment, but mentally, Stoback was still shut down. He would eat, drink, sleep and bathe when instructed, but that was it. Finally, after almost six months, he wandered down to the forge."

"The lad came down and watched me work for hours," Thorn said. "Then days. Then weeks. It was the only thing he showed any interest in, so I just let him watch. Didn't matter if I was smithing iron or carving stone, the boy was happy to watch. Then one day I had finished a piece I was working on. A tower shield for one of Dafoe's personal guard. Once it had cooled, I took it, and without thinking, began to enchant it. A simple spell, lighter weight and more durability. But as soon as I started, Stoback came back to life. He ran over to me and began asking a hundred questions. It surprised me so much I nearly lost the grip on my will and had to start the whole project from scratch. Once I got myself together, I began to answer the boy's questions. About fifteen minutes in, I realized I had myself an apprentice." He smiled slightly.

"Stoback is a mage?" Ashea asked.

"No, but he had the aptitude," Luness answered her. "As we said earlier, his natural abilities with a sword were far greater."

"The next ten years or so, his apprenticeship went along nicely. To be an enchanter, you need also to be a master craftsman. I can only enchant something I've created with my own hands, and the better the quality, the more powerful the enchantment. As such, each enchanter needs to be a blacksmith, a stoneworker, a carver, a jeweler and any number of other things. I think the innate magic that makes you an enchanter also helps you to learn the other trades more quickly, but I'm not sure. In any case, over those years, Stoback poured himself into his learning and was coming along nicely. At twelve, we smithed a beautiful sword and when it was done, the boy picked it up and gave it a few swings. He was clearly a natural and seemed to enjoy it. I asked some of the palace guards to work with him and before long, he was splitting his time with me and them. Well, by the time he was sixteen, the writing was on the wall. As talented as he was in magic, he was a force of nature with a weapon. We had an honest talk, and he admitted that fighting was where his heart was. He told me he wanted to find and stop the kind of people that killed his parents."

"Not sure he was being a hundred percent honest with you there," Torin said.

Thorn snorted a bitter laugh and shook his head ruefully. "Aye, I was a fool. I loved him so much, we all did, that I didn't want to believe that there was any lingering damage from his year of captivity. Solaire tried to warn us, but he seemed so happy in his studies. The time came that he wanted to leave, to go train with the elite soldiers in Casea. He wanted to learn all styles, he said. As a gift, I suggested we craft some armour and a sword together, so he could have a hand in enchanting the items. He helped design it and build it and poured some of his own will, bolstered by my own, into the enchantments. Chain mail that would repel forceful blows and a two-handed great-sword, light as a feather with an edge that would never dull. He'd found his average height and reach was a disadvantage and this was a way to fix that without comprising speed. The enchantment was one of my finest, likely because we both poured our wills into it," Thorn finished.

"After that, we didn't see him for a while," Dafoe said. "Then we started to hear stories about a great swordsman hunting down bandits, and we all assumed it was him. We thought he would return to Aquilo and join our army, but we figured maybe he needed to find his own path."

"Years passed and we started to hear other stories," Luness said. "Concerning stories of a great swordsman in filthy armour killing indiscriminately. We didn't believe it at first, but there were more and more reports. Finally, we sent some men to investigate. He sent back their heads with a note saying to leave him alone."

They each took up the story as if by spreading it around, they could shoulder the pain together. Ashea could almost feel the collective hurt at their failure.

"Solaire suggested we search his chambers," Thorn said. "As she suspected, we found a false bottom on his wardrobe that was filled with the bones of small animals. Some were old enough that they had to have been there from the time we found him. He'd been killing in secret, slaking a desire that was growing inside him. Now he was running around the countryside."

"After that, we tried to find him," Dafoe said, the same heavy tone in his voice. "Thorn taught Luness how to circumvent the armour and they drilled on it, but Stoback was a survivor and he became less and less obvious in his killing. Slowly he began to blend into Haven and we lost him completely."

"A monster we housed and made invincible by an enchantment we taught him how to create," Luness said, shaking her head.

"Well, his will was always strong, just not strong enough to come out of his childhood unscathed," Dafoe said.

"His will..." Thorn had that look on his face again; the thought he'd been chasing seemed to have come back to him. "Damn! I think I know what happened," he said, slapping his hand on the table.

Morley jumped as his plate bounced in front of him and he grabbed his glass of wine lest it fall over. He looked briefly around the table, appeared to decide he still didn't care what was going on, and went back to eating.

Torin turned back to Thorn as the man pulled something out of his breast pocket. He delicately placed a small wooden top point-first onto the table in front of him and started it spinning.

"This was the first item I ever enchanted. A simple toy, a top that won't ever stop spinning," he said.

Everyone watched as the top spun for a few seconds and then a few more, never wobbling.

"Okay, what does this have to do with Stoback?" Luness asked patiently.

"Just wait."

They all watched the top for a few more seconds and then it jumped, maybe three inches, off the table, landed and continued to spin.

"There! You see!" Thorn said triumphantly.

Everyone looked at each other, equally confused at the epiphany that only Thorn could see.

"That's very good, Thorn, very good!" Morley said, as if Thorn were a small child showing off. He then put a hand up, blocking his mouth from Thorn, and whispered to Torin in a tone that was loud enough for the whole table to hear, "It may be time to consider sending the old man up north. I hear your people send the senile out to sea on ice floats."

"Shut up Morley," Dafoe said.

Thorn just kept smiling.

31

TORIN

~

After silencing Morley — Torin decided he did not like Morley Swingle — Dafoe had probed Thorn a couple of more times, but the mage just sat and stared at the perpetually spinning top. Every thirty seconds or so, the top would hop again and Thorn would smile and shake his head. Finally, as if remembering where he was, he looked up at everyone staring at him and cleared his throat.

"Right, this probably requires some explanation. I don't know why, but immediately after I finished the enchantment on this top, I wished I had made it hop instead of spin perpetually. One of those weird circumstances where as soon as you make a binding decision, you think of what you really wanted instead. There was nothing I could do, however. When I enchanted this item, it was only within my abilities to get it to spin perpetually. Adding a second enchantment on an item is difficult even for a master, and besides, that wasn't the assignment. I was to carve an item from wood and enchant it. Once it was done, I moved on to the next task in my training. Being somewhat sentimental, I held onto the top. I was proud of my work and thought it would remind me of how far I'd come once I was a mage. Over the years, when I looked at the top, I would always wish that I had made the damn thing hop. It stayed on the nightstand in my chambers and, for a number of years, I would think about making it hop every night before I went to bed. As I got older, the trivial nature of my first enchantment receded from my mind until I forgot about completely," Thorn said, his eyes distant with memory.

"This really is a touching story, Thorn, but I'm wondering if it has a point?" Morley asked between bites.

"Morley, shut up," Dafoe said again.

"No, he's right, I'm getting long-winded. A few months ago, before I went to bed, I spun the top, just on a whim, and was watching it spin. To my surprise, it hopped, just like you saw today, and I had to wrack my brain to remember if I'd made it do that. It was late, and I fell asleep before I could remember and I haven't thought of it since. Then you mentioned Stoback's will, and it got me thinking. What if an enchantment isn't static?" Thorn posed the question to the room.

No one said anything. Morley continued to eat while the other mages contemplated silently. Ashea and Torin shared a look.

"If this is a solution to killing Stoback, we need to hear it now. He might not want our help, but we aren't going to let our friend die if we can help it," Ashea said.

"Yes, of course. So, the consensus has always been that an item, once enchanted, cannot be enchanted again. It requires a combination of crafting and willpower from a specific person to enchant an item. Once that item is complete, that enchantment, or enchantments if one is talented enough, is locked into it. It can't be changed or enchanted again or removed after the original enchanting window closes. It's static," Thorn said.

"Makes sense," Luness responded.

"So, what if we were wrong? I don't keep items for myself. I enchant them for whomever has commissioned me and I pass that item along. It's removed from me and my will. This top, however, stayed with me and for years I wished I had made it hop. Well, what if I had wished so hard that I actually willed, slowly, over the years, into adding an enchantment?" Thorn asked and looked around the room again.

"It's not so crazy," Mary mused. "What are we doing when we infuse our will into magic and make it real, if not fulfilling a wish?"

"Okay, so what does that have to do with Stoback?" Ashea asked.

"He helped craft and enchant his own armour," Luness said, eyes wide.

"Exactly!" Thorn said. "And for years we hunted him. So, for years, he probably *wished* that his armour was enchanted against other magic. Looks like now it is."

"Okay, so what you're saying is that the plan that you all had to stop that madman is out the window and, being users of magic, you're useless against him as well?" Ashea asked. Torin could tell she was losing her patience. He was too.

"Just because I am a master of the elements does not mean I don't know how to fight," Luness said, steel in her voice. "I was trained as a warrior in Casea before my powers were discovered. I am happy to elucidate Stoback on the subject."

"Luness, no one doubts your prowess as a warrior, but I'm afraid I need you here," Dafoe said. "Ashea's arrival is one of the final pieces in the reflection I have been working to understand for years. A reflection with the fate of our entire world at the heart of it."

"If she has to stay, that's fine," Ashea said, "but we're going to help Thomaras and unless there is another solution you can all offer, we're going now."

"Please, I will not force you to do anything and you are free to come and go as you please, but would you at least hear me out?" Dafoe said. "This information may well keep you safe, even if you don't stay."

"Fine," Torin said and Ashea nodded.

"Thank you. Luness, have you made the connection with your sister?" Dafoe asked.

"Yes, she's been with us since I arrived," Luness said, then turned to the confused faces of the newcomers. "My sister and I are twins, and we share a bond with our magic. We can create a telepathic link with the other and while linked, we can see and hear what the other sees and hears. That's how we knew to expect you today. After Torin and Ashea left her citadel, she contacted me.

"Good," Dafoe said. "I believe Stoback to be the symptom of a greater issue. The issue I brought all of you together to discuss before we were interrupted by Stoback."

"Wait, Felix isn't here yet, nor is his delicious husband," Mary said.

"Unfortunately, Felix is no longer a member of this council," Dafoe said, a sad look across his face.

The other mages looked surprised, except for Morley, who simply continued eating.

"Not a part of the council? Did he quit?" Thorn asked, bemused.

"No, but his absence is part of the discussion. There is a being of immense power, a dark being from another realm along the tiled plane that seeks to break into our own. It is called Umbra, and It is a plague. It was once a mage, though I don't know if It was a man or a woman, and Its magic manifests as the ability to consume the life force of living beings to grow Its own power. The mages of Umbra's plane tried to stop It, but by the time they realized the threat it was too late. When used on a mage, Umbra's powers allowed It to consume, and in turn be able wield, the mage's abilities." Dafoe paused and looked around the room, allowing his words to sink in.

"So It can command any type of magic?" Thorn asked softly.

"Any kind It has absorbed, yes," Dafoe said. "I have no idea what kind of magic existed in this other realm. Maybe exactly the same as we command here, maybe something completely different, maybe a mix of both. The infinity prism seeks balance, so it's likely that the magic It wields is similar. Let's hope we never have to find out."

"The presence in my dreams, that's Umbra, isn't it?" Ashea asked. "Why is It trying to get to me?"

"Yes, that is Umbra," Dafoe said. "The balance that I speak of is the reason that you are being targeted. More accurately, it's the reason that It is able to target you. I believe that the manifestation of your powers, specifically the fact that you can command multiple forms of magic, is the prism trying to find balance. Umbra knows this as well and is using the connection between the two of you as an attempt to enter this world."

"You know…" Ashea said, and stared at Dafoe.

"I am the prism reader, child. I know much."

"So if we killed her, would it stop Umbra from being able to get here?" Morley asked.

The fat mage seemed oblivious to the stare that Torin

was giving him, but just as Torin decided he might get up and see if that was a question Morley really wanted to have asked, Dafoe raised a pleading hand. "Morley, we aren't murdering one of our own," he said, addressing Torin as much as the other mage. "It wouldn't solve the issue, anyway. Umbra is attempting to make Its way through the barrier of the tiled plane in different ways. Those animals that you three ran into are another way Its attempting to flex Its influence. It could take decades without Ashea, but make no mistake. Umbra will get in eventually. It is an eternal being with limitless power and patience to match."

"Okay, so what do we do to stop It? If our magic isn't enough, then what is?" Luness asked.

"Ashea is the key and her training becomes all-important," Dafoe said. "Having a mage that can stand against Umbra with multiple forms of magic will give us the edge we need to stop It. She will begin training with Luness and myself. I can train her to strengthen her mind against Its attempts to infiltrate her and cross into this realm through her body. Ashea, it seems that you already have a knack for controlling the elements, so we might as well start there. What do you say?"

To Torin's surprise, it really did seem like a question. Torin wondered if Dafoe was really prepared to allow Ashea to walk away from all this if she chose to do so, but something told him he was.

"Are you saying the fate of the world rests with me? Because that seems like a lot," Ashea said.

Dafoe chuckled and got up from his chair to walk over and crouch down in front of Ashea. "It doesn't rest with you alone. Everyone in this room, every soldier in Haven, will have a hand in fighting this beast. You simply give us an advantage that the people of Umbra's world, the people that have been absorbed into Its being, never had. If you choose to walk away from all this, you may do so. I would only ask for a few days, maybe a week, so that I can train you to protect yourself from Umbra's attempts at your mind. Then you would be free to go."

"That seems fast. Even for one with Ashea's latent talents," Luness said.

"Umbra is able to enter this realm through Ashea because one of the many skills she has is the ability to read the reflections of the prism. The reason It is tracking her through dreams is because the dream realm is a key aspect of the reading the reflections. That's the bad news. The good news is that because she is a prism reader I can also communicate with her within the dream realm and help her learn the skills therein far faster than in the physical world."

Ashea looked at Luness and then back at Dafoe. "I'm a prism reader?"

Dafoe laughed. "Well, not yet. But with training, if you so choose, you could be. For now, though, we can use your talent in that area to protect you from Umbra."

Torin watched Ashea look at Dafoe and hoped she decided to stay and learn how to protect herself from Umbra. Ashea looked at him and smiled. She knew that he would support her either way.

"Okay, I would love to be able to have my dreams to myself again," Ashea said.

"Well, I'm glad that's sorted, but I still want to know what happened to Felix and Az'an." Thorn said.

"They're with the spider," Ashea said, a strange look on her face.

"The spider?" Mary asked.

"Yes," Dafoe said, "though the images of a spider that

many of Haven worship aren't entirely accurate. That is simply the form she takes on this plane of the prism."

"So wait, there really is an eternal spider weaving the will of the infinity prism and keeping the balance?" Thorn said. "I thought she was like an allegory, a physical symbol that represented the different ways the prism attempts to keep the balance."

"Well, you are correct that the prism seeks balance," Dafoe said. "One of the agents of said balance are eternal beings that have the ability to read and weave prophecy. The prism speaks to them, and through their weaving they are able to read and, to some small extent, manipulate its reflections. This allows them to help prevent things like Umbra from ever happening. It seems like the Weaver in Umbra's plane failed to do so and I believe that it is Umbra's ability to affect reflection himself that allowed this to happen."

"But if this being is an agent for balance, wouldn't she be an ally?" Ashea asked.

"Normally, yes, but I believe that Umbra is already influencing her. Manipulating her weaving so that she believes me to be her enemy and Ashea to be the cause of this plane's destruction. I believe you were introduced to her brood already," Dafoe said, turning to Torin and Ashea.

"You mean there's a spider out there that's bigger than those things? No thank you," Torin said.

Ashea just shuddered and reached out for Torin's hand, who took it obligingly.

"And far more powerful," Dafoe said. "Add to that the fact that she's seduced Felix onto her side and she is a formidable enemy indeed. Luness, in addition to Ashea's training, I need you here in case Felix and the spider come for Ashea."

"Felix helped Ashea and let us go. Are we sure they mean her harm?" Torin asked.

"I can't know with certainty what the spider has read in her weavings of the prism, but what I do know is that Umbra is manipulating whatever she sees. Whatever her plans are, know this; they will put Ashea exactly where Umbra needs her. The only place Ashea, and by extension our entire plane of existence, is safe is here with us."

"I don't relish fighting the Druid," Luness said. "He has always been a friend to me, but I will do what I need to. That being said, are you sure we have lost him?"

"Morley," Dafoe said, ceding the floor to the mage.

"Quite so," Morley said. "We were growing suspicious of his allegiance, so I arranged for some of my dolls to be placed throughout his woods. I began to see the spider's brood come and go and even caught a glimpse of the Orb Weaver once."

"That doesn't prove much. She could have been attempting to recruit him, but it doesn't mean he joined her," Thorn said hopefully.

"Well, he's stopped responding to any of our attempts to contact him and he slowly began to hunt down and destroy all of my dolls," Morley said. "I am blind to his woods now."

"I wouldn't have wanted your creepy dolls in my home either, Morley. I'm not sure that makes him guilty," Thorn said.

"I wish it weren't true either, Thorn, but all of this evidence, coupled with the reflections of the prism that I've read, is ironclad," Dafoe said sadly.

Torin's patience finally ran out. "Okay, so there is a greater threat here and Ashea is going to stay and help you fight it. How do I kill Stoback?"

The entire council turned as one to look at him. Torin

simply stared back with an implacable face. He was about done with their business.

"I'm not sure you have to. Thomaras may be successful and if not, all he wants is Ashea. A few deaths in a small town are a small price to pay for the fate of the world," Dafoe said.

"Unacceptable," Ashea snapped. "If you want my help, you'll help Torin and Thomaras with Stoback."

"Thomaras didn't seem too keen on our help," Luness said.

"Well, I am," Torin responded. "So help."

"I'm afraid I can't offer Aquilo's forces to stop Stoback," Dafoe said with finality. "My priority is the safety of the plane and focusing on him is exactly the distraction his master intends."

"Give me half an hour and I can fix your hammer," Thorn said. "It's not much, but it will help."

Luness spoke. "My duty is to Dafoe, despite my desire for revenge, so I can't come with you, but I can offer some small advice. The armour he wears deflects fast, hard strikes. Get inside and grab him, then don't let him go."

"My thanks," Torin said to Luness and turned to Thorn. "Half an hour?"

"Half an hour," Thorn said and stood.

"Dafoe, can someone show me to my chambers?" Ashea asked. "I think I need to rest."

"Of course. The guards outside the door will show you. I need to speak with my council, anyway."

Torin followed Ashea out the door.

∾

32

TORIN

~

"What should we do?" Ashea asked the moment the door closed behind them.

Despite what she'd told the council, it was clear that Ashea needed to consider what course of action she would take without Dafoe around.

"What do you want to do?"

"That's not very helpful!"

"Sorry. It's your choice, though. I don't think anyone else can make it for you," Torin said gently.

"I know, I know. I want to help Thomaras and Erica but—"

"But you have to stay."

"Yes. If Stoback is really working for whatever is hunting me in my nightmares, then I don't think I can go anywhere near him."

"They'll understand."

"What if they don't?"

"I don't think you can afford to worry about that. You're

too important," Torin said, and wrapped Ashea's tiny form in a hug.

"I don't want to be important," she said into his chest.

"We rarely get to choose things like that. Stay here. Learn how to kick some ass."

"Do you trust Dafoe?" Ashea asked.

"I don't know for sure. Do you? He's far less concerned about me."

"I think so. So far all he's done is help me. The Orb Weaver had me locked in a cell and Dafoe got me out. She had me poisoned so I could be taken to Felix and Dafoe warned me of the danger. Dafoe has given me choices and information whereas the Weaver has tried to move me like a piece on a chess board."

"Felix healed you and let you go," Torin offered as a counterpoint.

"Yes, but that was his decision. One he followed up by telling me he doesn't always like the spider's methods. So far, the only person who really didn't trust Dafoe was Thomaras and even he came around after learning more about him."

"So, you trust Dafoe?"

"More than the Orb Weaver at least. You just hurry back here so you can keep an eye on me, okay?"

"Always."

Ashea pulled out of his hug and stared up at him, smiling through the tears in her eyes. "Do you think we have time for—"

"Yes."

Ashea laughed and pulled his head down into a long kiss.

.   .   .

All too soon, an attendant knocked on the door.

"Torin, Thorn is waiting for you in the forge. Ashea, Dafoe would like to see you in the council chambers," the attendant said through the door before walking away.

"Be careful out there," Ashea said as they stood in the doorway. "Give Erica a hug for me when you save her."

Torin kissed her and held her for a long time. He wanted to promise he would see her again, but the words caught in his throat.

"Okay," was all he could manage.

Ashea's smile told him it was enough.

He didn't have to walk very far down the stone corridor before a servant, presumably the one sent to his room, met him and offered to take him to Thorn. Torin nodded his agreement and followed the young man.

The castle wasn't terribly complicated, but having never been here before, he was glad for the guide. After a few rights and lefts, Torin found himself descending into the lower levels of the castle where the familiar smell of a smithy filled his nostrils. He smiled and waited for the clang of steel on steel, but there was only silence.

"This hallway leads directly to Master Thorn's workshop," the servant said, and gestured down the hall.

"Thank you," Torin replied with a smile.

The servant looked a little uneasy at the tusks protruding from that smile, but did his best to return it before turning on his heel and making his way back to the castle proper.

Torin followed the hallway and as he got closer, he could see a blue light pouring out of the large, open doors at the end of the hall. When he walked into the room, he saw that the source of the light was Thorn himself. He was bent over what looked like a large worktable in the middle of the circular room. His back was to Torin, but Torin could see the hammer as it lay on the table surrounded by the same blue aura that was spilling into the hallway.

Abruptly the light faded and Thorn let out a long sigh before lifting the giant maul with both hands and inspected it.

"Looks good," Torin said.

Thorn jumped and nearly dropped the hammer as he spun to face Torin. "Gods, man! Don't sneak up on me like that. How does someone your size sneak up on anyone, anyway?"

As the shock of the surprise left him, and he saw the impish smile on Torin's face, Thorn chuckled lightly and walked over to Torin, handing him the hammer.

"Good as new. Better, actually. As you saw before you tried to scare the life out of me, I was putting an enchantment on your weapon. I know I didn't ask permission, but it was the only way to save the weapon and I figured you wouldn't mind."

"Nope. What does it do?" Torin asked.

"Well, fixing it would have been impossible for any normal smith. There would have been no way to weld the two pieces together again and expect it to have any kind of integrity. Best case, someone could have maybe salvaged the head and put it on a new handle, but fortunately for you, I've got some magic at my disposal. I fused the two parts together as best I could. It was almost perfect to look at, but I don't know how long it would have held up in use. To fix that issue, I enchanted it to be nearly indestructible. Now it doesn't matter if there is a flaw where we fused it..."

"Because now I have an indestructible hammer?" Torin asked with a grin.

"Nearly. The amount of force it would take to break it

would be extreme, but it could happen. Now, my enchantment didn't affect the head, of course. The shamanic magic used on the granite caused my enchantment to flow off of it like water, but I'd wager the granite is as close to indestructible as can be, anyway. An enchantment like this is hard to learn, harder to execute, and will probably keep me from performing any real magic for a few weeks. So do me a favour? Go and kill Stoback with it."

Torin's grin faded, and he met the gaze of the mage in front of him. "I'll do my best."

He turned from the mage and headed for the castle's exit. While he walked, he considered Thorn's request. Could he kill Stoback? He really wasn't sure. He had no illusions about being the best warrior in the land. He was primarily a doorman in a small mining town, but he had always known that his size and strength would give him an advantage over most people south of his homeland. Add to that the granite that was infused in his body and he had always felt confident going into any conflict.

Now, though...

Stoback had shattered the granite. That wasn't supposed to be possible. The Granite Ogre shamans had always warned that the magic the mages wielded was more powerful than their own. Torin supposed that this proved it. Stoback's enchantment had bested his. But none of that was what worried him. Even without the armour, without the enchanted sword, Torin didn't know that he could beat Stoback. The man was a psychopath, but he was a damn good swordsman. Maybe the best Torin had ever seen, and frankly, he wasn't too keen on dying at the hands of a madman.

He continued down the winding path that led from the

castle and out of Vees. The rain had abated completely now, but the roads were still wet and the sky remained grey. By the time he left the capital and was back on the Five Points Road, Torin was starting to formulate a plan based on what he'd learned about Stoback.

He even managed to convince himself it was a good one.

They're coming. The big one and the half-breed. Prepare yourself. The whisper in his mind grated like steel on a chalkboard, but Stoback was grateful for the information. He wasn't sure where it was coming from, but it was making him even more powerful than he was before. He turned and looked at the two people bound and gagged in the room he slept in.

"It's time. Now, which one of you shall I use first?" Stoback asked rhetorically.

He already knew the answer. The doorman was friends with the giant, sure, but the girl was the real emotional connection. He would save her until he could watch their faces when he ended it.

"It's time, Rolph. You're going to welcome your friends on their way into town. Well, part of you, anyway." Stoback drew his sword.

The short, broad man struggled as much as he could, but his strength was exhausted. Stoback had made sure of that. Any energy he had now was pure panic. It wouldn't matter anyway.

Thunk.

The severed head bounced off the floor. The body slumped over sideways and, in a turn of good fortune, fell right onto the girl, drenching her in blood. She didn't react, she just continued to stare at him with murder in her eyes. Stoback could respect that.

"Okay, little filly, you and your friend stay here. I've got a message to send," Stoback said. He bent down and picked up the head. "Want to give him a kiss goodbye?" He held the head, face first, in front of her.

She continued to glare.

Stoback started to giggle and walked out of the room.

33

ASHEA

~

Ashea stood in Thorn's workshop with Dafoe, Mary, and Luness. She was excited to begin her training in magic and particularly happy about learning how to keep Umbra out of her dreams. She hadn't spoken about it since she woke up in Felix's home, but every night had been the same set of dreams, dreams she couldn't quite remember upon waking, with the same cold darkness trying to consume her. So far she'd been able to stay ahead of what she now knew was Umbra, but she got the feeling It was getting closer each night.

More than that, though, she was worried about Thomaras and Torin.

She would have felt a little better if they were together, but the way Thomaras stormed out was the worst part of the whole situation. She really thought she and Torin meant something to him, but all it took was a little pressure and he fell back into his old ways.

"Alright, Ashea, are you ready to begin?" Dafoe asked

"Oh. Yes, sorry. What do you want me to do?" Ashea asked.

Dafoe smiled at her patiently and in spite of the circumstances, she began to feel better. "I know you're worried, but you're exactly where you need to be. I understand your concern for your friends, but you need to let them fight for themselves so you can fight for those who are more vulnerable. That is the burden that comes with the power possessed by you, me, and everyone in this room."

"I know. It's just... how do you do it?"

This time, it was Luness who answered her. "By understanding that if you aren't willing to make sacrifices, even for the ones you care for most, it's those very people that will suffer. You are part of something greater than yourself now. I know it seems as though it happened quickly, but it's clear that the prism had plans in place for you long before you drew a breath on this plane."

It was Luness, more than anything, who convinced her. She'd seen the anger burning in the mage when she'd heard of Robert's death. She'd heard the desire for vengeance in her voice when she offered to go with Torin to hunt him down. And yet, she was here. Because she knew she served a greater purpose.

Because she trusted Dafoe.

"Okay, I'm ready."

"Just lie down on the table. We'll need to be asleep for this to work. Just like I was able to reach out to your mind when you were sleeping before, it's the only way I'll be able to do so now. The realm of reflection shows itself to a mage in that space between waking and dreaming. That's where I will be able to meet and guide you," Dafoe explained.

Ashea lay down on the hard table. As exhausting as the

past few weeks had been, she didn't think she'd be able to fall asleep.

"I'm not sure I'll be able to just nod off."

"No, and we wouldn't expect it," Dafoe said. "The ability to slip into the space between waking and slumber is a skill that will take you some time to master. For now, though, Mary has something that should help."

Ashea eyed the bottle that Mary produced from her voluminous robes warily. It was small, only filling about half of Mary's hand, and had a round bottom that narrowed at the top that was closed with a cork.

"Not to worry, my dear," Mary assured her. "It will help you sleep but won't keep you asleep. Any loud sounds, or if you are physically touched, and you'll wake right up. I wasn't about to brew a potion that the unscrupulous could use to put people to sleep and do whatever they'd like with them."

Ashea propped herself up on one elbow and took the bottle that Mary offered her. She pulled off the cork and smelled the contents within.

"Smells like strawberries," Ashea said in surprise.

"Of course," Mary scoffed. "You think with the ability to suffuse my will into my work that I would choose to make a nasty-tasting potion? I have a business to run here."

Ashea could understand the woman's point. Her mother's potions and tinctures had always tasted nasty, but her mother also didn't have any magic at her disposal. Smiling an apology, Ashea put the bottle to her lips and downed the contents in one swallow. It tasted as good as it smelled.

"I don't feel anything," Ashea said.

"It won't kick in right away. Lie down and close your eyes. You'll feel sleep come," Mary said.

Her expression and sincerity reassured Ashea. She nodded silently and closed her eyes.

At first, she felt nothing but the hard table on her back. And then the warm feeling of sleep started to creep up into her chest, then down her legs, and finally filled her whole body. She felt her breathing deepen and then she was fast asleep.

The dreams started as they always did. Ashea was walking through the corridors of her foster parents' home. She was eleven. Suddenly, a golden light glowed and Dafoe shimmered into view.

"Hello, Ashea," he said calmly.

She was no longer eleven and the corridors of her old foster home melted away into a hazy nothingness. Everywhere she looked was obscured by fog, but she could still feel a cold darkness emanating out from somewhere in the mist.

"Umbra's out there, have no doubt," Dafoe said gravely. "This is where It can try and enter your consciousness and in so doing bring Its physical being into this plane of existence."

"But you're going to show me how to stop It?" Ashea asked anxiously. Being in this place made her feel exposed and vulnerable. Only Dafoe's reassuring presence kept her from panicking and trying to shake herself awake.

"I am. First, and this is going to sound counterintuitive, you must open yourself up to Umbra. Feel Its presence and allow It to find yours. Once It finds you, then do your best to shut It out. Sometimes it helps to picture a gate swinging shut or something along those lines."

Ashea stared at Dafoe in disbelief. Counterintuitive was

perhaps the biggest euphemism in the history of euphemisms. Abhorrent was a better description.

"You're sure you can stop It?"

"For now, yes. But Umbra grows in power with every passing moment. You need to learn how to repel It first. Then, we'll need to learn how to work together. Only then, on this plane, will we be able to stop It for good."

"Okay, as long as you can stop It," Ashea said, fear plain in her voice.

"Of course. Go ahead," Dafoe said.

Ashea took a deep breath and opened her mind to the presence that she felt out in the ether. It wasn't hard to find, and as soon as she cast her mind out, Umbra found her immediately. She was shocked at the speed with which It sought her out. Before she could even begin to think about a gate or a door, she felt Dafoe's presence extend itself and Umbra was held at bay. She could sense Its presence, but it was no longer barreling towards her.

"Now," Dafoe said, his voice slightly strained, "open yourself up to me. I can show you how to strengthen your mind and shield yourself."

Ashea followed the instruction. Despite her fear, Dafoe's presence in her mind was so comforting, she sought to let him in. Once she did so, it was as if a long-forgotten skill had been jarred loose. It was so simple. She followed the instructions now embedded in her memory.

And hit a wall.

It was a wall she'd felt before. Since meeting Thomaras and Torin, it had happened less, but it was a wall that prevented her from using her magic. It kept her from blasting her way out of the dungeons she was convinced would be her tomb and stopped her from killing the giant spider that had bitten her in Hannover.

Now it was stopping her from keeping Umbra out of this plane.

"Ashea..." Dafoe said urgently.

"I can't!" Ashea cried.

She felt a surge of power come from Umbra and then a moment later a much larger blast came from Dafoe, accompanied by a warm, golden light.

She woke up.

34

TORIN

~

The sun was getting low in the sky as Torin rounded the final curve on the road into Hannover. He was well-rested despite his journey. He had forced himself to take breaks along the way, even if his desperation to save his friends made him want to push himself just to get there. He reasoned that Stoback would need to keep them alive if he was planning on bartering for Ashea.

Looked like he was wrong.

A wave of nausea washed over Torin as he rounded the corner and saw Rolph's head on a pike along the side of the road. A cloud of flies buzzed around it, but even at this distance Torin could make out the doorman's telltale beard.

After successfully keeping his last meal down, Torin made his way over to his friend's head. They had been fairly close, certainly closer than a passing work relationship, even if that was their common ground. Rolph had a cutting wit and a thirst for knowledge that Torin had appreciated in equal measure. He didn't seem to consider Torin's obvious differences important aside from an opportunity to learn about new things that he didn't know before. Torin always appreciated the capacity for compassion and learning that filled a man that was also capable of violence when necessary.

"I'm sorry, my friend. I don't even know how he knew about you," Torin said softly.

Ignoring the flies, Torin lifted the head off of the pike. He walked a fair distance away from the road before digging a deep hole and burying his friend's head.

If Rolph had family, Torin didn't know who they were or where to find them, but he figured the least he could do was keep the animals from getting at what was left of him. Once he dealt with Stoback, he could figure out what to do with the rest of his friend.

Torin knelt on the ground for a moment and closed his eyes. Stoback wanted to make him angry, wanted him to fight recklessly. Torin wasn't going to give in. He would need all of his wits about him if he had any chance of stopping that monster. He slowed his breathing and thought of Ashea. He had to disarm him and get his hands on him.

Easier said than done.

Disarming someone of his talents would be a tall order. Torin didn't even know if he could be disarmed. Thorn hadn't said anything about that kind of enchantment on his sword, but Stoback had already shown he could change the enchantments on his tools.

One problem at a time.

Torin opened his eyes and stood. He was angry and sad about his friend, but now he was resolved to use that anger as a tool and not let Stoback influence him. He would give Stoback all that he could handle.

By the time Torin walked into Hannover, hammer in

hand and jaw set grimly, the sun had gone down and the main street was lit by torches. He'd hoped to see some sign of Thomaras but so far there was nothing. Torin looked around cautiously at the abandoned village. It was eerily quiet, and he couldn't see a soul. The torches were lit in such a way that the ones leading him to the town square were the only ones burning. The rest remained dark.

When Torin got to the main square, he could see that the torches were lit in a ring and standing in the centre was the unassuming, if filthy, figure of Stoback. He was holding a torch of his own that caused his shadows to dance and jump as it flickered. The smell of mothballs lingered in the air, mixing with another smell he couldn't place.

"Hey there, big boy! I don't see your skinny friend. Trouble in paradise?" Stoback asked with a giggle.

In response, Torin loosed his hammer and let the head rest on the ground.

"Right, right. Strong and silent. I forgot. Well, I also see that you didn't bring the girl along. Naughty, naughty. Now this one is in real trouble," Stoback said and gestured.

Tied to a chair on the front porch of one of the shops that lined the town square was Erica. She was slumped over, her hair dangled in her face, and she was covered in a concerning amount of blood, but he could see her shoulders rise and fall with ragged breaths.

"Don't worry, I'll deal with you first," Stoback giggled.

Torin took a deep breath and controlled his anger. He refused to rise to the bait. "Come on, then," he said calmly, without moving.

"Don't forget about us," a familiar voice said from behind him.

Torin spared a quick glance and saw Felix and Az'an walking up the dark path. The emerald in Felix's staff was glowing faintly, and Az'an had both of his curved blades drawn. While he wasn't sure of their intentions for Ashea, Torin suspected they were his allies in dealing with Stoback.

As soon as Stoback saw them, he grinned manically. "Now, now. This party is invite-only. Wait your turn."

Stoback tossed his torch, and Torin finally placed the smell. Lantern oil. Stoback must have soaked the ground with it. As soon as the torch hit the ground, a circle of fire sprung up, cutting Stoback and Torin off from his allies.

No sooner had the fire lit than Stoback was on him. Torin was ready. He gave ground strategically, making sure to move in a circle and not directly backwards, and parried Stoback's seemingly reckless blows with no intention of counter-attacking. He was determined to leave no opening for his enemy. After a flurry of blows that got him nowhere, Stoback disengaged and the sound of his giggling was all that filled the air that once rang with steel on steel.

Torin had thought a lot about their first encounter while on his journey to Hannover. He was used to being larger than his opponents and, even if he wasn't faster, he usually had the advantage of being faster than they expected. Stoback was not only fast, but the reach with his great-sword negated most of Torin's size advantage. Add to that his near-perfect and bizarre technique, and Torin had almost no advantage at all. That was without even considering the enchanted armour.

It was hard for Torin to admit his lack of advantage, but once he did, he realized that Stoback likely suffered from the same hubris. Countless battles being head and shoulders better than his opponents had probably made him overly confident that his combination of skill and magic was unmatched.

As Stoback came at him again, Torin once again took the

defensive, but this time, despite the extraordinary strain on his already damaged forearms, Torin kept Stoback at the very edge of the giant maul's length. He parried each blow with his maul and arm fully extended, using his deft footwork to continuously keep himself out of Stoback's normally superior range. As they disengaged a second time, Stoback's giggling faltered momentarily.

"Better than last time, big boy, but you can't stay on the defensive forever," Stoback spat.

Before Torin could respond, the ground began to shake slightly and the earth itself kicked upwards, dirt spraying into the air and then falling down, extinguishing the circle of flames.

"Fortunately, he has some help," Az'an said as he walked towards Torin and Stoback.

"Did you really think a little fire was a match for my magic?" Felix asked.

"That wasn't supposed to stop you, tree hugger. It was just a signal," Stoback said and started to laugh once more.

Behind Felix, the door to one of the darkened shops burst open and five men, bandits from the look of their patchwork armour and dirty clothes, stepped out. Felix quickly moved out of range of the men, his staff coming up defensively. Az'an only hesitated for a moment before running back to put himself between Felix and the new foes.

"It seems you three pissed off some of the local boys. It was surprising how amenable they were to helping me kill you," Stoback said between gales of manic laughter.

Torin had to assume that these were some of the remaining men from the bandit group that had waylaid them what seemed like ages ago. He didn't have much time to think about it, though, as Stoback advanced once more.

35

THOMARAS

⁓

Thomaras had been making his way over to Erica when Stoback tossed the torch and the ring of fire and encircled them. He had just managed to get into the shadows between two buildings before light exploded all around. As Torin engaged the madman, Thomaras had picked his way, painfully slow, closer to Erica. He resisted the urge to rush so that he didn't give away his position.

He'd spent too much energy getting here without being seen to give himself away now.

It was Morley Swingle and his damn doll that made Thomaras finally realize that this Umbra thing was watching them. It had to be. There was no other way that It could always know where they were. The ambush outside the Darkwoods and Stoback knowing exactly where to wait for them on the road to Aquilo was proof enough.

He'd felt a small pang of guilt at leaving Torin and Ashea, but Thomaras knew there was no way he could get all three of them here unseen. Besides, he spoke true when he said they were the cause of his problems. He needed to get to Erica and get away from this whole mess.

The din of clashing steel told Thomaras that Stoback was engaged once more, and he closed the final gap to Erica. Only a professional detachment cultivated by years of violent work kept him from recoiling at the sight of her.

Erica's face was swollen and beaten almost beyond recognition. Her chest was covered in blood, but Thomaras was fairly certain it didn't all belong to her. The way she held a hand over her stomach protectively threatened to once again break Thomaras. At his approach, the two slits that were her eyes struggled to open, and she smiled at him through broken teeth.

"Hi beautiful," Thomaras said and meant it.

"I promised myself I wouldn't tell him anything about you or where you went, but he never asked any questions. He just hurt us. Over and over," Erica croaked.

"Shh, it's okay. Let's get you out of here. The mage of light can help you." Thomaras moved to pick her up.

"No, you have to help Torin. I saw Stoback fight off Rolph and most of the city guard by himself. He forced everyone in town inside and told them if they left, he'd kill them. An entire town, Thomaras. Torin needs your help." Erica's strength seemed to be fading and her eyes closed once more.

Thomaras resolved to ignore her words and moved to scoop her up once more.

"No!" Erica's eyes snapped open and she weakly pushed him away.

"Erica, he doesn't want us. No one cares about us. The only reason you got hurt was because I helped them. We can just disappear into the west and forget all of this," Thomaras urged.

"We," Erica said so softly Thomaras barely heard it.

"What?"

"We helped her. I chose to help Ashea too, and I'd do it again."

"Okay, fine, but we can still leave now and be safe."

"I wouldn't go anywhere with this Thomaras," Erica said, lucidity clear in her eyes.

"What Thomaras?"

"This one. The one that's willing to cut and run. This Thomaras is fine for some company at night but I wouldn't go anywhere with him. I wouldn't introduce him to my parents. I wouldn't care when he left."

"I'm still that Thomaras. I'm just trying to keep us alive!"

Erica rested her hand on his chest and smiled painfully.

It was still the most beautiful smile he'd ever seen.

"We both know that's not true. Now go. Help you friend."

Thomaras stared at her as a flood of arguments rose within in his mind, cresting like a wave, only to crash futilely against the truth of Erica's words. Every rule he'd broken with Ashea. Every truth he'd confessed to Torin. All of it had been small steps on a path he'd never trodden. A path that led him to a place he never thought he'd want to be in.

A place where he cared about a group of people, as small as it was, more than himself.

He sighed heavily and kissed Erica gently on her ruined lips. "I love you."

"Who wouldn't?" she answered.

Thomaras allowed himself a chuckle before turning to the matter at hand. He would be no help to Torin if he just charged in and joined the fray. Their last fight had proven that he was no match for Stoback. He'd have to get in close.

Easier said than done.

The ring of torches lit the town square so completely that the only shadows left were thin ribbons dancing haphazardly in the night.

Thomaras watched Torin continue his battle with Stoback. Az'an and Felix had joined the fray as well and were dealing with the bandits Stoback had recruited to ambush them. He watched in frustration, trying to find a path that would lead him close enough to help.

He desperately wished he could somehow melt into the small shadows cast by the torches.

At the thought, he felt a strange pull on his body.

He watched the shadows dance some more and continued to imagine himself becoming a part of them.

He felt the pull once again and this time he could have sworn his arm faded slightly.

He looked up and saw Torin charging Stoback recklessly. He saw a path amongst the shadows. A path that would take him right behind the murderous bastard. He drew a dagger and visualized the route he would take if he could just dance from shadow to shadow.

He felt the pull again.

This time, he let himself go.

36

ASHEA

~

A shea sat bolt upright on the hard table. She was drenched with sweat and shaking with unspent energy. She frantically looked around for Umbra before she realized where she was.

"It's okay," Dafoe said. "You're safe."

"I tried to stop It. I did. I don't know what happened."

"That's okay. I didn't expect you to get it right away. That's why I was there. It takes a while to be able to follow the instructions, even when they are imprinted upon your memories. Perhaps, since you already have experience with elemental magic, you and Luness should work together," Dafoe suggested.

"Okay," Ashea said, though all she felt was exhausted and defeated.

Luness smiled warmly and extended a hand to help her off the table. The statuesque mage seemed to know exactly how Ashea was feeling. "Come, it will do you good to see some success. Magic is a hard thing to learn. Up until now, you've been acting on instinct and intuition. Both are crucial components to what we do, but learning to control your magic is infinitely more difficult."

Ashea did her best to take the comfort and encouragement Luness was offering. It was hard not to wallow, but she tried to remind herself what was at stake. Not just for herself, but for the entire world. The sooner she could master her abilities, the sooner everyone would be safe.

Including Torin.

It was thinking of Torin that finally steeled her resolve. Ashea had never fallen in love, so she didn't have anything to compare her feelings to, but she had to imagine that the way she felt about Torin to be a stumble in the right direction.

More surprising than how she felt about Torin was how he felt about her. Every word, every action and every small glance was filled with the affection he felt towards her. This was a foreign feeling for Ashea. As an orphan, she had spent most of her time getting rejected and moving from place to place.

Now, she had finally found love and acceptance once more and she'd been willing to let it walk out the door so she could gain the power to make a difference in the world. If she was willing to sacrifice all of that, then she'd be damned if she was going to quit when things got difficult.

She took Luness's hand. "Show me how to control it."

The two women moved through Thorn's workshop to an area that was clearly designated for testing spells and enchantments. The stone walls were charred black with soot in many places, and the debris from what looked like wood and straw dummies was strewn about the floor. Dafoe continued to watch from a safe distance.

"Thorn enchanted this stone to be more resilient to magic, so we don't knock down the keep," Luness said with a smile before raising her hand and throwing a fireball across the room.

Ashea flinched in anticipation of an explosion of heat, but the stone seemed to leech the magic out of the air. The ball of flame still crashed violently against the wall, but the resulting explosion was minimal.

"Now, your turn," Luness said and gestured.

Ashea raised her arm and tried to summon a cube of fire like the one she'd used to stop the boar that was charging Thomaras. She pictured it in her mind and, with all of her being, tried to suffuse her will into it.

Nothing happened.

Just like when she tried to follow Dafoe's instructions in her dreams, they met some kind of wall. She could feel the magic on the other side of it, but no amount of effort could bring it forth.

"I can't," Ashea said in frustration.

"That's okay. I didn't expect you to be able to call upon it at will. Feeling the magic takes time, effort and guidance. Those that are untrained tend to stumble upon it from time to time. When they do, they are able to visualize and form it to their will. It's the ability to sense the magic that takes practice.

"I can always feel it," Ashea said, confused.

"What do you mean?" Dafoe asked.

"The magic is always there. I can feel it whenever I try to use it. I just can't get to it."

"That doesn't make sense. If you can feel it already, you should be able to use it. Knowing where your magic is and being able to access it is the final piece," Dafoe said.

"I don't know what to tell you," Ashea snapped in frustration.

"I'm sorry, Ashea, I'm not angry with you. I'm just trying to understand. We've never seen a mage like you before. Would you permit me to enter your mind while you attempt to use your magic?"

"Will I have to go back to sleep?" Ashea asked. She shuddered involuntarily at the idea of returning to the plane where Umbra was so close.

"No, if you are awake, I can enter simply as an observer. I won't be able to guide you in any way, but perhaps I can better understand what's going on."

"You can peer into people's minds?" Luness asked.

Dafoe raised his hands as if to ward off the simmering anger he heard in Luness's voice. "Only another prism reader. Since my predecessor is the only other one I've ever met, it's not a talent I've used much."

Luness nodded, but Ashea got the sense that being surprised by her leader's abilities was not something she appreciated.

For a moment, the mage of elements' reaction made her hesitate, but she'd let Dafoe inside her head once and all he'd done was help. "Okay, go ahead."

Dafoe nodded and closed his eyes. After a few moments, he motioned that they continue. Ashea tried to sense a difference in her mind, but felt nothing. Perhaps with some training, she'd be able to sense the prism reader's presence.

"Alright Ashea, attempt to use your magic again," Luness instructed.

Ashea lifted her arm and tried to channel another cube of fire. Again, she visualized it. Again, she felt the magic. Again, she was blocked.

"Well, fuck," Ashea said in frustration and then smiled

as she realized she was using one of Thomaras's favourite phrases.

"There's a mental block in place," Dafoe said without opening his eyes. "Some kind of repressed memory that's preventing you from accessing your magic. I can't remove it myself, but I can find the memory that's affecting you and bring it to the fore."

Ashea felt a surge of panic. If she was repressing something, she wasn't sure she was ready to face it in front of Dafoe. "Can we wait?"

"There's no time, Ashea. The sooner we fix this, the sooner you master your powers. Then we can address Umbra."

"I understand, but I need a moment," Ashea stammered.

"I know you're scared, but you can handle this," Dafoe pressed.

"Dafoe, stop." Luness's voice was iron.

"Luness, I know what—"

"Stop." Her voice didn't rise in volume, but the iron in Luness's voice had turned to sharpened steel.

And it might as well have been pressed against Dafoe's throat.

Dafoe opened his eyes and met Luness's stare. The two held each other's gazes for a moment and Ashea was certain violence was imminent.

Finally, Dafoe's familiar smile returned. "Of course, I'm sorry. I just thought I could help."

"If there is a memory in her mind traumatic enough to prevent the use of her magic, then it is a deeply personal thing. One that she should explore on her own, rather than have someone she doesn't know rip it out of her subconscious. Perhaps she would be more comfortable speaking to me alone?" Although phrased like a suggestion, it was clear that Luness was insisting.

The steel mask slipped over Dafoe's face for a moment and then he was himself again.

Or was it the other way around?

"Of course. I'll leave you two," Dafoe said with a smile and left.

Luness waited until she was sure they were alone before continuing. "You don't have to talk to me either. If whatever happened is too much to handle and the cost is that you can't use your magic, that's your choice. We'll find a way to stop Umbra."

"Your kindness is appreciated, but what if you can't? Whatever happened to me can't be worse than Umbra entering this plane of existence. I may be scared, but I can handle it."

Luness smiled. "Good. You're right, of course, but it had to be your choice."

Ashea laughed. "What if I'd decided not to fight?"

"I wasn't worried about that."

"Why not?"

Luness looked at her as if the answer was the most obvious thing in the world. "Because you're a fighter."

37

TORIN

~

Torin continued his dance with the madman. His forearms burned as he kept his maul extended, its wolf's head flashing in the torchlight as it parried blow after blow. Every once in a while, Stoback would throw a feint and get inside Torin's guard and Torin would have to throw a kick, or one time a full-body check, before Stoback could bring the weapon to bear. He didn't hurt Stoback, but the force against the magical shield that his armour generated would knock Stoback back enough that Torin could get his guard back up.

He was beginning to tire, and Stoback faked a strike that turned into a forward roll that brought him well inside Torin's maul. As Stoback brought his sword up vertically for a backhanded cut that would have torn into Torin's face, Torin instinctively threw up his forearm to block the blow. The blade ripped through exposed flesh and grated across shattered granite, causing Torin to bellow in pain. Stoback had not expected the block and was just off balance enough that Torin, gritting through the pain, spun away from him and, switching to a two-handed grip on his hammer, completed the rotation and struck Stoback square in the chest.

Stoback didn't even stop laughing as he was thrown the full length of the town square and through the window of one of the buildings that lined it.

Torin's chest heaved as waves of pain washed over him. It seemed that his exertion, along with Stoback's blade, was reopening whatever wounds Ashea had been able to heal around the shattered granite. Worse, Torin needed to catch his breath, but he had to help out Az'an before Stoback returned.

Torin turned towards the couple and realized his fears were unfounded. One of the bandits was already dead on the ground and the other was struggling to join the fray as the surrounding earth seemed to have turned into quicksand. The man had sunk to his thighs and was clearly panicking as he felt himself continuing to sink deeper. Az'an, meanwhile, was holding off the remaining three bandits with a grim smile on his face.

Torin had heard that the desert folk were swordsmen beyond compare, but seeing it in action was a different thing. Az'an seemed to be continuously moving, but every step, every strike, was the picture of economy. No wasted energy, just precision turned into art, turned into death. His curved swords were a blur, parrying blows and delivering cuts while never over-committing or giving up his position. The three men, confident in numbers, were pressing the action but couldn't land a blow. Even in the short time that Torin watched, small wounds appeared on the men's faces and hands as if by magic. Every time they attacked and Az'an parried, they paid for it, in small amounts, with blood.

One of the three exhausted men made a clumsy strike and Az'an ran him through. The other two stepped back nervously as their friend died on the ground in front of them. Az'an took the moment's reprieve to check on Torin. When he met Torin's gaze, he smiled and then pointed with the end of his sword towards the building from which Stoback was emerging. Torin gave him a nod and turned back to his attacker.

He needed to end this.

Torin charged Stoback. Stoback would have to respect the sheer size and speed of Torin and, being the seasoned fighter he was, would ready himself to take advantage of Torin's commitment.

One step outside of Stoback's range, Torin planted his foot and came to a dead stop. Torin didn't savour the brief look of surprise on Stoback's face as all of Torin's momentum seemed to stop on the blade of a knife. Instead, he threw out his hammer horizontally, his forearm flaring up in pain as it bore the full weight of his weapon at full extension. Not wanting to once again be thrown away from his opponent, Stoback sidestepped slightly and brought up his blade to block the blow. At the exact instant that Stoback's blade touched the head of his hammer, he spun it in his hand, as he had so often done before a battle, and locked the spikes on the end of his hammer in the guard of Stoback's sword.

Stoback's eyes widened, and he attempted to extricate his sword from the hammer. His instincts and talent were such that he almost succeeded before Torin was able to pull his hammer back and with it Stoback's weapon.

The sword flew through the air almost lazily, and Torin caught it with one hand.

Stoback's laughter ceased.

Behind him, Torin could hear two bodies hit the ground and spared a quick glance back to see Felix and Az'an approach. All that was left of the attackers were four dead bodies, and one hand sticking out of the now solid ground, opening and closing desperately.

"Great. Let's kill him," Az'an said, and took a step forward.

"No." Torin put a hand out to stop the man. "There is no honour in this," he said and walked slowly towards Stoback. "Here, take it." He offered the sword.

Stoback looked from Torin to the men behind him and then back to Torin again. Slowly, like a wolf cornered by hunters, he approached Torin, clearly expecting an attack.

"An honourable man," Stoback laughed derisively.

As Stoback reached for the sword, Torin let it go. Stoback moved to catch it and Torin, as slowly as he could, reached under the chain mail and grasped his wrist.

"Not so much," he said flatly.

The panic in Stoback's eyes was deeply satisfying as he realized that Torin, with all the strength that his Granite Ogre blood gave him, was inside the protection of his armour.

Torin squeezed his hand and heard a satisfying crack as Stoback's wrist gave way underneath it. The madman screamed and the smell of mothballs washed over Torin. He ignored it and slowly moved his other hand to take Stoback's throat. Instinct kicked in and Stoback pulled a dagger, slashing at Torin's stomach in one motion. The blade glanced off his granite-infused skin.

Stoback seemed to realize what had happened and went slack in Torin's grip, his knees almost buckling in an attempt to wrench himself free. Torin let him fall a little while maintaining his grip. His forearm was in too much pain to hold all the man's weight.

Too late, he realized his mistake. Stoback wasn't trying to fall out of Torin's grip. He was repositioning himself. He bent his knees and then blasted the top of his head square into Torin's nose. First, he felt his nose shatter, and then he heard the telltale sound of Stoback's enchanted armour. The next thing he knew, he was sent flying. His iron grip ripped from Stoback's wrist with the force of the magic.

Torin landed on his back. His vision swam with tears, but he could clearly hear Stoback's laughter again. He forced himself to his feet and looked for his hammer. Stoback was between him and the weapon.

Az'an stepped in front of Torin, blades drawn. Felix was attempting to mire Stoback in quicksand, but it was ineffective.

"Felix, please stop him," Az'an said evenly.

"Won't work. Enchanted armour," Torin said.

"Against magic?" Felix was confused.

"Yup," was all Torin had the energy for.

"Looks like it's just you and me, sand man," Stoback said, laughing. "Just like old times. You look like you still know what you're doing with those and my left hand is broken. You might have a chance."

Az'an raised his swords but gave no response.

"You'll have to disarm him, then penetrate the armour's field slowly," Torin offered.

"Yes, well, you see, I helped train him back when he was in Vees," Az'an said. "He surpassed me when he was twenty or so. I can buy some time, though. You need to get back to Ashea. I love you, Felix."

Torin took in the resigned sorrow on the Druid's face and realized that these men were committed to a cause that was bigger than the two of them. He wouldn't cheapen their final moments with attempts to dissuade Az'an from a course they both knew to be correct.

"I love you too," Felix responded.

They kissed quickly and passionately. Torin was reminded of his kiss with Ashea before he had left the capital.

Az'an walked towards Stoback with his blades at the ready. The madman's laughter intensified and then suddenly turned into a wet gurgle. His eyes went wide with shock and the three men shared confused glances as a large, bloody gash seemed to open itself up, very slowly, across Stoback's throat. He dropped his sword and clutched the wound, as if hoping he could catch all that blood and put it back like nothing happened.

As the body collapsed, two perfect squares of light appeared like two eyes in the night. The shape of a man appeared around them and seemed to step out from what little shadows were dancing in the torchlight that ringed the square.

Tall and lithe, the figure appeared to be completely black aside from two blue eyes looking back at them.

"Sorry I'm late," Thomaras said with a grim smile. "Took the long route."

38

THOMARAS

~

Thomaras didn't have time to enjoy the shocked looks on the faces of his friend. He pointed towards Erica. "Felix, can you help Erica?"

For a moment, it appeared as though Felix was going to ask for clarification, but one look at Thomaras's face sent him in Erica's direction without a word.

"Thought all we did was fuck your life up," Torin said. "Why not just grab her and go?"

"I couldn't let you face Stoback alone."

"Erica made you help, didn't she?"

Thomaras couldn't help but laugh. "Yes. But I almost definitely would have helped anyway. Probably."

Torin nodded and Thomaras could sense he was still hurt. Despite wanting to get back to Erica, he was surprised to find he needed to make things right with Torin.

"Look, I wasn't sure exactly what I was going to do when I left you in Aquilo. All I knew is that if I was going to do anything against Stoback, I'd have to do it without him seeing me."

"You couldn't share your plan?"

"Honestly? No. I kept getting the sense that people knew way more about what we were doing than they should. When I saw what Morley could do with his magic, I started to wonder just how many of those guards, retainers and servants that surrounded us Umbra could use to see into our world. I had to put on a bit of a show as I didn't know what kind of agents Umbra had at Its disposal." Torin's steady gaze didn't change. "And I guess I was considering sneaking in to save Erica and running away. Sorry, old habits die hard."

Torin's face finally broke into his customary smile as he closed the distance between them and wrapped Thomaras up in a giant hug.

"Okay, okay. That's just fine. I'm glad you forgive me," Thomaras said as he tried futilely to struggle out of Torin's embrace.

"You saved our lives. Very tricky," Torin said, finally putting him down.

"You did pretty well yourself with some underhanded tactics. If he hadn't hit you with that head butt, I think you had him," Thomaras said.

Torin just grinned sheepishly and waved the comment away. His smile dropped, and he glanced over towards Felix. "How bad is it?"

"Looked bad," was all Thomaras could manage.

The two shared a look before rushing over to Felix. The Druid was bent over Erica, who appeared to be unconscious. He glanced over his shoulder when he heard them approach, but went back to work immediately.

"Her face looks bad, but it's all superficial. Stoback was

making a show of it. However, she is hurt badly; I just need to find the cause." Felix's voice was detached as he worked. A sharp intake of breath made Felix hiss through his teeth and he immediately looked up at Thomaras apologetically. "I'm sorry... it's just... it's bad." He wasted no time getting back to work.

Now that the blood was wiped away, Thomaras could see three jagged cuts in Erica's midsection. He went very cold. Felix produced a handful of long grass from one of the pouches in his robe. Thomaras recognized them from when Ashea had been poisoned, and he allowed himself some cautious relief.

Having found the worst of the injuries, Felix quickly began to feed a long piece of grass into each cut. Once the first few inches of grass was in each wound, he closed his eyes and the grass began to glow an emerald green. Felix raised his hands, and the grass began to work its way inside of Erica. Thomaras was worried it would hurt her, but a few moments later her short, ragged breaths became longer and slower. Her brow, previously knotted in pain, seemed to relax and it looked as though she had fallen into a more peaceful slumber.

Felix continued to work for a few minutes longer, and then he sagged and let out a long sigh.

"I've stabilized her for now, but she is bleeding more inside her body than out. A number of her vital organs have been punctured. From what I can tell, Stoback knew exactly what he was doing to make sure her death was as prolonged as possible. If I were to guess, he was planning on making you watch her die once he defeated you," Felix said, eyes hooded with sadness. "I've made her comfortable, but I can't save her."

"The mage of light?" Thomaras asked hopefully.

"I don't know if Erica will make it there. Even if she did... I don't think so," Felix said.

"I have to try. Torin, find me a carriage or a cart," Thomaras said.

Torin nodded and stood up, but Az'an raised a hand to forestall him. "There is much at stake here. I don't mean to be insensitive, but I think we need to discuss our next moves as a group."

"We're not a group," Thomaras snapped. "Torin and I have a friend to save. I'm not even sure what side you're on."

"Ah, I imagine our mutual friend Dafoe has been spreading tales about us?" Felix asked.

"He said you were working for some giant spider thing and that you were all under the influence of Umbra. Judging by Stoback's attempts to kill you, I'm guessing that wasn't true, but..."

"Half true," a silken voice said from the shadows.

Thomaras took an involuntary step backwards as the largest spider he'd ever seen emerged from a darkened alley between two buildings.

Torin readied his hammer and Thomaras cursed himself for leaving his bow stashed away in the woods.

"No need to fear, my friends. She's on our side," Felix said.

"He speaks the truth, though I understand it may be hard to believe me over what Dafoe has already told you," the spider said. "I know he is charismatic and charming; neither are my strongest traits."

Thomaras was having a hard time reconciling the beautiful voice that emerged from the mandibles sitting beneath eight disturbing, albeit intelligent, eyes. He had to agree that Dafoe was a little easier to look at.

"At this point, the only people on my side are the ones helping me save Erica."

"Thomaras, the chances are slim," Felix said gently. "I don't even know if she'd survive being lifted onto a cart."

"I have to try!"

"I'm afraid we don't have the luxury of time," the spider said. "Dafoe is acting out Umbra's plan as we speak, and we will need all of your help to stop it."

"She needs my help. You can go deal with Umbra yourself, spider," Thomaras fired back.

"You may call me Orb Weaver and you will address with more respect, mortal." The Orb Weaver seemed to expand slightly in size and Thomaras became pointedly aware of her giant mandibles and the razor-sharp claws that adorned each of her eight legs. Still, he held his ground.

"I can't lose her. We can't just let her die," he said, more gently this time. "Why do you need us, anyway? What do we have to do with this grand plan?"

"You and Torin seem to be somehow masked from the reflections of the prism. You disrupted my plans because I didn't know you existed. I had thought it was Umbra's doing, but judging by events here, I'm assuming you are equally hidden from Umbra and Dafoe. That makes you two very dangerous tools in this battle."

Thomaras had heard enough. "I won't be used as a means to an end for anyone. Especially if it means sacrificing someone I care about."

"I think you should hear her out," Erica said in a weak voice.

"Erica! Hold on, we're going to help you," Thomaras said, ignoring her words.

"I'm not sure you can. If what Felix says is true, I likely

won't make it to anyone who can help. Just hear her out," Erica pleaded, her eyes still closed.

"Fine. But then we take you to get help," Thomaras said.

"I will make this quick," the Orb Weaver said. "I have finally understood the weave that the prism is trying to show me. Dafoe sees himself as the hero of this plane of existence, but he is young and foolish. Umbra's abilities in reflection rival my own and far surpass that of Dafoe. Umbra has manipulated what Dafoe sees and shown him a path that will only hasten Umbra's breaking into our plane. Dafoe believes that his mage of enchantments has created an item, an amulet, that will allow Dafoe to siphon Ashea's powers and give Dafoe the ability to control multiple forms of magic. He believes he will then be able to defeat Umbra. In truth, Umbra has shown Dafoe each step of this plan with false reflections of the prism. If Dafoe attempts this transfer, he will allow Umbra to slip into this plane unhindered. If that happens, Umbra will be unstoppable."

The Orb Weaver finished speaking, and a heavy silence fell over the group. Thomaras looked at Torin and then they both looked at Erica, now lying with her head on Thomaras's lap. Her eyes fluttered open.

"Shut up," she said as Thomaras was about to speak. "You have to go. If not to save the world, then to save Ashea. My chances of living through this are slim, but you can still save her. Don't throw away her life just for me to die anyway. I won't allow it."

Thomaras didn't fight the tears welling up in his eyes. He wanted to argue with her. Convince her that she was being silly, that he could save her and Ashea, too. He'd find a cart or find a horse... hell, he'd carry her if he had to. But he knew all of those arguments were false. Simple manifestations of the love he had for Erica.

"Why do you always have to be right?" he asked instead. Tears clouded his vision as he looked down at her beautiful smile. She even managed a small laugh.

"Can't help it. Someone has to tell you what to do," she replied.

The tears were flowing freely now as he bent down and kissed her dry, swollen lips.

"Come on, let's give them some space," Thomaras heard Torin say and then a giant hand fell briefly on Thomaras's shoulder.

The Granite Ogre reached down and took Erica's hand in his. Thomaras helped her up into Torin's embrace and the two shared a brief, whispered conversation, the contents of which belonged to them alone. When they broke their embrace, Torin kissed Erica gently on the forehead and Thomaras could see tears streaming down the ogre's cheek. As Torin walked away, grieving for his friend, Thomaras was hammered with guilt.

"I'm so sorry," Thomaras said as he held Erica.

"For what?"

"For coming into your life. I never deserved you. You could have met a normal person whose life wasn't full of risk and danger. I've kept people away from me for my whole life for a reason. Now, here I am, endangering the one person who's ever been worth a damn. Selfish. Fucking selfish."

"Stop that," Erica said firmly. "Stop acting like I had no choice in the matter. I knew what you were. I didn't know everything, but I know a dangerous man when I see one. I also know a beautiful and gentle soul when it's hidden beneath that danger. Selfish? Selfish would have been denying me everything we had together. Selfish would be pretending that our love is something I would have been better without. If I could go back a thousand times, I wouldn't change a thing."

As she spoke, Erica's words became softer and softer. He felt her life fading from her and tried to hold her even tighter. As if his grip on her body could keep her from leaving him. Even for just a little longer.

"I love you," he whispered.

"I love you too. Say it again."

"I love you," he said and looked into her eyes one last time before they closed forever.

Thomaras's world fell into a haze of tears and grief.

39

TORIN

~

Torin stood a little apart from Felix and Az'an and allowed himself to weep for his friend. He had known Erica for as long as he'd been living amongst the humans, and she'd always been kind to him. She might have been the first to be kind to him, actually. Torin couldn't help but feel the world dim a little as he watched Erica's unique light slowly extinguish.

He suspected it was a light the world would never fully recover.

Torin's grief surged as he saw Thomaras dissolve into tears and racking sobs and he knew his friend was gone for good. Once he had collected himself, he moved to comfort Thomaras but was stopped by Az'an.

"You have your own grief, and it's one the two of you can share, but for now permit me to speak to him?"

Torin nodded and watched the Nomad approach Thomaras. Torin was poised to step in if Thomaras lashed out, but whatever bond the two men had forged in the

Darkwoods seemed to hold and before long, Thomaras was embracing the shorter man. The two men then walked back together and Thomaras seemed to be, at least, in control of himself.

"I can't believe he found her. Or Rolph," Torin said.

"Umbra sees more than we assumed," Thomaras said.

"So how did you sneak up on Stoback?" Torin asked in response.

"I made my way through the backcountry until I was certain that a few of those black puppet animals saw me. That part was easy. I made camp under the watchful gaze of the creepiest squirrel of all time and waited for nightfall. I pretended to fall asleep and then slipped out of camp. I had to double back a few times to avoid Umbra's animals, but once I found a small creek, I was able to get some mud on me and the going got easier. A few times I thought I was caught, but then some predator would take out Umbra's minion. Lucky, I guess. After that, it was just a matter of waiting for an opening where I could get close enough to kill the asshole." Thomaras punctuated the story by pointing over his shoulder at Stoback's corpse with his thumb.

"It was not luck but my intervention that aided you," the Orb Weaver said, breaking into their conversation.

"What do you mean?"

"Since the two of you have been blocked from my weavings, the only way that I've been able to track you is through the last of my brood." As the Orb Weaver said this, a smaller spider appeared out of the shadows and walked beside her. Thomaras noticed that it only had seven legs. The eighth ended where one of Thomaras's arrows had taken it off the body of the spider in this very town.

"I have been watching through his eyes as he tracked

you," the Orb Weaver explained. "I didn't allow him to follow you too deep into Aquilo for fear of him being discovered by Dafoe's forces. Once you two split up, I had him follow Thomaras since I knew where Torin was headed. He is the one that took out Umbra's vassals who searched for you."

"Uh, well thanks, then. And I suppose I owe you an apology for the leg," Thomaras said awkwardly to the spider.

The spider, to Thomaras's surprise, bowed in supplication and then seemed to wave away Thomaras's concerns with one of its good legs.

"He bears you no ill will. We were mistaken in attacking you and you were merely defending yourselves. None of us had all the information, but we do now and we can't dally."

"Not sure if you saw what happened here, but I'm very much in need of a drink," Thomaras said and turned towards The Jilted Maiden.

"Please, there is no time," the Weaver snapped. "Torin, Ashea may be in danger. You have to come."

"With all due respect," Torin rumbled, "we'll decide what we have to do."

Torin walked away without waiting for a response. He was, of course, worried about Ashea, but he wasn't going to leave Thomaras here if he could help it.

Along the way, they ran into Earnest and Thomaras broke the bad news. Torin asked the man if he could make arrangements for Erica and Rolph's bodies. Then, he followed Thomaras into the empty common room. Torin, familiar with the establishment, walked behind the bar and helped himself to a bottle of Bard's Tears that Thomaras was so fond of. He poured two glasses and then sat down beside his friend.

"To Erica," Thomaras said and raised a glass.

Torin clinked his own against his friend's without a word and the two finished their first drink in one swallow. Torin poured two more glasses, but they sipped that round in silence.

"I killed him." Thomaras finally broke the silence.

"Yep."

"I don't feel better."

"No."

"He killed her. So I killed him. But I don't feel better." Thomaras's words were quiet and even, but he threw his glass against the back wall of the bar. "Maybe if I kill Umbra."

Torin kept his silence.

"I know what you're going to say. I should let it go. Revenge isn't good for you. Blah. Blah. Blah."

"No, I say we kill It."

"Really?"

"Yep."

"Can we?"

"I don't know, but I think Ashea can. The spider seems to think she's important. Will you help me help her?" Torin asked his friend.

Thomaras looked down at the bar in silence for a while and then took a pull directly from the bottle of whisky. A few times he looked like he was about to speak but instead would take another drink. Whatever was happening with Ashea, Torin was certain time was of the essence. As patient as he was, it still took every ounce of discipline for Torin to hold his tongue while every fibre of his being screamed at him to run to Ashea.

Still, he stayed quiet.

Thomaras spent his life weaving a set of rules around

himself so tightly that it kept any human connection out. Now that one of the few people he had let in was gone, the weave was unraveling, and it threatened to take Thomaras apart with it.

Finally, Thomaras turned his head and looked at him through red, swollen eyes.

"If I had any sense, I'd take off right now. Leave all of this behind. Have you ever been to Zozo?"

"Nope."

"It's smack dab in the middle of the salt marshes. A lawless town run by a brutal cutthroat. Do you have any idea how much fun a man like me can have there?"

"Nope."

"More than I can explain. And I'm well liked there, in the right circles, of course. I could disappear there and be happy until the world ends or you fools save it."

Thomaras's forced smile was so sickly and broken that Torin felt tears prickling his eyes once more. "But?"

"But... after Erica... you know I've never cared for someone..." Thomaras looked at Torin and took a breath. "I'm on a precipice, Torin. The footing is precarious and if I fall off, I don't know that I can get back up. You and Ashea... you make me so much better than I am on my own, but so did Erica. And if I lose either of you two like I lost her..." Thomaras trailed off.

"You won't. I promise," Torin said.

"But what if I do?"

Torin shrugged. "You're asking the wrong question."

"What's the right one?" Thomaras asked, hope brimming along with the tears in his eyes.

"Erica saw you in a way that you could never see yourself. What would that man do?"

For the second time that night, and for all Torin knew

the second time in his entire life, Thomaras broke down into uncontrollable tears. This time, though, Torin held him and shared his grief with the tall, enigmatic man. Together they wept for the light that was taken from the world this day and somehow, when they were both done, that dimness seemed to recede just a little.

Without another word, the two men stood up and headed for the door. Thomaras turned back and gave a grim nod.

Torin considered all the mages and eternal beings that had filled his life recently and decided that Thomaras could be the most dangerous thing on Haven right now.

And no one could even see him coming.

40

ASHEA

∿

L uness led Ashea away from Dafoe and into a corner of Thorn's workshop that contain a few plush chairs and a sofa. The mage lowered herself into a chair and gestured for Ashea to do the same. Ashea leaned back on the sofa and sighed as the sheer pace of events over the past few weeks seemed to catch up to her.

"So, are you going to jump into my brain and dig up my memories?" Ashea asked.

"No, that's beyond my ability, but even if it was something I could do, I don't think it's the best way to help you."

"What is?"

"We're just going to talk, Ashea. I get the sense that there is much you don't share. I wouldn't normally rush something like this, but as you know, time is short."

"Okay," Ashea said, steeling herself, "ask away."

"Take a moment, child. You must be weary."

Ashea chuckled a little at the understatement. "I've

spent my life on the move, but I don't think I've ever been this tired."

"Umbra has always pursued you?"

"It's hard to say. When I was young, I was always moving from place to place. It wasn't until I found a real family and stayed in one place for a few years that I remember the dreams starting."

"And your magic? When did you first start using that?"

"I don't really remember. It seems like it was always there in a small way. I could conjure a spark or a small gust of wind, but that's all."

Luness nodded. "That's typically how most mages first manifest their magic. Do you remember the first time you did something of any consequence?"

Ashea thought for a moment. "I guess it was when one of Umbra's puppet animals attacked Thomaras and me. It was charging Thomaras and he wasn't going to be able to get out of the way in time. I didn't really think about it. I just raised my arm and a cube of fire appeared."

"And then your fight with Stoback? The one I felt?"

"No, there was another time before I left Hannover. Torin was going to go charging into a stable full of giant spiders to get his hammer, so I used air to bring it to him instead."

Luness nodded again, as if her suspicions were confirmed. "It seems whatever is preventing you from using your magic doesn't stop you when you are using your magic to aid others. What we need to do now is try to discover the event that's keeping you from using your magic in service of yourself."

Ashea sat in dumfounded silence. All her life, she had been a survivor. Someone that was willing to do whatever it took to stay alive and stay safe. She couldn't believe that all this time she could have had magic at her beck and call to protect herself, and something inside her kept her from using it. "No, that can't be right. I've always done anything necessary to survive."

"What do you mean, anything?"

"I lied and stole. I framed foster parents for crimes in order to get rid of them. Eventually, I fled the entire system and travelled from Granniston all the way to the salt marshes by myself!"

"That final foster family. How did you escape?"

"I... ran away one night."

"Just slipped out in the night?"

"No... he kept the door locked."

"Who did?"

"My foster father. They warned him that I was a runner so he kept me locked in. I was there for longer than any other place."

"How old were you when you left?"

Ashea struggled through the memories. They were there, but she didn't want to see them. "Maybe ten? Eleven?"

Luness's expression looked pained as she pressed Ashea. "What happened?"

"He tried to... he broke into my room. Drunk. I didn't really know what was going to happen, but I knew enough. I... hurt him. With my magic. I hurt him badly."

"Badly enough that he wouldn't survive?"

"Badly enough that his wife could finish the job," Ashea said, and burst into tears.

Luness was beside Ashea with her arms wrapped around her in an instant. Ashea leaned into the mage and sobbed so long that she lost track of time.

Eventually, she got control of herself. "I've never told

anyone about that. I almost think I forgot that it happened. He was going to…"

"Shhh, child. We both know his intentions. Just as we both know that what you did was the right thing. The problem is that it was something no child should have to do. Likely, your mind has tried to protect you by burying the memory. Unfortunately, by burying that memory, it also covered up the path your mind needs to take to call upon your magic. It appears that it compensated at times when others were in grave danger but didn't break down the wall entirely."

"So, how do I break down that wall?"

Luness smiled. "I suspect you are close now. Come."

Luness led her back to the testing range, but this time she set up one of the wooden dummies against the wall. "Now, you said you used a fire cube to save Thomaras? Do it again, this time for yourself. Imagine this dummy as someone trying to hurt you."

Ashea nodded and raised her arm. She pictured the cube perfectly, a flaming version of the blocks she played with when she was too young to be scared of the things that plagued her life. She suffused the image with her will and reached into the well where she could feel her magic pooled.

Again, she slid off an invisible wall.

"Picture the danger, Ashea. Picture someone trying to hurt you."

Ashea tried with all her mental force to break the wall. To feel the danger. Nothing worked. Sweat beaded on her forehead with the effort.

"Picture him, Ashea. Picture the man who wanted to hurt you for his own pleasure. Who wanted to take every ounce of your innocence on his terms. Remember your strength, Ashea. You didn't let him take it. You gave up your innocence on your terms. Gave it up so he wouldn't ever hurt anyone again."

The mage's words were low and even, but they seemed to roar inside Ashea's mind.

Her innocence.

Her terms.

Ashea screamed in rage and a cube of fire burst forth and struck the dummy with such force that the splinters of wood and straw struck the opposite wall of the workshop. The enchanted wall glowed a bright red as it absorbed the heat.

"Very good," Luness said. "How do you feel?"

Ashea smiled. "Powerful."

41

FELIX

～

The remainder of the night was both tragic and surreal to Felix. For years, he had been working with the Orb Weaver to try to prevent what was coming about. His connection to the forest kept him from all but the most important meetings of the mages council and that distance had insulated him from Dafoe's influence. Even so, it had taken the Orb Weaver some time to convince him that Dafoe could be compromised. The man's power and charisma were hard to deny. Seeing everything they had feared coming to a head here and now was difficult to wrap his mind around.

Thomaras was taking his loss hard. They had all given him space to say his final goodbyes, and after the woman died in his arms, he had broken down uncontrollably. Felix suspected that he had spent so many years creating a distance from anyone that losing what he had finally allowed into his heart was something he wasn't equipped to handle.

Surprisingly, it had been Az'an, his quiet, measured husband of all people, who had finally gone to the young man and offered comfort. Felix wasn't sure what Az'an had said, but Thomaras slowly began to calm down and was finally able to get control of himself. When Az'an returned to Felix, he simply smiled, and Felix knew not to ask what had transpired between the two. Felix thought that Az'an had never looked more handsome than he did in that moment.

After the Orb Weaver had tried to win Thomaras and Torin to their cause, the two friends disappeared into The Jilted Maiden. He watched as the innkeeper set about making arrangements for Erica's body.

Stoback's body was of greater concern to Felix.

The spiders had made themselves scarce once the crowd started to grow, but before they went, Felix had convinced the Weaver to give them a few hours to get themselves settled before they headed out of town. The Orb Weaver had agreed to meet them at Thomaras's camp up the road. Before she left, she made it clear she felt it was best that the enchanted items be destroyed. Felix didn't think anyone would be too keen on trying to use the filthy gear, but he agreed and assured her it would be done.

He and Az'an stripped the stinking body of the armour and sword. Felix noticed that the eyes, open and dead to the world, were now completely black. Tendrils of the same matte black colouring seen on the puppet animals had begun to reach out from them and colour the madman's face. Shuddering, Felix ordered a handful of the townsfolk to take the body into the scrublands and bury it.

Deep.

Az'an got his hands on a large burlap sack to put the chain mail in, and the two of them made their way out of town. As they moved farther into nature, Felix felt his magic begin to grow again. Even a small town like Hannover was a drain on his powers. Once they were far enough, Felix focused his magic, and the earth began to give way into a hole. He continued to dig out the earth until he hit bedrock. Once there, he opened up the bedrock, and Az'an tossed all of Stoback's gear into the hole. Felix then placed the rock on top of the items. Because of the resistance to magic, the bedrock did not immediately crush the armour and sword and Felix could sense the bubble of magic protecting it. Felix then sealed the earth back on top and the moment that he removed his will from the earth, he could sense that bubble begin to buckle. Over time, with his own magic removed, the natural pressure of the earth would crush the cursed items. Until then, it would take a tremendous effort to dig them out, if someone even knew where to look.

"How long until they are destroyed?" Az'an asked.

"Not soon enough," Felix answered glibly, and then added, "Within the year they'll be crushed into nothing."

Now, Felix stood in front of The Jilted Maiden Inn, arm wrapped around his husband's slim, taut waist, and waited for Torin and Thomaras to join them.

"I thought we were saying our final goodbyes back there," Az'an said.

His voice interrupted Felix's thoughts of the evening and brought him back to reality. "Yes, you got my hopes up. I was looking forward to having the house to myself," Felix joked.

Az'an smiled at him and they kissed deeply.

"I'll have to thank Thomaras. I wasn't ready to lose you," Felix said, all joking aside.

Before Az'an could respond, the men he'd sent to bury Stoback's body approached them. They looked scared.

"Sir, I'm sorry, sir... we... I don't know what happened,"

one of the men said. He had clearly been nominated by his peers to do the talking and wasn't happy about it. He was wringing his hat and looking at his feet.

"You can call me Felix. Now, what happened?" Felix asked gently.

He was hoping to put the man at ease, but it didn't seem to work. Only then did Felix realize that the man wasn't scared of upsetting a mage.

He was scared of whatever he had seen.

"We took the body out of town, like you said. We started to dig and then we heard something in the darkness. We figured it was wolves or the like, come for the body, so we took the torches to try to scare them off."

"Okay," Felix said, gesturing for the man to continue.

"Well, there were some wolves, but also deer and a boar... only they were all... black and they... they smelled like clothes that had been left in a closet too long," the man continued sheepishly.

"Like mothballs," Felix said.

"That's right! Mothballs. Anyway, we tried to scare them off, but they didn't act like normal animals. They didn't even move right. So we backed away, and they went straight to the body. One of the wolves grabbed it and started to drag it away. We didn't know what to do, so we just let it happen. We thought about fighting them off, but they weren't right, Felix. Something about them wasn't right." The man had panic in his voice now, and Felix raised his hands to calm him down.

"It's okay, you did the right thing. Those things would have been hard to kill. Why don't all of you head home?" Felix suggested.

The men all nodded and rushed off. Felix cursed himself. He should have seen to the body himself, burned it or something. He was so worried about the enchanted gear falling into the wrong hands that he never considered what Umbra might do with the body.

Sensing his thoughts, Az'an laid a hand on his shoulder. "Nothing you can do now. We'll tell the spider what happened and go from there."

Felix nodded, but before he could answer, Torin and Thomaras emerged from The Jilted Maiden.

"If we walk through the night, we should get there by dawn. Torin and I don't need much sleep, but are you gentlemen going to be okay?" Thomaras asked.

"We're well rested. Long journeys are standard fare for us," Az'an responded.

His husband was right; they were used to long travel, often on little sleep. Felix would have loved a good night's rest before going into another fight, but he would be fine.

"Sounds good," Thomaras said curtly.

Felix needed only one look at the resolve in the young man's face to know he would be okay after losing one so dear. They set a brisk pace, and not for the first time, Felix was glad of his ability to draw energy from the elements of nature around him. Once they were out of Hannover and walking through the country, he was able to do so even more efficiently. The group elected to move off the main road and take a more direct path to Vees, one that would take them to the camp to meet the spider and that bypassed the Crossroads altogether. Torin and Thomaras seemed to have no problem seeing in the dark, and Felix could feel every inch of the surrounding land. He couldn't see with his eyes, but he simply allowed nature to show him the way.

After about an hour, Thomaras seemed to notice something was going on and he turned around, stopping so abruptly that Felix had to grab Az'an lest he bump into Thomaras in the dark.

"We've been walking for an hour straight, and I feel more rested than when we left. What's going on?" Thomaras asked suspiciously.

"I am able to draw on the energy of nature and replenish my strength, as well as that of anyone close to me. It will only work to a certain point. Bodies need sleep no matter what, and I have to do it slowly or the effort it takes for me to draw out the energy becomes more than the energy I'm putting back in," Felix explained.

Thomaras nodded, accepting the explanation and the help.

Shortly after their brief pause, they met the Orb Weaver at Thomaras's camp. Thomaras acknowledged her with a nod and then went about collecting his things. Once he'd put an assortment of stashed items into the numerous pockets in his cloak, he sat down and began stringing his bow and checking his arrows.

The Orb Weaver watched him briefly and then made her way over to Felix. "I know you're worried about him, but I don't think he'll abandon this cause. I cannot see him in my weavings, but I have watched your kind long enough to know that he has given up too much not to see his sacrifice through to the end."

"True enough. I just worry that his emotions might get the best of him," Felix replied.

"He seems the calculating sort. Professional and detached. Besides, his heritage makes him powerful, even more so than he knows."

"A little Arahana blood has never made much difference in my experience," Felix said dismissively.

The signs were clear for any to see that Thomaras had

some of the ancient blood in him. His eyes, in particular, were that of the legendary people that once ruled Haven. Thomaras probably had more of those features than anyone he had ever seen, though he clearly took steps to hide them. But Felix wasn't prepared to get worked up over a little Arahana ancestry.

"More than a little, Druid. He is as much Arahana as Torin is a Granite Ogre."

Felix detected some satisfaction in the spider's tone. She really did enjoy knowing what others did not. "Being smug is not an attractive colour on an eternal being, you know," Felix said, mostly to hide his shock. "How could he be half? There aren't any Arahana left."

"I am not at liberty to share all that I know, Druid, but believe me when I tell you that one of his parents was a full-blooded Arahana."

Before Felix could react, Thomaras was up and ready to go. He should have looked ridiculous, covered in mud as he was, but Felix was looking at him with a new perspective. He considered the way Thomaras had been able to move through the flickering torchlight and get behind Stoback without any of those assembled seeing him. Even after he killed Stoback, Felix wasn't sure he'd really seen Thomaras until he stepped out of the shadows. Thomaras was obviously skilled in moving around without being seen, but he had been in a ring of torches. The shadows were far too small to conceal anyone, no matter how practiced they might be.

"Magic?" Felix whispered the word.

"It comes in all forms, Druid. Think on it." The Orb Weaver's silken voice was laced with satisfaction, but Felix was too wrapped up in possibilities to be annoyed. As she left his side, Az'an approached.

"What's on your mind?" Az'an asked.

"I'll tell you as we walk... I think Thomaras may be more dangerous than we first thought," Felix replied.

His husband simply nodded. Felix filled him in as they walked towards his old family, ready to do battle.

42

ASHEA

~

Before Ashea could say anything, Dafoe crossed the room and wrapped her up in a brotherly hug.

"Yes!" he exclaimed loudly. "I knew you could do it!"

It wasn't hard to get caught up in the mage's enthusiasm. Ashea had been trying to understand the fickle nature of her magic for her entire life, and it took these mages less than an afternoon to unlock the problem. She finally felt whole.

"Easy Dafoe, you're going to break her," Luness said lightly.

"Right, right. Sorry." Dafoe let her go and stepped back, still beaming. "Are you ready to learn how to keep Umbra out of your head?"

"Yes!" Ashea said with a grin.

"Are you sure she shouldn't rest a little first? She's overcome much in a short period," Luness said.

"Time is of the essence, I'm afraid. It took longer than

expected to get you here, Ashea. But if you need rest, we can, of course, take some time."

"No, I'm ready," Ashea blurted. She was tired, but the idea of being able to protect herself was too tempting to wait. Besides which, she didn't want to let Dafoe down.

His smile of approval warmed her. "Very good. Then let's begin."

Ashea had been so wrapped up in her training, she hadn't noticed that Thorn and Mary had joined them once more. Mary was holding a familiar bottle in her hand, and Thorn had two matching amulets.

"What are those?" Luness asked.

"I had Thorn create a focus item for Ashea and a matching one for myself so that I could guide her without having to enter the dream realm," Dafoe explained.

Ashea nodded, but noticed that Luness's face had taken on a very neutral expression.

"Thorn?" she asked.

The burly mage smiled and nodded encouragingly, but remained silent. Luness raised an eyebrow before turning to Ashea. "If you need time to rest, it's okay to say so."

"I'm fine," Ashea said before anyone else could chime in. She needed these mages, her peers, to know she could handle her business.

"See? She's fine. You can see how strong she is, Luness."

Luness seemed poised to make another objection, but after a moment's consideration gave a curt nod instead. In that moment, she appeared to Ashea like a dutiful soldier following orders.

"Thank you, Luness," Ashea said. "I wouldn't be here without you."

"You're welcome, child," Luness said and the term that

made her bristle before made her feel more connected than ever to the implacable mage.

"What do you need from me?" Luness asked Dafoe.

A strange looked passed over Dafoe's face. "It seems you will have a few moments' rest after all. An event that affects the reflections of the prism has occurred. I need to read them."

With that, Dafoe turned and walked to the corner of the room where he sat down cross-legged and closed his eyes. Ashea looked at the other mages. "How long does this usually take?"

Mary shrugged. "Depends. On what, I don't know, but sometimes it's minutes and sometimes it's days. I wouldn't imagine he'll be keeping you too long, though."

"Is he in a hurry?" Luness asked.

Mary's face remained casual. "Seems like it. You're his favourite. If he hasn't told you his plan, what makes you think he'd tell me?"

Luness said nothing, but Ashea could tell something was bothering her. Before she could press the mage on the subject, Dafoe stood up and returned to them.

"Luness, collect Johnson and his unit and wait at the gates. I'm afraid we can expect some company," Dafoe said, and then turned to Ashea. "You'll be happy to know that Thomaras and Torin were successful in stopping Stoback. Your friends are safe. Unfortunately, they are being given some bad intelligence and they are on their way here to do something rash."

"What's that?" Ashea asked.

"Save you."

"Save me? They believe the Orb Weaver now?"

"I'm afraid so. I don't know what happened, but they've been swayed to her side."

Ashea was silent. The certainty she felt moments ago seemed shaky.

"I understand this makes your decision difficult, but you have to trust me. She's an eternal being and so sure of her abilities that she can't even fathom they could be manipulated. She knows the danger Umbra poses to this realm but underestimates Its danger to her."

"What will you do to them?"

"I won't hurt them, Ashea, I promise. Not if I can avoid it. Luness and our forces will do their best to take them in without any deaths. We'll keep them in a cell until you're ready to help stop Umbra, and then we can show them the truth of the situation."

Ashea found it hard to believe that Torin and Thomaras could be manipulated like that, but Dafoe could have kept that information to himself. At every turn, he had allowed her to make her own choices and been open with the events surrounding those choices. It would have been easy for him to just tell her that her friends were on their way to help.

Instead, he told the truth.

"Okay," Ashea said.

Dafoe nodded and then turned to Luness. "Please, Luness. As peacefully as possible.

The mage of elements looked at Ashea for a moment before answering Dafoe. "You're just teaching her how to keep Umbra out of her mind, right? When it comes to fighting that monster, I'll be here?"

"Of course. We won't be able to stop It without you."

Luness nodded and gave one last look at Ashea before striding purposefully out of the room.

"Thank you, Ashea. I'm sure it's not easy to trust me," Dafoe said and hugged her warmly.

Ashea never had a brother, but she imagined if she did, this hug would remind her of him.

When he broke the embrace, Dafoe led her back over to the table she had lain on the last time she had attempted to learn how to use her powers of reflection. She shuddered involuntarily.

"It's okay, you're ready now and I'll still be here. These amulets should make it even easier for me to guide you."

"Why didn't we use them last time?" Ashea asked.

"I needed to assess your abilities on their own. These amulets will allow us to share our powers, but without having learned what your own power feels like, they would make my influence almost indistinguishable from your own. The amulets should be an aid, not a crutch."

Ashea nodded and accepted the potion that Mary handed her. She pulled the stopper and sniffed the contents. "Blueberry this time?"

"It's a new flavour. You'll have to let me know what you think," Mary said with a grandmotherly smile.

Ashea smiled back and quaffed the contents of the glass bottle. Before she could report on the flavour, sleep was taking her, and she lay back on the table gently. The last thing she saw was Dafoe smiling down at her.

The light must have changed as she drifted off, because just before her eyes fully closed, the smile seemed almost predatory.

43

THOMARAS

~

Thomaras knew that he was barely holding himself together. He didn't know that losing someone could feel like this. When his father died, he'd been more relieved than anything and since then he'd never been close enough to anyone to warrant any kind of emotions when they were gone. Az'an's kind words had helped him. He was a soldier and accustomed to loss. Felix had not been his first love and his past was more painful than Thomaras could have imagined.

Torin's large, seemingly unshakable presence helped as well. Part of him recoiled from the idea of continuing a friendship with the ogre lest he lose him, too, but there was another part, a much larger part, that was inextricably joined with Torin. He had been friends with Erica long before Thomaras had met her. They would forever be connected in their loss.

"We were told we'd find you here," a voice said from the darkness of the woods.

They had left his makeshift camp about an hour ago and had been traveling through one of the thin forests that dotted the scrublands. Umbra must have somehow told these men where to lay an ambush.

Had Thomaras been paying more attention, he would have seen them easily. Twenty men, all armed, and they looked pissed.

"Did you think you could kill our men and our leader with no repercussions? Didn't you realize who you were dealing with?" the voice asked smugly.

"No, and frankly I don't care," Thomaras responded.

Suddenly, the darkness faded away, and the forest lit up as what seemed like every firefly in the woods descended upon them at once. The bandits looked around in surprise; they had thought the dark would be their ally. Thomaras's eyes adjusted quickly and he noticed that both Az'an and the spiders were missing from the group.

Thomaras didn't waste any more time as he began picking off targets with his bow. Three men fell before the rest even realized what was happening. When they finally put it together, the closest men rushed Thomaras, only to find Torin between them and their prey.

As his hammer spun, men screamed and died. Their leader stepped back, strategically looking over his shoulder to see where his remaining allies were. He stopped his retreat as he watched Az'an dance in and out of six of his men. They swung clumsily at the air as Az'an cut them down one at a time.

Realizing he was soon to be the last of his men, the previously smug bandit picked another direction and took off sprinting, only to stop so abruptly he fell on his ass.

"Unlucky for you, human, I have decided that the time for machinations behind the veil is over. I'm going to be taking a more direct hand from now on." The Orb Weaver's silken voice was ever at odds with her intimidating visage.

"Um..." was all the man could manage as the telltale smell of urine filled the air.

"She means you're fucked," Thomaras offered in explanation.

"Indeed, though I would never have been able to put it so eloquently," offered the spider. "Now you said you were told we were here. By whom?"

The man looked up into the spider's eyes for a moment and immediately spilled his guts. "A voice in my head told me. It sounded like granite scraping against granite and it told me where you were and that we should kill you since you killed our men. Well, they killed them. You weren't there... I didn't know you were here... I didn't know..." The man's babbling turned into sobs.

"It seems Umbra knows that Stoback failed. We should move quickly and be on our guard. I don't know that he'll tell Dafoe, however. Such an overt act might tip the mage off that Umbra has been influencing the reflections," the Orb Weaver said.

"What about him?" Thomaras asked, knife already drawn.

"We can leave him, I think. You'll be a good boy from now on, won't you? You'll try to help people instead of killing them?" the spider asked the sobbing man.

"Yes mistress! Yes, I promise!" he almost screamed.

"Good, good. Off you go, then," the Orb Weaver commanded.

The man immediately got up and sprinted off in the direction to which the spider had randomly gestured.

"How...?" Torin asked.

"Most mortals don't do so well when looking into the

focused gaze of an eternal being. Your brains... break. He'll be good from now on," the Orb Weaver said dismissively.

"Good. Let's go."

He cared little about what happened to the bandit. He needed to get to Ashea in time. If he didn't, then... he didn't want to think about it.

The rest of the trip passed without much trouble and before long, their small party was hidden behind a hill overlooking the gates to the capital.

"So, if Dafoe is working with Umbra and he sent us away to battle Stoback, is it safe to assume that he wants us dead?" Thomaras asked the Orb Weaver.

"It is difficult to say what his intentions are. The man is arrogant and certain in his mastery of reflection. If you are shielded from him the way you are from me, then he likely can't plan for what your actions might be. I think it is more likely that he believed your role was to stop Stoback than that he sent you to your death. Umbra, on the other hand, was probably pulling strings in such a way as to move you off of the board," the spider explained.

"So, you have no idea?" Thomaras asked.

"Reflection is not an exact science, mortal. What I do know is that he is planning on draining the magic out of your friend's body and taking it for his own. Under those circumstances, do you think he was hopeful that you would return?" she replied, acid in her tone.

"Fair point. Well, I'm up for suggestions..." Thomaras turned to look at the group.

Before anyone could answer, a bell started to ring. When Thomaras looked back towards the gates, a group of fifty soldiers, led by the unmistakable form of Luness, was walking right towards them.

"There's no way they saw us. How do they know we're here?" Az'an asked.

"My broodling swept the area for those animals Umbra controls and there were none. It's likely another of his mages found you. I suggest not running. Perhaps once you're in the gates, a path forward will present itself. I must go, but I will help you as soon as I can." As she spoke, the Orb Weaver was spinning silken webs in a ring on the ground. Once that was done, the ring shimmered once and the ground inside it took on a liquid form. She stepped through gracefully and was gone. As soon as she passed through, the ground returned to normal and the strands of web dried up.

"Um, what?" Torin asked.

"Don't ask me how it works, but her connection with the tiled plane allows her to travel from one place to another through those portals she makes," Felix explained. "She says that the distance on that plane is much shorter, but that the energy it takes her to cross it is far greater. She does it in only the most dire circumstances."

"Well, that's a good sign. Alright, I guess we go get caught? I don't fully trust the spider, but this tactic has worked for me in the past." Thomaras tried to sound confident.

"We are greatly outnumbered and I'm afraid my full attention would have to be on Luness," Felix said. "Outside of my own forest, I don't truly think I'm a match for her. I don't think we have the option to fight."

Az'an nodded, and Torin looked at Thomaras and shrugged. He'd follow Thomaras's lead.

"Okay, let's get ourselves captured," Thomaras said.

When Luness crested the hill, the three silver spheres floating above one hand and a deadly-looking spear in the other, Thomaras and his companions were sitting cross-legged on the ground waiting for them.

"Um... halt?" Luness said, confused.

"Already done," Felix said. "You can arrest us now. Nice to see you, by the way."

44

ASHEA

∼

Ashea opened her eyes and was surprised to find herself in the bedroom where her one-time foster father had tried to hurt her. She looked around the room and noted how small it felt.

And how little power it seemed to have.

This was the scene of an event so impactful that it had created an invisible wall that kept her from using the greatest gift she possessed. Had she awoken here even a day ago, it would have made her skin crawl, but now it only strengthened her resolve.

She felt the amulet around her neck warm up slightly and then Dafoe appeared, sitting cross-legged on her small bed. He looked around the room. She noticed a small tether of magic connecting the two amulets. She examined the spell that made up the tether and noted that it was simple enough to recreate.

"Why did you bring me here?" Ashea asked.

"It wasn't me. This is your dream. Your creation. You brought us here. To prove that you could, I would suspect."

Ashea considered that for a moment. Most of what happened here seemed to be processed by her subconscious. It made sense that it would bring her here to face what happened a final time. "Doesn't seem so bad now."

Dafoe smiled. "That's because you're stronger. What happened here will never happen to you again. You have the power now. Therefore, this room can hold none."

Ashea matched his smile. She liked being the one with power.

"Now, are you ready to learn how to keep Umbra out of your mind? To take power away from It as well?"

"More than ready."

"Good. As you remember, you'll have to draw Umbra to this place. Know that I'll be here to help, but I doubt you'll need it."

Ashea closed her eyes. Like last time, she opened herself up to Umbra and, like last time, Umbra sought her out like a predator hunting through the night. She felt Dafoe's presence open up to her, but the technique he'd laid out remained in her mind as if the memory were her own. Instead of opening up to him, she drew upon her own magic and slammed the gate to her mind shut. What used to be the door to the small bedroom was replaced by massive gates that were able to fit the room only through the illogical physics that accompanied dreams. Her body recoiled as Umbra slammed into the gate with Its full force.

But it held.

"Very good, Ashea. Now, let me in so I can help reinforce the spell."

For a moment Ashea hesitated. The gate she created was

holding. Why did Dafoe need in? The moment passed, however, when she felt Umbra begin to exert Its power against her mental barricade.

When Dafoe's power merged with her own, she felt the barricade reinforce and she could see, very clearly, all the ways in which he had bolstered her own spell. Dafoe had been correct when he said the amulets would muddy their respective powers, but Ashea could still make out the distinct nature of the mage's abilities. Then, Dafoe's power flared.

"Hold on, Umbra's trying to break through."

Ashea's full attention was drawn back to the image of gates that she had erected to protect her mind. She saw the doors bowing inward slightly as Umbra unleashed its powers against them. In her mind, she pictured thicker steel and more bars across them. They shimmered into place on the gates and the doors bowed less dramatically.

"Incredible," Dafoe said with awe in his voice. "Your natural abilities in this realm are unlike any I've seen. I think you're ready. We can end this, here and now, if you want to."

"I want to." Ashea didn't hesitate before she answered. She was standing, toe to toe, with a being that threatened her very plane of existence, and holding it at bay.

Of course she wanted to.

"Good. First, we need to open that gate. Umbra will come in fast, but together we can stop It. The moment you feel the shield I throw up, be sure to match it."

The last thing Ashea wanted to do was remove the barrier between herself and Umbra, but she took a deep breath and prepared herself. Scared as she was, she wanted to end this now. If she could stop Umbra here, then she could ensure that her friends would be safe. She felt every knot and barrier of the spell that made up the gates before her.

And let them all go.

The moment the gates were gone, Umbra burst into the room. The sheer force with which It entered blew the tiny bedroom away like a hay bale caught in a cyclone of wind. Ashea felt her body being blown into a black void that surrounded her. She was toppling backwards into nothing when she felt Dafoe's steadying presence stop her.

"The shield, Ashea!" he called.

Ashea's focus snapped into place and she looked for the pattern in her mind that Dafoe had left and then copied it. Umbra, Its form simply a black blob, battered against the shield. Ashea could see cracks forming already. Even with the strength of Dafoe's magic combined with her own she could tell they couldn't match the sheer force of nature that was Umbra's magic.

"The amulet is more than a focus, Ashea. It will serve as Umbra's prison. We will separate Its consciousness into two and hold them from each other. It will be trapped for eternity."

"What do I need to do?" Ashea asked.

"Just let it in. It will try to enter your body but will instead be drawn into the amulet. You have to trust me, Ashea."

Ashea nodded. She was past the point where she could doubt the mage. If she was going to stop Umbra, it was with his instruction. She felt Dafoe lower the shield and copied his spell. Umbra was on her immediately.

Her mouth went dry as the sheer power Umbra possessed buffeted her back. She gritted her teeth and put up no resistance as a dark tendril reached out to penetrate her chest.

The amulet opened wide and began to pull Umbra in instead.

The infinite creature tried to recoil but was caught fast. The amulet began to draw Umbra in despite Its efforts to pull away. Ashea gave a cry of joy before a wave of weakness dropped her to her knees. She looked over at Dafoe, who was smiling sadly.

The creature wasn't being absorbed into his amulet at all.

"I'm sorry, Ashea."

45

THOMARAS

∼

B y the time the confused look was off Luness's face, ten more soldiers had crested the hill behind her.

"Nice to see you too, Felix," Luness said. "You understand that you're outnumbered and I'll set you on fire if you try anything, yes? Give your weapons to the soldiers and I won't need to chain you all up."

Thomaras looked around at his companions. "We're fine. Just take us in."

"Perhaps you should show a little more gratitude, or at least less defiance," Luness said. "I could just as easily have you chained like common criminals. I'm trying to show a professional courtesy here."

Something in her tone made Thomaras pause, and he nodded. She nodded in turn and spun on her heel.

"Alright, loose circle around the prisoners. No one gets too close. Sergeant Moore, you have point," Luness barked.

Without needing to be told, several men approached

and warily took their weapons. Thomaras still had a few concealed on his person, but his bow, daggers and brace of throwing knives were taken.

Thomaras looked at Sergeant Moore when Luness called him by name and recognition dawned on him. He had been the soldier leading the party that had tried to stop Stoback.

When they came into view, the remaining soldiers were formed up with weapons drawn.

"At ease, men, they've surrendered," Moore said. "Johnson, run ahead and prepare separate cells for each of them in the dungeons. The rest of you clear the main road up to Castle Vees. Keep all civilians back. They've agreed to come quietly, but I don't want to risk the general public." He issued his orders in a crisp, practiced tone.

"Sir, are you sure you don't want a few more men with you? We were told they were extremely dangerous," the man that Moore had identified as Johnson said.

"Johnson, is it your job to question orders?" Moore barked back.

"No, sir!" Johnson immediately clapped a salute and sprinted off towards the capital. The remaining men formed up and headed that way as well, but at a more controlled jog.

"Let's go. No one speaks. I still have the chains if we need them." Luness didn't bother waiting for an answer before she turned and walked ahead of them. Thomaras shared a look with Torin before following along silently.

The soldiers that went ahead did their job efficiently. By the time Luness led them into the city proper, the main street was once again cleared for them to pass through. Most of the citizens looked on with little interest at what was slowing down their daily routine. Torin earned some extra looks and whispers, but aside from that, the people seemed to accept what was happening as mage business and left it at that.

When they entered the castle, Johnson was waiting for them.

"The dungeons are ready for them," he stated.

"Excellent. Now collect the rest of the squad and sweep the countryside surrounding the city. We were told there could be more of them," Luness ordered.

There was a brief question in the young man's eyes, but after a quick glance at Sergeant Moore's stern face, he simply saluted and went about carrying out his orders.

They continued to walk into the castle towards the dungeons.

After a few twists and turns, they descended some stairs into the cleanest dungeon Thomaras had ever seen. Dafoe's obsession with order and neatness seemed to extend even to areas that were intentionally tucked away out of sight.

Two men were standing crisply at attention, likely forewarned of their arrival by Johnson, and both snapped smart salutes to Luness.

"Gentlemen, how much longer left on your shift?" Luness asked

"About two hours, ma'am," one of the men answered.

"Today is your lucky day. These prisoners are under my care and, as such, will remain under our supervision. You two feel free to hit the pub early. If anyone asks, it was on my orders," Luness said with a wink.

The two men only hesitated for a second before saluting again and happily walking out of the dungeon. It wasn't often that you were on a mage's orders to get a drink.

Once the two men had passed out of sight, Luness turned to the group.

"My orders are to lock you up until Dafoe can come down here and convince you that the spider is lying to you," Luness said.

"But?" Felix asked, unfazed by the directness of her approach.

"But something feels off. I can't place what it is, but my gut tells me Dafoe isn't being completely honest."

"If you're unsure of Dafoe, should we be speaking so openly in front of his men?" Az'an asked.

The circle of guards began to chuckle and Luness even smiled herself.

"My position here is a strange one. On the mages council I am Dafoe's second in command, but because I am a commanding officer and general in the east it precludes me from that title here. My command here is respected as a mage carrying out the orders issued by Dafoe, but if it came down to it, the men would follow Captain Hanson or General Hudson's orders over my own. Given the amount of time that I spend here, it wasn't a situation I was comfortable with. So, over the years, I slowly filled the ranks with a few soldiers from Meridias that I knew would be loyal to me. Some 'new' recruits, some transfers from border units and some fudged paperwork allowed me to get a unit of soldiers loyal to me assigned to duties within the castle, all under the command of Sergeant Moore. Unfortunately, we lost a number of those soldiers to Stoback and what's left is before you," Luness explained.

"Clever. I see you didn't trust Dafoe fully, either," Felix said.

"Up until today, I trusted him completely. His general? The captain of his personal guard? They're just two more soldiers in an army that I don't know. I just wanted to make sure I had some assets I knew I could count on, mostly in case I had to defend Dafoe from some kind of internal betrayal," Luness countered.

"Well, your mistrust is well founded. I think I have much to tell you," Felix said.

He explained the Orb Weaver and her belief that Umbra was influencing Dafoe's view of prophecy, and of his plans to steal Ashea's powers for himself. Once he was done, Luness looked concerned but seemed to be making an effort to remain unconvinced.

"If Umbra is obscuring Dafoe's view of prophecy, then how does this Orb Weaver know that he isn't obscuring her own?" Luness asked.

"She is an eternal being, Luness. She's been on this plane of the infinity prism since it sprang into existence. Umbra is a powerful foe, yes, but reflection is what she was made for. Her view is clear."

Thomaras could tell that he thought he almost had Luness convinced, but it seemed as though he didn't want to be too harsh with her. Considering how strongly she appeared to believe in Dafoe, Thomaras could understand his approach.

"But he seemed so concerned about Ashea's well-being."

"As long as I've known Dafoe," Felix said, "he has believed that he was Haven's best defence against whatever might threaten us. He truly believes his place is to stand between Haven and whatever may come. Umbra has manipulated reflection to make Dafoe think that there is a way for him to possess Ashea's powers. With the ability to control multiple forms of magic, I have no doubt he *believes* he can be an ultimate force for good. His concern over Ashea's well-being is genuine, both because if she dies, he loses his chance at her powers, and if Umbra gets her, then we're all finished."

"The easiest way to sell a lie is to lean into the parts of it that are true. If it makes you feel any better, he fooled us too," Thomaras offered.

Luness waved Thomaras's words away as if remembering something more important. "Did the spider explain how he was going to steal her powers?"

"She said Umbra made him believe Thorn had created something for that purpose, but that it wasn't what he believed," Felix answered.

"An amulet?" Luness asked frantically.

"Yes, how did you…" Felix had walked forward while speaking and was interrupted when Luness swept him up in a hug.

"I've missed you," she whispered to the Druid, and then she was giving orders. "Alright, we'll keep up the prisoner act until we get over to the workshop. Then we'll give your weapons back. Sergeant Moore, you and the soldiers take up position at the bottom of the stairs leading to Thorn's workshop. If anyone tries to come down, you tell them the mages council is in the middle of a meeting. If they try to force their way in, you've got a defensible choke point to hold them. As for the rest of us, let's go have a little chat with Dafoe."

"Wait, you believe us all of a sudden?" Thomaras asked.

"Yes. I've known Thorn for a long time. He didn't want anything to do with those amulets. Something isn't right, but Ashea is all in on Dafoe. She needs our help."

Salutes were clapped, weapons were returned and in a flurry of organized movement they were on their way again.

"Ready yourselves," Luness said to the group. "Thorn and Mary are formidable enough on their own, but as I left,

I saw Captain Hanson leading some of Dafoe's personal guard down there and Morley's got one of his damn dolls stashed in every room. This is going to get ugly."

Thomaras nodded grimly and unlimbered his bow. "Good."

46

THOMARAS

〜

Thomaras rounded the corner and entered the large chamber that served as Thorn's workshop with his bow at full draw. Beside him, Felix had his staff in one hand and the other was buried in a satchel that he had slung across his shoulder. Luness led the group with Torin and Az'an, flanking her to either side.

"Dafoe, what are you doing?" Luness exclaimed in surprise. She was ahead of Thomaras and rounded the corner first. Now that he was in, he could see what she was reacting to.

Ashea lay motionless on a wooden table in the centre of the large room. Dafoe was standing behind her head with his hands raised in the air and his eyes closed. They wore matching amulets. A matte black tendril of energy was flowing from Ashea's amulet into Dafoe's.

"Oh dear Mary, it seems we have company." Morley's voice issued forward from what looked like the same tiny doll that was in the meeting chambers earlier. He was sitting on the edge of the table, tiny legs dangling off the end and one hand resting on Ashea's foot.

"They're here, Thorn," Mary said. "Buy us some time. Luness, I know what this looks like, but it's the only way that we can stop Umbra. You have to understand."

Thorn, who was clad in plate mail that was so thick it looked it would be impossible for him to move, nodded and lowered the visor on his helmet. He bent down and picked up the handle of a flail that was about three sizes too large for the mage, burly as he was, to even think of lifting, let alone swinging as a weapon.

In response, Luness lifted her hand and a fireball the size of a watermelon sprang forth and flew towards Morley's doll. Faster than Thomaras thought possible for a woman her age, Mary pulled a potion out of her bag and smashed it on the ground at her feet. What looked like thick white smoke erupted in front of her, but when the fireball came into contact with it, the smoke turned into a thick foam and smothered the spell as quickly as it had formed.

"Now, Morley!" Mary called, and threw a second potion onto the floor in front of the table. At the same time, Morley's doll leapt down and landed in the puddle of liquid left behind by the shattered bottle. The liquid first clung to the doll, making it look like it was covered in silver, and then the doll started to grow until it stood almost as tall as Torin.

"See, this is why you aren't allowed in on our plans, Luness! Your first reaction to an idea you don't like is to throw a fireball at it!" Morley said through his avatar as it started walking towards Luness.

Luness took a step back and lifted her arm again, but before she could, Torin stepped in front of her and unlimbered his hammer.

"Nope," Torin said.

He lifted his hammer but was forced to take a step back as the giant spiked striking head of the flail zoomed inches from his face. It struck the opposite wall, cracking the stone, and then returned just as quickly to the handle of the flail. The chain itself retracted completely into the handle so that the weapon appeared more like a giant morning star in Thorn's hand.

"I'm sorry, lad. I really do like you, but I can't let you interfere," Thorn said. His voice echoed deeply inside the helmet. He must have activated whatever enchantments were on the armour because he now stood almost twelve feet tall. Only the cavernous ceilings of his workshop allowed him to stand fully erect.

He flicked his wrist almost casually and the striking head of the flail whipped out again, this time causing Torin and Luness to dive out of the way. Az'an had taken a step back and was now beside Thomaras and Felix.

Thomaras, unsure of which target to pick, had the decision made for him as five soldiers, all dressed in blood-red armour accented with black trim, emerged from another cloud of smoke that one of Mary's potions had created. These five joined the five that were already in the room and a short, stout-looking man whose armour was completely black got up from the chair he was sitting in and drew his longsword. "Defend Dafoe!"

The man, Thomaras assumed it was Captain Hanson, gave the orders and immediately had to duck out of the way as Thomaras's first arrow flew through the space where his head used to be and struck the man directly behind him. He took out two more men immediately after and was drawing a fourth arrow when a bottle broke at his feet. He completed his draw, pivoted his body to the place where he last remembered Mary being, and fired. The arrow was true, but

Mary had just finished drinking a potion and her body shimmered as the arrow passed through her like air. She then ran through the wall closest to her and was gone.

Thomaras was about to draw again when an acrid smell hit his nose. He glanced down at the broken glass at his feet and saw green tendrils of air rising up in front of him. Thomaras recoiled, but wherever the tendrils had touched his bow, the wood began to rot and melt. He dropped the weapon before it could touch his hands and watched in dismay as it dissolved into a sludgy puddle on the floor.

"Fuck," Thomaras said and drew his daggers. He wasn't keen to engage Dafoe's personal guard without his bow and decided instead to end the threat at the source.

Thomaras calmed his breathing and found the place within himself where the shadows called to him.

He opened his eyes and answered.

Torin was peripherally aware of soldiers appearing out of thin air and then dying from Thomaras's arrows, but he was mostly focused on Thorn. The man's armour was ridiculous enough without the added reach from his flail. He certainly seemed to keep the best enchantments to himself.

Not wanting to give the rest of the soldiers time to join the fray, Torin tried to push the action against the mage, but every time he made a move, he would be pushed back by the whip-fast flail. Torin had been trying not to parry the weapon — after Stoback, he was somewhat leery of enchanted weaponry — but he couldn't close the distance if he didn't try.

Before he could, however, Dafoe's personal guard found him. Two men engaged and Torin was forced to give them his full attention. They were clearly skilled, but weren't used to dealing with an opponent with his size and speed. He blocked and parried blows, but whenever he went on the offence, Thorn's flail head would smash the ground in front of him, forcing him back a step and allowing the two men to renew their attack.

Torin looked around for help, but his companions seemed to be equally engaged. Torin couldn't see Thomaras, but Az'an was fighting with three of the guardsmen, and while he didn't appear to be in any peril, his style of fighting made for slow, deliberate victories.

Torin watched in amazement as Felix pulled a long branch from his satchel and threw it at Captain Hanson and the two remaining guards. The first guard managed to jump out of the way, but the second guard, more out of reflex than any conscious thought, caught the stick out of the air. As soon as he touched it, Felix's staffed glowed green, and the branch began to grow, wrapping the guard and Captain Hanson up in wooden branches that bent around them and started to squeeze.

Then the guards were on Torin again and his attention focused on the matter at hand. The two men seemed to be in good shape and Torin was concerned that, given his rather long night of travel preceded by his rather long day of fighting a psychopath, he would tire before they did. He needed to force the issue now.

Torin blocked a few more blows and was finally able to whirl his hammer in both hands, parrying both men's attacks. He feinted a step forward, but stayed where he was. Thorn's flail came as expected, but this time Torin swung his hammer into the ball and it exploded towards his two attackers. It struck them with such force that when their armour hit the wall behind them, what was left of their bodies leaked onto the floor.

Torin turned towards the mage and readied his hammer.

"I don't want to hurt you, Torin!" Thorn bellowed.

Then it hit Torin; the mage really didn't want to hurt him. All he was doing was keeping Torin occupied so that he couldn't affect the battle overall. Torin wondered if the man had ever killed anyone before and a wave of sympathy washed over him.

"It's okay," Torin said. "You won't."

Thorn took an involuntary step back that looked almost comical in that giant, imposing set of armour.

Torin put on a burst of speed and charged the mage. Thorn flicked out the striking head, but Torin was ready. He knocked it aside with his hammer and before the chain could retract, he grabbed it with his off hand and pulled it out of Thorn's grip. Before the mage could react, Torin brought his hammer around and extended it horizontally towards him. He speared Thorn with his hammer, his full weight and momentum driving the head of the hammer into the armour and caving it in. Thorn went flying and when he hit the ground limp, the armour returned to its regular size. Torin turned to survey the rest of the battle.

Luness was about to get to her feet when Morley's avatar was on her. His abnormally long arm pushed her to the ground and his other arm pulled back to strike her. The end of the doll's hand morphed from a wooden fist into a wooden spike.

"I'm not supposed to kill you, but I'm allowed to hurt you enough that you can't fight. I don't normally like compromise, but in this case I think it works," Morley sneered at her.

Before he could strike her, she pushed him backwards with a gust of wind. The force of the wind she had willed forwards should have sent the doll flying, but instead he was only pushed back a few feet.

"Some fight in the old girl," Morley chuckled.

As he came forward, Luness opened her palm and willed forth fire. Not a ball, an explosion this close would likely hurt her too, but a stream of fire that would turn the wooden doll into kindling.

The gout of flame engulfed the creature and after a few moments, she let up slightly, assuming he had caught fire. Instead, the thing stepped forward through the flames, a manic smile on his face. Luness frantically renewed the strength of her spell. The force of the flames seemed to slow him somewhat, but he wasn't burning.

"Oh, Luness, don't you understand? I am born of magic!" Morley exclaimed through the avatar.

"Well, let's see if you're born of hammers."

The doll's surprised face swiveled towards Torin for a moment before the Granite Ogre smashed it with the full force of his hammer. The doll shattered at the impact and the remaining pieces flew across the room.

"Thanks," Luness said.

Torin nodded and extended a hand, which she took so he could pull her to her feet.

She turned to see Az'an cut down the last of his attackers and step beside Felix.

The Druid was concentrating on his magic. Captain Hanson and another guard were trying to hack their way out of an ever-growing tree branch, but Felix kept cleverly growing the branch in such a way that if they were to cut themselves free, they would have to hack through each other. A vine appeared to have grown out of the Druid's empty hand and it completely enveloped a third guard, who was writhing on the floor trying to get free.

"If you two could give me a hand here," Felix gasped. "It's awfully difficult to draw on the power of nature whilst in the centre of a stone keep that resides in the centre of the largest city in Haven."

Luness smiled. She really had missed the Druid, and raised a hand towards the guard on the floor. She willed forth a hard-packed ball of air and flung it on the man's head. It struck him and he stopped moving.

Felix immediately dropped the vine but Captain Hanson, having tired of being out of the fight, elected to cut through the portion of branch that was holding him and in turn severed the other guard's arm. The man screamed in pain and fell to the floor, but Hanson was free of the branch and advanced towards them.

47

UMBRA

~

The remaining humanity in Umbra's brain was screaming out in panic. This should have been a moment of triumph, but instead something was going wrong. The foolish mortal had taken Umbra's bait and created the amulet to steal the girl's power, but instead of facilitating Umbra's entrance into the plane, it was drawing Umbra in. As if they were expecting it to come through the girl.

It shouldn't have been possible.

The immortal portion of Umbra's mind, strengthened by the knowledge and the power of mages and eternal beings alike, took over and began calculating. However Dafoe may have manipulated the plans for the enchantment didn't matter. It was still Umbra's enchantment. All It had to do was find a weakness in the mortal's magic.

Ah, there.

Umbra allowed itself to be drawn into the amulet. Dafoe had taken the design and changed it slightly, but the foundations remained and through them Umbra could enter the girl and gain access to this plane. It cast Its mind out and sought the weakness in the enchantment.

Umbra flexed Its power, and the amulet shattered.

The girl screamed in pain, but Umbra paid her no heed. She would be silent soon. As the amulet's magic faded away, Umbra's essence flowed into the girl. Filling her mind until her essence slowly began to fade.

In a burst of power, Umbra was repelled.

Umbra looked around and was surprised to find Itself standing in the girl's dream realm in Its corporeal form. This was the closest it had come to entering another realm on the tiled plane, but It was still being held at bay.

"How are you doing this, girl?" Umbra demanded of the tiny mortal in front of It.

"Stay out of my mind!" she screamed in defiance.

Ah, defiance. It had been so long since Umbra had heard it. The small part of Umbra's brain that still enjoyed such things was elated at the prospect of crushing the defiance out of another mortal. "Whatever skill you might have is a star in the sky compared to mine."

Umbra renewed Its attack on her mind and was met with resistance. In truth, It was impressed with her strength. Few had put up such a fight. It would have loved to absorb her powers, but It needed her body whole in order to enter into this realm. Once It did, she would be destroyed along with her power, but that was a price It was willing to pay.

"GET. OUT," she screamed again and pushed It back.

If Umbra's face had been capable of grinning, the sight would have been terrifying. It flexed a portion of Its true power and burst through the girl's defences. She screamed in pain as Umbra's essence invaded her body and mind.

"Your sacrifice is appreciated, girl," Umbra said as he

weaved the spell that would allow his corporal form to finally enter a new plane of existence.

"Fuck you," she said calmly.

The moment It cast the spell it felt a final burst of effort from the girl. In the space of a fraction of a second, It tracked her spell. She connected some kind of ethereal tether to Umbra's essence. It did rapid calculations to decide what effect the spell might have and determined that once Its own spell was complete, hers would be meaningless. She would be destroyed completely by Its spell and her tether would attach to nothing at all.

Then she was gone and Umbra stepped into Its new plane of existence.

Something was wrong.

Umbra felt it as soon as It looked around at the black nothingness. This wasn't Its new plane of existence. Something was holding It out. But how?

"Sorry, that would be my fault. I'm afraid I can't let you into our plane of the infinity prism," a voice said.

Umbra looked around the inky blackness, trying to see where the voice was coming from.

"Oh, here. Allow me," the voice said.

Suddenly, It was in a small stone room. There was a bed and a chair, but neither had any cushions or blankets on them. The walls of the room seemed to curve in a circle and when Umbra looked at where they should meet the ground, they seemed to just continue to curve.

"What is this place?" Umbra asked.

"Home, I guess?" The man, Dafoe, appeared sitting cross-legged on the bed. "See, you're trapped in an amulet that a friend of mine made for you. The infinity prism showed me how to do it; it's no big deal, really," he said lightly.

Umbra considered the mortal for a moment. It had beaten the changes Dafoe had made to the amulet.

"Yeah, here's the thing. I saw through that little ruse of yours and the infinity prism showed me the upgraded version of that trick. Also, you can't hide your thoughts from me here. Anything you think, I know," Dafoe said.

Umbra swept forward faster than any mortal person's eyes could track. In the blink of an eye, It had the arrogant man by the throat and was holding him so that his head reached the ceiling. Umbra looked into his eyes and saw... amusement?

In an instant, Umbra was sitting in the chair looking at the human sitting comfortably on the bed.

"No," he said.

Umbra tried to get up but found that It couldn't move. "How?"

"You eternal beings are always so confident! I really admire that trait but sometimes, like now, it gets you into trouble. You think because you took every ounce of power available in your plane of existence that your own power is absolute. Yet, here we are."

"I could turn you to ash with a thought!" Umbra roared.

"See? There it is!" Dafoe said, pointing at Umbra. "There's the confidence I love. And you're right. In a battle like that I would lose in an instant. Unfortunately for you, my view of the infinity prism is unparalleled."

"I fed you every reflection you read," Umbra responded.

"I know you think that's true but you and the spider were moving pieces on a board that I created for you. Here, it's easier to show you, since I'm in your brain anyway." Dafoe gestured and the small room melted away.

Umbra stared in wonder as images of Itself reading the reflections of the prism appeared before him. It remembered each reading and the machinations that It put into place in response. Now, though, It could see that each reflection, represented as a point of light bouncing through the prism, had gone through a prism of Dafoe's own creation before reaching Umbra.

"How is this possible?" It asked.

"The prism reader you absorbed in your own realm was good; they just weren't nearly as good as me. So far as I can tell, no one is. And I made a point of looking! Didn't want to become so arrogant that a life form I believed to be below me trapped me and prevented my life's work. Know what I mean?"

Umbra searched with all Its might against the mental bonds that were holding it but couldn't move.

"Yeah, you know what I mean. So, this is your life for... eternity, I guess? I'm not sure how long... whatever you are... lives but that life is going to happen here. So enjoy that. No universe-eating for you." With that, Dafoe stood up, winked and was gone.

Umbra stood up and looked around at the tiny room. It paced the entirety of the floor once and then sat back down. It began to probe out with Its mind. It was a patient being. It had all of eternity to figure this puzzle out. It probed a little more, looking for cracks, looking for imperfections... Its mind flashed in brilliant pain, and then there was darkness.

48

THOMARAS

~

Thomaras stepped into the shadows.

He moved from one to the next with his daggers drawn. He watched the captain of the guards and his remaining soldiers move towards Torin and Luness, but he let them pass. Those two could handle themselves, and he only had eyes for one victim.

Dafoe.

The mage still stood behind Ashea's prone form on the table, the strange black tether connecting his amulet to hers, with his eyes closed. Thomaras closed the distance, invisible to everyone in the room.

Dafoe's eyes snapped open and seemed to look right at Thomaras.

Then there was a soundless explosion that knocked Thomaras onto the ground. The impact caused him to lose his concentration, and he fell out of the shadows. He looked up from the ground and saw a tear in the fabric of the world.

Within the tear, he saw Ashea, impossibly small,

standing against a matte black giant. It had to be Umbra. The being towered over her, and while it had no face to speak of, Thomaras still seemed to see a wicked grin slashed across the terrible visage. The two seemed to be staring at each other, and then Umbra rushed forward and entered her body. A moment later, Ashea's amulet shattered and she winked out of existence. The black tendril flowing into Dafoe's amulet surged forward and knocked the mage down onto one knee.

He looked up and smiled sadly.

"Where's Ashea?" Torin bellowed.

"I can answer that," Dafoe said.

Thomaras brandished his daggers. Torin readied his hammer, but they both waited.

"You better hope we like that answer," Thomaras said.

Dafoe stood up and waved off the soldiers. "You may take the men out of here, Hanson. We shouldn't have any more need for you."

"As you say, Dafoe," the captain said. His expression gave the impression that he didn't agree with his master, but he didn't bother to argue. In a moment, they were all gone.

"First of all, I'm sorry, Luness. It killed me not to include you in all of this, but every reflection I looked at told me that if you were told about this from the start, you would die. You must believe me. This was the only way to keep you alive," Dafoe said.

"Or maybe you just knew that I'd kill you if found out that you were going to bleed that child of her powers," Luness said, walking forward.

Dafoe raised his hands imploringly. "Please, Luness, hear me out. You've been lied to. All of you. Even you, spider. You can come out now," Dafoe said, looking around the room.

After a few moments, one of the walls shimmered, and the giant spider made her way gracefully out of the portal.

"Speak, mage," the spider said. "The only reason I don't attack you myself is that I sense no new powers in you."

"Because there are none," Dafoe said. "That was never my aim. Umbra manipulated reflection so that I would think the only way to stop him was to steal Ashea's powers and make them my own. In this way, It pitted us against each other, even though we should have been allies in this fight. Fortunately, I was able to see through Its clumsy machinations and form a plan of my own that would allow me to stop Umbra. I was able to hide Torin and Thomaras from both you and Umbra and use them to bring me Ashea. It was the only way to stop him. I'm sorry for the deceit."

The Orb Weaver looked like she was considering his words carefully. "What proof do you have? It is hard for me to believe that a mortal would be more talented in reading reflection than I am, but arrogance serves no one."

In response, Dafoe approached the Orb Weaver and extended the amulet out to her. She reached out one leg tentatively and rested it on the amulet for a moment. She immediately recoiled.

"That's the being that threatens our world," the Orb Weaver said. "That feeling is the same as the black silk that came out of me..." She trailed off.

Thomaras wasn't sure how he could tell, but the spider's face looked disgusted.

"Likely Umbra's attempt to throw you off from his true manipulation of reflection," Dafoe answered.

"But how did you trap him?"

"Through the most intricately crafted piece of jewelry and accompanying enchantment that I've ever made," Thorn said.

The seasoned mage had extricated himself from his armour, and the beginnings of what was going to be a nasty bruise could be seen on the part of his chest that showed through the collar of his shirt.

"The infinity prism showed me the plans, and I passed them on to Thorn. It took years of attempts until we got it perfect, but it worked. It worked!" Dafoe gripped his fellow mage in a tight hug.

A ghostly incandescent form appeared through a wall and looked around the room. "Everything sorted here, Dafoe?" Mary asked.

"I think we're getting there," Dafoe responded.

The ghostly form of Mary reached into her satchel and pulled out a bottle which incongruously turned completely corporeal once it was out of the bag, seeming float in the air before the misty figure. She removed the stopper, and as the contents poured into her mouth, her body returned to corporeal form as well. "I'm sorry, Luness, all of you. It was the only way to stop that monster," she said.

"You buying this, spider?" Thomaras asked.

The Orb Weaver was quiet for a moment before answering. "I will not know for certain until I return to my grotto, but I believe what he says is true. I was mistaken and for that, I am sorry. I will go now and consult the weavings of reflection. Know this, mage. If I find there are any lies here, you will be dealing with me." The spider didn't wait for a response before she spun another portal and was gone.

"She really needs to work on her people skills," Dafoe quipped.

Thomaras gestured at Dafoe with one of his daggers. "None of that explains where Ashea is, so before you start getting witty, I think you better start talking."

"You're right," Dafoe said. "I'm sorry. Torin, Thomaras, I

am so, so sorry. There was no way to stop Umbra and have her survive. You never have to forgive me, but please know that her sacrifice saved this entire plane of existence."

Thomaras threw one of his daggers with a scream of rage. Dafoe had killed her. At the very least, he had let her die. Thomaras waited for the satisfying thunk of his dagger penetrating Dafoe's chest.

Instead, the weapon hit an invisible wall and clattered to the ground.

Thomaras blinked and then swung to face Luness. He surged forward with his remaining dagger, but before he could take a step, he was mired in a thick wall of air. "Torin, kill him. Kill that motherfucker," Thomaras screamed.

"Please, Thomaras, calm down. Your friend needs you right now," Dafoe said.

Thomaras turned to see that Torin had slumped to his knees and was staring at the table where Ashea's body had lain. "Don't tell me what my friend needs. You killed my friend. Not by accident, not in the heat of battle, but by years, YEARS, of careful manipulation! You're a dead man." Thomaras railed against his invisible restraints.

"Thomaras, you don't have to like him for it, but he did save our world," Felix said gently. "Umbra was a scourge like nothing we could imagine. Ashea wanted to fight him. In this way, she did."

"Thank you, Felix," Dafoe said.

"Don't mistake my acceptance of these circumstances as support," Felix said. "I find your methods abhorrent. The only reason I am speaking in your defence is because I was so clearly fooled by that thing. I believe that you did what you had to do to stop It, and for that I'm grateful, but I know you well enough to understand that your willingness to sacrifice Ashea to achieve your goals would have precluded you from finding a different way."

"Felix, there was no other way. I assure you."

"Maybe that's true, Dafoe, maybe. But I refuse to stand idly by and allow you to dictate which means justify your ends. I will continue to search for a better way," Felix said to Dafoe and then turned to Thomaras, "so that we don't have to sacrifice someone like Ashea ever again."

Something broke inside Thomaras in that moment. The ground under his feet that had been giving way since Erica died finally slid out from under him. He sagged in the thick magical air that held him and his head fell forwards.

"Okay," was all he said.

"Luness, let him go." Thomaras heard Dafoe say the words, but they seemed to echo inside his head as blood roared in his ears. He nearly fell to the ground when Luness released him, but Az'an's steady grip held him up. Thomaras shook the man off without looking at him and turned to walk out of the room. Hesitating, he turned back to Torin, kneeling on the ground and staring at nothing. "Hey."

Torin turned and looked at him, red eyes wet and broken.

"You promised. Now I've fallen off the precipice."

The half-Granite Ogre half-human giant closed his eyes and hung his head. Thomaras turned his back and walked out of the room.

He didn't look back.

∾

EPILOGUE

~

The winds howled relentlessly across the cracked and broken landscape that was once a lush and diverse world. They howled as they descended from the peaks of mountains that cracked and shuddered as earthquakes ravaged the land. They howled through the ever-churning oceans that spit and crashed against rocky beaches. They howled across vast deserts turned to sheets of glass by the cascading lightning strikes from the ever-present storm clouds above. They howled and they buffeted a small, motionless form lying on the ground.

Ashea woke to her face being pelted with rain. She covered her face with her arm and then stood up to look around. As she took in the desolation, the memories of her fight with Umbra came back to her, though she wasn't sure she could call it a fight. Umbra rolled over her like a wave destroying a sandcastle. The only reason she was still alive was the spell she had cast out in desperation. The tether she was able to follow into Umbra's plane of existence.

Or what was left of it.

As she took in the devastation that Umbra wrought here, she shook her head at her own hubris. Dafoe had convinced her she was powerful enough to stand against something that could do all of this, and she had believed him. Even Dafoe, with all of his abilities, had needed to rely on lies and subterfuge to stop Umbra.

Ashea sighed. Had she been asked if she would sacrifice her life to stop Umbra, she would have said yes, but that didn't make being used as a pawn hurt any less. At the end of the day, she had helped to stop Umbra and took solace in that. Besides which, both Umbra and Dafoe had expected her to lie down and die as their respective plans took form and instead she had survived.

And ended up in the worst place imaginable.

Nailed it.

A particularly loud clap of thunder caused her to look around for any kind of cover. Though desolate, the landscape was dotted with plenty of rock formations. After some searching, she was able to find one that could be called a shallow cave. She sat down inside, grateful for the protection it offered from the elements. She wrung the water out of her hair and clothes as best she could and closed her eyes. Without the constant roar of wind in her ears, she was finally able to hear herself think.

The calm brought on by the silence also brought an awareness of another presence. One too powerful to belong to anything else. She followed the presence and realized she was still connected to it through the tether she had created. She reached out to Umbra's presence and realized that It, too, was trapped. She did her best to absorb all the information she could before Umbra noticed her and slapped her away casually.

She opened her eyes and considered what she had felt. The prison Umbra was in was most certainly the amulet. Ashea recognized the enchantments within. She also felt something else.

Dafoe was drawing on Umbra's power.

It appeared the spider's belief that Dafoe was after power wasn't completely unfounded. Suddenly, any solace Ashea had taken in defeating Umbra disappeared. She had been used as a pawn, yes, but not for the greater good. She had been used to make Dafoe the most powerful man within the infinity prism.

She couldn't let that stand.

She reached out and felt for the tether. She feared Umbra would detach it but It either lacked the ability or the will to do so. She could still feel Umbra brooding.

"Listen. We're both trapped. Maybe we can work together to get out of here," Ashea said through the tether.

"Quiet, ant," Umbra responded in Its gravelly voice. "I will find my own way out of here."

Ashea's heart leapt. If she could communicate, maybe she could convince Umbra to work with her. The enemy of my enemy...

"Will you? Dafoe outmaneuvered you at every turn. He knows everything you can do."

"His power is insignificant to my own, as is yours. I will find a way."

"Maybe, or maybe you've met your match. In either case, Dafoe thinks I'm dead. Off the board. The one thing he won't be prepared for is us working together."

Umbra slapped her away again and Ashea assumed she'd failed. She couldn't say how long she sat in the cave fighting against despair before she felt the tether activate from Umbra's end. It didn't say anything, but, much as

Dafoe had shown her the scaffolding of a spell to protect her mind, Umbra showed her a spell of Its own.

Smiling, Ashea strode forth from the tiny cave into the raging elements. The winds howled and broke upon a sphere of perfect calm surrounding the last living being on this plane.

THANK YOU!

There are many things that I love about writing. Creating a new world, writing that perfect line that gives you goosebumps when you read it, and even the painstaking process of editing down a first draft, all bring me joy.

But favourite thing is sharing my work.

Putting my stories out into the world for others to enjoy is the reason I do this. So, a heartfelt thanks to you, intrepid reader, for taking a chance on my book. The worlds I weave would be hallow without you here to explore them. I hope you come back and explore some more.

STAY IN TOUCH

Thanks again for reading! If you enjoyed the book, reviews are the lifeblood of independent publishing, and I would be grateful for your feedback.

If you'd like to learn more about Taylor you can check him out here:

Taylor: www.taylorcrook.ca

Be the first to get your hands on Taylor's solo work, sign up for monthly newsletters or just check out some short stories. You can also keep up with Taylor a little more frequently by following him on instagram and twitter.

twitter.com/TaylorC68001927
instagram.com/taylorcrookwrites

ALSO BY TAYLOR CROOK

Path of the Eternal Sun

CPSIA information can be obtained
at www.ICGtesting.com
Printed in the USA
LVHW022025210423
744817LV00001B/1/J